# SHATTERED & SCARRED

## Sacred Hearts MC Book I

AJ Downey

Second Circle Press

First published on Kindle 2014
Print edition published 2015 by Second Circle Press
Book design by Lia Rees at Free Your Words (www.freeyourwords.com)
Cover art by Clarissa Yeo at Yocla Designs (www.yocladesigns.com)

ISBN: 978-0692333884

# DEDICATION

To Tracie, the strongest woman I know. You are your own Trigger in a lot of ways. I'm proud of you.

## THE SACRED HEARTS MC BOOKS IN ORDER

**1. SHATTERED & SCARRED**

2. Broken & Burned

3. Cracked & Crushed

3.5. Masked & Miserable (a novella)

4. Tattered & Torn

5. Fractured & Formidable

6. Damaged & Dangerous

# CONTENTS

# PROLOGUE

I was entranced by the rush of pavement beneath the luxury car's tires. My high heels, abandoned and forlorn on the passenger side floor board where I sat, had my feet sighing with relief. I watched the darkened landscape pass by the tinted glass in a blur. It was warm in the car and I was grateful. The nights were cool, if not downright chilly and my dress wasn't made for the weather. It was made to make me look good, and by extension, make *him* look good.

"I mean, are you *trying* to start with me?" he demanded. I blinked long and slow and watched the reflection of his hand move off of the gear shift in the darkened glass. I flinched and turned wide fearful eyes in his direction. My hands remained clasped primly in my lap, the skin on my knuckles mottling white, the harder I gripped, the more they started to shake and he hated it when I shook but I couldn't help it... I was scared and rightfully so.

Chadwick Granger was a beautiful monster and most definitely something I should fear. I took in his profile. Short wheat blonde hair and hazel eyes that penetrated the soul. His jaw was square and strong the angle leading to a generous mouth that had, at first, said the sweetest things until I had found, much too late, it had the capacity to say things infinitely more cruel.

"I'm not... I didn't... I..." I closed my mouth resolutely on my murmured words that were meant to appease him when I saw the spark of victory in his eyes. The generous mouth that had long ago been sweet twisted into all too familiar cruel lines.

"So now you want to argue?" I swallowed convulsively... He was a master at manipulation, at twisting how things were to meet his own ends and I had walked right into it... again... I should have just remained silent.

"Answer me!" he snarled.

"No. I'm not trying to start with you, I'm not trying to argue… You're absolutely correct Chadwick, you're always correct. I don't know what I'd been thinking." I forced a smile but I knew it was heavily watered down and halfhearted at best. I had never been good at lying with my expression or, for that matter, of lying with my eyes and truthfully I think that was partially why he'd chosen me in the beginning, all those years ago.

He took his eyes off the road and looked at me. He returned his gaze out the windshield and I relaxed marginally, but then he looked at me again, and any semblance of warmth seeped from his gaze and desolation crept into my heart. His hand shot off the gearshift and knotted in the back of my hair. I cried out but willed my hands to remain in my lap.

*I've earned his correction…* I thought bitterly as he wrenched my head to the side and back. Searing pain went up the side of my neck behind my ear, down to my shoulder as the muscle cramped.

"Just remember darling. You've *earned* my correction," he said, pulling the car off to the side of the lonely highway. Tears poured from my eyes, down my face, hot and slick as panic seized in my breast making it hard to breathe.

"What do you say!?" he shouted into the small space, shaking my head by the fistful of hair he had ahold of. I cried out, fire alighting along my scalp. My eyes burned with the fresh sting of tears.

"Yes, sir!" I screamed and covered my mouth with my hands.

"How many times do I have to tell you, Ashton?" he demanded, turning the wheel sharply onto the shoulder. Gravel and debris pinged the underside of the car and I closed my eyes, sobbing. His voice had taken on the frozen steel quality that I had only heard a time or two before, the times he had hurt me bad enough I really thought I was going to die.

"How many times do I have to tell you, you stupid whore, that you don't raise your voice to me!" he stomped on the emergency brake and flung open his door, I shrieked in pain and terror as he dragged me across the center console and into the still cold night by my hair…

*Please God… don't let him kill me this time…* I silently begged.

# CHAPTER 1

*Trig*

The thrum of the bike beneath me, the open road in front of me, I was a little disappointed that I was coming in early from my solo run. This was fucking freedom and I loved it. I gently twisted the handlebars to guide my bike into a curve when the sweep of my headlight caught on something moving up ahead along the shoulder. I took a drag off the cigarette pressed between my lips and cursed under my breath letting out a cloud of that vapor shit instead of the smoke I so seriously craved.

I still couldn't believe I let Reaver talk me into this e-cig shit. I blinked and angled my bike across the lane so my headlight went more toward the shoulder and cursed again. That was no deer, it looked like a kid. I downshifted and slowed my roll pulling up alongside the girl, who wasn't a kid after all, she was just that fucking small.

She hugged herself, teeth chattering uncontrollably as she stomped resolutely along the shoulder, bare fucking feet slapping along the glass strewn pavement.

"Whoa, sweetheart! What the hell are you doin' out here!?" I called above the chug of my engine. I walked the bike alongside her and grimaced as my boots crunched over the freezing asphalt, sparkling in the moon and my headlamp light with frost and bits of glass. Early spring my ass, it was mid-March and we were still freezing over.

She cringed and I was cringing too. Her dress was a halter style and her upper back and shoulders were exposed as well as her shapely legs from the thigh down. She was small but proportionate. Her hair was a bit of a tangle and dark. It hid her face from me but I could tell she was crying from the odd sniff and the way her shoulders hitched.

"Hey, hey, hey, stop a minute!" I tried, she didn't stop, but she spoke.

"I can't be seen talking to you," she intoned, "He'll come back and when he comes back he won't like it if I'm talking to you," her voice cracked.

I stopped my bike and put down the kickstand switching it off. I swung a leg over and caught up to her in two long strides, easily keeping pace beside her.

"Hey, wait stop!" I pulled off my gloves and stuffed them in the pocket of my motorcycle vest, or cut.

"Stop a minute!" I tried again.

"I can't!" she wailed, "I've earned his correction and I have to be home by morning, but he'll come back! I'm sure he will…" she picked up her pace.

"Let me give you a lift!" I blurted to buy time, just what the fuck was going on here?

"I can't! He'll know, and I've earned his correction. I have to walk he told me so," her breath plumed the air and I stopped cold. Just what the fuck was this crazy broad talking about!? I caught up to her and grabbed her arm.

"Just stop a minute and look at me!" I said and she whirled, a high frightened cry emanating from her that rose the hair on the back of my neck. The only time I had ever heard anything like it was when I had been out trapping with my granddad one winter and we'd come up on this fucking fox trapped in a snare… this was just like that only worse somehow because damned if she wasn't pretty.

A pair of the loveliest dark eyes looked up into mine with way too much white showing. Her face was smeared with tracks of eye makeup and her lip was busted and swelling. Her skin was petal soft beneath my work rough hand and as cold as ice.

I grimaced at the necklace of bruised fingerprints raising on her pale throat. Her cheekbone was swelling and I swallowed back the bitter bite of anger. Someone had worked her over pretty good and left her out here in her pretty party dress to freeze to death.

"What's your name?" I asked her gently.

"Ashton," she breathed, frozen in place. I gave her another once over from head to toe.

"Ashton, I'm Ethan but nobody calls me that. You can call me Trigger or just Trig." She swallowed and let out a whimper.

"Please just let me go… I have to…"

"No," I said it gently but firmly. "No Baby, you're coming with me. I gotta get you looked at." I sniffed and pulled off my jacket and cut and wrapped it around her slender shoulders.

She blinked her dark eyes up at me and said, "I don't know what to do…" she looked dejectedly up the lonesome highway like it would provide her answers, but seeing as not a single other soul had driven by since she was, presumably, abandoned out here… I doubted there were any for her.

"Well Ashton, let's start by getting you someplace warm where I can get a look at you," I said. My mind was racing. What I *should* have done was call the cops, but that was kind of hard to do with a key of smack in my left saddlebag and a sawed off in my right.

"Come on Baby, let someone take care of you, huh?" I used a tone of voice that I would use on a spooked animal and guided her resolutely towards the bike.

*Fuck! Fuck! Fuck!* I was so not in the business of taking in fucking strays and this particular stray stank of money. Her rich asshole husband likely *was* coming back for her but man… I couldn't leave her like this. No woman, no matter how much of a pain in the ass she might be, deserved this kind of treatment.

"I don't… I…" she was resisting my pull as she looked at the bike. This ride was going to be cold as fuck, but we were only ten minutes or so out from the clubhouse. The party would be in full swing when we got there, I'd bet money on it, but I would worry about that when we arrived.

"I'm going to pick you up and put you on it…" I started, I explained exactly what I wanted from her, how to lean with the bike not against it, how I wanted her to hold onto me, all of it in great detail. I placed her feet where I wanted 'em and winced, they were a shredded bloody mess.

"Don't you dare move your feet off of these bars you got it?" I asked. She nodded mutely, her face as white as snow. I didn't want her to burn herself on the pipes.

*What the fuck was I doing?*

I got on in front of her and kicked the bike into life. My baby roared and Ashton's slender arms pulled her small lithe body tight against my back, the sleeves of my jacket rucked back and huge around her fine boned wrists. I spared a thought that at least she was cooperating before I pulled out onto the highway in a spray of gravel. I had one singular thought. I hoped Doc was sober enough to help me take care of her injuries. I didn't know a God damned thing about patching up the damage, just how to dish it out...

About ten minutes later I pulled into the gates and up the steep drive of the compound. A prospect dragged the chain link fence closed behind us. I backed my bike into its place in the line out front and killed the engine. Ashton shook, her entire body trembling against my broad back. I could feel the side of her face pressed in the hollow between my shoulder blades. My shirt stuck to my back there with her tears.

I had no fucking idea what I was doing. None. I was way off the fucking reservation with this one. I pulled off my gloves for a second time that night and covered her icy hands with one of my much larger ones which were only marginally warmer.

She was like a little fucking china doll. It was unreal. She clung to me, and trembled like one of those little fucking rat dogs that celebrity skanks carry around in their purses and I started doing a slow burn.

Burn. Yeah... that's what I'd like to do. Burn whatever motherfucker had done this to her to the motherfucking ground. I took off my brain bucket and hung it on my handlebars, the wraparound glasses with the clear lenses went into the overturned helmet and I raked fingers through my thick unruly thatch of blonde hair.

"Welcome back Trig!" the prospect jogged up the drive, gravel crunching beneath his boots.

"Go find Doc," I ordered by way of greeting. A furrow appeared between his brows.

"You hurt?" he asked.

"Not me, now go find fuckin' Doc and hope like hell he's sober enough to fuckin' help!" Ashton jumped at my raised voice and shook harder, her arms were locked around me and I was kind of impressed at her strength despite her diminutive size.

The prospect jumped too and went immediately for the club house, music blared out into the night and softened to a dull roar as the door opened and shut.

"Ashton," I said, speaking to her like a spooked animal again. It had worked before…

"Ashton Baby, you gotta let me go," I soothed. I pried her arms from around my waist and stood up. I got off the bike and turned. She looked as freaked out as someone could get. Her eyes were far too wide and her skin so pale it was luminous in the light of the moon. The door to the clubhouse opened and the prospect and Doc came out.

Doc strode forward, he was in his typical uniform of unrelieved black, from boots to pants to tee to cut to the black do-rag that covered his shaven head. His salt and pepper handlebar mustache nearly vibrated with irritation and his light colored eyes peered into the dark in my direction.

"Chuckie here says you got wounded?" he asked.

I stood to the side, revealing Ashton, still perched on my bike.

"Eh?" he blinked and looked her over.

"Bring her inside, can't do shit out here," he grunted, adding, "I'll go get my kit."

"My room, five minutes?" I asked.

"Better make it ten, but yeah, your room 'll do fine." He went to his bike and I turned and looked down at Ashton. She was shaking like a god damned leaf and looked like she was about to lose her shit. I slid my coat and cut off her and threw it over the saddle of my bike.

"I'm going to pick you up, Baby. Put your arms around my neck," she didn't want to comply, her head shaking violently back and forth. Too bad. I put an arm behind her back and scooped her off the bike with my other beneath her knees.

"Chuckie, take my coat, cover her up." He jumped, and scrambled to comply and I made note of it. It almost made up for the Q&A rather than just going to get Doc when I'd asked. He covered her and I jerked my head to indicate he should cover her face. He nodded and did what he was told.

"Get the doors then find Dray and have him deal with my bike." I looked at him pointedly and he nodded. He didn't know why, but at least he didn't ask this time. He was back in the black and earning points with me again.

"Didn't make it to the rally?" he asked. I cursed in my head, he was just a prospect and shouldn't know about that kind of shit yet, but damage apparently done so I didn't deny it.

"Naw man, found her on the way past here, needed to stop. Couldn't exactly call the cops…" he opened the door and we were swallowed by a rush of heat and noise. I barreled into the thick of it, rushing towards the back and the rooms set aside for members on the council. I was on the council, I had a room.

Dray, the VP of the Sacred Hearts MC gave me a chin lift from across the room and started shoving towards me. He fell into step beside me.

"Whatcha got there?" he asked with a crooked grin.

"Not what you think man, you gotta get out to my bike, like double time," he gave me a cold hard glare.

"You didn't deliver?" he asked.

"Tell you about it later, I was ahead of schedule, if you move it you can easily make it on time." Dray raked a hand through his chin length straight black hair and nodded. His equally black eyes were seething in my direction.

"You and me, we're going to talk about this brother," he was pissed, I was pissed, we would talk and then we could both be pissed together. Sacred Hearts had one rule… No women, no children and fuck if Ashton wasn't some weird amalgamation of both.

"Yeah. I feel you," I said and he broke away and went out.

The further back into the sprawling compound I went the quieter it got until I reached my room, kicking the door open after stooping to turn the knob. Chuckie had peeled off when Dray had come up. He was smart. The music was a dull and distant throb back here and it was quiet enough that I could hear Ashton's teeth clacking together along with her ragged too fast intake of breath.

"How you doin' Baby?" I asked, I set her down on the bed and pulled my jacket and cut off her face and around her shoulders. She blinked up at me under the harsh overhead light and I sucked in a breath. Her eyes weren't dark, they had just been fully dilated out on the road… I had never met a woman, or man for that matter, with eyes like hers.

They were gold… light gold, like twin suns set in her delicate heart shaped face. Her long auburn hair, windblown and tangled as it was, with its reddish highlights in it made the gold of her eyes that much more intensive. I swallowed, lost in them for more than a minute.

"Where's my patient?" Doc asked from the door and the spell she had me under snapped with a damn near audible pop. I stood aside and let him into the room. Ashton crab walked backwards up the bed and away from Doc until her back pressed flat against the headboard.

"Easy Darlin'." He put his bag down by the bed.

"Ashton this is Doc, he's here to help," I soothed.

"Nobody can help me…" she moaned, "He's going to kill me…" to which my first thought was, *the fuck he is.*

Several minutes later she was out and Doc was looking her over.

"She's hypothermic, her feet are pretty wrecked… how long was she out there?" Doc had had to administer a tranquilizer, which hadn't been easy, and now Ashton lay small and frail in my bed. I stood, arms crossed and watched him assess. Holding her down while he had jammed a needle in her arm, all the while her howling like that wounded fox had scraped my damn nerves raw.

"No way to tell," I said tersely.

"Well it was more than a minute. I'm getting her out of this party dress, you strip down she needs heat and you picked her up so you're it Trig." I scowled at him.

"The fuck you talking about Doc?"

"She needs to get warm. Stop worrying so goddamned much

about your womanly virtue and get undressed!" he commanded. I gave him a look that should have been able to strip flesh from bone and pulled my shirts over my head.

He expertly stripped Ashton out of her skimpy black party dress and grunted. Her delicate yet curvy body was discolored in more places than not by deep ugly bruising… Scars ran horizontal across her ass and high up on the backs of her thighs where she'd endured past whippings from a switch or a belt. My blood began to boil the more discoloration and scarring my eyes picked out on her small body.

"Can't find anything broken that I can see… fucker knows how to make it hurt. Lot of liver and kidney shots. Belly is soft, don't think she's bleeding inside… Get in the bed with her." Doc looked up and looked about as pissed as I felt.

*No women.*

*No children.*

Fuck.

I did as the old man ordered and got into the bed behind her, pulling her into the cradle of my much larger frame. Her skin was beyond cool, just plain frigid against my own.

"Right. I'm gonna take care of these feet then I'll leave you to it. I need to get my drink on after this shit." Doc set to work cleaning, disinfecting and bandaging her feet while I held her. Her shudders eventually diminishing to shivers and her shivers finally gave up after a small gasp of relief.

"She's gonna sleep 'til morning. Best get some rest yerself." Doc got up and pulled the blankets over us.

"Thanks Doc," I murmured.

"Glad you found her when you did." He shouldered his bag and went for the door.

"No women," he grunted.

"Yeah, no women," I echoed.

He flipped out the overhead light and shut the door firmly behind him and I was left in the dark with a nearly naked girl I didn't know a damned thing about clutched to my chest.

What the hell was I doing?

# CHAPTER 2

*Ashton*

I woke in an unfamiliar bed fetched up hard against an unfamiliar body. Chadwick had never been soft, no, he was extremely fit but the body pressed to my back was nothing short of sculpted granite. All hard planes and angles, putting off a heat to rival the hottest day.

I blinked, the room was as dark as the inside of my eyelids. I tried to swallow which was hard with as dry as my mouth and throat were. I moved cautiously, slowly, and meeting no resistance, I pulled myself to the edge of the bed. I sat up slowly, every muscle screaming in protest. Everything hurt, from the roots of my hair to my very nails. I set my feet to the floor and gasped.

Oh God! This was going to be sheer misery but I had done it before and likely, would have to again.

I forced myself to my feet and bit back a cry, sinking my teeth into the tender flesh of my bottom lip until I tasted blood. I stood stock still, letting myself adjust, trying to find the limits of this new, much more abused body. Again, I had been here before... I would adjust, I would heal and I would do better, *be* better, for his correction. I had to be.

I cracked the door and looked about for something to cover myself with by the limited light from the hallway. The room was neat, orderly except where the clothing from the night before had been discarded on the old shabby brown carpet. I looked back to the bed and couldn't help the blush that heated my cheeks. The man in the bed, he was magnificent to look at...

The bar of light from the cracked door fell across his chest which was chiseled and cut to a degree that he rivaled a Greek statue. He could probably snap the likes of me in two with very little effort but he hadn't. Instead, I recalled how he had taken me from the side of the road, seen that I'd had medical attention, obviously, by the bandages I bore... I tried to remember everything that happened but it was foggy. I remember him holding me to the bed, the sharp pinch of a needle and then... I sighed quietly and spied something serviceable to cover me.

I bent slowly and picked up his discarded tee, slipping it over my head. I took a moment to do a more thorough assessment of my body and I sagged with relief when I realized that I experienced nothing to be alarmed about. I didn't feel violated in the slightest and when it came to Chadwick... well... that had been something I had experienced as well.

The man on the bed shifted and I froze in place, I didn't even breathe for several long moments waiting for him to speak, to sit up... to be caught. Thankfully, none of those things happened and I slowly exhaled in relief. I shuffled to the cracked door and slipped out into the hallway shutting it firmly but silently behind me.

I let out another breath I hadn't realized I'd been holding and took in another slow and deep one. I had no idea where I was. None. I crept down the hall silently in search of a bathroom which my body was urgently crying out for by now. I found one and breathed a sigh of relief shutting myself inside.

I quickly did my business, relieved that I indeed had nothing to worry about when it came to my virtue at the hands of the man whose bed I had woken up in.

I caught myself thinking, *Thank you God... Chadwick would never take me back if...* but I stopped cold. In the eight years Chadwick and I had been married... This was the first time I'd ever been without him outside of our home. I lowered myself back down onto the closed lid of the toilet, equal parts elated and terrified.

All of these questions and more went through my head... *Where was I? What was I going to do? Where was I going to live? How was I going to survive? What would he do if he ever found me?* That one stopped me cold. He would kill me. Of that I had no doubt. It may not be that moment or that hour or even that day, but eventually he would kill me. There had been so many times in the last year or two I would have welcomed death as an escape from that man but now… right now… with this tiny taste of freedom… I wanted to live. A tiny flicker of hope flared to life inside my chest.

I helped myself to standing, using the edge of the sink and tried to formulate a plan as I stared into the cracked mirror above it. He'd hit my face. He was always so careful to avoid the face before but his control had been slipping more and more as of late. As I stared into spider webbed silvered glass, I realized just how far he and I had come. I was no longer a wife to him, I hadn't been in a very long time. I was simply his piece of property, his plaything to do with what he willed. I didn't know what was worse, the fact that I had come to this conclusion or the fact that I wasn't even startled by it.

I stared at the split in my lips, the spiral pattern of bruises emanating from it, taking up the majority of my chin, travelling along the curve of my jaw and up my cheek. I tongued the teeth in the back where the blow had landed and winced. Some were loose but thankfully none were missing. I sighed. It hurt being up and about but the pain really was there to let me know I was alive, so in a weird way I was almost grateful for it. I let my eyes rove my damaged face and decided that I couldn't go back. I needed to find a way out somehow. A way to disappear.

I left the tiny bathroom and shuffled back out into the hall, moving wraith like through the sprawling building until I found myself out front, where we'd come in at. There were other people here, behind those closed doors in the back. I could hear the odd cough or grunt, the slap of flesh hitting flesh in the rhythm of sex and the cry of a woman at the height of her climax, but none of these things held answers as to where I was.

This room did. A grotesquely fascinating mural on one cinderblock wall proclaimed this to be the lair of The Sacred Hearts MC. All of the bikes lined up outside the picture window set in the front of the building told me what the MC stood for. The mural depicted a red bleeding human heart veined in blue, wrapped in silver barbed wire. The valves of the heart morphed into tailpipes that spewed fire which hovered above the heart's image, I took it in and swallowed hard, grimacing, wondering briefly if I may have gone from bad to worse.

I went behind the bar and found a glass and a tap and poured myself a glass of water, drinking greedily. I looked around the wrecked facility, empty glasses, bottles, cans… and let out a slow breath. I needed to do something. I needed to feel useful and so I cleaned. All the while thinking furiously, wondering how I would convince my savior on his iron horse, to let me stay.

He found me some time later in the building's kitchen, fixing breakfast for the masses. Doc, the man who'd come to my aid, and a few others that I didn't know were lined up at the bar drinking black coffee out of chipped mugs bearing the eerie logo on the back wall. I hadn't found my voice to speak to any of them, but rather did what would have been expected of me at home, passing out coffee and food silently while doing my best to remain a ghost.

"You see Ash…" my name died on his lips as his gaze traveled through the kitchen door and landed on me, standing at the industrial cooktop, spatula in my hand. He raked a hand through his shoulder length blonde hair and leveled me with his silvery eyes.

"What are you doing?" he asked.

"I cleaned and now I'm cooking breakfast. I didn't know what else I should do," my voice was low and quiet, what Chadwick would expect of me in the morning. I closed my eyes and turned back to the frying bacon.

My savior turned around, surveying the club house and his friends who all looked at him with raised eyebrows. I tried to remember his name, but couldn't. I wanted to say it was something simple, like John or… The bacon popped and sizzled and I jerked my hand out of danger.

"You did all this?" he asked. I turned and looked at him plaintively.

"Yes," I said softly. He nodded and took a seat at the bar, several of the men nodding their respect. I shuffled forward slowly and poured him a coffee.

"You don't have to do any of this Ashton," he said and I looked up into his face. Ruggedly handsome. I had heard the phrase before but Ethan was the first man I had ever met that I would apply it to and it would fit. He was the image of Nordic perfection. Blonde, light eyed with a strong square jaw and mouth set into firm lines. He had angular cheekbones and a strong nose that looked as if it'd been broken a time or two. I was surprised to see it didn't detract from his good looks but rather added to them.

"I know Ethan," I said faintly, proud I'd remembered his name, and set the coffee in front of him.

"Sugar? Cream?" I asked and his gaze drilled into mine. I swallowed resolute that I would not cower but I could feel the trembling starting anyways. I shot my gaze to the floor where it belonged and took a step back, surprised when his hand didn't shoot out to stop me.

"I take it black," he said finally, puzzlement clear in his voice.

I plated up each man bacon, eggs and hash browns, all made from scratch. The kitchen didn't have much but it had the staples. I had found the bacon in the freezer, eggs in the fridge and the potatoes in the pantry needed to be used or they would have been a lost cause so I had gone with preparing them over using the pancake mix I'd found in the pantry.

I set down paper plates and plastic silverware with paper towels for napkins to a round of surprised and grateful nods.

"Ashton, is that your name?" one of the men asked.

"Yes," I murmured, Ethan scowled.

"Thanks for cooking Ashton. No one's ever done it before," the man smiled at me and I gave a tremulous smile in return.

"You're welcome…" I didn't know his name, so I paused and he smiled.

"Data," he supplied and my brow wrinkled for a moment. What kind of name was that?

"You're welcome Data," I murmured. He was a lanky man, tall and thin with a mop of greasy brown hair and liquid brown eyes.

I refilled all of their coffee cups and stopped in front of Ethan's and topped his off.

"Sit down Ashton," he said.

"More people will be up soon. I should fix some more…"

"Please?" he asked and it caught me off guard. I looked at him in soft surprise and the intense look in his silvery eyes had me moving to comply before I could think of another excuse as to why I was needed elsewhere.

He pulled out a stool next to him and slapped a hand on it. It was tall and I captured my lip between my teeth as I contemplated how to get up on it without hurting myself even worse. I must have waited too long because he sighed and stood and without being able to help myself I flinched.

"Easy," he said, large hands descending on my shoulders, "No one is going to hurt you here." He stooped and placed his hands on my hips and helped me up onto the stool.

He retook his seat and I folded my hands in my lap. His tee shirt hung past my knees so I was comfortable enough in my state of dress. I settled my gaze on the center of his chest, which was bare without the benefit of his shirt. He had a tattoo on one side of his chest of the Motorcycle Club's logo and so I focused on that.

"What were you doing out there, Baby?" he asked me and I could feel my cheeks grow warm under his scrutiny.

"I upset my husband," I whispered.

"I'm going to need more than that, Sweetheart," he stated.

"We were coming back from a charity dinner and I contradicted something he'd said in front of another couple, which was stupid, I know better than to upset him…" I closed my eyes, tears welling. There was a long moment of silence and I could feel all of their eyes on me.

"Please, I'm not in the habit of causing trouble," I began to babble, to say anything that would end that awful silence. "I'm normally very cooperative, this is really the first time we've ever disagreed," I was lying through my teeth and it died on my lips when Ethan scoffed. More incredulous sounds were made down the line of men at the bar and I closed my eyes, the words turning to ash in my mouth. I was a horrible liar…

"Baby, he beat the shit out of you." The heat and venom in his voice scalded my mind and I forgot to breathe. "Look at me, Ashton." My body warmed at his nearness as he stood from his seat and closed some of the gap between us. I tipped my face up and reluctantly opened my eyes. The look in his eyes as he looked at me was like a shock of ice water to my system, if ice water could leave a puddle of heat curling low in my belly.

"This," he trailed a fingertip along my jaw and I winced pulling away from the slight touch. *That hurt...* but I suppose that was his point. "Is more than a disagreement and in case you've forgotten," he put his lips beside my ear, his warm breath flaming against my skin, slightly stirring my hair.

"You woke up in my bed mostly naked... now nothing happened, you know that, I'm sure, but we both know this wasn't the first time he's hurt you. Not by a long shot." I closed my eyes and twin tears slipped hot and salty slick down my face. So he'd seen the scars. He drew back and looked at me. His words hurt, but they were the truth, and so it was that the truth hurt...

"Ashton, look at me," he intoned and I opened my eyes, shoulders slumping in defeat.

"May not have been the first time Sunshine, but fuck, it damn sure was his last." He got back up onto his stool and left me sitting there in silent shock.

"You can't promise that," I whispered.

"I think he just did Sweetheart," the voice was low and rumbling deep and came from the far end of the bar. I jolted and took in yet another man standing there, almost equal to Ethan in size by breadth of shoulders but, shorter and the polar opposite in coloring. Where Ethan was light in every aspect, hair, skin and eyes, this man was dark.

He wore unrelieved black from head to toe, his chin length black hair stick straight and shiny like a crow's wing with those blue highlights. He was all square angles and was decidedly Hispanic and leveled me with death's own gaze. I hopped off the stool immediately and hissed, Ethan's hands flying out to steady me.

"Easy Sunshine, that's Dray, he's our VP." I drew in a breath and inclined my head.

"I'll get you some breakfast and coffee. It's a pleasure to meet you, Sir." His eyes narrowed and I swept into the kitchen and away from his penetrating gaze.

17

"Nice to meet you, too?" his voice was dripping with sarcasm and I quailed.

"Ashton," Ethan supplied.

"Ashton," Dray repeated, "Christ even her name sounds rich," I heard him mutter and I flinched inwardly. Chadwick was loaded... I, on the other hand, had come from nothing. When I had met him my sophomore year in college, it was by virtue of a full ride scholarship I had earned while under the roof of a foster home. I set a plate of eggs, bacon and hash browns in front of Dray and gently placed a cup of coffee near it. He looked me over and nodded at whatever he was thinking.

"Church in fifteen minutes," he told the men and I blinked in surprise. I didn't think bikers were the type to attend church.

Ethan smiled behind his coffee cup and I returned to the kitchen to clean up. By the time I had finished, the men had disappeared into a small room they called their chapel. They had been in there the better part of an hour. I had cleaned up their plates and taken my meal in the kitchen when a leggy woman appeared in the doorway.

"Who're you?" she asked, eyeing me speculatively.

"Ashton," I murmured. She was taller than me, which wasn't saying much, most of the world population was. I am five foot even but she, she was easily five foot nine, taller with the red heels she was wearing. Her long legs went up forever before stopping in the shortest pair of army fatigue patterned shorts I had ever seen. Her midriff was left bare and she wore a cut off white tee that stopped just below her breasts. The sleeves had been removed somewhere along the way too.

She swept long platinum blonde hair with dark roots which had been processed to within an inch of its life over her shoulder and looked me over with muddy gray-blue eyes. She was older than me, maybe late forties early fifties to my thirty. Fine lines and wrinkles bracketed a mouth that was used to smiling and eyes that had spent too many summers squinting under the sun.

"I'm Chandra," she said, followed by, "Got any coffee?" She sat at the end of the bar so she could see into the kitchen and pulled out a cigarette. I set down a cup of coffee in front of her and blinked.

"Should you be doing that?" I asked softly.

"Private club sweetie." She lit the end and sucked on it, the tip flaring bright orange. "You the one Trig brought in last night?" she asked, exhaling a plume of smoke in the direction of the ceiling.

"Trig... Trig... Trig..." I repeated softly, searching my memory...

"Yeah Trig, Trigger... Blonde haired pile of delicious muscle. You can't miss him honey."

"Oh! You mean Ethan." I blushed and she arched a dark eyebrow.

"*Ethan?*" she asked, "Who the hell is that?"

"I am. How you doing Chandra?" The small room was letting out and Ethan was one of the first out the door. His eyes locked onto me and I tried to look smaller, because I was rooted to the spot.

"Trigger! Why's this bitch calling you Ethan, Baby?" she asked. I recoiled at being called a bitch but kept my mouth shut.

"Take it easy on her Chandra, she's had a bad night." Doc came out from around Ethan and went to Chandra and kissed her.

"Ashton," my name brought my eyes back around to Ethan.

"C'mere Sunshine," he crooked a finger at me and I swallowed and shuffled forward to comply.

"Dray and I want to talk to you." He put a hand on my shoulder and I cringed out of habit. He dropped it to his side and indicated I should go into the room they had just been in. I went in and Ethan shut the door behind me. Dray sat at a large metal slab of a table, a booted foot on top of it. He looked positively stormy.

"Sit down," he shoved a chair out with a boot and I jumped at the sound it made scraping across the floor.

"Damn it Dray, go easy," Ethan growled. I sank into the chair and licked my lower lip, the cut on it stinging faintly.

"What's your story, Princess?" Dray asked me.

"I... I... I don't have a story," I whispered. Dray's eyes narrowed.

"Uh, yeah, you do," he said.

I fixed my eyes resolutely onto the scarred table top and thought to myself this was a funny set up for a chapel before the thud of Dray's booted feet hit the floor. I near came out of my skin. My breath coming faster and faster as my anxiety ratcheted up yet another notch.

"Who are you?" he asked after a moment of silence.

"Ashton, Ashton Granger," I whispered ashamed.

"What were you doing out on the road?" he asked.

"Accepting my husband's correction, that's what he calls it when I... overstep my bounds," which sounded a lot better than 'when I misbehave', still the sting of humiliation burned my eyes.

"You want to go back to him?" he asked and I looked up sharply.

"He'll kill me! This time for certain. Please don't send me back there?" I couldn't stop the pleading desperation from creeping into my voice.

"Well, what the fuck am I supposed to do with you!?" he demanded. He shot a look over my head at Ethan when I didn't answer immediately.

"I... I can cook, I can clean..." he slapped a hand onto the table top and I jumped.

"Fuck man! You know the rules. Only club bitches and old ladies in the club house. Last night was a one off thing but we can't keep her here!" Dray turned his smoldering dark eyes onto me and I went back into my seat as far as it would allow.

"Can you fuck any brother who wants you?" he asked.

"What?" I asked.

"Will you..."

"Dray, man fucking stop! You're scaring the shit out of her!" Ethan knelt down next to my chair.

"I'm not asking for her to stay here permanently just until I can get a place, like a week man. A week max. I'm not taking her back to that fucker." Dray speared me with his gaze and I blinked stupidly at him.

"Let me call Dragon," Dray said finally.

"Fine," Ethan said.

"I don't think he's going to like it any more than I will," Dray said dryly.

"I'll take my chances," Ethan seethed.

"Yeah. Get her the fuck out of here and find her some fucking clothes," Dray waved his hand in dismissal and I stood up and blew past Ethan and out into the main room.

"Easy Sunshine," Ethan said, voice low behind me.

"Is he always that... intense?" I asked quietly.

"Dray? Yeah. Usually I am too," he admitted. I sat heavily in a seat near the window. The sun streaming through the venetian blinds warming my skin.

"I don't have anything," I murmured staring out over the gravel drive.

"I know, but hey, I've been there. It's not so bad." Ethan slid into the seat across from me.

"What isn't?" I asked.

"Starting over, " he replied and something loosened in my chest.

"I'm really free?" I asked.

"For the most part... I mean you are still married to the man." He folded his hands on the Formica tabletop.

I pursed my lips and closed my eyes breathing in a long slow breath.

"I'm scared," I admitted.

"Yeah. I figure you are," he said and neither of us said anything else for a long time.

# CHAPTER 3

*Trig*

I sat across from her and realized that she was probably one of the most heart stoppingly beautiful creatures I'd ever laid eyes on. We sat in silence for a long time, her golden eyes trained out the window while I just drank her in. She needed a shower, her hair needed to be combed, and she needed some clothes of her own.

I wondered what she was used to wearing. Did she wear dresses or jeans? Did she usually put all that thick auburn hair up or did she leave it down? Was she a woman who wore makeup every day?

I needed to stop thinking like this. I closed my eyes to block her sun soaked image out and went back to last night on the side of the road and that god awful sound she made. That bone chilling wounded animal sound that had turned my blood to ice water in my veins. I took a deep breath and tried to get her attention without scaring her.

"Ashton," I said, and there was a slight flinching around her eyes but nothing else. I tried again.

"Ashton, Baby look at me." She turned slowly, her face moving first, her eyes reluctantly following.

"You need a shower. I'm gonna try and scare up some clothes for you then we're going to go buy some of your own to get you started," I said.

Her eyes dropped to her hands where they rested in her lap. When she brought them over the lip of the table she had her engagement and wedding ring clutched between her thumb and the side of her index finger. I looked at her and she looked at me.

"I don't have any money but you could pawn these," she murmured. I covered her hands with mine.

"Naw, I got this. You keep those so you always have an insurance policy. So you know you can hock 'em if you ever need to. I may

22

not be able to afford much more than Walmart, when you're used to a bunch of fancy shit but –"

"No, don't do that Ethan," she said sharply but gently.

"Look, let's get you cleaned up, get you some of your own clothes and then we can go from there but I'm not taking your rings. So put them back on your fingers and let me go find Doc so he can look at those feet after you get out. Okay?" I searched her face.

"Okay?" I asked and she nodded, sniffing back tears. I wondered, as I led her up the hall to the bathroom and found her some towels, how long it would be before I would see her smile. While she was in the shower Dray moved up the hallway like a thunderhead.

"Call Dragon?" I asked.

"Yeah," he answered and the look he directed at me was heated and I knew that I had won my way.

"One week you fucking prick! You undermine me in front of the rest of the fucking crew like that again over a fucking gash and I'll nail your goddamned balls to the fucking bar." I loved our VP as much as I loved the thought of having a VD when he was like this, but he was young so I gave him a pass.

"Sir, yes, sir!" I handed him a half assed salute and his expression darkened.

"She stays in your room and pulls her weight around here." My back straightened.

"Cooking and cleaning, not necessarily on her back," he intoned, "Although I sure wouldn't mind those eyes lookin' up at me while she sucked my cock." He grabbed his crotch and shook it up and down once and I took a step forward.

"Watch it there Trigger man!" he warned.

I nodded once and he finished going up the hall, moving around the bend and out of my line of sight. I continued standing sentry outside the bathroom door and sighed. Dragon, our club president was Dray's daddy and the only reason Dray was VP. Dragon kept hoping Dray would come around to the rest of the club's way of thinking but I saw that happening, oh say, about the time hell froze over. Dray had a thing about damsels in distress and keeping them as far away from him as possible. Probably wasn't a bad policy.

Women tended to complicate things. I could attest to that myself.

The noise of the shower stopped and I straightened. A few minutes later Ashton poked her wet head out into the hallway.

"C'mon Sunshine, Doc is waiting," she looked up at me.

"Bandages are wet, kind of hard to avoid in a shower and I didn't want to take them off," she murmured. I could barely make out what she said but nodded just the same and scooped her up before she could protest.

Her arms tentatively went around my neck and I kind of relished that I could do this. Not often you encountered a woman as lush and small as her that was also light enough to carry if you wanted to. The movies were full of bullshit. Doc was waiting in the common room at the bar and I set Ashton down on it, admittedly, a little reluctantly. Doc immediately went to work.

She was wearing a clean shirt of mine. A light blue button down with the sleeves rolled back that had come from the depths of my closet. Last time I'd worn the damn thing was for a court date. It wore on her like a dress.

"Found these, they might fit her," Chandra came in with a pair of shorts and a ladies cut Sacred Hearts tee that was a size small.

"Where the hell you get those woman?" Doc asked looking over his half-moon glasses.

"They're Desiree's," she said by way of answer then told Ashton by way of explanation, "That's my eleven year old granddaughter."

"Oh, thank you… you know I think they just may fit," she murmured taking the two items from Chandra.

"I'll wash them before I return them," she promised solemnly.

"I'm going to go see about borrowing the truck," I said.

"Don't bother, Dray's panties are in a wad," Chandra said, cigarette bobbing between her lips. She pulled a set of keys out of her cleavage and handed them to me.

"Take mine, it's the gold Taurus," she crossed her arms.

"You're all being so nice to me," Ashton whispered brokenly, hiding behind a curtain of her lank, damp hair. She brushed away a tear.

"A lot of lost souls find their way here sweetheart," Chandra said, taking a drag. "You ain't the first." She blew out a long stream of smoke and I was just about dying for one of my own. I pulled out the unsatisfying e-cig and she smirked at me. I frowned at her but sucked on it anyway blowing out a weak ass cloud of vapor.

"There you go darlin', go get dressed." Doc leaned back and I lifted her down off the bar gently, but damned if Ashton didn't go into the kitchen. She came back out with a bottle of kitchen cleaner and a roll of paper towels and deliberately cleaned the bar where she'd been. Chandra laughed and I fought not to grin.

"Sunshine that bar is cleaner than it's ever been even after your pretty little ass has been on it. Go get dressed so we can go," I said and she stood there and blushed all the way to the roots of her pretty auburn hair. Her eyes welled with tears.

"I'm sorry, sir," she whispered.

"Hey, no. It's Trig or keep callin' me Ethan. There is no 'sir' here. Not anymore." My lips compressed into a thin line and she nodded, eyes wide and bolted for a different room. She came back a minute later. The tee fit, the shorts were a bit tight and she wore the button down open over it all. It wasn't the best look but it wasn't enough to land her on the Walmartians website or anything. I nodded, satisfied. Chandra threw down a pair of oversized leopard print flip flops onto the floor and Ashton jumped at the sharp slap but obediently stepped into them. She looked like a child playing dress up.

"How old are you Ashton?" I asked. She looked up sharply.

"Thirty, why?" she asked. Shit I was only six years older than her.

"Just curious. Ready?" she sucked in a long breath and let it out slowly.

"I suppose," she said nervously. That made two of us.

When we got to the store Ashton looked around herself dubiously and her small hand found mine as soon as we set foot inside. Didn't take me long to figure out she'd never been to a Walmart. We went into the clothing section; she stopped cold.

"What?" I asked, startled.

"I haven't bought my own clothes since I graduated college… since Chadwick and I got married," she whispered.

"Get what you want Babe," I said as soothingly as possible.

"What would you like?" she asked and I could tell it was an automatic trained response. It made my heart heavy to hear it and I touched her shoulder lightly. She flinched and turned looking up at me with those wide golden eyes.

"Doesn't matter Sunshine, you just pick what you want," I nudged her towards the racks of clothes and she turned back to me.

"I don't know what to get, I mean what..." she looked near tears and I couldn't help but smile. She didn't know what I could afford.

"Just get what you need, Baby. I'll figure it out," I said.

She selected a pair of those black stretchy work out pants, a pair of jeans and some other things. I stopped paying attention. She got herself bras and underwear and socks and a pair of running shoes and a pair of sandals. She looked so damned solemn and lost moving through the aisles and I was doing a slow burn.

One, I wanted to kill her asshole ex. Two, I just plain wanted *her*, which was fucked up all on its own. I scrubbed a hand over my face and asked if she was done. She looked at me and asked softly about a toilet and I looked at her confused.

"What?" I asked.

"I asked if I may please go to the toiletries section... toothbrush, toothpaste... that sort of thing?" she was trembling again and I found myself nodding.

"Yeah, yeah whatever you need Babe," and I was surprised to find I meant it. I mean I was no rich fuck like her hubby but I wasn't no slouch either. I could afford this trip and I was surprised to find that I really didn't mind paying for her things. Just something about her, I wanted to fix it. She was too pretty, and from everything I had been able to see so far, too sweet, to have something like this happen to her.

I took her over near the pharmacy and she picked out an inexpensive toothbrush and some toothpaste on sale and I smiled. We rounded to the shampoo section and she went immediately to the brand I'm pretty sure she'd always used. She opened the top and smelled it, she closed it and put it back on the shelf and seemed to be at war with herself.

"What's wrong, Sunshine?" I asked in the way I'd used on the road, Jesus, not even twenty-four hours ago…

"I can smell like whatever I want now right?" she asked. Jesus fucking Christmas, he'd even controlled what she'd *smelled* like? I looked at her and blinked and before I knew what I was saying it was out of my mouth,

"Sunshine, if you want to smell every fuckin' soap, shampoo and lotion in this fuckin' place until you find what you like well then I'm going to stand here and wait until you're done. Go to it." I leaned on the cart and watched my words sink in, and I gotta tell you…

So. Fucking. Worth. It.

Because she fucking *smiled*, and it was like the sun had come out from behind the clouds, lighting up her whole face to the point she fucking *glowed*. I knew right then that one man's loss had just become my treasure because there was no way I knew what I was doing. Still, at the same time, there was no way I was letting her go. The attraction was just that strong.

I told my inner cave man to get back in his hole and I smiled back at her and made myself as good as my word. I stood there and waited for her to figure out what she wanted to smell like, although when I'd carried her from the shower, smelling like my body wash hadn't been a bad thing. I'd kind of liked my smell all over her. Way more than I should have for having just met her. Hell, I think I was sunk the moment she'd looked at me with those bright golden eyes of hers. I sighed. I watched her move carefully up and down the aisle and decided to make it a priority to learn more about her.

Finally, satisfied with her decisions she returned to the cart with a bottle of shampoo, conditioner, body wash and I think lotion and hairspray or some shit. I didn't really care. I smiled at her again and asked if she was ready to go. She nodded carefully but I could tell she thought she was forgetting something. Her face was an open book.

"I think so," she said softly. Damn she was hard to hear, and I nodded and we hit check out.

It was a relatively short drive back to the clubhouse and mid-way there her soft voice floated across the interior to reach me.

"I'll pay you back."

"You think about what you want to do for work?" I asked her.

"I don't know what I can do with a liberal arts degree," she said and my eyebrows went up.

"Not a fuck of a lot," I said and laughed, she sobered; her face turned toward the glass and it reflected panic back at me.

"Don't worry about it right now. You have to heal up and look presentable before you can even start looking. That's going to take a couple of weeks. We'll be at the clubhouse for one of 'em. I got to find a place for us after that. So just... don't worry about a thing until then. Okay?" I looked over at her and she was staring at me with this strange sort of awe on her face.

"Okay," she whispered, and we finished the rest of the ride in silence.

# CHAPTER 4

*Ashton*

"I'm just going to set 'em on the bed," he said pushing through his bedroom's door.

"You take your time going through things, get square and come out and join the party if you feel like it. If not, I'll be in later tonight. No pressure either way." I nodded dumbly and belatedly registered what he'd said.

"Something to sleep in…" I mumbled as he was headed back out the door.

"What?" he popped his head back in and I cringed.

"I forgot something to sleep in," I said a bit louder for his benefit and waited for the yelling, the screaming…

"Use the dress shirt. Keep it, it's yours," he said with a shrug and ducked out the door. I blinked after him and sank slowly to the bed. I closed my eyes while the room spun for a moment. Just so much was happening in too short of an amount of time… I swallowed hard and began to sort through the many bags our shopping trip had yielded.

Ethan had bought a plastic caddy for my toiletries to go into, to make it simpler to carry them back and forth to the restroom. I spent several long minutes loading it with what we'd purchased until I was satisfied, then I went and brushed my teeth. I stared at myself in the mirror for a long minute and took the brush he'd bought me to my hair. I brushed it until it was only slightly wavy and it shone and then peeked into the hall.

I waited until it was clear and then ghosted up its length to Ethan's door, shutting the door tightly behind me. I closed my eyes and felt torn. I wanted to be safe, where no one could judge or hurt me but I had to admit to myself the only person I felt safe around so far was Ethan… and maybe Doc and by extension Chandra.

I pulled out clothes and tore off tags, hanging things neatly in the closet while I made up my mind. I turned back to the bed and decision made, I set about getting dressed. New bra, new panties and it was amazing how much better I felt just with those things. I hung up the dress I'd arrived in, hiding it in the back of the closet, apart from my new things.

I trailed fingers along the crisp cotton of the dress I'd chosen today and told myself I really didn't need to be brave. That I could stay here, in the room and wait for Ethan to come back and that would be okay… but I found myself picking up the dress anyways. I stepped into it and shrugged into the straps and with a deep breath, reached around back where I zipped it almost all the way up.

I couldn't make it all the way, I wasn't flexible enough in my current state so the top three inches of the zipper stayed down. I let my hair cover it and slipped my feet into the plain brown sandals which hurt but I was used to the pain by now. Or at least that's what I kept telling myself.

It was a white sundress in the baby doll style and fit like a dream. The edge was hemmed in white eyelet lace and the lines of it were crisp and clean. It fell to just above my knees and was more modest than what I had arrived in which pleased me. I found myself hoping it would please Ethan as well and that startled me.

While it was true I was afraid of this new life… I wasn't looking to replace Chadwick with Ethan. I swallowed. That would not only be wrong, horribly twisted, it would also be completely unfair to Ethan. I sat down on the bed and sniffed even as bass beats began filtering through the wall from the common area of the club house out front.

God help me I was so confused. I didn't know what to do and after so long, so many years of being told what to do, of being a prisoner in Chadwick's home, I didn't fully know how to operate out here. On my own… I closed my eyes and wiped away some more stray tears. A soft knock came at the door.

"Come in…" I said softly and realized whoever it was couldn't hear me. I got up and cracked the door. Chandra gave me a one sided smile.

"Oh look at you!" she exclaimed, "Can I come in?" I nodded and opened the door wider and she slipped in. She lightly grasped my shoulders and looked me over.

"You go out there, you need to stay close to Trigger, you understand me?" she asked.

I nodded and turned around to pick up the white headband that had come with the dress. She snapped my zipper up the final three inches for me without being asked and I jumped but turned back around smiling, grateful.

"I mean it darlin', you don't want anyone mistaking you for a club whore." I nodded gravely and slid the headband into my hair so it would hold it back from my face. Chandra fluffed some of my hair forward over my shoulders and smiled.

"Look a lot better without all them bruises but you're lovely." She smiled at me and I gave one back in return hoping it wasn't as weak as I felt it was.

"Ready?" she asked me and I nodded meekly and followed her into the hall, closing the door tightly behind me. I followed Chandra to the common room and was immediately assaulted by the noise and laughter. It was crowded. The sharp crack of pool balls from over at the table made me jump but I don't think anyone noticed.

Chandra led me out the front door. A group of men stood to one side smoking and talking softly and I stopped short. The Sacred Heart emblem emblazoned on the back of Ethan's vest seemed larger than life against his broad back. Chandra called out to him, "Yo, Trig!" and he turned but his eyes weren't on her, they landed immediately on me and something feral and frightening passed through them before being swallowed up into their depths. I'd seen looks like that before from men, from Chadwick even, but where the look from Chadwick had caused a slow curl of dread to constrict my heart, the look from Ethan did something entirely different.

Butterflies swirled in my stomach and my hand unconsciously went there, smoothing down the front of my dress. Ethan looked me over from head to toe and back again and all conversation had ceased between the men. Chandra dragged me forward and my legs

31

felt leaden but they went. I drew even with Ethan and looked up at him.

"You keep a close eye on her Trigger, now I mean it," Chandra admonished.

"Yes Ma'am," he said and took my hand in his much larger one. "Ashton, you look great," he added.

"Thank you," I murmured, he turned back to the men and they resumed talking in low tones and so I did what I was best at, I stood at Ethan's side as a decoration with no mind of her own. I listened of course. I couldn't help that. They were speaking on details about a run. Where they would stop, how long it would take but were carefully neutral on where or what they would be doing exactly.

Ethan kept stealing looks at me and finally turned to me.

"I'm doing it aren't I?" he asked.

"What?" I asked startled.

"Guys, I'm gonna catch you later," he said over his shoulder, "Ashton's feet are a mess and I don't want her standing here." He took me gently by the elbow and led us slowly inside out of the growing chill. The music was loud and the laughter louder. He found us a pair of chairs at a smaller table and asked me what I'd like to drink. I asked for water and he came back with one and a beer. He settled across from me.

"What did you think you were doing?" I asked genuinely curious.

"Treating you like the fuckwit," he said and I arched a brow.

"You're worth more than simply standing there looking pretty on my arm while the grownups talk." He grinned and I was struck by how straight and white his teeth were.

"That's all right…" I said and he took a pull off his beer.

"Bullshit," he said and I fell quiescent.

"What?" he asked.

"I'm sorry for arguing," I said, "Of course you were right I…" he laughed and shook his head incredulously.

"Don't fucking apologize to me for having an opinion Sunshine, you're fine," he leaned back in his seat and I nodded staring vacantly at the scarred wooden table top. He sat across from me watching me and I took a sip of my water.

"Ask me something," he said finally and I looked up startled.

"What do you want me to ask you?" I asked and he laughed.

"I want you to ask me something *you* want to know about me," he said.

"Why did you stop?" I asked. His eyes softened and he looked over my face.

"Because I had to... I couldn't just let you keep walking. You were going to freeze to death, or worse... Couldn't let it happen Babe," and he took another drink of his beer.

I closed my eyes and allowed myself just a sliver of a moment of self-pity, just a millisecond of wishing that he could have driven right by and that I froze... Chadwick was still out there and I would be a fool to think he wasn't looking for me. That he wouldn't do something...

"What are you thinking?" Ethan asked me and I looked up sharply.

"About what would have happened, had you not stopped when you did," I said.

"You ain't gotta worry about it Babe, because I did. Okay?" he gave me a pointed look and I nodded carefully.

"You want to tell me about it?" he asked and I opened my mouth and did... All of it, from the time Chadwick and I met, to when it started to go downhill, all the way up until now.

I tired quickly and it wasn't long after that, I fell silent. A shadow fell over me. I jolted and looked up fearfully, I'd been lost inside my own head, but it was Ethan. He bent and scooped me up before I could protest. I sort of loved that he carried me like he did. I felt safe in his arms and could almost pretend for a moment that I was something to be treasured. He took me back to the room and set me carefully on the edge of the bed.

"Ethan," I called before he could duck back out the door.

"Yeah Sunshine?" he asked. I blushed, I could feel the warmth flood my face.

"What is it Ashton?" he asked, his voice kind.

"Um, can you help me with my zipper?" I waved at my back and he smiled.

"Sure," he murmured.

I stood carefully and turned and the fabric of my dress parted smoothly. I turned to say thank you but the room was empty, the door swinging wide where Ethan had been. I shut the door and hung the dress neatly in the closet. I put my bra back in the bag with the rest of my unmentionables and hung it on the inside of the closet doorknob as a sort of impromptu underwear drawer.

I pulled on Ethan's dress shirt and buttoned it and flipped out the overhead light. I took the side of the bed furthest from the door and was asleep before my head could even touch the pillow.

# CHAPTER 5

*Trig*

*Shit, that had been way too hard…* I thought to myself as I strode down the hall back to the heat and noise of the party. I kept visualizing the parting material revealing the smooth perfect skin of her back. It had been an exercise in self-control not to unhook her bra and bring my lips to the side of her neck which was so fucking wrong on so many levels given what she'd just been through. I went to the bar and ordered a Tequila. Doc turned on his stool and looked me up and down.

"She all right?" he drawled.

"Yeah," I tossed back the shot and let the burn go down, fiery but smooth.

"You all right?" he asked, eyes twinkling with laughter.

"Yeah," I grunted and took a second shot immediately after the first and grinned.

"Under your skin?" he asked.

"Yeah," I nodded and my smile soured.

"It's about time boy, and from what I've seen so far, not a bad choice," he slapped me on the back and I closed my eyes.

"I'm not ready for anything and she's *damn sure* not ready for anything." I shrugged off his hand and Doc leaned back.

"Well like it as not, yer in it for the long haul with this one," he reminded me.

"I know," I grated shooting a look over in Dray's direction. He'd forced my hand in Church that morning. Only way I could have her here and *not* be passed around was to declare her my Old Lady. Really it was meaningless, a formality on paper only, but damned if I wanted to explain it. She'd been owned by her husband for far too long as it was and I didn't want that stink on me.

"She know?" Doc asked.

"Nope and I'm going to do my best to keep it that way. She was owned by her husband for the better part of the last ten years of her life, she deserves freedom." I didn't want to talk about Ashton or club business anymore. I just wanted to go to bed which was tough as hell with her in it.

"So what're you going to do?" Doc asked.

"I'm going to find us an apartment, get her into her own room, her own space, then I'm going to help her find a job." The world was becoming slightly fuzzy around the edges from the alcohol.

"Got it all planned out then, huh?" he asked.

"Yeah," I took two more shots in rapid succession.

"Good luck with that," he commented sardonically and I snorted.

I got up and staggered down the hall, back to my room. I leaned against the wall outside the door and slid to the floor. By no means was I passing out drunk. I just wasn't ready to face Ashton's soft lithe body tucked into my own. I let the shots blur out the sharp edges of my consciousness before I staggered to my feet. I opened the door and the light fell across Ashton's sleeping face. She looked like an angel and I felt torn. She stirred and her golden eyes blinked up at me in confusion.

"Ethan..?" her soft voice asked.

"Yeah Sunshine, just me. Go back to sleep," my voice was rough with tequila and a jumble of emotion. She reached out a small hand and patted the mattress beside her and I felt my lips curve into a smile.

"You want me in there with you?" I asked, pulling my arm out of the sleeve of my jacket.

"It's your bed," she sighed out.

"Yeah," I murmured, awkwardly toeing off my boots, stumbling as I did it.

I almost missed it when she murmured, "You make everything safe."

I stopped and the taste of tequila suddenly went sour in my mouth. Me, make everything safe? Christ if only she knew how much I wanted to do some very unsafe things to her. I hung my head and ripped my belt angrily out of its buckle, unbuttoning and unzipping my jeans with more force than necessary. The proof of my desire for her springing free of my undone fly almost immediately.

I tried thinking of anything to get it to go down and really all it took was catching sight of the bruises and swelling marring her cheek and jaw. I looked her over one last time before I shut the door and got into bed beside her. I turned onto my side and closed my eyes. Wishing there were just a little light in here for me to see her by.

It wasn't long before she shifted, scooting closer to me. I lay on my back and she snugged herself into my side. Her breathing deepening smoothing evenly back into sleep. I asked myself, not for the first time and probably not for the last just what it was I thought I was playing at but like all the times I had thought it before I came up empty on answers. Ashton twitched against me and I put my arms around her, gathering her close. I sighed. I had a lot to do tomorrow…

When I opened my eyes, for the second morning in a row, I found myself alone even though I hadn't gone to sleep that way. I coughed and sat up, wondering where Ashton had gotten to now. I pulled on the pair of jeans from the night before over my boxers and leaving them undone, went for the bathroom. I needed to hydrate so my next stop was out to the common room for some water and like the day before, that's where I found Ashton.

I leaned a shoulder against the door jamb and watched her move, wraith like through the room. A giant black trash bag her only companion. Bottles clinked softly as she slid them in, cans rattled as she moved from table to table cleaning up the MC's mess. Her expression was heart breaking. Withdrawn and solemn and I couldn't fucking stand it. I raked a hand through my hair and pulled it back. I fished in my pocket for a hair elastic and tied it off.

"Ashton, Babe, stop," I said and she froze.

"It needs to be clean," she said and looking lost she went back to picking up.

"Yeah, I get that but it doesn't need to be cleaned up by you Babe," I strode to her and she backed up a step.

"I need to do it," she said plaintively.

"Why?" I asked.

"Because it's normal, it's the only thing I'm good for and it's…"

"It's what? What's expected?" I stooped to capture her far off golden gaze with my own. She looked at me and her shoulders slumped.

"Yes," she answered solemnly, "It's what he would have expected."

"It's okay Sunshine," I said pulling her into a hug. She was stiff in my arms.

"You don't have to do it if you don't want to. No one expects it out here…"

"…but we appreciate it." Doc called from the doorway. Ashton jumped in my arms and I let her go, forcing a smile onto my face.

"That we do," I said. She nodded but wouldn't look at either of us and continued picking up after the festivities. She wore those black workout pants that kissed her every curve. She also wore a lavender tee that fit her like a dream. Her feet were clad in her new sneakers and her hair rode in a braid over her slender shoulder, a thick rope of auburn that I wanted to twine around my hand as I pulled her mouth to mine… God damn these were some intense urges for a woman I didn't even know! I needed some distance, clear my head, the *big* one.

"I'm going out," I said abruptly.

"Would you like me to fix you some breakfast or coffee?" her soft voice drifted across the common room to me, barely audible, but soothing to my frayed nerves.

"Sure Babe, yeah. I'd like that," I said. The fiery rush to get out of there cooled a bit. "I'm gonna grab a shower while you work on that. Okay?" I asked and she nodded and graced me with a watery smile.

This was going to suck so hard but it was totally necessary. I went back to my room, picked up my shower caddy and my towel and went for the nearest shower. I turned on the cold water as far as it would go and showered in record time. I dressed in my last pair of fresh jeans, a worn but comfortable USMC heather gray tee and my boots. I moved my wallet and chain and my belt over to the fresh pants.

I sat on the edge of the bed that Ashton and I were sharing and propped my forearms on my knees. Okay. I couldn't deny the total lust I was feeling for Ashton but damn. She deserved a hell of a lot better than the likes of me. I hung my head and closed my eyes. I was surprised to find that despite how hard I was kicking my own ass not to touch her, not to take her any place either of us would regret going, that I didn't for one minute regret picking her up off the highway. But man, picking her up was a huge responsibility.

She was seriously fucked up in the head and I didn't always have the patience required for this sort of thing. Like it or not though, I was responsible for her and right now, the best thing I could do was get her out of the club. I was starting on that today. I sat up and there she was standing in the doorway, plate of food in one hand, cup of steaming coffee in the other. I smiled.

"This is hard for you," she whispered.

I patted the bed beside me and sighed. She set the plate and coffee on the dresser and sat down obediently and it almost killed me to see it.

"Not why you think," I said and worry creased her brow.

"Have I done something wrong?" she asked.

"No," I said.

"Then what?" she asked and I let my gaze sweep her pretty, if troubled face.

"I have a week to find us someplace to go, we can't stay here forever," I said. She nodded carefully.

"I have to be back to work this afternoon," I added "And I'm worried about leaving you here," I frowned.

"I'll be okay," she whispered.

"You sure?" I asked. God I wanted to do bad things to her. I concentrated on the problem at hand.

"I'll stay in here if you like," she murmured.

"Yeah. Unless you're with Doc or Chandra. Use the nearest bathroom and get right back in here. The T.V. isn't hooked to cable but the DVD player works. Anything you like to watch? I'll go get it for you," I searched her face and she looked relieved.

"Thank you," she breathed.

"For what?" I asked.

"For not sending me away."

I blinked, "Naw, not going to do that to you. Now what do you like to watch?" I asked.

"I like musicals," she said tentatively.

"What like Phantom of the Opera?" I asked."

"And Les Miserables." She smiled and it was a genuine one and it changed her whole face.

"Okay. I'll get them for you." I drank some of my coffee and she stood up. She bent at the waist, one hand on the swell of my shoulder and kissed my cheek softly. It was my turn to jump.

"What was that for?" I asked gruffly, secretly thrilled.

"You're good to me," she said in her soft lyrical voice and she drifted out the door. I picked up my plate of pancakes and syrup, and followed her out to the common room where she returned to the kitchen. I sat at the bar and watched her move around the stainless steel industrial setting. She seemed lighter somehow. I shook my head and shoved a bite of pancake in my mouth. She was a good cook, and I needed to hurry up and get those damned movies.

More people filtered in from the back, no doubt enticed by the smell of food and coffee. I hit up Doc and Chandra and told them what I'd told Ashton. They both agreed it was best and nodding to the woman in question I went out into her new namesake.

About half the day later I sat on the back of my bike and contemplated buying a real pack of smokes instead of this e-cig shit. I figured finding an apartment would be easier but it was turning out to be a giant pain in my ass. I tipped my face up into the sun and closed my eyes letting the deep red glow of the inside of my eyelids suffuse me with the warmth the air lacked.

It was beautiful but still crisp out. Spring was trying like hell to come in but hadn't quite made it to temperature. I started my bike. I had time to swing by the club house and only be about ten minutes late to work. Ashton's movies rode in the inside pocket of my cut and I wanted to give them to her before she died of boredom. I merged into traffic and rode, comfortably in tune with my bike, the road and the wind.

Once back at the club, I backed the bike into its place and cut the engine. I got up and slipped into the dim interior of the club house and blinked when I was assaulted by the strong antiseptic smell of lemon cleaner. Three brothers stood talking in the entry way. Everything fucking *sparkled*...

"Trigger," Doc called, Reaver, my best friend, was grinning at me and Dragon, the man, the president himself, turned around; teeth bared in a grin of his own, nestled in his dark beard.

"Your stray's been busy man," Dragon said holding out his hand. I clasped his forearm and was pulled into a bone crushing hug. We slapped each other soundly on the back and I went back to surveying the common area.

"She did the bathrooms too," Reaver said and I kind of cringed at that. The bathrooms here were disgusting.

"Where'd she get the stuff to do it?" I asked.

"Found it laying around, if I had to guess," Dragon spun in place.

"Hope you don't mind," I grunted.

"Naw brother, I'd like to meet her," I nodded.

"She's in laying down, she tired herself out," Doc let me know.

"Yeah, okay, I'll see if she's up for it," I said, Dragon and Reaver nodded.

I went down the hall and opened my door. Ashton sat up quickly.

"Easy girl, just me." I held up my hands where she could see them. She looked up at me, her face still sleepy, hair tousled and it was hot. I smiled and reached into my cut, plucking the two DVD's out of the pocket there and held them out.

"You brought them!" she said in surprise and half reached out.

"Sure did, go on take 'em," soft wonder filled her eyes and she plucked them gently from my fingers.

"Got a couple brothers out here that want to meet you. You up for it?" I asked. She looked up at me and nodded getting to her feet off the bed. She was in my dress shirt again and I held out my hand. She set her movies lovingly on the covers and put her hand in mine and we went out into the common room.

"Holy shit! That little thing did all of this!?" Reaver asked. Ashton shied behind me like a child would and I gave him a look.

"Sorry," he said and looked chagrined.

"Ashton," I said, pointing at him, "That there is Reaver and this is Dragon. Dragon is President of Sacred Heart MC." Ashton blinked up at the two men.

"It's a pleasure to meet you both," she said gently and Dragon laughed.

"Likewise," Dragon said as he dropped into a chair so he could get a better look at her. "Would you look at them peepers?" he commented.

"Never seen eyes like that," Reaver agreed.

"Ashton," I said and she looked up at me.

"Yes?" she asked.

"You doin' all right?" I asked.

"Yes, I'm sorry," she came around so that they could see her but her trembling belied her words.

"Nothin' to be sorry about," Dragon held up his hands.

"Listen Babe, as long as Dragon or Reaver here are around you're good to go, just as if Doc or Chandra were here. You get me?" I asked. She nodded a touch too quickly.

"I gotta get to work," I said and pulled my hand from hers. She looked a little lost for a second but then turned the full force of that golden gaze on me.

"Your lunch," she said and I frowned.

"What?" I asked.

She scurried off into the kitchen and came back and I noticed she was in her bandaged feet… then I noticed the floor was clean. I blinked. Damn she had been busy. She returned a moment later with a brown paper bag and handed it to me.

"I made your lunch," she said softly and I looked dumbly down at it. Three masculine chuckles. She blushed and I frowned.

"Thanks," I said. Could she be any more fucking adorable?

"Go on man, Ashton you want to stay out here or go back to Trig's room?" Dragon asked and I couldn't respect the man more for giving her the choice.

"If I'm allowed I would like to return to Ethan's room please," she murmured and I smiled.

"You can do what you want around here. You don't need no one's permission." Dragon leaned back in his chair and it creaked under his bulk. Dude was still cut at fifty.

"Thank you," she whispered and beat a hasty retreat. Dragon's expression darkened, Reaver's clouded over too.

"You got your work cut out with that one Brother," Reaver commented.

Didn't I know it? I looked down at the sack lunch in my hand. The guys laughed at me.

"Fuck off," I muttered and went for the door.

The three of them howled with laughter after me. It *was* pretty funny. Who makes a bad ass biker a sack lunch?

Apparently Ashton did.

# CHAPTER 6

*Ashton*

I sat on the bed and held the plastic cases with shaking fingers. He'd bought them. He hadn't forgotten, or changed his mind. He'd asked me, I'd told him and then he'd gone out and bought them for me. I blinked. I must have been staring at the two DVD's in my fingers for an hour or more. My mind spinning and whirling. A knock came at the door, I startled and stuffed the movies beneath the pillows to hide them out of old habit. Had it been Chadwick he would have taken them away just to be spiteful. He could be like a little boy ripping the wings off a fly, and usually *I* was that fly. I cleared my throat.

"Yes?" I called softly.

Chandra poked her head into the room.

"These boys are bitchin' they're hungry out here. You want to get out for a minute and get something for them?" she asked.

"Do you think it would be all right?" I asked.

"Please!" she said, rolling her eyes, "You're not a prisoner here sweetie. Get dressed if you want to come," she slipped out the door leaving it open a crack and I swallowed. I made a decision and scrambled to the end of the bed and dressed quickly in jeans and a long sleeved shirt that swirled with scrollwork pattern and blushes of color in grays and pinks.

I shoved my feet into socks and my new sneakers, which still hurt but couldn't be avoided, and crept out into the common room. Dragon, Dray, Reaver and Doc sat around a table playing cards.

"There she is!" Dragon called.

"Cool. What do you guys want?" Chandra asked.

"I don't know, what do we want boys?" Dragon asked and I could see the resemblance between himself and his son. There was no mistaking their blood relation.

44

Reaver was younger than Ethan, early to mid-twenties, with short brown hair that was shorter on the sides but longer on top giving the illusion of a Mohawk without actually being one. It hung low in the front, reminding me of a horse's forelock, resting on his forehead between his eyes which were warm despite their light blue. Bluer than Ethan's which were more silver. He had a dark blue teardrop tattooed at the outside corner of one eye and it was at odds with his easy smile.

The men traded notions of fast food restaurants and I grimaced and before I knew I had opened my mouth I suggested,

"I could cook for you." I was met by four sets of eyes, two dark, two light... one of those deep, dark pairs smoldering with barely suppressed anger. I shuddered at Dray's expression and licked my suddenly dry lips.

"Yeah. Okay. Pony up fellas," Dragon said and wallets came out and bits of green were put onto the edge of the table.

"Use it all, stock the kitchen," Dragon grunted and pushed the money towards me. I was frozen to the spot. Speechless. Chandra's heels clicked across the floor and she picked up the money and thrust it into my hands.

"Come on Babe, don't want these boys to starve to death," she winked at me and I followed her silently out to her car.

"What's wrong?" she asked. I looked at her.

"They just gave me money," I said a little stunned.

"Yeah, so?" she asked. I rubbed my fingers across the bill's surface. How do you tell someone when it's been more than three years since you last held any sort of money in your hands?

"I..." I closed my mouth. I didn't know what to say.

"Wow, your husband was a real piece of work," she complained, pulling out onto the three lane highway.

I counted the money and thought about what to do. The kitchen with Chadwick was always just... stocked. I hadn't had to do it myself. Chandra took us to a grocery store and I chewed my lip.

"Know what you want to do?" she asked.

"I don't know what they like," I murmured and she snorted.

"They like anything. Those boys will eat just about whatever you put in front of 'em as long as it has some kind of meat in it." I nodded and decided what I was going to do. I knew what the kitchen had and didn't. We started in the produce section. Chandra chattered on about each of the men and how she'd met Doc.

"Dragon founded the club about thirty years ago or more, before Dray was even thought of. He hooked up with Dray's mom a little under ten years into it. They had Dray when Dragon was in his early thirties, late for him but not so much for Tilly. Dray was a good kid, not always like what you see now," she sighed and chattered on. I listened politely and moved up and down the groceries aisles feeling oddly exposed. Soon the feeling grew into the pricking sensation of being watched. Finally in the dairy section Chandra broke off mid-sentence and turned.

"What are you looking at?" she demanded of a man, who was indeed staring.

"Nothing!" he exclaimed uncomfortably.

"Then take your ass over there!" she told him, pointing off in a direction that was away from us. "Creep," she muttered.

We finished shopping quickly after that. At the check stand the woman checking us out was staring at me too.

"What?" Chandra asked.

"Nothing!" The clerk said hurriedly, "It's just, she looks like the missing woman on TV." She said and I felt the blood drain from my face.

"Missing?" I asked, breathy.

"Yeah two nights ago off the highway after a disagreement with her husband. Are you her?" she asked.

"No!" I said hurriedly but could taste the lie.

"Does she look like she's missing?" Chandra snapped. The clerk looked at me, her eyes locking on my bruises.

"Didn't see a thing," she said resolutely, pursing her lips, and she and Chandra traded knowing looks. My hands shook like crazy as I counted out the money for our things, I was almost surprised I could even do it. Chandra grabbed our bags. I took the change and we both hurried from the store. I never in a million years dreamed he would go to the news...

"Don't worry about it, Baby," Chandra said, interrupting my thoughts as she backed out of the parking stall. I knew he would look for me. That he would find me... I closed my eyes.

"He hasn't found you yet. The boys will know how to get ahead of this," she said, pulling the thoughts right out of my head.

We drove back to the club house, Chandra immediately got onto her phone as we pulled out onto the main thoroughfare. It sounded like she was talking to Doc. I sank into my seat and tried to sort through my feelings. I had far too many of them to deal with. One of them stood out desperately clear from the rest though...

I had no desire to return to Chadwick Granger. None whatsoever. I was as sure as the day was long that doing so would be the death of me and I didn't want that life, the fear, anymore.

Three somewhat anxious males and one angry one met us at the clubhouse door. I stepped out of the car and automatically began picking bags out of the back seat to bring in. Doc stopped me.

"You all right, Sweetheart?" he asked. I nodded miserably.

"You want us to call Trig for you?" Reaver asked and I looked up alarmed and shook my head.

"No. There's nothing to be done for now, let him work. I've disrupted his life too much as it is." I turned to unload more groceries and heard Reaver mutter...

"If anyone's life needed a shakeup it's that fucker's." I looked at him sharply and stopped my mouth before it could open. He was smiling and there were at least two grunts of agreement. I put confusion somewhere on the list of things I was feeling.

"Put those down," Dragon ordered and I immediately complied.

"C'mon boys, let's get these in the house so Ashton can fix us some grub. I'm starving." I blinked. Just like that they moved around me and I followed Chandra into the club house. I went into the kitchen and washed my hands, my mind whirling and clicking and pulling in a thousand directions.

No one seemed phased by this new development. I thought of all that could befall them from hiding me from him and grimaced. Chadwick was devious, he would figure out some way of spinning things to make him look like a saint, me out to be a victim and these good people out to be vile kidnappers… if he wanted to. That was the thing about my husband, he was unpredictable. Went with whatever whim or fancy overtook him at the time.

Still, he had one iron clad rule that he never deviated from, and I had broken that rule. Obedience always, in all things. I wore the chain of his obedience around my neck even now and my defiance, my not returning to him when I had been expected to… I closed my eyes. I didn't even want to think of the consequences. If I were fortunate he would just lock me in a room. That had been the last time I had disobeyed him, and the last time I had ever been allowed to leave the house unaccompanied.

Once upon a time I had been given a small allowance, I had been allowed to go out and have my hair and nails done, of course to his specifications, still I had been allowed the illusion of an afternoon of freedom… My hair stylist, she and I had gotten along quite well and I'd gone off of the regimented schedule to have lunch with her.

Maynard, my husband's head of security had told Chadwick of my transgression. I'd been dragged by my hair to our bedroom. He'd taken a switch to me until I'd passed out and when I woke it was to realize I'd been locked in. All of the books, music, writing implements, all of it had been removed. He would come to me in the evenings and would have me spend all night on my knees, forcing me to recite over and over my marriage vows of 'love, honor and obey'. Food was withheld for the first week. I got water from the bathroom tap. I'd remained in the gilded prison of my room for I think a month, all though at some point he'd stopped locking the door. He'd just never told me I could go and I was terrified of crossing him again. Only when he'd told me I could did I leave the room, but I was never to leave the house outside of his presence ever again.

I returned to the here and now after a long time of staring out the window over the kitchen sink. I dried my hands and set about putting things away, leaving out what I would need to fix a good dinner for the men. I washed my hands again after handling the packages of food and set to work preparing baked herb chicken and broccoli. I prepared a salad to go with it and lightly dressed it with oil and balsamic and plated everything, bringing it out to the table and serving everyone carefully.

"Whoa, hey!" Dragon cheered.

"Thanks, Doll," Doc said.

"Awesome, you're the best!" Reaver said around a mouthful of chicken. Dray just glowered at me and I nodded, secretly pleased by the majorities' appreciation.

I returned to the kitchen and Chandra who sat at the counter with one of the bar stools. She had her reading glasses perched on her nose and was reading some kind of romance novel. I set a plate beside her and joined her with one of my own.

"Brought these for you," she said, setting two of the volumes down by my plate. I smiled and said thank you.

"You scared?" she asked, looking at me over her glasses. I nodded and folded my hands in my lap.

"Honey let me ask you something," she pulled her glasses off her face and closed her book, sliding both aside. "Do you honestly think Trigger is going to let anything happen to you?"

"Why do you call him that?" I asked, to buy myself some time to sort through what I thought of and how I felt about Ethan.

"He was a sniper in the Marines," she answered and took a bite of her food.

"Oh," I said and ate some of mine.

"Now answer my question," she said.

"I don't know honestly," I murmured and it was the truth. I didn't know anything about the man really, I knew that he was kind and that he went out of his way to care for me but I didn't know why.

"I've known Trigger for a few years now and I've never seen him look at anybody the way he looks at you. He's gone all fierce male protector on your ass and that's a good thing, Sweetheart. Trig's a good man. He'll look after you. You ain't got nothing to worry about," she ate the rest of her meal in silence and so did I, mulling over what she'd said.

As I was washing plates and cleaning up I caught myself

wondering why I couldn't have met Ethan ten years ago instead of meeting Chadwick. I sighed. There really was no use thinking along such lines. I was tired again and my whole body ached from my husband's beating and all the cleaning I'd done. It was time for me to go to bed.

I slipped past the men at their poker game and into the back and Ethan's room, changing once more into his shirt. I hung everything up and sat on the bed. I pulled my two movies out and put on Les Miserables and laid down to watch. I don't remember at which part I fell asleep. I think it was when Fantine was dying, and Hugh Jackman as Jean Valjean was at her side. Either way I never heard him come in.

I woke to a silent and dark room and strong arms lifting me gently against a solid chest. I settled in against Ethan and sighed in contentment. The tempest of emotion raging in my heart and head momentarily quieted.

"You awake?" he asked softly voice husky.

"Mmm," was all I could put out, I was awake but not enough to for coherent sentences.

"Okay Babe," He kissed my forehead, a soft brush of lips against my skin and I felt like it swept down my whole body. Like I lit up with a luminescence from the inside out. I drew in a long breath and let it out slowly and with my cheek resting against the swell of his chest, I fell into a much more fitful sleep. I woke again midmorning but Ethan was gone. A note was tucked into the corner of the television screen that read 'Ashton' on the front in flowing script. I blinked and plucked it down, opening it to read it.

*Hey Sunshine,*
*Glad you're up. You smell like orange blossoms and I fucking love it.*

I smiled and continued to read.

*Reaver, Doc and Dragon filled me in when I got back last night. You don't have anything to worry about. I'm here, he's not. I'm out looking for a place and then I'm heading to work. Maybe you'll be awake when I get back tonight, maybe you won't, either way I'm glad you're in my bed.*

*Relax.*

*You're safe.*

*-Ethan.*

The bottom of the note had an intricately drawn rose and stem that was so lifelike it took my breath away. I felt a stab of guilt for not having any breakfast ready for him before he went out. I got up and got ready for the day.

Showered and dressed I headed into the common area. Dragon sat at the bar smoking a cigarette and I ghosted up beside him.

"Can I fix you some breakfast, Sir?" I asked and he jerked back as if I'd slapped him.

"You scared the shit out of me!" he said.

"I'm sorry." I dropped my eyes to the floor and blushed.

"Don't be, just make some fucking noise next time." He put a hand over his heart and I bit my lip.

"What's your story?" he asked.

"I'd better make some coffee," I huffed and went into the kitchen. He leaned over so he could watch me.

"You ain't gotta tell me. Best you tell Trigger first, he's the one that found you," he said as he settled himself again.

"I did, the night of the party… Breakfast?" I asked.

"Got any eggs?" he asked.

"Of course," I murmured, "How would you like them prepared?"

"Over easy," he grunted. I moved about the kitchen, I was growing comfortable in it. If anything, with Ethan gone, it was becoming my safe place. I knew what I was about in the kitchen. I could make my own decisions for the most part. Chadwick had only once gotten me about something I'd done wrong in the kitchen and I really hadn't… he had been in a bad mood.

I had slaved preparing a beautiful, no, *flawless* braised pork roast and had served it to him with pride. He'd demanded to know what it was that I had thought I was doing. Said he'd specifically requested the dish Chicken and Forty Cloves for that night and when I had disagreed, when I had tried to stand up for myself… Well I had to be corrected.

Hands gripped mine gently and I looked up into sorrowful dark eyes. I blinked, and the imposing mountain of a man thumbed a tear from my cheek.

"I can't eat six eggs Chica," he said gently. I looked down into the pan and burst into sobs, tears falling like rain.

"You got a lot going on in that head of yours, yeah?" he asked when I'd calmed down. I nodded.

"Want me to call Trigger?" I shook my head violently. I didn't want him to have to come running back every time I had a little melt down.

"That's the second time you've said no to that, wanna tell me why?" I sniffed and turned back to the stove.

"Scrambled is fine, not answering my question isn't." My shoulders slumped.

"He can't save me all the time…" I murmured, "I have to learn to save myself too." I was startled by a boom of laughter.

"Sorry, just you and Trig are gonna make a pair," he wiped a tear from the corner of his eye.

"Why do you say that?" I asked.

"Girl, you're three days out of hell and you're acting like you should be just fine. Shit like that takes time. Trig was the same way when he came back from Afghanistan, took him a few years to get back to any kind of normal. Helped me turn this club around." He crossed his arms and it didn't look completely right with how massive his arms were. I plated half the eggs and set about making some toast.

"I don't know much about him," I confessed.

"Give that a little time too," he said. I plated his toast and went

52

and got him butter and jam out of the fridge. He sat at a table and I joined him with the rest of the eggs and some toast of my own. We ate in relative silence.

"What were you planning on doing today?" he asked.

"Laundry," I answered softly.

"I'll show you where the machines are at," he said.

"Thank you," I murmured.

I cleaned up the breakfast dishes and followed Dragon on a tour of the clubhouse, specifically where the laundry machines were, which was out back, on a covered porch. He left me back at Ethan's room after showing me where he could be found should I need anything.

It was quickly made apparent to me that Dray was nothing like his father, which was a shame. I liked the older man. He was more like Ethan, having much the same vibe. I checked Ethan's pockets and washed his clothes along with the few things I'd worn so far. I cracked one of Chandra's romance novels while the clothes washed and was decently engrossed in it when I switched them over to the dryer.

I folded and put everything away and watched Les Mis all the way through from the beginning. I got up after that and went into the kitchen and prepared a meal, then went in search of Dragon. I knocked softly at the edge of his open door. He looked up from a book of his own and said,

"What's up Chica?" I chewed my bottom lip.

"I would like to take Ethan some dinner. He didn't come back and I think it's safe to assume he's at work," I said.

"Yeah, he should be," he looked me over.

"Dress as warm as you can. Meet me out front," he said and heaved himself up.

I was already in jeans and my sneakers I went and grabbed a sweater from the closet and then snatched one of Ethan's hooded sweatshirts down. If Dragon said to dress warm I felt a motorcycle ride in my future. I pulled it on and went out front. Dragon looked me over.

"It'll have to do," he said looking me over. I picked up the plastic grocery bag with Ethan's dinner in it off the bar and looped my wrist through it.

"Come on."

We went outside and he put a helmet on my head, fastening the chinstrap, all the while giving me instructions on what he expected out of a passenger. I listened gravely to what he was saying.

"Last, but most importantly," he said, putting a finger in my face and I listened, rapt. "Enjoy the ride, Baby," and I smiled. He grinned and got on. I got up on my own with a little trepidation and held on for dear life as he started the machine. I felt the vibrations in my tailbone go all the way up my spine and he stuffed my hands in his pockets.

"Since you don't have gloves, keep 'em there!" he shouted. I nodded and we lurched forward. I bit down on a yip of surprise and tried not to stiffen up and to go with the flow.

My heart pounded the whole thirty minutes to where Ethan worked and I realized I had no idea what he did. I was surprised when we pulled up outside a tattoo shop. Though after the artwork on his note that morning, I really shouldn't have been. I just imagined him doing something more physically labor intensive I guess. Shame on me for stereotyping.

# CHAPTER 7
*Trig*

I laid some blue ink into the piece I was working on when I heard the door open. Chris, my counter man, didn't say a word. Goddamned lazy fuck. I shook my head and continued working. I caught sight of movement out of the corner of my eye in the entry way to my station and looked up. I pulled the gun away from my customer and killed the power by stepping off the pedal.

"Hey," I said startled.

"Hi," she replied softly. She was wearing her jeans and sneakers but was wearing one of my sweatshirts.

"We cool for a break Donnie?" I asked my customer.

"Fuck yeah, I need a smoke," Donnie pushed up and staggered toward the front. I stripped off my latex gloves with a snap and tossed them.

"What're you doin' here, Babe? Everything all right?" I asked.

She nodded and held out a plastic grocery bag tied at the top, "I made you dinner," she said gently.

I blinked, "You brought me dinner?" I asked. She nodded, eyes wide.

"Lasagna," she murmured and looked like she was about to panic. I stood up and she flinched and I probably should have been gentler but I pulled her into a hug.

"Thanks," I whispered gruffly against her hair and breathed deep her orange blossom scent. Her small arms went around my waist after a moment and hugged me back. I smiled and let her go, taking the bag from her.

"How'd you get here?" I asked.

"She asked me, Brother." I looked up, Dragon stood there, arms crossed in that ungainly way of his and I raised an eyebrow. Ashton was blushing a delectable light pink and I smiled and before I realized what I was doing I asked her,

"You wanna stay?" her beautiful sad face broke into one of those rare but brilliant smiles and she nodded.

"You mind?" I asked Dragon.

"Naw, man. I'll see you two back at the club house, give me a chance to stop by Sugar's." He grinned. Sugar's was the local tittie bar but Ashton didn't need to know that. I nodded.

"I'll leave her helmet on the counter, you have fun Chica." He winked at her and she gave him a smile and waved.

"There's lasagna in the kitchen back at the house. It's in the foil wrapped pan on the counter," she murmured at him. He grinned.

"Thanks, Baby Doll," he said and turned around, I heard him whistling as he went out the door. I put the food in the bottom drawer of my filing cabinet.

"Why don't you go on and have a seat up there," I pointed to the dentist chair, raised and laid flat against one wall. I had Donnie sitting in the massage chair.

"What made you come all the way out here to bring me dinner?" I asked when she was settled. She hugged her knees and a ghost of a smile flickered across her mouth.

"I think I missed you," she said and that made me smile.

"I been meaning to ask you," I searched her face, I had her attention; her expression was rapt. "Isn't there anyone I can call for you? Your folks or a brother or sister?" I almost regretted asking, grief clouded her expression for a moment and she hugged her knees.

"Folks are gone, I was an only child… I grew up in foster care from the time I was eleven," she answered. Her eyes were affixed on her knees and she picked at one of the drawstrings for the hood of my sweatshirt.

"What happened?" I asked her.

"My mom got cancer, my dad skipped town, too much for him I guess." She shrugged one shoulder.

"You said you met your douche bag ex in college," I said. "Don't know many foster kids that go to college," I commented. I snapped on another pair of gloves and started cleaning up my area some.

"Full academic scholarship," she smiled triumphantly.

"You stay in touch with your foster parents?" I asked. Mostly to get the measure of how they'd treated her.

"At first, the Tuckers were really good to me. They had two boys but Mrs. Tucker had a lot of love to give and really wanted a girl around and so they took me in," she was smiling faintly.

"She taught me how to cook," she said.

"A damn fine job she did, too." I smiled at her and she lit right the fuck up like a thousand watt bulb under the praise and the sight was enough to thaw out a part of me I thought was long cold and dead.

Donnie returned and sat back down, eyes closed; "Who's the chick?" he asked.

"I'm Ashton," She murmured and he cracked open one eyelid. I could tell it had cost her to speak up but she'd done it anyways, she was a fighter this one, in her own way.

"Donnie," he grunted and I started back in on his shoulder.

"Pleased to meet you, Donnie," she could barely be heard over the buzz of my gun. Quiet as a damned mouse this one. If her eyes hadn't already done me in with their burnished gold hue, she probably would have been tagged 'Mouse' rather than 'Sunshine' in my brain.

She stared transfixed at what I was doing. Golden gaze locked, as I pretty mercilessly ground some blue ink around the image on Donnie's shoulder. He was into MMA fighting and had requested an arctic fox on the swell of his left shoulder. The blue was going around the fox to bring it out more. Donnie Fox was his fighting name, hence the tattoo.

"Doesn't that hurt?" she asked when I paused to reload on ink.

"What do you think, Princess?" Donnie grunted and I wiped the area a little harder than was necessary. He cracked an eyelid in my direction. I shook my head and gave him a warning look. He frowned.

"I've never been in a place like this before," Ashton murmured and looked around. Donnie and I both looked at her. Come to think of it, I'd seen her pretty much naked and she didn't have any ink.

"How old are you anyways?" Donnie asked.

"Thirty," Ashton murmured.

Donnie snorted, "Bullshit!"

Come to think of it, Chris had let her right on back here, I would have checked her ID and made sure she was eighteen... Fuck that lazy fucking fuck! Of course Dragon had been with her, so that would have pretty much put a stop to any questions. Chris knew better than to question the big man. Dragon may not be as tall but the fucker was built like a brick shit house. Chris, for a stoner, was a twig by comparison. Ripe for the snapping.

"Last December," she affirmed. Donnie looked at her, and I mean really looked at her this time.

"What happened to your face?" he asked, eyes narrowed. Ashton averted her eyes, staring up at a piece of stencil artwork I had framed up on the wall, the mat had several holes cut for photos of the piece alongside it, show casing four of the stages. Before, stencil, line and shading art and finally the finished colored piece. I watched Ashton and wondered if she was going to answer.

"My ex-husband happened," she said simply and I was proud of her. She'd said ex. Not 'my husband happened' but 'my ex-husband.' I wanted to cheer.

"You tune him up yet?" Donnie asked me.

"Naw," I said and went back to work on him.

"Call me you want a hand," he said. Ashton looked a mixture of awed and horrified but remained silent. Her golden eyes were haunted and I sighed. She was still afraid but hopefully given enough time that would fade. I finished Donnie up, slathered his tat and bandaged it.

"Two hours, take off the bandage. If it's stuck, soak it in water. If you shower, avoid getting it directly into the spray for a while. Keep it moist, make an appointment in three weeks for any touch ups," I said.

"Thanks man," Donnie got up and we clasped hands. He pulled me into a man hug and slapped my back.

"See you around, pay Chris on your way out," I said.

"Will do," he picked up his hat and put it on backwards over his closely shaved head. I cleaned up quietly while Ashton looked on.

"Um dude, I think your counterman is passed out," I looked up, Donnie was standing at the entry way to my space and he didn't look happy. I scowled and got up, stripping off my gloves. I cursed, low and heated and saw Ashton flinch out of the corner of my eye. I put a lid on my growing anger fast and stalked out front.

Sure enough Chris was leaned back as far as his chair would go, eyes closed, mouth open, drooling on himself. I kicked his Converse All-stars out from under him and he crashed backwards.

"What the fuck man!" he spluttered.

"What the fuck is right, douchebag!" I growled at him, "I'm tryin' to run a fuckin' business here!"

"Dude, chill out. It's not that serious, Bro," he picked himself and the chair off the floor. Ashton ghosted up along the wall, I caught her out of the corner of my eye. I resisted the urge to beat the fuck out of the little prick.

"Dude, you're fucking fired," I grated. "Get your shit and get the fuck out." I crossed my arms and glowered.

"Seriously!?" Chris laughed, the fucker actually laughed.

"I would do what he says," Ashton said gently, "I know that look." I grimaced inwardly as Chris looked at her, probably for the first time that night and he backed down immediately.

"Sure, yeah, what the fuck ever, Man," he got his coat and slammed out the front door. Donnie looked at Ashton like she'd done an interesting trick. She was blushing.

"What?" I asked.

"Dude, she's smart," Donnie said with respect.

"I know that but I'm missing something here," I frowned.

"I'm sorry, that wasn't very nice of me to do after all you've done for me," Ashton looked stricken.

"What'd you do?" I asked.

"She let dimwit think you did that to her face," Donnie grimaced.

I blinked with surprise and rewound the entire exchange in my brain. I started laughing.

"Yeah, he obviously doesn't know me very well. C'mere

Sweetheart," I crooked a finger in her direction and she pushed off the wall. I sat her down in the vacant office chair.

"How you paying man?" I asked.

"Plastic," Donnie handed me his debit card.

"Okay, this is how you do this…" I showed her how to run the card and how to do all the paperwork involved, at least the bare bones of it. She quailed at first but picked it up pretty quickly. Donnie left and I smiled at her. This might work actually. I'd have to put some more thought into it.

"Come on Sunshine, I'm starving," I went back to my station and showed her where the break room was. She sat with me and I shared my food with her. The woman could cook.

"Are you the only one who works here?" she asked.

"Naw. The rest of the guys are doing a show at the convention center this week. I own half of this place with a buddy of mine," her eyes widened.

"Oh," she took another small bite of her food.

"Found an apartment today," I said and she looked up sharply, I was graced with two smiles in one night.

"Where at?" she asked.

"Not far from the clubhouse or the shop so it's pretty ideal," I said.

"It's a two bedroom so you'll have a room of your own," she leaned back in her seat and I tilted my head, looking at her.

"What's the matter, Babe?" I asked.

"I really don't have the words to say thank you for everything you've done for me," she murmured.

"Just live," I told her. She cocked her head and looked at me curiously.

"Get away from him, get a divorce, just live a life," I put my hand on the small table between us. She looked at it plaintively.

"I'm scared. I'm his property, he's not going to let me go without some kind of fight and he's cold, calculating, he doesn't fight fair," her voice was toneless, desolate and saturated with too much of her ugly reality for my tastes.

"Then we fight, and we fight dirtier," I said. Her hand crept up over the edge of the table and she put it within touching distance of my own.

"I'm not very good at fighting," she said, shifting in her seat.

"I think you're better at it than you realize," I said, thinking back on what she'd told me... full ride scholarships as a foster kid weren't easy to come by. Living under her monster ex's roof for over eight years as his punching bag, wasn't a walk in the park either. I went the last bit of distance and covered her hand with my own.

"You got people in your corner now, Babe. Think about it," I gave her hand a squeeze and heard the door chime out front. I got up and left her in the break room. It was my next customer. Some chick wanting a butterfly on her hip. I told her to come on back and asked Ashton to watch the front. She slipped into the desk chair Chris had been in not an hour before and I took my client and her guy back to my work space.

Ashton rang them up like a pro after having only been shown how to do it once and when they left she turned to me, golden gaze far too serious.

"I want to fight," she murmured and I gave her a good hard look.

"Okay, Babe," I told her. "We start tomorrow so we gotta get up early." She nodded and I went back to my station to clean up. I was proud of her. The next client went smoothly and I finished ahead of time but I had a walk in right before the shop was supposed to close. Ashton said she was game to wait so I put a few extra bones in my pocket and did what the chick wanted. A little flower on her ankle.

We rode back to the club house, Ashton pressed tight against my back which had my cock pressed tight against my jeans. We slept soundly and in the morning I was woken by her crawling back up onto the bed, a cup of steaming, strong black coffee in her hand. She held it out to me.

"What time is it?" I groaned.

"A little after seven," she said softly.

"What the fuck, Ashton?" I asked and she went very still. I cursed myself when she slipped off the bed, putting distance between us.

"You said we had to get up early," she reminded me gently.

"Shit," I swore softly. Partly because she was right and I was

61

being an ass, partly because I was sporting some serious morning wood and her sitting there in my shirt wasn't helping any.

"I'm sorry," she whispered and I shook my head, my hair brushing along my shoulders. I scrubbed my face with my hands and sat up, putting my back against the scarred wooden headboard.

"Nothing to be sorry about Sunshine, you're right and I'm up," I looked her over.

"Breakfast is in the kitchen… I hope oatmeal is all right," she picked up her caddy of shower supplies.

"It's perfect…" I said leaving the rest of my thought silent… What I wanted to say was *It's perfect, kind of like you,* but to be honest, that kind of scared the hell out of me. I shouldn't be thinking those things. I took a hefty swallow of coffee and she nodded once and slipped out the door.

It dawned on me that she didn't know what I had planned and that she was ready and willing to go along with whatever I said at this point. That took a hell of a lot of balls for someone in her position. I finished off the coffee in three long gulps, got my ass out of bed and found a vacant shower. I'd be lying if I said I didn't take an extra-long one to relieve some of the… tension that being near Ashton, with her sunlit eyes, caused me.

I dressed in a newer looking pair of light jeans, my usual boots and a white crew neck tee. I pulled on a black and red checkered flannel with the sleeved rolled tight above the elbow and pulled my hair into a pony tail. I tucked my digital camera into the breast pocket of the flannel and went out to the common room.

I found Ashton out near the kitchen and looked down at her. She was polished in her white sundress and sandals, her long hair French braided tightly down her back. Her fading bruises still stark against her pale skin.

"How are we doing this?" she asked, placing a bowl of oatmeal in front of me when I sat down. She sat across from me with her own.

"We're going to the cops. That way you can tell them you aren't missing, and then we're showing them these," I turned on the camera and flashed through photos of her injuries when they were fresh. She paled.

"When did you take these?" she asked.

"After Doc sedated you, before he patched you up," I said quietly. She looked like she was trying to swallow one bitter fucking pill. Finally she nodded.

"Thank you for thinking ahead," she murmured.

"No problem," I said, tucking the camera away.

"How is this fighting dirty?" she asked.

"What's the only thing your husband cares about?" I asked quietly.

"His image," she responded immediately.

"Yeah?" I asked. I saw her eyes light up as what I was proposing dawned on her.

"He'll kill me for sure," she murmured.

"He's gotta go through me and probably the MC first, Babe," I said and she stared at the table top.

She was scared. I could see it all over her face. The woman was an open book that way, but finally she looked up, eyes misting with tears and she nodded. I borrowed Dragon's truck to take her. He and I had discussed at length involving the cops ad we both agreed it was the best course of action. We'd put it to a vote and had barely eked out a yay vs nay on suspending our other operations until this blew over.

Doc had swung the vote like I knew he would. Still we had one more run in the next few weeks, something we'd worked too long and too hard on, so we would go through with that one. I'd worry about it when we got there though.

I pulled up in front of the sheriff's department and went in with Ashton. She went to the front desk.

"Can I help you, ma'am?" The deputy asked looking from her to me and back to her.

"Yes, my name is Ashton Granger," she said gently and followed it with, "… and I'm not missing, I'm hiding."

Goddamn, she was a fighter all right.

# CHAPTER 8

*Ashton*

"You say you took these when?" the detective was speaking to Ethan, not me but still, I could feel my pulse throbbing at my temples. I felt hot and cold at the same time, and my chest was tight. I could barely breathe...

"Friday night, just after I found her," he grunted.

We had stuck completely with the truth with only one minor embellishment. Rather than explain why Ethan hadn't taken me to a hospital, which truth be told, *I* didn't even know why... we'd said that I had begged him not to. We'd been here over an hour, the detective in charge of my missing person's case going over every detail of our story forwards and backwards. I felt ill. I felt like I was a suspect, rather than a victim, even though I really didn't want to be either.

"I just want my driver's license, birth certificate and social security card," I said finally, "Then I want a divorce attorney and to walk away from this whole ordeal." I looked the detective in the eye. "You can't know what it's like living with him," I said, tears spilled hot and fresh down my cheeks and I didn't bother to wipe them away.

"You understand your husband has to be notified you've been found," he said.

"Yes, but do you have to tell him where I am?" I asked.

"No..." the detective drawled.

"Then please don't," I said.

"You understand that you wasted a lot of people's time and valuable police resources by not coming forward sooner, don't you Mrs. Granger?" he asked, and I didn't at all care for his tone. Ethan didn't either.

"That's it, we're done," he said standing.

"Sit down, Mr. Howard!" the detective said sharply and I stood up.

"I would like to speak to your superior," I said softly and that shut him up.

"Mrs. Granger…" I huffed out a breath. If I was going to learn to fight, I supposed now was as good a time as any.

"No. We are quite done detective. My husband has been keeping me prisoner in our home for the better part of the eight years of our marriage. He has beaten me, he has taken…" I stumbled over the ugly truth, "He has taken me by force, and you… you stand there affronted, when I finally escaped him, over attempting to find me when I didn't wish to be found? I don't think so. Send in your superior officer. I am done with your admonishments and I refuse to take your corrections," I dropped into my seat, chest heaving.

At no point had I risen my voice. I had not yelled, I had not screamed though every fiber of my being wanted me to, yet still I felt as if I had run a marathon. I swallowed and clutched my hands together in my lap to quell their shaking. Ethan was looking at me, concern etched upon his face until he turned to a very pale and very speechless Detective Olurund and said.

"I think you better do what the lady asks," and amazingly, things went much more smoothly after that.

I filed charges through a detective in the domestic violence unit and was told if there was anything that I needed to retrieve from my home with Chadwick that a Sherriff's Department detail would accompany me that afternoon to do so. I had stated that I would like that very much and a time to meet had been appointed for four o'clock. Ethan had guided me out of the building, a fat sheaf of papers riding in his back pocket. We stepped out of the dimly lit police station into the warm sunlight yet I remained chilled to the bone.

I had done it. I had stood up for myself, so why did all I want to do was fall apart screaming and crying onto the sidewalk? I didn't understand.

"Ashton, Baby, what's wrong?" Ethan knelt down in front of me to bring us eye to eye.

"I don't know," I murmured and my voice sounded far away even to me.

"You did it, Babe and I am so proud of you. So, what's got you down?" he asked. "Tell me what you're feeling," he gripped my shoulder lightly and his warm, clear eyes snapped into focus.

"I feel..." how did I feel? Lost, angry, confused sure, but also fierce and proud and even a little elated but looming beyond all that? Scared. Scared about how Chadwick would react, would he let me go? Would he try to kill me? Would he put on his angel's mask and make me out to be a raving lunatic? I stared into Ethan's silvery blue eyes and felt so terribly guilty that he had become my lifeline in all of this. I must have spoken all of these things aloud because he smiled and said to me,

"Don't you worry about any of that, I knew what I was signing up for and I'm here, aren't I? Truth be told, there's no place I'd rather be. Now c'mon, I'm not going anywhere on you. We gotta go back to the club house. We're bringing some reinforcements to go get your stuff," he took me gently by the hand and we went back to the truck.

As scared as I was about what was going to happen to me, I believed in what Ethan said whole heartedly. He was here and he wasn't going anywhere. Don't ask me how I knew that those words above all others carried weight, but they did.

We drove back to the club house in silence, hands linked, resting between us on the old pickup's bench seat. That afternoon in what Ethan had called "colors" but was really just him, Doc, Dragon and Reaver in their motorcycle club vests came out. The old pickup, with me and Chandra in it, was escorted by four motorcycles, two in front and two in back through the rich suburban neighborhood I had lived in with Chadwick.

Dragon and Ethan were in front, Doc and Reaver followed up behind. A county Sherriff's cruiser sat in front of the gate when we arrived. I got out of the truck and went to the key pad. I punched in the five digit access code and the gate rolled aside. I had seen

Chadwick punch it in often enough to know it was his birthdate, 52781. Chadwick and our head of security, Maynard, were waiting at the top of the drive.

My husband's hazel eyes smoldered as I got out of the truck, my knees turning to jelly. He strode towards me. I plastered myself flat against the truck and threw up my hands in defense as he started screaming at me but Ethan was suddenly there as were the two Sherriff deputies, a man and a woman, placing themselves between me and him.

"You stupid fucking whore! What did you do!?" he screamed.

Ethan folded me up against him. Strong arms going around me, sheltering me from the storm. The two deputies were yelling at Chadwick to calm down and to stop yelling. Maynard stood by and nodded once in my direction.

"Ma'am," he said plaintively, and that one word held so much. It was cold, and dispassionate and dripped with his disapproval and disdain. I opened my mouth before I could stop myself.

"Truth is, I don't much care for you either Maynard," I said and was surprised I didn't burst into flames, spontaneously combust, from his look alone. He'd known what Chadwick was doing, had known from the start; had even participated to some degree in 'correcting' my behavior.

"Sir, if you don't stop screaming at your wife I'm going to put you in handcuffs and take you in on a charge of disorderly conduct," the female deputy snapped. Chadwick stopped screaming and looked at her, realizing that this time his money and affluence held no sway.

"What the fuck are you here for?" he demanded, face red, vein in the side of his neck throbbing at the perceived indignity.

"I want my papers. That's all. You can have everything else. I just want my license, my passport, my social security card and my birth certificate." He tugged his sleeve cuffs and adjusted them smartly, pushing a hand through his hair.

"They're in the safety deposit box at the bank, darling," he lied.

"They're in the wall safe in your office," I said flatly. He was going to make me work for this. Ethan had taken up position

67

behind me, his arms still around me, holding me on my feet. I was grateful.

"No, they're at the bank."

"Then you won't mind showing us," I said coolly.

"Fine!" he snapped and stomped into the house. The deputies, Ethan, and I followed. Dragon, Doc, Reaver and Chandra stayed outside with Maynard.

"Your boss is a dick," I heard Reaver say.

"Don't bother Reaver, this one's a dick too," I heard Chandra's voice clear and loud as I went into the house.

Ethan was a warm comforting shadow at my back. He loomed over me and I drew what strength from him that I could. I was terrified, I didn't want to be here. With every fiber that I was I wanted to tuck tail and run, far away from here... but Ethan was behind me, pushing me inexorably onward until we stood inside Chadwick's study. I trembled and shook and felt like I couldn't get enough air. Ethan's hands descended on my shoulders and he kneaded them gently and suddenly I felt calm. I could do this.

Chadwick took down the painting behind his desk, it was of some revolutionary warship battle, and he keyed in the safe's combination. He opened the door and pulled out file folders, slapping them on the desk.

"See, I told you. Not here," he crossed his arms and I went forward, slipping from Ethan's grasp and went through the first file. Nothing, the second file held my birth certificate and marriage license as well as my social security card and mother's death certificate. I sighed in relief. In the third file I found our passports.

"I guess you were wrong," I breathed. I met his cold gaze and stood my ground.

"So it seems," he scowled at me. He had expected me to cow down and take his word for it. That wasn't going to happen.

"Anything else, my darling wife?" he asked, acid lacing his tone, a barely suppressed caustic rage emanating from every pore.

"Yes," I said defiantly, straightening, my important papers clutched to my chest. I went for the second floor and our bedroom.

Ethan, the Sherriff's deputies and my very angry husband hot on my heels.

I snatched my iPod off the dresser and stuffed it in my dress pocket before anyone but Ethan could see. He smiled at me and I went to the closet. I pulled an old file box down and Ethan took it from me. It held a few mementos from my life before Chadwick Granger. Some high school yearbooks, photographs... that sort of thing. I pulled out the largest suitcase and began throwing clothes into it, from underthings to my yoga gear to jeans and sweaters and blouses to summer dresses until I could barely close it.

"Like me to carry anything ma'am?" the female deputy asked and I nodded once and hefted some things on hangars. She threw them over her arm and I knelt in the back of the closet and pulled up the carpet there, revealing my secret stash.

Chadwick looked apoplectic when I pulled out the journals. I stared across the short distance between us, coldly, and I put them into the box Ethan carried. He handed me the box and heaved the overstuffed suitcase by its handle.

"C'mon Sunshine. Let's get you out of here," he said.

"Yes. I'd like that," I said and took Ethan's hand, grateful for his strength. We all trouped downstairs. Maynard looked like he was seething and Chandra lit up.

"Hey Baby! We've been having a good 'ol time at the rent-a-cop's expense out here. You missed it!" I blinked and gave a tentative smile in return. The suitcase, and clothes went into the back of the truck, the box I held Ethan took from me, sliding it into the truck.

Chandra got in the driver's side. I got in the passenger's and took one last look at Chadwick. The look he gave me, chilled me to the bone. He had murder in his eyes and I knew without a doubt that none of this was over, not by a long mile. Ethan looked from me to Chadwick then back to me. He leaned in the open door of the truck.

"I'm right behind you, Babe. It's going to be fine," he said and then he kissed me.

My world stopped spinning, everything that had felt so out of control and completely mad the moment before simply fell away. It was a quick, chaste press of his lips over mine. My hand flew of its own accord, the scruff of two days growth scratching against my palm as I gently cradled his face and returned the press of his lips against mine. The universe seemed to hold its collective breath and all too soon he pulled away.

He pressed his lips in one final kiss to my palm, his hand warm against the back of my own where he pressed it to his mouth before relinquishing his hold. My fingertips trailed across his stubble and skin and fell limp with shock and wonder into my lap. He shut the door to the truck with a hollow metal clang and I jumped.

I looked across the drive way to Chadwick one last time. He'd gone very still and very cold. A snake in the grass.

"I bet you won't be so smart mouthed when there's no one to stand behind you Ashton," he said, crossing his arms.

"Oh boy," Chandra said rolling her eyes and she started the old pickup, the motor rumbling to life. The overwhelming growl of four motorcycles starting in unison filled the warm spring afternoon, shattering the idyllic silence. I spared a final look at Chadwick but he wasn't looking at me anymore. He was staring at Ethan and the look on his face sent icy fingers of fear ticking down my spine.

I sat back into the old worn bench seat as Chandra put it into drive and pulled down the long circular drive. A new kind of fear took root in my mind, planted by the seed of his chilling words; that one look. I sent up a fervent prayer that whatever bad thing that was going to happen would happen to me and not Ethan, because I knew my husband… I knew the monster that lived inside his head and the monster was hungry. I closed my eyes and prayed that I would be enough to sate it, and that Ethan would be spared.

*Please God, let him be spared.*

Much later on we were inside Ethan's room at the club house.

"Why did you kiss me?" I asked suddenly. We were trying to sort through the pile of things I had grabbed.

Ethan looked up sharply from a photo of my mother and me, silver eyes startled.

"Because you're beautiful, because you're amazing and because I wanted to," he said, searching my face.

"Oh," I said softly.

"Are you upset that I did?" he asked me. I thought about it for a moment.

"No. I'm just... I... Are you..?" I sighed frustrated.

"Babe, take a deep breath," he said, placing a hand on my knee. He'd taken off of work for me, said he hadn't had any clients today anyways which was a lie, I'd heard him cancel his one appointment for today when he'd thought I hadn't been near.

"Are you afraid this changes things?" he asked. I closed my eyes. I didn't want to see his face...

"Yes." I opened them changing my mind and found he was smiling.

"I'm still here," he said, taking my hand, "I'm still me and you're still you," he added and sighed. He shoved everything ingloriously off the bed into a pile at the foot of it and stretched out. "Come here," he patted the bed beside him. I crawled up the mattress and sat beside him. He patted his chest and I lay down, snug against his side, cheek resting on the flannel of his shirt.

"I like holding you like this," he said, truth was I liked it too, "I'm going to miss it when you've got your own room."

I nodded against him and closed my eyes breathing deeply his smell. He smelled like antiseptic from the tattoo shop and working machine parts from his motorcycle, he also smelled of fresh clean air and faintly of cigarettes. He smelled like he lived and I could appreciate that after years of overpowering aftershave and sterile lifeless suburban living.

"You did good, Sunshine. I'm proud of you," he said quietly and my heart swelled from the praise.

"Only because you were there to hold me up," I whispered.

"Naw, you could've done it on your own. You were fan-fucking-tastic today."

I sat up and looked down into his face. "Only because you were there to hold me up," I reiterated and I took a deep breath and I kissed him.

His lips moved slowly, sweetly under my own and I closed my eyes. I pulled back gently and whispered "Thank you," before I laid back down. His arm around my back tightened, holding me to him, his fingers on the hand opposite stroked my hair back from my face. He sighed and relaxed.

"You're welcome," he said and we stayed like that, warm and comfortable until both of us fell asleep, though mine was uneasy, plagued by Chadwick's threat.

# CHAPTER 9
## *Trig*

I woke up and she was gone again. How she managed to move around the room and *not* wake me up was a fucking gift from the gods. I sat up and sure enough, the room was immaculate. I was still wearing the same clothes from yesterday. We'd fallen asleep and I think, had stayed asleep. It'd been a long time since I felt so well rested. I went out into the hall and heard music, well, singing. Loud and clear it came from the common room. I padded it sock covered feet down the hall and found Dragon and Reaver standing in front of the bar, looking into the kitchen.

"What's up guys?" I asked and Reaver put a finger to his lips in the classic sign for shush and waved me over to stand with them. I stood by Dragon and felt a slow smile overtake my lips. I'd never heard anything but hushed tones and faint whispers come out of my Sunshine girl, but there she was, standing at the stove, voice loud and clear as a bell singing her little heart out.

Her voice was high and clear and perfect but the song was incredibly sad... We stood there dumbfounded and continued to listen as she sang and cooked at the stove. Her voice dropped and deepened... She poured everything she had into the song and it was both beautiful and heart breaking at the same time.

She sang one specific part about some douchecanoe leaving and all this other shit and I caught myself muttering "Bullshit," Reaver elbowed me in the ribs.

"Quiet man, I want her to finish," Dragon whispered harshly and I bit back a laugh.

Her voice softened and broke elegantly at the end and I swear to Christ a tear sprang to my eye. Reaver sniffed and I looked over at him incredulously but that was when Ashton decided to turn around and saw all of us standing there like the eavesdropping idiots we were.

She started hard and dropped her spatula with a clatter, letting out a little shriek. Dragon and Reaver fell out laughing and I couldn't help but smile and chuckle with them. She pulled her earbuds out of her ears which were hidden beneath her hair and smiled, blushing a furious shade of pink.

The two men started clapping and whistling and I went over to her. She was breathing hard from her fright and I pulled her into a hug.

"You got a set of pipes, Kid," Dragon commented.

"Thank you," came her embarrassed reply, her face buried in my chest. I laughed.

"Sorry we scared you," I said.

"It's okay, sorry if I was being disruptive…"

She was met with a round of "No!", "Naw!" and "Not at all," from the three of us.

"Sing any time you like," Dragon said, "Anyone gives you trouble you send 'em to see me," he took a seat at the bar, Reaver joined him and I reluctantly let her go, bending and retrieving her spatula for her. She washed it quickly at the sink.

"What was that anyways?" I asked.

"'I Dreamed a Dream' from Les Miserables," she smiled and held up the pot, "Coffee?" she asked and was met by three caveman grunts in the affirmative.

"You know its nice Pee Wee, but you don't have to serve us," Reaver said as she poured.

"Oh it's okay! I like to," she put her headphones in and turned back to the kitchen. When she started singing again, softer this time, we traded looks.

"How bad did I bone that last run?" I asked Dragon quietly.

"You didn't, my boy pulled it out," Dragon answered.

"Yeah, worth it," I said.

"Yeah, I don't disagree," the older man said.

"Was that the last one?" Reaver asked.

"For now, we got one more," he grunted. "Then it's time to cool it. We do any more they're going to catch on and then this'll turn into a real clusterfuck. Leastways now we got people to worry about," Dragon nodded in Ashton's direction and I couldn't help but smile.

We weren't your typical MC, at least not anymore. Once upon a time we'd done it all, running drugs, money, guns… you name it. The turnaround came about five years ago after Dragon's Old Lady, Dray's mom, got killed. A rival gang had shot up the old club house. She and two members had gone down in the fire fight.

I was still just a prospect, fresh out of the military and off deployment looking for a home, trying to tame some demons of my own. After Dragon lost Tilly he decided to go legit, saying if he'd done it sooner than maybe she'd still be alive. We'd gone from an outlaw club to legit inside two years.

Then last year we decided we could maybe do more and the pendulum swung the opposite direction. We went from illegal, to legit, to vigilante. The key of smack that I had failed to deliver, I had failed to deliver to the rendezvous point where we destroy those kinds of things. We had a strict rule about not bringing that shit near our house and I'd broken it bringing Ashton here.

Never was I so grateful to be a member in good standing with the rest of these guys. Because of the circumstances I had not only managed to save her but my own ass from a serious beat down for breaking the rules. The votes hadn't even been slim. Dray was the only one to vote in favor of kicking my ass. He was a hardcore stickler for the rules, which wasn't a bad thing, it's just not everything was so black and white.

Dray was pissed off at the fucking world, quick to anger and quicker to violence since his mom had died. Dragon kept him in line, but just barely. He still had hope for his kid and the rest of us humored him, but Dray just wasn't cut from the same cloth. He was fiery and hot headed and hadn't embraced the atonement the rest of us were trying to make for our past sins. He held a big fucking grudge that we hadn't gone after the men that had got his mom, right away. We'd done it but he'd wanted his retribution fast and bloody.

Ashton set plates of French toast, bacon and eggs in front of Reaver and I, and I smiled. She was going to make us too fat and bloated to ride with all these carbs...

"Feel like hitting the weights after this, Brother?" Reaver asked.

"Read my fucking mind," I said, shoveling a fork full of eggs into my mouth. She set a plate in front of Dragon.

"Over easy. Thanks darlin'," he grinned and dug in.

"That's disgusting," I commented as yolk oozed like snot across his plate.

"Shut it, you ain't eating it," he said.

"Yeah and I never will." Ashton's laugh was a bolt out of a clear blue sky and all three of us froze.

"What?" she asked.

"First time we've heard you laugh," Reaver supplied.

"Looks good on you Sunshine," I said and she smiled and it lit her up, like her namesake.

"Why can't I be you?" Reaver asked.

"Because there's only one of me why?" I asked.

"Because only you go out on a run and come home with a hot chick that you just found on the side of the road," he complained. Dragon laughed and I ate my breakfast. Ashton moved through the kitchen blushing and I smiled.

*Yeah, only me.*

Hours later, I stripped off gloves, stood and stretched. I peeked out front and found Ashton engrossed in adding up receipts. She needed a job and just so happened I needed a counter man. It was a pain in the ass training her from scratch but at the same time that was a blessing too. This way I got someone guaranteed to do it my way.

The boys got back from the show today and were a bit dumb founded at first, but I called a shop meeting and explained what was up. Everyone agreed Chris had been here way past his expiration date and it didn't hurt that Ashton was easy on the eyes. They gave her a month to see if she could learn the point of sale system but she exceeded even my expectations and had it figured out in like two hours.

Of course, what did I expect when she'd spent the last ten years of her life with a perfectionist prick who was quick to whoop her ass if she got it wrong? She was damaged but amazingly, not beyond repair.

She sat quietly at the desk and greeted customers softly and warmly. She booked appointments for five of us and cleaned the shop to within an inch of its life. So what if we caught her staring at this piece of art or that for long minutes? She got shit done a hell of a lot faster than Chris' lazy ass ever had.

"What are you thinking?" she asked and I snapped out of my reverie.

"Thinking about you," I said honestly and laughed.

"Oh," she looked worried.

"You're doing awesome. Better than expected," I smiled and she glowed from the small praise.

"Are you sure you want to live with me?" she asked.

"Never been more sure of anything in my life, why?" I asked.

"Insecure, I guess," she gave me a weak smile.

"Don't be," I said then switched subjects, "When's my next appointment?"

"Not for another hour," she didn't even look at the date book but she knew.

"In that case, can I take you to lunch?" I asked. She smiled.

"Okay."

We went next door to a sandwich shop. Once seated in a back booth, she relaxed some.

"Excited?" I asked. It was moving day for the both of us tomorrow.

"Yes," and I could see that she was. A full week out and the bruises on her face had faded to a muddy yellow and green. Barely there. Few more days and she'd be flawless. The rest of her was still pretty thrashed, I could see the dark wine colors on her lower back when she bent to file something and her shirt rode up.

"You're quiet," I observed.

"A lot has been happening in a very short amount of time," she said.

"Yeah," I agreed, then asked, "How you holding up?"

"Okay, I guess. Still scared, a little jumpy," she chewed her lower lip and I pulled it free of her teeth with the pad of my thumb reflexively. What she did shot a speedball of desire straight into my veins. She kissed it, my thumb, and leaned her cheek into my curled fingers. She watched me while she did and I swallowed hard. I surreptitiously adjusted myself in my pants beneath the table. She drew back from my hand and I pulled it back over to my side of the table. The moment, delicate as a soap bubble floating in the air, snapped, but the memory of it remained, hanging in the air between us.

"I'm sor..." she started but I put a stop to it quick.

"Don't apologize Ashton." I searched her face and tried to show her what she looked like to me, through my eyes.

"Never apologize," I whispered.

"Okay," she said and we both went back to eating, the silence heavy between us.

I don't think she knew any better than I did what we were doing. Both of us were just playing it by ear. I wanted to do right by her, I really did, but I honestly didn't know how long my self-control would last. Not when she did shit like that. I just didn't want to push her, or worse, take the place of her douchebag ex. I looked at her delicate hands and realized she'd stopped wearing her wedding set. When had that happened? I guess it didn't really matter.

We went back to the shop and I worked late. I had Chandra come and give her a lift back to the clubhouse for our last night spent there.

I was going to miss her body pressed against mine in the night.

I really was.

Fuck me, man! I had it bad...

The next day, a group of us guys were at the new place.

"You sure you want to do this man?" Derek asked for the third time since that morning. I wiped the sweat off my forehead with my arm. We were getting the last of my furniture from storage and moving it up to the third floor apartment.

"For the last fucking time man, I'm sure," I said.

"Okay bro, it's your funeral if the bitch turns out to be crazy and stabs you in your sleep." I scowled at him.

If anyone was gonna get stabbed in their sleep it was going to be Ashton. I had woken in the middle of the night with her tight little ass pressed to my cock as I'd spooned her. It had taken everything I had not to move her leg just so, her panties aside and...

"Hey Trigger! What're you thinking about so hard over there?" Reaver looked over at me and I was jolted back into action. He laughed at me and turned to Derek, an old Marine Corps buddy of mine.

"Naw man, wait 'til you meet her. She's sweet as fucking pie. Cooks for the damned MC morning, noon, and night. Even cleaned the clubhouse bathrooms," he took an end of my box spring and I took the other. We hefted it up the three flights of stairs and there was no more talking for the moment.

Derek set down one end of my couch, one of the guys from the shop set down the other. I motioned for them to put it against one wall. They slid the black leather monstrosity back and straightened.

"Yeah man," Squick said, "He's got her working the counter at the shop. She's quiet and freaking tiny! I think my eight year old niece is bigger than her," I gave him a look like he was being ridiculous which he was... but not entirely so.

"Okay, other than 'quiet' and 'tiny' what's she freaking look like?" Derek asked as we trouped down the stairs to get more stuff.

"She's got eyes like the sun," I said and Derek barked a laugh.

"Dude, that's not him being poetic and shit, she really does; her eyes are gold. Never seen anything like it," Reaver affirmed.

"Okay, what about the rest?" Derek asked.

"Long auburn hair to her butt," Squick said.

"She's a member of the itty bitty titty committee," Reaver said and I glowered at him.

"What!? She is," he said defensively.

"You still don't have to put it like that," I said.

"Dude, you in love with this chick or something?" Derek asked laughing. I stopped and thought about it, I cared about her, sure and she'd done a pretty spectacular job of getting under my skin in all the right ways… but love? Derek's face fell.

"Holy shit. You've known this bitch all of a week! I mean fuck man, if you have to think about it…" he didn't finish the thought probably because I had a look on my face that screamed if he did I would break his fucking arm.

"Look, I like Ashton, a lot. I want to make sure she's safe and that she can put her douchebag ex in the rearview once and for all. I'm just doing what I've done from the moment I met her, playing shit by ear and going where the road takes me. Whatever happens, happens." I shrugged and the three of them exchanged looks and shrugged too.

"Now hurry the fuck up so I can go get her. She was so excited when I left she's probably about ready to pee herself by now." The guys laughed and I joined in this time, a little bothered by my recent introspections.

Ashton kept saying everything was moving really fast and she wasn't wrong but this was the first time *I* was thinking along the same lines. So far everything had been comfortable, had felt right even. Now I wasn't so sure. We hustled through the last of what was on the truck and I left the guys putting furniture together. I jogged out to the truck and started it.

Truth was, despite my afternoon's misgivings, I was excited for her to see the apartment, to claim the space for her own. I couldn't afford to get her a bed so I got her one of those air mattress beds that inflated in a minute. I'd set it up in her room along with some white sheets for tonight and a gift card for a hundred bucks at Walmart for her to pick what she wanted blanket wise. She should be able to get some cheap ass particle board furniture for the room too.

Nothing fancy, but at least it was a start.

I felt a pang about not having her in my bed anymore. I'd slept better in the last week than I had in months, if not a couple of years. I turned onto the highway and drove towards the club house.

I was beginning to think Ashton was as much a tonic to some of the broken parts of my soul as I was to hers. Her broken was just a lot fresher than mine, more noticeable. Still, comfortable or not, sleeping better or not, it was time to take a step back, give her some time to recover. I could still be there for her but she needed some space.

I guess in some ways I felt like a parent trying to teach their kid to ride a bike, only with stakes much higher. The training wheels had to come off but I was still holding on to the bike running alongside. Eventually I would have to let go and she would either pedal down the street on her own or she would fall. I hit the signal and turned into the clubhouse driveway.

I didn't have to let go today and despite my unease on if I was really doing her a solid or becoming a crutch for her, I wanted to enjoy this, hopefully see her smile. Yeah, that would be good.

# CHAPTER 10

*Ashton*

I stood just inside the door way to Ethan's room and made sure I had gotten everything that was moving to the new apartment. The bed and bedding remained as did the small television and DVD player. A change of his clothes hung neatly in the closet but everything else was piled in the common room waiting for Ethan to arrive and take us home…

I sank down onto the corner of the bed.

Home…

It felt foreign in my head. I hadn't had a home in a very long time. When my mother died, I had been bounced from temporary foster home to temporary foster home, two or three times before landing permanently with the Tuckers. I had been lucky. Nothing bad had happened to me to remove me from any of the homes. You hear horror stories all the time of abuse or molestation… none of those things had happened to me, it had just been a matter of supply and demand. The need for good foster homes vastly outweighed the homes available. So I'd had to play a short game of musical homes until one came available.

Living with the Tuckers from eleven to eighteen had felt like home after the first year or so. Then it was off to college and no matter how much you personalized a space, a dorm room was just that… a dorm room.

Then I had married Chadwick, right after graduation and I had thought that finally, I would have a home of my own. A family. I had been an absolute fool. The first few months of our marriage had been good. We'd honeymooned in the South of France, made love just about every night, then about eight months in things began to change.

At first, Chadwick had decided that he didn't like me going out

82

with my friend Alley. He'd declared her trashy and a bad influence. He began nagging me after a fashion, lecturing me every time I went out, told me that he was disappointed in me which had hurt. I didn't want him to be disappointed and so I began to see her less and less until eventually I didn't see her at all.

Then he became too busy for us to visit home, which for me, was the Tuckers, just two states away and he wouldn't hear of me going alone. What if something happened to me? He'd ask, and then he would tell me how he couldn't live without me, how much he needed me in his life.

Then after a year or two of married life he had become critical of my appearance, stating I required diet and exercise that he hadn't married a fat woman and he wouldn't *be* married to one. Instead of letting me go to a gym he'd had one put in at the house and had hired a personal trainer. Handpicked a woman who had taught me yoga. She and I became friends and he fired her. Told me that people like us didn't make friends with the help. I argued with him and that was the first time he hit me.

"Ashton?" Ethan knelt down in front of me.

"What's wrong?" he asked. I looked up from my lap to his silvery eyes and smiled. His expression softened.

"Just thinking about how I got here," I murmured.

"About out on the road?" he asked.

"No, about college and how everything just got so... lost," I sighed.

"Tell me?" he asked and sat down cross legged on the floor. I took a deep breath and I told him, about my mom, about foster care and about how I had worked my ass off in high school to make my mom proud. About the essays and scholarships and grants... About meeting Chadwick at one of his fraternities rush parties.

About how sweet he'd been, taking me on dates and talking long into the night, about how he'd proposed on Valentine's Day our junior year. How we'd gotten married just after graduation and how he'd immediately gone to work for his father. He listened patiently as I stripped myself bare, about how I'd grown increasingly isolated, about the first time Chadwick had hit me, about how he'd brought flowers afterwards and how he'd apologized and how I had wanted so hard to believe him. How I had believed him until it happened again…

Ethan gently thumbed tears from beneath my eyes and smiled sadly at me. He struggled for a time, fishing for something, anything to say. He looked lost and so I bravely smiled and stood up. He got to his feet and pulled me into a hug.

"I know it's been said before but I'm gonna say it anyways, Sunshine," he leaned back and tilted my face up to his, gently cupping my face with his broad hands… "Things are going to be different from now on," he said softly and I nodded, his fingers sliding against my skin sending a wash of goose flesh down my spine.

"I'm gonna keep saying it and spend every day proving it until you finally believe it too," he smiled. I smiled and wiped my eyes and sniffed.

"Ready to go see the new place?" he asked gently.

"Yes," I nodded.

We went out to the common room. The door was opened wide and the pickup backed to it. Doc stood in the back of the truck while Dray handed him up boxes and suitcases and duffels of clothes. I had put trash bags over the hanging clothes, poking holes in the top for the hooks of the hangars to go through. Those hung off of the empty gun rack inside the truck against the back window.

"Thanks," Ethan grunted at Dray and the darker man gave him a curt nod. I didn't even pretend to understand their relationship. More often than not they seemed to butt heads and yet, Dray still helped Ethan despite their ongoing thinly veiled animosity.

"Thank you," I murmured as I went past and Dray grunted.

"Whatever gets the club house back to man-land faster," he said and I smiled despite his grumpy attitude.

"See you over there, Darlin'." Chandra blew out a plume of smoke as she spoke and I smiled. She and Doc were coming too. I bit my lip and turned back to Dray whose expression was storm clouded. I was going to invite him but lost my nerve. I got into the truck and Chandra got in beside me. Ethan was riding his bike over.

We drove along and sang to the radio and the raincloud over my heart slowly moved off. By the time we were pulling into the apartment building's driveway behind Ethan and Doc's bikes I was suffused with the warm glow of excitement, fairly vibrating with it. I was out of the truck before Ethan could reach for the handle. He laughed.

"Excited?" he asked and I nodded emphatically.

"Hey! There she is!" I heard from above me and shading my eyes from the sun with my hand saw Andy from the shop, though for some reason everybody called him Squick.

He was a lanky fellow, tall and rail thin and nothing but knees and elbows. He was covered in a myriad of colorful tattoos large and small, all patch worked together on both arms. The colorful cartoon-like images he explained to me were "new school" climbed both sides of his neck and cascaded down his ribs, leaving his narrow chest and stomach bare. He favored faded band tee shirts with the sleeves cut out, leaving gaping holes down his flanks so his tattoos were visible. He paired the shirts with holey jeans, the knees ripped out and frayed, ending over the top of his black Converse, more threads trailing at his heels where he'd walked off the back cuff of his pants.

I smiled and waved up at him. A man I didn't know stood beside him. He was shorter than Andy by a lot, but who wasn't? He was built sturdy, and carried himself like a soldier. Back straight, shoulders back. He wore jeans and a green tee shirt, and peered down at me speculatively. His brown hair was hidden under a black baseball cap turned backwards on his head. It was the kind with a solid back, without the adjustable plastic thing some of them had. A small silver logo rode between his brows, too small to be seen from this distance. I couldn't make out his eye color from here, but Andy's I knew were a warm brown.

"Ashton," Ethan called and I went to where he stood and took the banker's box with my yearbooks and photos from him. He heaved his big green duffel bag over the side of the truck and nodded that I should go ahead. Doc and Chandra followed, each carrying something.

I took the stairs carefully. My sneakers quiet on the wooden treads, all the way up to the third floor. Andy stood outside the open apartment door and ushered me in with a flourish. I smiled at him and went in. Standing just inside the door it smelled strongly of fresh paint, the living room was to my left, couches and the television already in place. A fireplace was in the corner, the window set into the wall beside the fireplace was wide open overlooking the parking lot below and letting in the fresh spring air.

To my right was the small kitchen and in front of that, sharing space with the living room, was a dining area. A table and four chairs, correction a *nice* table and four chairs were set up in front of the open breakfast bar leading into the kitchen. A liquor cabinet hugged the wall by the front door, though as of now it was empty. A hallway was directly across from the front door and held four doors. Two on the left and two on the right.

"Stuff is getting heavy honey you might want to step aside," Doc called from behind me.

"Oh! I'm sorry!" I called and stepped to the side, into the dining area. Ethan, Doc and Chandra filed in passed me. The strange man I didn't know was watching me from the living room, arms crossed, hazel eyes coolly assessing. I swallowed.

"Hi," I ventured.

"Hey," he answered.

"Ashton, Derek... Derek, Ashton," Ethan said and disappeared down the hall. He went into the second door on the left and I nodded politely to Derek who raised an eyebrow at me. I went down the hall, the air in the apartment cool against my legs. I had chosen a pair of shorts and a tee based on the sun shining outside. While it was warm in the direct sun it was still too cool for shorts which I had belatedly found out but it hadn't been worth it to go digging through everything for pants.

The first door on the right passed the kitchen was a bathroom. It looked stark without a shower curtain. Everything was white. The walls, the bathtub, the toilet, the sink even. The only thing breaking up the stark white monotony was the tan counter top and the earth toned linoleum.

The door across from it was the linen closet and so I went passed it and looked into the room Ethan had disappeared into. He was standing beside his bed, a king size by the look of it. It was made of a rich dark cherry wood, a four poster with large round cannonballs atop each post at chest height. A matching dresser sat against the wall at the foot of the bed. His back was to me as he pulled clothes from the duffel bag which was almost as big as me. He was separating them into piles on top of the bare mattress and I crept further down the hall to the last door on the right.

The walls were white like everywhere else in the apartment. The carpet a light cream. An air bed covered in a white bottom sheet and white top sheet sat in the middle of the floor, the head pressed up against one wall. The closet was just inside the door to the left and I set my box inside it on the floor. A blue square of cardboard sat on the foot of the bed and I picked it up with shaking fingers. I sank to the floor and opened the gift card envelope.

*For blankets and whatever else you can get out of it. Welcome home. —Ethan*

...was written in his careful printing. I sank cross legged the rest of the way onto the carpet and looked around the stark and empty room, the window in the back wall was closed, the venetian blinds drawn but turned so that the natural light illuminated the room.

"You okay?" Ethan asked softly from the door way.

I turned to look at him, he was standing, shoulder propped against the door jamb, arms crossed over his chest causing the fabric to strain across his broad shoulders, the sleeves tight around his biceps. His long hair was only half pulled up and hung behind his ears, down his shoulders. He was watching me, carefully considering, his expression schooled into one of neutrality as he waited to see what I would do. I turned back to the empty room and looked it over again.

"So this is what it feels like to start from the beginning?" I asked.

"Yeah," he said, tone neutral.

I wanted to laugh, I wanted to cry, I wanted to sing and I wanted to scream all at the same time. I felt swamped by emotion and yet I felt numb. I didn't know what to do with myself and so I did what came naturally… I was unerringly polite.

"Thank you for my gift card," I whispered.

"You're welcome, Babe," he said.

"Hey, she in here?" I heard Andy ask.

"Oh good!" he exclaimed and I turned at the sound of rustling paper. He held a flat rectangular object wrapped in white birthday paper, colored balloons and streamers printed on its surface, cursive script proclaiming 'Happy Birthday!' flowing between them. I couldn't help it, I broke into a smile and frowned at the same time.

"My birthday is in December," I said.

"Yeah well, it's a housewarming present," he said and shrugged, "And it's sort of like your birthday too… I guess," he smiled and I laughed and that made Ethan smile for some reason.

"Can I come in?" Andy asked and I looked at him and Ethan both, just outside my bedroom door and sobered.

My bedroom door… they were asking if they could come in… I nodded rapidly, my throat suddenly squeezed tight by unshed tears. They came in and sat on my floor with me. Andy put the large housewarming package in my lap. Doc, Chandra, Reaver and the man I didn't know, Derek stood in the door way. I looked at Ethan.

"Don't look at me Babe, this is all Squick," he said. I looked at Andy and down at the package in my lap and worked a fingernail under a bit of tape.

"You're killing me!" Andy said and I looked up at him, he was grinning and I felt my lips spread in an answering grin of my own. I tore the paper indelicately, ripping a diagonal swath across the glass of a framed picture.

Not a picture, a drawing… A poster sized drawing. At the bottom of it was the logo, perfectly rendered, for the musical Les Miserables. Rising behind it was every character, lovingly rendered from Andy's imagination, all of them completely obvious to me… Jean Valjean, Fantine, Javier, Cosette… my vision blurred and a keening sound escaped my throat. I thrust the image at Ethan and tackled Andy in a fierce hug.

"Thank you so much!" I cried and there was broken laughter from outside the room.

"I haven't finished the other one but I'll get it to you as soon as it's done. I did one for Phantom of the Opera too." He was grinning and I wiped my eyes and laughed, taking the framed poster in its simple black frame back into my lap. It was colorful and vibrant and so amazing that I couldn't stop smiling. Ethan clapped Andy on the back and his expression was one of pure gratitude and I think it was in that moment that I fell a little in love with Ethan "Trigger" Howard.

"C'mon Babe, let's get the rest of what's in the pickup in here. I want to get you to Walmart before it closes so you'll have some blankets tonight." Ethan stood up and reached down for my hand. I let him pull me to my feet and I stripped the rest of the paper from the frame and lovingly leaned it against the wall. I smiled at Andy and he put an arm across my shoulders as we walked out into the rest of the apartment.

"How did you know?" I asked.

"Dude, I heard you singing that shit your first day around the shop when you thought no one was listening. My sister was in choir all through high school. I know all about Les Mis and Phantom," he grinned down at me and I smiled up at him and gave him another hug around his lean frame.

"You're awesome," I said and he laughed.

"Don't you forget it!" He wrinkled his nose at me and tweaked mine and I laughed incredulously.

"Come on! Some of us are gettin' hungry!" Reaver yelled from the top of the stairs and for some reason I burst into a fit of giggles.

We made the run to Walmart in record time. I selected a comforter set and a microfiber warm fuzzy blanket. The blanket was a light lavender, the comforter set a gray background with a deep purple damask pattern. It was only fifty dollars and so I used the other half of the card on a small white chest of drawers that Ethan promised he'd put together for me. It was cheap particle board but better than the nothing I had.

Ethan let me pick the shower curtain and matching bathroom

rugs and towels but only on the condition that he would let me pay him back with my first real paycheck. We were back in the apartment, pizza had been ordered and Reaver and Andy had gone on a beer run. I had asked Reaver his real name once upon a time, oh say, four days ago but he had refused to tell me.

"Why?" I'd asked him.

"Because I hate it and you wouldn't call me Reaver anymore," I'd conceded the point but still, he didn't look like a Reaver to me. I didn't know what he looked like, honestly, but Reaver wasn't it.

Chandra and Doc had been gone when Ethan and I had gotten back from the store and Derek was alone in the apartment, kicked back on the couch, one foot propped on the simple black rectangle that was the coffee table. Ethan picked up the heel of Derek's white and blue Adidas on the way by and dropped it to the carpet.

"Really?" Derek asked.

"Yeah. Really," Ethan had said. I went for the bathroom with the bag containing the shower curtain.

"Just as anal as when you were in the corps..." I heard Derek mutter and I paused, looking at them both. Ethan was frowning.

"Can one of you help me with this?" I murmured to break the tension.

"Yeah, what are you doing?" Derek asked.

"Hanging the shower curtain," I held up the bag with the supplies.

He went into the bathroom and Ethan went his own way. I handed Derek the rings to put on the rod and fluffed out the liner, matching it up with the curtain which was a minty green.

"Not bad," he commented.

"Well its Ethan's space too," I murmured.

"You ever get above a whisper?" he asked, clipping the curtain in place.

"Only when I'm singing," I answered.

"Excuse me, what?" he stopped mid-motion. I blinked up at him suddenly afraid to repeat myself. He saved me by saying,

"Did you just say 'Only when I'm screaming'?" he asked.

"Oh! No, I said singing… but uh that too," I blushed furiously. He grinned.

"Trigger been getting you pretty loud?" He asked grinning and I blinked up at him and shock must have registered on my face.

"Sorry none of my business," he said.

"Uh… no… We aren't… Uh…" I was speechless.

"Hey sorry, I didn't mean to…"

"My husband hasn't touched me except to correct me in two years. I'm not even sure I remember how sex works when I get to be a willing participant," I shrugged a shoulder indelicately and handed him the next opening in the shower curtain.

"What the fuck?" I heard from the open doorway and shame erupted under my skin, prickling in a fiery pink tirade from my chest to the roots of my hair. Ethan was scowling at me and I felt tears spring to my eyes.

"Oh, hey, no Sunshine, not mad at you," he captured my wrist and pulled me into a protective hug. "You on the other hand, what the fuck, man?" he asked Derek, frowning.

"Dude! I didn't ask!" he put up his hands.

"He didn't," I said, voice muffled by Ethan's shirt, "It just sort of came out. I'm sorry!" Ethan sighed.

"It's okay Babe, how many times I gotta tell you, stop apologizing? There's nothing to apologize for," he gave me a squeeze and let me go.

"This moment of awkward brought to you by the letter 'D'," Derek said and I smiled. Sesame Street had been a favorite growing up.

"'D' for Derek?" I asked. He shrugged.

"I was thinking more 'D' for douchebag," he admitted. Ethan laughed.

"That fits too," he said. Derek frowned.

"I meant her ex," he clarified.

"I didn't," Ethan said and walked away. I handed Derek another part of the shower curtain so he wouldn't go after Ethan. He looked me over for a minute before taking it.

"Thanks," I whispered.

"No problem. I'll get his ass later," he frowned and I laughed.

Reaver and Andy came back about thirty minutes later, fifteen minutes after that there was a knock at the door.

"Pizza!" Andy cried clapping his hands together and rubbing them briskly. Ethan got the door and I rooted through the kitchen for a roll of paper towels.

Ethan put the two boxes on the table and Reaver opened beers. I came around with paper towels and the guys took seats around the table. Ethan pulled me onto his lap. I didn't protest and no one said anything. Everyone helped themselves using two or three paper towels as plates. I smiled and took a bite. Reaver reached down next to him and pulled up a bottle unlike the beer bottles in front of the guys and twisted off the top.

"Figured beer wasn't your thing but you're drinking," he commented and handed me a wine cooler. I laughed.

"You were right and thanks," I clinked bottles with him and took a drink of the sweet alcoholic drink.

"Good?" he asked. I smiled.

"Haven't had one of these since college," I said.

"Jesus, what *did* that prick let you have?" Derek asked.

"The occasional glass of wine. Only in public and only on special occasions," I shrugged. The table got quiet as they processed the information.

"What made you happy?" Reaver asked.

"Not a lot," I answered honestly. I thought about it, "Cooking. Mostly because that reminded me of Mrs. Tucker, singing if Chadwick wasn't in the house to hear me." Andy frowned.

"Why do you call him Chadwick?" he asked.

"He didn't like Chad. Chad was a mongrel's name... He comes from a family of pedigree and shortening his name like a commoner simply would not do," choked laughter greeted that response.

"Sing us something," Derek said and I blinked.

"I... I don't know..." I said.

"C'mon please?" Andy said.

"Yeah, sing us something," Reaver put in.

"Why?" I asked.

"I want to hear something above a whisper come out of you," Derek said and crossed his arms. I looked at Ethan, his arm around my waist tightened.

"Just not that song you were singing in the kitchen," he said to me and his silver eyes clouded... Okay, so no help there. I chewed my lip.

"*Don't you fret, M'sieur Marius...*" I sang the beginnings of the death of Eponine and I looked to Andy and he grinned and helped me out. Singing Marius' lines. The guys looked at him surprised.

I looked at Ethan and closed my eyes, voice stronger and sang, asking to be held, to be sheltered and Andy picked up, then I cut in, as we sang 'A Little Fall of Rain' from Les Miserables.

"You want to finish it?" Andy asked and I nodded, and he sang the next line and we sang Eponine's death together and I smiled because right then I was singing the death of my old life with Chadwick and welcoming a new life full of new friends. Ethan was watching me, his hand where it rested on the top of my thigh, massaging. I sang out the last of the piece with Andy and as the last note died, silence overtook the small apartment.

"Wow," Derek said, breaking the spell. He cleared his throat and took a drink of his beer.

"Powerful stuff. What was that?" Reaver asked.

"A Little Fall of Rain' from Les Miserables," I said, "It's the part where Eponine who is in love with Marius dies after being shot."

"Dude, sucks for Marius," Derek said. I shook my head.

"No, Marius is in love with Cosette. Was completely blind to what Eponine felt for him." I ate a bite of lukewarm pizza.

"Marius was a dumbass," Ethan grunted.

"Maybe so but he marries Cosette, who was hot..." Andy said and I laughed.

"Your sister, huh?" I asked.

"Maybe I was a choir kid too," he said grinning around a mouthful of pizza, "Don't tell anyone," he said after swallowing.

"As long as you'll be my Marius or Jean Valjean from time to time," I said.

"Deal," he held out his fist and I reached across the table and bumped it with my own.

"Nerd love is such sweet love," Derek commented dryly.

"Very funny. While you were out on the football field, I was cozying up with some hot chicks. Who's the bitch now?" Andy asked.

"He's got you there, man," Ethan grunted. I slid off his lap shaking my head.

"Don't you ever sing anything happy?" he asked me and I cleaned up my mess.

"I don't know, is there anything happy in Les Mis or Phantom?" I asked Andy. He grinned...

"That's a negative ghost rider!" he said.

"Masquerade, but that one's just too campy to sing acapella," I said.

"Aca-what?" Reaver asked.

"She means singing without the benefit of music," Andy said.

"Oh."

"What did you want to be when you grew up?" Ethan asked me suddenly.

"A singer," I said simply.

"Why?" Derek asked.

"My mom. She loved all things musical. Was a music teacher but I wanted to be on Broadway."

"Ever see one?" Andy asked.

I pursed my lips. "Les Mis, in concert. Chadwick took me when we were dating in college. Before I became his dutiful housewife." I threw the soiled paper towels away in a stray grocery bag in the kitchen.

"Feel like kicking his balls in so he can't reproduce," Derek grumbled and I missed the grocery bag completely and dropped the bottle I was holding. It crashed against the kitchen floor and I knelt to pick it up. Ethan came around and knelt down with me.

"I'm sorry," I said hastily.

"Don't apologize," he said gently and helped me pick up the large shards of glass, at least it hadn't shattered. We deposited the glass into the plastic sack and I sighed.

"Enough diving into Ashton's past for one night," Ethan declared and bottles were raised in salute.

"I'm going to take a shower if that's all right with everyone," I said.

"Yeah, sure, why wouldn't it be?" Ethan scowled.

"I don't want to be a bad hostess," I murmured and he grinned.

"Go on, I'll keep these animals in line," he nudged me in the direction of the bathroom. I went to my room first and found my night shirt which I packed on top of the suitcase. I pulled it free and picked up my toiletries.

I showered long and thought hard, scrubbing every inch of myself. I sighed in contentment as the warm water beat down on my shoulders and scalp, washed and conditioned my hair and shaved my legs and underarms.

When I was as clean as I was going to get I shut off the water and dried myself, wrapping my hair in the towel to pull on Ethan's dress shirt. I'd washed it and it didn't smell like him anymore, just clean laundry soap and dryer sheets. I pulled the towel off my hair, and rubbed it over the long strands before brushing it out. I opened the bathroom door. The guys were talking in low murmurs so I ghosted up the hall to my room and put everything away where it belonged. A soft tap came at the door's edge and Ethan cleared his throat.

"Guys are leaving," he said. I nodded, followed him out and hugged everyone goodbye, thanking them all for their help and Andy especially for my picture.

"Night Doll," Reaver said and kissed me on the top of my head.

"Ashton, listen… if you uh, ever want to remember what that's like, call me," Derek said, referencing our conversation in the bathroom. I sputtered…

"I…" I blinked, speechless.

"Yeah, smooth move numb nuts," Ethan said and slammed the door in Derek's face but when he turned around he was smiling and I realized keenly that we were alone.

"Tired?" he asked me.

"A little," I answered.

"Want another?" he asked, moving over to the table he picked up one of the wine coolers.

"Sure," I said. Why not? He twisted off the top with a flick of his wrist and handed it to me.

"Thanks," I murmured.

"Welcome," he said and hung his head and laughed.

"When did this get awkward?" he asked and I swallowed a mouthful of the sweet alcohol and shrugged.

"Probably about the time I admitted how long it's been since my husband wanted to have sex with me," I nudged the carpet with one of my toes noting the white polish of the French manicure was chipped. Chadwick had me do it because the shoes he'd selected for the charity dinner we'd attended were open toed. Usually I did my own polish and he didn't care but he'd wanted French tips and so I had done them that way.

"Ashton, where did you go?" Ethan's gentle voice popped me back to the present.

"What?" I asked.

"I said 'yeah but we all know he's an idiot' and suddenly you just weren't there," he said. I frowned.

"I was thinking about my nail polish," I confessed, he was confused so I explained, he sighed.

"We gotta get you some new memories, some *good* memories," he said.

"I have some," I smiled.

"Yeah? Name one," he said and dropped onto the end of the couch. I went over and curled up on the cushion next to him and took a drink of my wine cooler. He took a drink of his beer.

"When you kissed me," I said finally and he looked at me, really looked at me.

"I'm not sure I should have done that," he said and I cringed inwardly and tried not to let it hurt. "Damn I want to so much, though. Think about it too much," his eyes were fixed on where his thick fingers peeled the label from his bottle of beer.

"Me too," I said softly, but I wasn't ready and we both knew that so I rose as gracefully as I could to my feet and with as much dignity as I could salvage from airing my painful, humiliating, ugly truths I murmured, "I'd better go to bed."

He caught my hand as I walked by and looked at me deliberately as he brought my palm to his mouth. He pressed a kiss to its center, his eyes drifting shut as he breathed in deeply and reluctantly let me go. I smiled, and let it show how much the gesture touched me before I trailed up the hall to my bedroom.

I gently shut my bedroom door and sat down in the center of my air mattress and finished my drink. Leaving the empty bottle atop one of the boxes, I lay down. A minute later I heard Ethan's door shut. I sighed, got up and turned out my light and lay down again. Hours later I woke to the sound of panicked shouting. I jolted awake sitting up sharply in bed, every hair standing on end.

"Move! Move! Get down!" I threw back the blankets and padded to my bedroom door and flung it open. I threw open Ethan's door and found him twisted in his sheets. He was screaming and clutching at his right leg, up high on his thigh. I flipped on the light and bounded up onto the bed.

"Ethan wake up!" I shouted, grabbing his face between my hands but he twisted and writhed.

"Ethan! Ethan please wake up!" I shouted desperately. Still nothing I straddled his hips and gripped him by the shoulders and shook and screamed,

"Trigger wake up!"

Ethan's eyes snapped open fear clouding his vision before they finally focused on me.

"Ashton?" he asked and his voice sounded far away, lost... I stroked the side of his face which was slick with sweat. His chest heaved with great gasps for air.

"It's okay," I soothed. He gripped my upper arms with both his hands firmly, not quite enough to hurt.

"Shhh, Its okay," I soothed again and rested my forehead against his. I closed my eyes and waited for my heart rate to go back to normal.

"What happened?" he asked.

"I think you had a bad dream," I murmured. His arms went

around me and pulled me down onto his chest.

"Did I scare you?" he asked after a moment.

"Only because I didn't know what was happening," my voice was quiet, barely above a whisper.

"I'm sorry," he said only slightly out of breath now. I sat up and looked him in the eyes, searching his face to reassure myself he was back, that he was here...

"If I don't get to apologize then you don't either," I said and he pulled me back down, holding me against his body, one hand on my back the other tangled in my hair. I stayed like that and soaked in his warmth.

"What was that?" I asked him.

"Flashback," he said, "I get 'em sometimes."

"How come this is the first time I've seen one?" I asked.

"I don't know, I just sleep better when you're with me," he answered.

"Why didn't you say so?" I asked.

"I wanted you to have your own space," he said finally.

"Fine, then give me the kitchen," I murmured and he laughed. I sat up. I could feel what our position was doing to him, pressed along where my leg met my body. I let him see the seriousness in my eyes and the laughter died in his.

"Ashton I..." I put my fingers over his lips and sat up straight. I climbed off his body to the floor and went and switched out the light, then resolutely climbed back up into the bed.

"Are you okay?" I asked.

"Yeah, I will be but," I cut him off.

"Good," I said. Then, "Good night Ethan." He chuckled and pulled me tight to the side of his body.

"Night Sunshine," he murmured.

# CHAPTER 11

*Trig*

Ashton fell asleep before I did. I lay awake, sweat cooling on my body and stared at the ceiling for a long damn time. She had impressed the hell out of me. After all she'd been through to climb up on me when I was thrashing like that, to put herself in danger of getting hit, accidentally or not... that took balls.

I closed my eyes and wished for some water but didn't want to disturb her. Her soft even breathing puffed out against my chest and I couldn't help but smooth the crisp cotton of my shirt over her svelte frame. She sighed out in her sleep and relaxed under the touch and I smiled.

I'd taken her on not knowing what the hell I was doing, intending to fix her like some kind of fucking project or something and here she was fixing one of my hurts. Kind of incredible. I'd never been a religious man, but I did believe in God and I found myself wondering which one of us was the gift from Him. I closed my eyes and thought about *my* ex. She hadn't been able to handle the night terrors.

I'd done everything I could to keep her safe. Meds, counselling... Took the VA up on everything they had to offer. Still, I'd caught her in bed with another club member and that I could not abide. My fault, sure... some of it, but whatever happened to stand by your man?

I looked down at Ashton, her face lax and angelic from the parking lot lights down below my window. She'd stood by her man and look where it'd gotten her. Seven or eight years of hell that I was glad to get her out of. I trailed a fingertip down her cheek and she moaned softly in her sleep. My cock twitched at the sound and I closed my eyes and let out the breath I'd sucked in. I was painfully hard with nothing to be done for it.

Fuck.

I wanted Ashton like a dying man wanted the final kiss of death. We just needed to put more distance between ourselves and the ugly disaster that had been our meeting. She needed time to come down from that mountain of shit her husband had piled under her. She needed a fucking divorce, which was my final thought before I managed to go back to sleep.

When I woke up it was to a brilliant pair of golden eyes framed by a luxurious mane of auburn hair. Ashton's arm was across my chest, her chin resting on it.

"Morning," she said softly.

"Morning," I grunted. Silence ensued.

"What're you looking at?" I asked finally.

"You," she said. "I'm trying to decide if you're really okay."

"I'm okay Babe," I smoothed her hair back from her face and she nodded reluctantly.

"I don't want to get up," she murmured.

"Why not?" She closed her eyes, her slim shoulders rising and falling in a gusty sigh.

"I want you to touch me," she said finally, golden eyes flickering open, rooting me where I lay.

"Ohhh-kay?" I said, not quite getting what she was asking of me.

"It's been a long time since anyone has touched me without meaning for it to hurt," she whispered.

"Yeah," I said.

"So I want you to touch me. Doesn't have to be now, doesn't have to lead to sex, I just… need you to touch me. Please?" she asked so sweetly, how the fuck was I supposed to say no?

"I get you, I think," I said and she looked relieved.

"We have some unpacking to do, so how about this… we unpack, we go to work and when we get home tonight let's put on that movie you were singing from with Squick last night," I suggested.

"And you'll touch me?" she asked.

"Babe you don't have any idea how hard it is for me to keep my hands off of you do you?" I asked.

"No," she whispered.

"Jesus," I muttered and covered my face with my hands and scrubbed. Her weight on me diminished as she sat up and I pushed myself into a sitting position.

"I don't want to be the thing that finally breaks you," I told her.

"Sometimes it feels like you're the only thing holding me together," she murmured. "I know that's not fair to you," she went on, "and I want to get to a place where I don't have to rely on you so much but..." she looked rough, conflicted.

"Hold up. Maybe we're making this more complicated than it needs to be," I said. She looked up hopeful.

"Let me ask you something... and I want you to think about this," she nodded, "What do you need Ashton?" I asked her. She chewed her bottom lip and looked at me, her sun light eyes steady and sure.

"I'm tired of hurting. I want to feel good. I need to feel like I'm something special. Like I'm worth something again," she looked at me and her expression was haunted. She didn't speak the words but they were written all over her face. Without ever even parting her lips she said to me *I need to feel loved...*

I leaned forward and she went so very still. I patted the tops of my thighs sharply and she came forward carefully. I didn't let her eyes go with mine as she came to sit on my lap. I adjusted her so she was straddling my hips like she had the night before. I pulled her tightly against me, one arm behind her back the other tenderly cradling the back of her head.

Her hair was like spun satin between my fingers as I brought her lips to mine. I could feel her heartbeat, a rapid fluttering thing trapped in the cage of her ribs. Her lips were warm and soft beneath my own and parted so sweetly in invitation. Her arms twined around my shoulders and neck, her fingers tugging my hair gently and I moaned into her mouth, plunging my tongue inside. A small sweet sound, not a whimper, not a moan, I don't know what, crawled up her throat and spilled into my mouth and my cock jumped.

She was hot where she pressed against it and I wanted inside her so damned bad it hurt but not yet. She needed to feel special, cherished, desired and I had every intention of delivering, slowly and sweetly. I broke the kiss after long minutes and held her against me.

"Tonight, Les Miserables and I touch you," I promised her.

"Okay," she whispered.

"Only way this is gonna work is with full frontal honesty," I told her.

"What does that mean?" she asked.

"It means, you have any misgivings, you need to be honest about them. You need to stop you have to tell me, you need to tell me how you're feeling even if you don't know. No doing anything you aren't ready for just to please me. You gotta tell me where you're at even if you think it's something I don't want to hear. You get me?" I asked.

"I get you," she whispered.

"You got a room across the hall. You need time to yourself, you need your own space, then you go there. I don't go in there unless invited, no one does. Ever. Deal?" I asked.

"Deal," she said.

"Ashton I have no fucking idea what I'm doing here," I told her honestly.

"Me either," she whispered.

"As long as we're on the same page," I huffed out a sigh.

"I think we are," she said.

"I hope we are," I said and crushed her to me. Her head fit perfectly beneath my chin. She clung to me and I held her.

This was way beyond me but life doesn't come with an instruction manual. I was willing to see where the road took us and it seemed like Ashton was up for the ride so we would do this, whatever this was, and hopefully both of us would come out better, not worse for it.

We stayed like that for a bit until I couldn't stand it anymore. I gave her a gentle pat on the butt and she got down. I went to the bathroom, showered, shaved and generally did my thing. She had breakfast and coffee started by the time I was out. As soon as we'd eaten it was her turn. She showered and dressed and spent some time unpacking her room.

"Ethan?" she asked me at one point.

"Yeah Sunshine?"

"You and Reaver work out right?" she asked.

"Three days a week, sometimes more, why?" I asked.

"At the clubhouse?" she asked. What was she getting at?

"No, usually at the 'Y'," I answered.

"Do they have yoga classes there?" she asked.

"I can find out for you," I said.

"I'd really like that," she said and smiled.

"Consider it done," I plucked my cell out of my back pocket and called Reaver.

"Dude, what fuggin time is it?" he answered by way of greeting.

"No clue. Ashton wants to know if they have yoga classes at the 'Y'."

"Yeah, Man. Where did you think those hot chicks in the spandex were going?" he asked.

"Didn't know, didn't care, just enjoyed the view," I answered.

"Well, now you know," he yawned.

"Cool, we going today?" I asked.

"Yeah man, let me get some breakfast," he groaned.

"Ashton, feel like feeding Reaver?" I asked.

"Sure," she said gently and smiled and I loved that I put it there.

"Come on over bro, Ashton's got you covered," I said into the phone.

"No carbs!" he yelled into the phone.

"Meat and eggs only, Babe," I told her. She frowned but nodded.

"See you in a few, Bro," I said into the phone.

"Yeah," he hung up.

"Have I been doing something wrong?" she asked.

"Not at all. We're just trying to maintain," I said.

"Okay, do you have a specific meal plan?" she asked.

"Yeah," I said.

"Write it out for me?"

"Yeah," and I did.

She looked it over and nodded slowly setting about the kitchen and I smiled. First time in a long time my home life had been harmonious. Felt good. We may still be in unchartered territory but we'd figure it out. One day at a time. Reaver showed up and it was like old times, he knocked twice then tried to open the door but it was locked. I heard a muffled curse as I went to throw the bolt and let him in.

"What the fuck over?" he asked.

"Ashton," I said quietly.

"Ah..." he looked into the kitchen and said "Hey Baby! How was your first night in the new place?" Her eyes met mine and she smiled.

"Better than I expected," she said, keeping my secret. I smiled. I suppose it was our secret that she would be sleeping in my bed, with me. Whose business was it anyways?

"What made you decide to do yogurt?" Reaver asked. She laughed.

"Yoga helps with the stiffness after a correction," she said softly.

"Babe," I said and she looked up.

"Yes?"

"Don't call it that, call it what it is if you've got to call it anything," I said and raked a hand through my hair. She pursed her lips and nodded.

"Yoga helps with the stiffness after my husband beats the crap out of me," she said, her perfect lips twisting in distaste.

"Thanks," I said. Reaver looked like he wanted to cut a bitch. I was with him. She fixed him breakfast and when she set the plate in front of him, he pulled her down into his lap. I tensed.

"What are you doing?" she asked.

"Hugging you kid. You look seriously hug-deprived," he said and grinned. She gave an incredulous laugh and smacked his forearm with one of her small hands. He let her up and ate with gusto. I smiled.

We were at the gym inside an hour, I bought Ashton a membership and admired her tight little ass in her tight black yoga pants and purple and lavender tank tops as she ghosted up the hallway with a few other women taking the class.

"Heavy bag?" Reaver asked.

"Yeah."

"Good, I need to beat the shit out of something," he said and his gaze was far away, locked on where Ashton had gone. I nodded. My sentiments exactly. He dropped his bag at a bench and sat down, I joined him and we began the tedious process of wrapping our hands.

"You tell her about declaring her your Old Lady, yet?" he asked.

"No," I said shortly.

"Man you better explain it," he said.

"I know Bro, I just don't want her feelin' like she's owned, even if it is just on paper to appease club politics," I said.

"You mean to appease our cock-weasel VP." Reaver's eyes, bluer than mine by a mile, turned cold as a winter's sky.

"Yeah," I punched a fist into a palm and repeated the process on the other side. I think all of us were getting tired of Dray's shit. Reaver grinned at me and it was not a nice smile.

"Let's do it," he said and bounded to his feet.

We put in a heavy work out. We didn't know how long we'd been at it, nor did either of us notice when Ashton had gotten out of yoga. My arms felt like lead and I'd turned around and there she was, sitting on the floor against the wall, golden eyes watching us curiously. I kicked myself and let my eyes sweep over her, assessing her mood and to see if what we were doing was distressing in any way.

Her eyes met mine and she gave me this serene little smile and I blinked, surprised. Whatever she'd been doing for the last hour or however long seemed to help. She seemed more together, like she'd found some glue to bind her pieces together. I smiled and turned to Reaver. We were both sweat soaked and breathing hard. He nodded and I gave him a one sided grin. Yeah. We were done for today.

"We're gonna hit the showers," I told her and she nodded and lithely rose to her feet. The movement more fluid and graceful than I thought her battered frame was capable of. Huge difference. She trailed us to the locker rooms and slipped into the women's.

"I gotta ask…" Reaver said and turned to me.

"You got any thought to making her your Old Lady, for real? 'Cause if you don't I'd sure like to try," I thought about it for a second. Thought about her beautiful face tipped up to Reaver, to any other man, his hands on her trim waist, his lips descending onto hers and my blood ran cold.

I could feel that creeping stillness fill me, the kind I'd cultivated behind the scope. That place I went right before I pulled the trigger seeping into my veins, flowing through my system until it reached my eyes which were trained hard on my brother in leather. He put up his hands.

"I had to ask, no need to go all creepy psycho motherfucker on me," he said.

"Sorry, Man," I said and the words felt like they had to fall a great distance before leaving my mouth.

"No problem, it's why I asked," he said and slapped me on the back of the shoulder, disappearing into the locker room.

I stared at the closed door of the women's locker room and clawed my way back to the surface. I'd wanted to kill him for even suggesting putting his hands on her. What the fuck was wrong with me? Hell, I'd even shared women with him before. Now I was rooted to the spot by sheer force of will alone, when what I really wanted to do was punch something. Okay, what I *really* wanted to do was go in, lift Ashton and press her against the wall, take her right then and there, claim her body for my own.

I pushed into the men's locker room instead, stripped in record time and plunged headlong into a cold shower. The heat of my lust for the woman sufficiently quelled, shocked out of my system by my shivering. I turned the water to a more comfortable temperature. Reaver eyed me sidelong.

"You're so fucked, Brother," he said, laughing at my sour expression.

"Don't I know it?" I said. Damn didn't I…

# CHAPTER 12

## *Ashton*

I showered for the second time that day and put my soiled gym clothes into the plastic grocery bag I'd brought what I'd intended to wear that day in. I felt so much better. More centered, more limber, just... better. Like a whole person, less like I was going to fly apart at any moment. It was at once soothing and invigorating. I brushed my hair and sighed into the mirror. I wished I could dry it.

"Here, use mine," I turned and smiled at a woman from my yoga class. She held out her hair dryer to me.

"Are you sure?" I asked.

"Yeah!" she smiled, her short chestnut pixie cut hair already dry and I murmured my thanks. She did tastefully understated make up in the next mirror while I dried my hair, wrapped in one of the large white towels. I shut off the dryer and handed it back once my hair was dry.

"Thank you," I murmured.

"Hey, you're welcome," she said cheerfully, "My name is Hayden," she stuck out her hand. She seemed to be about five years younger than me, which pretty much meant we looked to be about the same age with my stature. She was a few inches taller than me and a bit thinner. I took her hand and shook it.

"Ashton," I murmured.

"First time I've seen you around here but you look familiar," she tipped her head to the side considering.

"My picture was on the news," I said. Her mouth opened in a little 'o' of surprise.

"That's it!" she exclaimed.

I went over to the bench where my clothes were laid out and pulled on panties beneath the towel. I let it go and picked up my bra. I turned back around to face Hayden at her sharp intake of breath.

"Your husband did that, huh? I saw him on the news being arrested," she said. A mixture of sadness and concern marring her pretty face. I felt my stomach drop out, he would be furious. Steel climbed my spine. *Serves him right*. I thought and I was surprised.

"My husband did yeah… Ethan, the blonde man out there, he saved me," I pulled the straps of my bra up onto my shoulders and slipped into the dress I'd selected.

"Wow, for real?" she asked. She was pulling on slacks and a blouse.

"Yes," I smiled and felt a swell of some deep and undefined emotion in my breast at the thought of him.

"So who was the other guy?" she asked.

"That's Reaver," I smiled.

"Reaver? What kind of name is that?" she asked, her light green eyes curious.

"They're bikers, everyone calls Ethan Trigger or Trig, I just can't think of him that way. It just doesn't fit in my head. Reaver won't tell me his real name," I explained.

"You were rescued by a biker?" she asked. I laughed.

"Sounds like something out of a fairy tale," I confessed.

"Well both of them look like a cross between prince charming and the big bad wolf," she admitted and I laughed.

"They're both very sweet," I confessed, slipping on my sandals and buckling them.

I smoothed down the dark blue with white polka dots material of my Havana dress and twisted in front of the mirror. I was able to get the zipper up all on my own which I was pleased about. It was one of the dresses I'd salvaged from Chadwick's and one of my favorites. I blinked in the mirror and realized, even though it was from my old life, that it was something I likely would have chosen myself.

"It was nice meeting you Hayden," I murmured.

"Likewise Ashton… here, if you ever want to talk or hang out sometime, this is my number," she handed me a white business card. I smiled.

"Thanks," I said and belongings in hand we both went for the door.

*Hayden Michaels Interior Design* the card read and had her phone number and email on it, as well as a website. We slipped out the locker room door where I slipped right into Ethan's arms. He pulled me into his chest and kissed the top of my head.

"You all right, Sunshine?" he asked, "You were in there a long time," he murmured against my hair. I cuddled into him and hugged him back.

"Hayden let me use her hair dryer. We were talking," I said and leaned way back to peer up at him.

"Hi," Hayden said from just behind me. Ethan and Reaver turned.

"Helloooo," Reaver said, drawing out the word. His eyebrows shot up into his hairline. Ethan rolled his eyes.

"Hi," Ethan said.

"You must be Ethan, and that makes you Reaver," she laughed and stuck out her hand. Reaver took it and bowed gallantly over it, pressing a kiss to the back of her knuckles.

"Pleased to meet you, Hayden," he winked at her.

"Oh wow, I need to look out for you!" she said and laughed. Ethan made no move to let me go. "Call me, Ashton!" she said and smiled broadly before stepping lightly down the hall and disappearing around the corner.

I nodded but my eyes were captured by Ethan's, silver on gold, something swam in the depths of his gaze and he lowered his forehead to mine closing his eyes. I closed mine and simply enjoyed being in the circle of his arms.

"Who was that?" Reaver asked, staring after Hayden a little awestruck. He turned back to us and said, "Whoa, sorry. Take your time," he backed out of the small alcove housing the locker room doors and gave us the illusion of privacy.

"What's the matter?" I asked softly.

"Nothin' babe. Just doing what you asked me to do," he smiled at me, a slow almost shy smile and I felt an answering smile grace my lips. He was touching me. Holding me against him sweetly, tenderly like I was something precious, not fragile, not broken. His big hands resting at the small of my back.

"Thank you," I whispered.

"I think I need to take more moments out like this," his voice was low and warm and evoked an answering heat low in my body. Butterflies unfurled their wings and took flight in my stomach.

"I'd like that," I said. He kissed me tenderly a quick press of lips and straightened sucking in a slow deep breath like a swimmer long under coming up for air.

He led me out of the alcove and I smiled shyly at Reaver who winked at me. He fell into step beside us and we went out to the truck.

"They arrested Chadwick, Hayden said she saw it on the news," the men exchanged a look over my head, eyes glinting fiercely with grim satisfaction.

"I need a divorce," I stated dryly and their faces erupted into feral grins.

"Courthouse it is, Babe," Ethan said and helped me into the truck. I was small so I sat center, sandwiched between both men.

"Fuck yeah," Reaver echoed getting in beside me. I smiled. Between these two the road ahead didn't feel so scary anymore. Ethan's fingers found the spaces between mine and I smiled. I felt stronger than I had in years and I didn't think that my hour long session of yoga had much to do with it.

It had helped, sure, but I think my realization that I was going to be okay had come watching Ethan lay into the punching bag, a sweating Reaver held for him. Ethan had let fly with a single minded fury that I had seen plenty of times before on Chadwick's face but watching him lay into the bag of sand, I realized quickly the difference between the two men.

Where Chadwick was cruel, his fists landing into me to inflict maximum pain and damage, Ethan was calculating in his rage. He let fly at that bag with blows, had they been placed on a body, would have done so much more physical damage, yet when he turned to me his gaze was filled with such sadness and tenderness.

I knew beyond any shadow of a doubt in that moment that Ethan

Howard would never intentionally hurt me. He may get frustrated, he may get angry, he may yell and scream and punch a bag or wall but he would never, *never*, let that fist fly at me. Not consciously. My suspicions were cemented when I stepped out of the locker room into his warm embrace. He'd said I'd been taking a long time but no impatience, no anger tinged his voice. Only concern, I didn't want to go as far as to say love but as he'd pressed his forehead to mine, soaking up the moment letting it be what it was, I know that there was *something* there.

"What are you thinking about so hard over there?" Reaver asked. I smiled and he raised an eyebrow.

"I'd tell you, but then I'd have to kill you," I murmured. Both men barked an incredulous laugh.

"Did you just tell a joke?" Ethan asked, mystified. I smiled impishly and felt a ghost of my old self from before Chadwick settle on my surface.

"Maybe," I said softly.

"Nice," Reaver said, tone light and a little triumphant. Ethan raised the back of my hand, eyes fixed on the road and pressed a kiss to the back.

"I think I'm going to love my new life," I said, feeling lighter, freer than I had in an age. My pronouncement was met with twin masculine sounds of approval.

We went to the courthouse and got all of the paperwork required to file for divorce and information on how to go about things so, we could keep things quiet, as in my address, all of that. I could file, Chadwick would be served and then the long legal battle would begin because I knew in my heart of hearts that he wasn't going to just sign the papers even if I didn't want anything, which I didn't. I just wanted to be free of him.

We left the courthouse, my mood a lot less elevated than when we'd arrived.

"Don't worry about it. We'll get there," Ethan promised, squeezing my hand.

"Wish we could just kill him," Reaver commented dryly I looked over at him sharply but he and Trigger were exchanging a look that made the blood chill in my heart, the cold spreading through my veins until I physically shivered.

I blinked, realizing that I had finally thought of Ethan as Trigger... It was the first time I'd ever seen it.

"Have you?" I asked them.

"Yeah,"

"Yep," they answered in unison. I paused and considered them.

"They deserve it?" I asked. They exchanged looks.

"Yes," Reaver said.

"No, not all of them," Ethan said and I looked at him. His eyes were haunted.

"Thank you for your honesty," I murmured and I hugged him tight. I needed him to know that I knew... It changed something in me, sure, but only marginally. I still cared deeply for him, maybe even loved him and I was pretty sure he'd done something in the military besides... which wasn't exactly in his control. He hugged me back but it was halfhearted at best. Today was turning into an emotional rollercoaster and I don't think either of us were enjoying the ride. Ethan took us home, Reaver left us there.

"I don't understand, but I think I do," I said when the awkward silence stretched too long between us.

Ethan frowned at me. "That doesn't make any sense," he stated flatly.

"Doesn't it?" I asked. He thought about it, brow furrowed and finally his forehead eased with realization.

"You're a civilian, you can't ever understand," he said.

"...but I do." I murmured. He smiled and it was sad.

"But you do," he agreed.

"We both know what regret tastes like," I said softly.

"Yeah," he laughed and stated the obvious, "Tastes like shit."

"Yeah," I smiled.

"How'd you get to be so smart?" he asked.

"Trial and error," I said, "Mostly a lot of error."

"That makes two of us, Sunshine," he said and held out his hand. I took it and we left the apartment, locking the door behind us.

"I can't afford an attorney," I sighed.

"We'll figure it out Babe, trust me," he said.

"I do," I said and it was the truth. We rode in comfortable silence the short distance to the shop. The sky was clouding over with thick dark clouds and I smiled.

"I think it's going to rain!" I said.

"That has you excited?" he asked.

"I love a good rain storm, even better if there is thunder and lightning!" he laughed and the darker mood of earlier lifted.

"Why?" he asked.

"I don't know. Just something about the energy of stormy weather, I especially like it in the spring and summer when it's warm and I can go out in it," I smiled.

"That's nuts," he said looking at me sideways.

"Nuh uh!" I said and stuck out my lip in a pout heat flickered through his eyes.

"Don't do that, Babe," he warned and I froze.

"I'm…" he put his hand out over my mouth.

"Don't apologize, you pout that lower lip out and it makes me want to come across this seat and find out what you got on under that pretty dress you're wearing." He took his hand away, my mouth hung open in shocked surprise.

"You want me?" I squeaked.

"Every way I can get you," he said and pulled into a space in front of the shop. He got out of the truck and went in and I realized that I affected him that strongly. He didn't trust himself to get my door…

I got out and shut the truck door and trailed him inside as the first fat drops of rain started to fall. I stopped under the overhang over the shop door and breathed deep the smell of ozone and fresh, cleansing, falling rain. I turned and caught Ethan, Andy and a man I didn't know staring at me through the shop's front window. I smiled and stepped back, out into the rain and tilted my head back and laughed. Not caring if I looked like a certified lunatic. I heard the shop bell and the scrape of the door opening.

"What are you doing!?" Andy shouted.

I looked at the men and grinned.

"Living!" I answered and Ethan laughed, deep and rich and full bodied the laughter left his broad chest in harmony with the falling rain. A clap of thunder and a flash of light made me shriek and I dove for the cover of the overhang. The four of us stood there laughing and watching the rain for a few minutes before going into the shop.

"Sunshine, I want you to meet Zander. He's the other half of Open Road Ink," I held out my hand.

"Hi," I said a little shyly now. So this was my other boss...

"Hi," Zander was grinning from ear to ear. He had a chipped tooth and a crooked smile. His nose was crooked too, broken once upon a time. Mine had been crooked for a while once from a fall out of a tree when I was seven... until Chadwick had insisted upon surgery to correct the perceived blemish in my appearance.

Zander was shorter than Ethan and Andy, maybe five foot seven or eight which was still taller than me. He had black hair, cut short, that winged out from beneath his red baseball cap. He had well developed shoulders and a trim waist and wore a gray tee-shirt and frayed jean shorts that ended just below his knee. Red Converse covered his feet and warm brown eyes traveled over me from head to toe.

He had colorful tattoos on one arm and the other was done in black and white. The colorful arm was fire and brimstone while the black and white, excuse me, grayscale arm was all fluffy clouds and angels.

"She's pretty," he commented, Andy elbowed him in the shoulder.

"She's standing right here," he said out of the side of his mouth. I smiled, rainwater dripping from the ends of my hair and the hem of my dress onto the black and white checkered linoleum floor.

"You probably think I'm a lunatic," I said.

"Have to be to put up with his dumb ass," he said jabbing a thumb in Ethan's direction. I captured Ethan's gaze with my own and pouted out my lower lip, the effect ruined some with my smile. He sucked in a breath.

"He's not that bad," I said softly flicking my eyes to Zander's. It was his turn to suck in a breath.

"Liquid fucking sunshine," he breathed. I blinked.

"I'm sorry?" I said.

"Talking about your eyes, Baby," Ethan said gently.

"Oh," I felt a blush creeping up my face. Andy's head jerked.

"Show time folks," he said and I looked to see two people approaching the shop door through the rain. The boys scattered and I sat behind reception a little self-conscious that I looked like a drowned rat but not sorry.

A man and woman ducked into the shop and I smiled and did my job. She wanted her nipples pierced and I set her up with Zander, who was our resident piercer. Ethan had been filling in while Zander had been away, first at the convention and then while he visited family. I still blushed at the thought of having such a sensitive area done but I really wanted to watch one of these times. The idea secretly intrigued me.

Hours later the shop was quiet except for the buzz of tattoo guns from Ethan and Andy's cubicles. Andy started it, he really did. His rich voice carrying through the shop as he worked on his client…

*"No more talk of darkness…"* and he began to sing from Phantom of the Opera. I smiled and without any prompting or urging sang Christine's lines… I let my voice lilt and trail and Andy's soared over the divider… It looked like he was intent on singing the whole thing. I was game.

As soon as he finished his lines, I smiled and sang out, mine. I stapled the paperwork I was processing and slipped it where it belonged. It was Andy's turn at the end of 'All I Ask of You', he stood up, put one gloved hand against his chest and threw out his other hand dramatically and sang boldly, *"Ashton! That's all I ask of you."*

I clapped and dissolved into a fit of hysterical giggles.

"Watch it, Man!" Ethan called, "Hate to have to kick your skinny ass!" but his words were tinged with laughter and humor, belying any real threat.

"All right, all right! Back to work you clowns!" I heard Zander call and smiling and feeling all glowy I resumed concentrating on what I was being paid to do, I was excited for my first paycheck which I would see this Friday.

The rain had stopped and the sun had come and gone. Dusk hung low over the parking lot outside and I sighed, the day couldn't end fast enough. I wanted to go home so Ethan could touch me. Hands descended on my shoulders and I jumped. They kneaded my shoulders and I tipped my head way, way, back to look up into Zander's smiling face. I blinked and stiffened up a bit. Not used to near strangers and casual touching yet.

"Got a question," he said.

"Uh, sure," he continued to knead my shoulders and it felt really good, but I really wished it were Ethan's hands.

"Can I use your face?" he asked. I blinked.

"What?"

"To draw, I want it here," he turned his arm to reveal an unfinished angel. I blinked.

"Why me?" I asked.

"You're beautiful," he shrugged one shoulder. I colored, it was suddenly way too warm in here.

"I suppose," I said.

"Cool," he put his head back and yelled "Yo, Trigger!" towards the back of the shop.

"Yeah!?" Ethan called back.

"Time to finish it!" Zander yelled. He looked down at me and jerked his head to indicate I should follow. I got up and followed him back to Ethan's station. Ethan looked up from where he was bandaging his client. A skinny young man who had asked for a band symbol on his calf.

"How you payin'?" Ethan asked, the kid peeled off some bills and looked at me. He said.

"Thanks man, no receipt," and walked out.

"Sit over there, Sweetheart," Zander said. I obediently did what I was told. Ethan cleaned up his station and started prepping needles and guns.

He was looking at me in a way that was starting to thoroughly creep me out. Eyes cool and distant, appraising... I felt my heart throb painfully in my chest, as if a weight were upon it, squeezing it down to where my heart didn't have enough room to expand.

"Stop, please," I said and threw up my hands. Ethan's warmth washed over me as he rolled his chair to just in front of me. He took my hands in his and brought them down into my lap. My eyes were closed and he whispered,

"Ashton, come on look at me," I opened my eyes and Ethan was back, his clear silver eyes warm again.

"What's wrong?" he asked and I swallowed. I did what he'd asked me to do and I told him what I was feeling.

"You were looking at me like I was a thing, not a person. It makes me uncomfortable," I pulled in a deep breath and he smiled.

"I'm sorry Sunshine, I was working," he said gently and it made sense. He drew nearer and placed his lips against mine, I closed my eyes and concentrated on the warm feeling of his lips on mine. The knot of anxiety loosened and I felt myself relax. His warm finger tips resting gently on either side of my neck.

"You're a person, Baby. The most beautiful, brave, strongest, person I know," he whispered against my lips. He drew back and smiled.

"Better?" he asked and I closed my eyes and nodded.

"Thank you," I murmured.

Zander cleared his throat at the opening to Ethan's space, "That was hot," he said and dropped into the chair, putting his hand on his leg and bending his arm at an angle to make it accessible to Ethan. I blushed and averted my eyes to the ceiling.

"About time man," Zander said to him softly. Ethan smiled and I dropped my gaze to his face, warmth and light spilling from his eyes as he searched mine.

"I know," he said and I sat quietly while he perfectly freehanded my face onto Zander's arm.

# CHAPTER 13

*Trig*

Ashton had fallen asleep tucked in the corner on my dentist chair. Her face angelic and at peace. I think we'd be skipping Les Mis tonight but I'd be damned if I was going to miss out on touching her. I patched up Zander's arm.

"She's sweet," he whispered.

"Yeah," I said carefully.

"Damaged," he observed. I looked him straight in the eye and said,

"Aren't we all?"

"Yeah, Brother, yeah," he got up and patted me on the shoulder before he went out into the shop. I cleaned up and looked over at Ashton.

I went out and opened the truck door then went back in and picked her up. Her arms went around my neck and she cuddled into my shoulder as I took her out and tucked her into the passenger side.

I waved at Andy and Zander through the window and took us home, they could finish up closing down the shop. I wanted my girl nude and in my bed, my hands on her. There wouldn't be sex tonight, I wanted her awake and moving with me for that. I drove us home and tried like hell to get the image of her riding my cock out of my head.

"Did I fall asleep?" she asked as I parked the truck. I smiled.

"Yeah, Babe."

She yawned and I laughed a little. It had been a pretty long and emotional day. I picked her up and carried her up the stairs. I got the key in the lock and got the door open, kicking it shut behind me. I took her straight into the bedroom and set her gently onto the bed. She sat up and struggled to wake up.

"Don't," I whispered. I kissed her quick and soft and knelt down putting one foot on my knee, slipping her out of her sandal then then other.

She blinked down at me and I reached out my hands. She took them and I stood her up. I unzipped her dress carefully and slid my hands along her back, pulling the dress off of her, letting it fall to the floor. I stripped off my shirts and pulled her in tight against my body and her slender arms went around me. I smoothed my hands over her silky skin and she sank into me.

I took off her bra and kissed her, cradling her face between my hands. I touched my tongue to the seam of her lips and she opened to me, a small whimper escaping her throat. She tasted divine, like spring time and fresh rain, and I explored her mouth leisurely. Taking my time. I let my fingers trail down her neck, tracing her collarbone and shoulders.

I pressed my palms over her breasts and she arched into me. Her mouth moving with mine wantonly and I nearly lost my shit. She was glorious. Beautiful, soft, and yielding to my touch. I undid my pants and let them fall, toeing out of my boots and leaving the whole pile lie there.

I dropped to my knees, breaking our kiss and she made a soft sound of protest. On my knees I was just below her chin and I pulled her to me, placing a kiss over her heart, between her breasts. Her small hands wound into the back of my hair and she tugged gently. I leaned my head back and she looked down into my face. Her golden gaze soft with wonder.

"Is this what you wanted?" I whispered.

She nodded, and I smiled at having robbed her of speech. I trailed fingertips down her back in a barely there touch and her eyes closed. She shivered but not from cold and I loved that I could do this. Hell, I could kneel at her feet like this and worship her until the end of time.

I hooked my fingers into the backs of her panties and pulled them down, letting my nails lightly scratch down her supple ass cheeks, down the backs of her thighs, over the ridges of scars there, before uncurling them to lightly trail behind her knees. She was gripping my shoulders, her knees shaking as I let her panties fall. I pressed a line of warm kisses down her orange blossom perfumed skin, stopping just above the auburn curls at the apex of her thighs. I straightened and hugged her to me and she opened her eyes to look into mine.

"You are so fucking beautiful," I breathed and she let her fingertips trace my cheekbones. I closed my eyes and let her fingers do the walking, trailing across my cheekbones, my eyelids, the arch of my brows, down the sides of my face, and across my lips. When I stood up I picked her up and lay her back on the bed. I kissed down her body and across the arch of her hip bone. God she had hip bones I could gnaw on like a dog! High and perfect, the dip between them smooth and flat and begging for the caress of my lips.

She was muscular and toned, slender without being stick thin. She was so perfect. I felt myself hot and thick and stiff in my boxers, straining so hard I thought my skin would split. I ached to be inside her, could feel every throb of my heartbeat echoed in my cock, but that wasn't for tonight. Tonight was for touch. To give her what she needed. To kiss her, taste her and love her with my hands and lips. I climbed up her body, bracing myself on my hands and knees over her.

"How do you feel?" I asked.

"Loved," she ventured and I nodded slowly.

"Good," I whispered and I kissed her deeply. She kissed me back and moaned softly into my mouth. I got into bed beside her and pulled her against me, my cock pressing hotly through my boxers into the soft skin of her lower stomach. She gasped.

"You feel what you do to me?" I asked, kissing the side of her throat. Her hands roamed my chest and shoulders unbidden.

"One of these nights, when you're ready, I'm going to make love to you," I whispered the promise into her ear and she buried her face in the side of my neck nodding emphatically. I chuckled low and deep. God she was a treasure.

I let my hands roam her delicate body, fingertips skimming her back as she lay against my chest, her fingers tracing spiral patterns on my ribs and stomach. It took everything I had to keep it at sensual petting and to go no further. We lay in each other's arms silently exploring for God knows how long until finally, exhausted and relaxed we both fell into oblivion.

When I woke up the next morning it was to her singing in the kitchen. I lay there a minute and soaked it up, a double tap came at the front door and it burst open, she shrieked and I pulled my forty caliber out of the bedside table rounding the bedroom door and aiming.

"Reaver! The fuck, Man!?" I pointed the gun at the ceiling and stared at my friend's back. He was turned around hands in the air.

A blur of movement as Ashton streaked past me into my room and slammed the door. I blinked. What the fuck just happened?

"Sorry Dude, I'm sorry! Didn't expect *that*," he muttered turning around slowly. I blinked.

"Ashton, you all right?" I called. The bedroom door opened and she came back out red as a beet in one of my shirts and it finally dawned on me what happened. I started laughing, then Reaver started laughing, all the while Ashton stood there, waves of humiliation coming off her like heat patterns off of a summer sidewalk.

"I was making you coffee," she said quietly. Naked. She was making me coffee naked. Reaver howled and I wiped tears from my eyes. I gestured at her to come here with the Glock in my hand, she looked dubious at first but tucked herself against my side. I kissed the top of her head, a mixture of adrenaline, elation and honor a heady cocktail in my blood.

"Thanks," I said.

"Do *me* a favor, dude?" Reaver said waving at me to get my attention.

"What?" I asked.

"Put some damned pants on or something. I got no interest in seeing *your* junk," he winked at Ashton and she blushed a deep crimson.

"I hate you both," she muttered and Reaver lost his shit all over again.

"Me!? What did I do!?" I asked, taking my gun back into the

bedroom and putting it back in the bedside table. Ashton crossed her arms, arched a brow but the whole effect was ruined by the smile tugging at her lush mouth. She went back into the kitchen and resumed what she'd been doing, back straight, trying to muster as much dignity as possible. I pulled on some straight legged, black warm up pants and went out to the dining table.

"So are you ready, my brother?" Reaver asked, grinning knee bouncing under the table. I frowned.

"For what?" I asked, frowning.

"The run... next week..." Reaver looked shocked as hell that I'd forgotten but he shouldn't have been. I looked into the kitchen and was met by a sweet golden gaze. I'd been sort of busy. I grunted and nodded. It was our last one before suspending operations, we'd put too much into it to pass on it. I needed to get Ashton square before I took off on what would be a two or three day run. I wondered if Squick would give her a ride to the shop and home for a couple of days.

It was a shock to the system when I realized that for the first time since joining the MC... I didn't want to go. I wanted to stay here with Ashton. I was staring at my hand on the table when a cup of coffee clicked against the wooden surface. I looked up into Ashton's gentle expression and she lowered herself into my lap, her small arms twined about my neck and I looked at her, really looked at her. The bruises had been healing up nicely and were barely a ghost of a shadow on her fair skin. Her eyes shone with some undefined emotion but whatever it was, you could be sure it was positive.

"You don't have to worry," she smiled tenderly, "I've disrupted things enough for you. You should go, have a good time with the guys," she smiled wider and it turned sweet and warm.

"Yeah, I have to go," I said.

"How long will you be gone?" she asked.

"Leave Sunday, be back by Wednesday night," I answered. We had Sunday and Monday off from the shop. Today was Friday, so she'd pretty much be on her own for two days around here. I wasn't sure I liked that.

"Maybe I'll call Hayden," she said brightly. I could see a bit of sorrow in her golden gaze but there she was, two weeks out from an ordeal of a lifetime, being my brave girl. I didn't care Reaver was sitting there looking at us, I pulled her mouth down to mine and kissed her but good.

"Sounds like a good idea. Chandra will be around too. Maybe you two could do something," I said. She smiled and nodded.

"It will give me a chance to finish unpacking this place too," she looked around at boxes in corners, mostly my random ass stuff from storage. I nodded, essentially giving her permission to put it where she thought it should go.

"Settled then. I'll see if Squick can keep you working," she smiled and for a second I wondered if I needed to be jealous. She slid off my lap and I felt the loss of her softness and warmth keenly, like I was letting go of a part of me. Reaver was looking at me with an amused expression and I scowled at him.

"We hittin' the gym today?" he asked. I was about to protest, say we'd gone yesterday when Ashton' excited voice floated over from the kitchen.

"Can we!?" Well shit that settled that.

"Yeah, you want to hold off on breakfast until after?" I asked.

"Sure we can do that. I'll go change!" She sashayed that sweet heart shaped ass of hers down the hall to her bedroom and as soon as the door shut, Reaver turned on me.

"You totally tapped that last night, didn't you?" He demanded, voice a harsh whisper, look stormy. I wondered if he had a hand anywhere near one of his knives.

"No," I said and crossed my arms. We stared each other down over the dining room table. I could feel myself slipping into that silent zone again, the place I went when shit was serious and I could see Reaver was going there too. To be honest I was pretty touched that he was so fiercely protective of my girl. Wait hold up. I raked a hand through my hair and swore harshly under my breath.

"That's what I thought man, you *did* go there." He crossed his arms and looked murderous.

"No, I didn't, Bro! My cock never left my shorts, I swear it," he frowned then looked disgusted.

"TMI, but you got your point across so what the fuck *did* happen?" his cool blue eyes burned with curiosity but it'd have to wait, Ashton was back and smiling. She was in an exceptional mood this morning and my chest swelled with pride that I'd put her in it.

I got up, "Be out in a sec," I said and went to change myself. When I came out Ashton was looking at Reaver suspiciously, eyes narrowed.

"Charlie," she said.

"Nope," he shook his head, his devil may care grin firmly in place.

"Earl," she said and he laughed.

"No, that's almost worse," he said.

"You'll tell me if I get it right?" she asked.

"I swear on my grandmammy's grave," he said.

"Your grandmother is alive and well two towns over you jackass," I said, laughing. Ashton frowned.

"I got two grandmothers asshole," he smiled as he said it. Ashton got up and clipped her iPod to her waistband, hanging her headphones around her neck.

"No yogurt today?" Reaver asked as we piled out of the apartment.

"No, it's running today," she said.

"Don't you want to do that outside?" I asked. She looked at me surprise across her lovely features and blinked.

"I can do that now, can't I?" she said softly. I sighed inwardly. Two steps forward one step back it felt like sometimes but whatever, we still gained ground with that one step.

"Yeah Babe, you can." Reaver said. Ashton let out a joyous whoop and crashed down the stairs.

"I guess we're running today," he said with a shrug. I grinned. Guess so. I let her get a head start but not too much of one. Her legs were shorter and it wouldn't be too hard to catch up.

"I don't think she's in a good place for you to be fucking her just yet," Reaver said bluntly about a quarter mile later.

"Not fucking her," I said, "Not going to fuck her," she was just ahead of us, her headphones in, making long strides. What she lacked in stride compared to us she was making up for in stamina.

"What did you do then?" he asked.

"Touched her," I said. He looked at me dubiously.

"You put your hands all over that body..." he paused for breath, "and didn't fuck her?" he asked.

"Told you, not going to fuck her," I growled irritated.

"Then what the hell you gonna do?" he asked.

I debated for a second and finally settled on the truth, "If or when I do anything... I'm going to love her," I said and pushed up my stride until we were both too out of breath to talk anymore. Reaver was looking at me with something akin to respect and nodded, I nodded back; glad we were finally on the same damned page.

Ashton ran our asses ragged, but once we got back to the apartment, after we were all showered and in fresh clothes, she fed us like fucking kings. Reaver and I dropped onto the couch and he flipped on the TV, taking up a controller. I expected Ashton to sit with us but she declined in favor of doing laundry. Even threw Reaver's sweaty gym clothes into the mix. As her footfalls disappeared down the stairs he made a sidelong glance at me.

"We both fucking know there's no 'if' in this equation man. It's only a matter of when," He said. I grunted in agreement as we shot each other to shit on the big screen.

Yeah. I knew it, I just had to make damn sure that when 'when' came, it was right for *her*. I wasn't going to lie though, she was fucking flourishing like a flower left too long in the shade that had finally been given some sun. It was a hell of a sight to see too.

I looked down the pixelated scope on my half of the screen and lined up a head shot, pulled the trigger. Reaver's side of the screen went red in a wash of pixelated blood and I gave him a tight lipped grin.

"Fuck man, not fair you're as good as that in the virtual world as you are in the real one," He griped and my grin lost some of its measure. It was a mark of how far I'd come, that I could even play this fucking game without puking my guts out from an unwanted flashback. Just when I started to feel that sucking pull into the black hole of despair I harbored inside, Ashton came through the door and lit me up with her golden eyes and smile. She sat on the floor between my knees and ducked, coming up inside the circle of my arms where I held the controller. She nestled there and put her hands over mine.

"Teach me," she whispered and I kissed her temple.

"Okay, take the controller."

She was a shit shot and had me and Reaver in stitches inside ten minutes. We played for the better part of an hour before she and I had to go to work.

"You guys coming to the club house tonight?" Reaver asked.

"Church, isn't it?" I asked.

"Yep."

"Then I'll be there. You want to go?" Ashton nodded happily.

"Cool. See you there," we parted ways.

"Ethan?" she asked softly, getting into the truck.

"Thank you," she smiled and I smiled back last night coming up fresh in my mind.

"Anytime," I grunted, and she blushed. I laughed and got us to work on time.

# CHAPTER 14

*Ashton*

Andy leaned over my shoulder and clicked the mouse through the webpage he wanted to show me and an image of a girl in a dress rendered. It was black with white lace edging the hem, neckline and sleeves. Printed in bright cheery reds and greens across the material were bunches of cherries in twos and threes. I tilted my head to the side and considered it, smiling. The cut of the dress looked like it had come out of the forties or early fifties and was similar to the Havana dress style I liked.

"They have it in white and pink too," he said, flicking the mouse pointer over blocks of color below the image. I blinked and pointed at the white one.

"I like that one better, the black would make me look like a ghost," I whispered. He grinned.

"Yeah, that dress, frilly ankle socks and some white Converse would look hot. These guys wouldn't know what hit 'em and that style is right up this place's alley," his eyes sparkled with mischief.

"What made you think of this?" I asked.

"Tired of you looking all self-conscious and worried that you don't fit in here. Thought maybe a bit of a wardrobe changeup might do it. After I saw you in that dress the other day, I thought this might do the trick, seemed right up *your* alley. Crossover is a beautiful thing."

"What the hell you two whispering about over there?" Zander demanded. Andy looked panicked for a second and closed out the window we'd been looking at.

"Just showing Ashton some features on the calendar," he lied and kept my eyes on the screen so Zander wouldn't see it on my face.

"Oh. Okay."

"Monday?" I breathed and Andy held up his fist. I smiled

conspiratorially and bumped it with my own like I'd seen the guys do a million times before and we giggled.

"Calendar features my ass, what are you two up to?" Ethan asked, popping up over his work station eyes narrowed, but he was smiling.

"I've been sworn to secrecy," I murmured boldly. Andy looked proud, Ethan frowned but I could tell it wasn't real. He ducked back down and continued whatever prep work he was doing.

The shop was slow, really slow and we ended up closing early. I stretched luxuriously, my midriff peeking out from under my tee shirt over the low waist band of my short white shorts. Zander had found a small ladies tee in black with the shop's logo on it in a box somewhere and I had slipped it on over my camisole, discarding the cardigan I'd been wearing over it in the bottom of my file drawer. I fished it out and shrugged into it.

"Payday girly," Zander said from behind me. I turned around and Ethan, Squick, Zander and Moe, the other artist in the shop were standing behind me. Ethan held a check in his hand, Andy held a cupcake. I laughed.

"First paycheck ought to be celebrated," he said with a shrug and held out the confection. Vanilla, my favorite. I licked the icing and was met by three groans. I looked up at Ethan startled and swallowed, the naked heat in his eyes was met by an answering one at the apex of my thighs. I blushed. Zander rattled something off in Spanish and I blinked. He was met by noises of agreement.

"I have no idea what you just said," I looked at all of them in turn, the frosting covered treat forgotten in my hand.

"Some very not nice things about your husband," Andy supplied.

"Oh, well in that case, share," I said boldly and the laughter broke the layer of tension that had settled over the gathering like ice. I took the slip of paper from Ethan and stared down at it for what felt like long minutes. It was too much. I set the cupcake on my desk and looked up, confused.

"This is too much," I whispered.

"Yeah, some of that is royalty," Zander cleared his throat.

"What?" I asked.

"Modeling fee," he said, holding up his arm where my face smiled out from his skin.

"I don't want..." I started but he held up a hand. I stopped.

"Say 'thank you,' Sunshine," Ethan smiled kindly at me.

"Thank you," I said automatically.

The little crowd around me dispersed until it was just me and Ethan. I smiled up at him.

"Ready to go?" he asked, "We'll get that cashed tomorrow."

I put the check in my back pocket and got up, retrieving my cupcake. I licked off some frosting and smiled with no little satisfaction at his sharp intake of breath.

"God damn woman," he uttered ushering me out the door.

"If it helps, I want you too," I whispered. He laughed incredulously.

"No. That doesn't help at all, Baby," he said and drove us home. He ordered me to dress for the road but I think that was more because he wanted me to cover up. I pulled on some form fitting jeans and a low cut, long sleeved, fitted emerald green top. I swept my hair into a high ponytail and set my check on top of my press board chest of drawers, weighting it with my body mist after I had spritzed a generous amount across my chest and throat.

The air was lightly perfumed with orange blossoms and I smiled, remembering my mom. I met Ethan in the living room he looked down at me and bent, inhaling sharply. His silver eyes slipped shut and he smiled.

"Got you something," he murmured, looking at the floor.

"What?" I asked, curious.

"If you're going to be on the bike with me you need better protection than denim and sweatshirts," he lifted a shopping bag over the back of the love seat and held it out to me.

"When did you find the time to..." I started to ask.

"Had it moved in here before you even got here, Babe." He smiled and I opened the bag. A lot of black and the smell of new leather wafted up to meet me.

"I didn't know how to..." he started then stopped abruptly before rushing out, "I don't want you thinking I'm trying to dress you like he did, I just want you safe if you're going to be on the bike. Got you some pants, a jacket and some boots," he cleared his throat and looked incredibly uncomfortable. I looked down into the bag, dropped it on the floor and wrapped my arms around him, sniffing back tears.

My voice trembled when I said, "What you did, buying me these things, you do it because you care about what happens to me. Not because you want to control me. I know the difference," I squeezed him and he held me tight.

"Go change, I'm dying to see you in what's in that bag," he said gruffly but with no little emotion of his own.

I went into my room and pulled out a pair of leather pants and sturdy women's sized boots. I wondered how he'd gotten the sizes correct. I put the pants on and they fit like a second skin. I sat on the floor and pulled on the boots, dragging the cuff down over the top of them. They were the kind with the silver buckle on the outside of the ankle and were surprisingly comfortable. I kept my green top on, retrieving my black belt with the silver buckle from my closet and threading it through the loops. More for aesthetics than an actual need to hold the pants up. I tucked in the shirt and shrugged on the jacket with its silver snaps and zippers, pulling my hair free of the collar. I stepped out and down the hallway and he looked me over nodding.

"Between this and watching you lick the frosting off that goddamned cupcake, I don't know how much more my self-control can take," his statement sent electricity pulsing through my core in a pleasurable little throb.

He held out a helmet and I took it with numb fingers and followed him out of the apartment. He locked the door behind us and took my hand as we clattered down the stairs. He put me on the bike and got on in front of me after making sure my helmet was on securely. I put my hands in his pockets and snuggled close to his back as the engine roared to life.

"You good?" he called over the angry chugging.

"Yeah!" I called back.

"Enjoy the ride!" he called and pulled out into the lot. I smiled and held on as he pulled out into traffic.

The ride was too damned short.

All too soon the wind stopped and the world became still and I was back on solid ground missing the feeling of being fetched up tight against Ethan's strong muscular back. I followed him into the clubhouse which was relatively quiet. He had Church before the other, non-council, members arrived and the weekly partying started. I waved at Chandra inside the door, she was sitting at a table with a bunch of other women and Ethan nudged me in their direction.

"Look at you!" she crowed, then asked, "Have fun?" I nodded enthusiastically and sat down.

"I'm Candy," a girl next to me said, eyeing me speculatively. She looked to be barely twenty and had long straight dark hair and a gap in her front teeth. She was a little on the skinny side with long, long legs that ended in clear plastic platform heels. She wore dark denim daisy dukes and one of those wife beater tank tops shorn off which barely hid the swell of her breasts, some of the roundness peeking out below the sheared off edge of the fabric. She had on a neon pink bikini top under it, which was really just triangles of material enough to hide her nipples, with a string around her neck and peeking out below the tank top in a bow in the back.

"Ashton," I murmured.

"You Trigger's?" she asked and I must have thought about it too long because Chandra started introducing the other two women at the table.

"Ashton, this here is Moira and Shelly," she said, indicating the other two.

Moira was a red head but it was out of a bottle, the shade of red clashing with her tanned skin. Natural red heads didn't really tan, they burned and then were infested by freckles. Being I shared a ginger's skin tone, I knew this unfortunate truth all too well. Moira wore a denim vest and bra with no shirt, the scarlet straps of the sexy lingerie peeking out from under the light denim vest. It was paired with a short denim skirt that didn't do much to make her legs look longer. She smiled at me and I wish I could tell you what her eye color was but they were hidden by purple contact lenses.

Shelly was a natural blonde, her hair short and sassy. She wore bright red lipstick that looked right on her and she had on a black leather vest that laced in the front like a bodice. Her push up bra worked some serious magic and displayed her cleavage perfectly. She wore a short, black leather mini skirt and black combat boots. Her eyes were a clear light blue that reminded me entirely too much of Reaver's.

"Are you related to Reaver?" I asked Shelly quietly.

"Yeah he's my cousin. How'd you know?" she asked.

"You have the same eyes," I smiled and she smiled back.

"What's his name?" I asked and she laughed.

"Nuh uh, he'd flay me alive," she said flatly. I smiled.

"I'll guess it eventually," I said with a shrug.

Chandra was in a tight army fatigue Harley Davidson tee and denim skirt. Instead of the green of regular fatigue colors, her shirt was in grays and pinks with the Harley logo done in pink glitter on the front. She wore pink high heels and her lipstick matched the shoes and eye shadow the shirt. She'd cut her hair short and it curled, gently rolling back from her face. It looked good and I told her so. She smiled and lit her cigarette.

"Thanks sweetie," she said, sucking in a drag.

"You don't wear makeup?" Shelly asked.

"I did, but I don't have any, I got my first paycheck today and I kind of can't wait to go buy some. All though I'm not nearly as good at it as you are," I confessed. Her make up really was stellar.

"Want me to do yours while they're in there?" she asked.

"Could you? It wouldn't be too much trouble?" I asked.

"Naw, come on," Chandra laughed and Moira and Candy looked slightly put out that they hadn't been asked. I felt a tad guilty but Shelly was herding me into the nearest bathroom with her purse under her arm. She took her time and I felt a little tingle of pleasure that someone would do something so nice for me. Bass started thumping through the wall as the music was turned up and I smiled. The party was getting started and I was glad that this time I could really be a part of it rather than crashing it or going to bed early.

Shelly put some clear gloss on my lips and let me look in the mirror. My eyes stood out in stark relief. Whatever she had done made them seem huge. Wide and open, the gold coming alive, glimmering like treasure. I smiled and hugged her.

"Best go out and have Trig get a look at you," she looked smug and I laughed, not quite sure why. We went out into the common room and his silver eyes locked on me from across the room. I ducked my head, hoping he wasn't cross for my not being here when he got out of his meeting and I threaded my way through the people crowding the space to where he sat at the end of the bar.

"Where'd you go Sunshine?" he asked, and when I heard his voice I knew he wasn't upset, just relieved.

"Shelly did my make up for me," I said and looked up at him. He dragged his eyes across my face and looked poleaxed for a second. He stood up and led us to a table and sat down pulling me into his lap.

"What's wrong?" I asked and he grinned at me.

"Nothin'. I just want to be the man with the prettiest girl in the room in his lap all night," I smiled and he yelled out, "Yo, Reaver!"

"Sup!"

"Bring me and Ash a couple of beers!"

Reaver turned back to the bar and said something to Data, who was tonight's bartender. Dray turned from the bar and looked me over, frowning.

"Why doesn't he like me?" I asked Ethan and he sighed.

"Dray's just pissed off at the world Baby, he doesn't like anybody right now, least of all himself," I cuddled into Ethan and looked at Dray from across the room, he leaned on the bar scowling, eyes roaming the room and the people in it with a predatory and unfriendly gaze. His shoulders hunched in a sort of familiar way that tickled at the corners of my mind.

Reaver set down two beers and handed me a brightly colored drink in a pint glass that looked like it was mostly fruit juice. I smiled and took a sip. It was sweet with a bitter bite of alcohol at the end. Rum, I think. I nodded and he grinned. Whatever I had been thinking about Dray chased clear out of the front of my brain.

"Tucker," I guessed and he smiled, shaking his head.

"You ask Shelly?" he asked me. I frowned and nodded.

"She wouldn't tell me," I said.

"Good. I'd flay her alive," he said.

"That's what she said," I said and both of them laughed. I frowned, "What?" I asked.

"Nothing Babe," Ethan said and kissed my throat, which was all he could reach with the way we were sitting. I didn't miss the cool rush of air across my skin as he breathed me in.

He pulled out that electronic cigarette he always had and sucked on it, the end flaring blue, releasing a plume of cherry scented vapor at the ceiling. He frowned dissatisfied with it and yelled. "Somebody get me a damned cigarette!"

I laughed and told him, "You light it and I'm not going to sit on your lap." His blonde eyebrows arched in surprise.

"Oh really?" he asked, smiling.

"Yes really! They're gross," he laughed.

"Fine, you win for now," he said and went back to the e-cig which was only marginally better. His hand snuck up the back of my jacket and he jerked my shirt out of my waistband, his hand flattening against the naked skin of my back. I jerked with surprise and pressed back into his palm. He squeezed the top of my thigh with his other hand and my pulse sped up. I sucked down more of my girly drink and listened as Reaver told a story about his and Dragon's last run. Apparently they'd gone a state over to talk with another charter, I guess that was another group of Sacred Heart men only in a different location.

"So Dragon tells this club whore twin thanks… but calls her by her sister's name," he was saying. I blinked and sipped my drink.

"So this broad hauls off and slaps the shit out of him and Dragon just stands there with this look on his face like…" Reaver made a face and it was pretty funny, Ethan and I laughed. I let the fingers on the hand wrapped around his shoulders idly play in the ends of his thick, shoulder length locks.

"Hey! You telling stories over here Reaver?" Dragon hooked a chair with his boot and pulled it out, dropping into it.

"Don't worry, it was only mildly humiliating," I said, tongue loosening under the effects of the alcohol I'd consumed, Dragon laughed.

"Speaking of mildly humiliating…" Reaver said, a wicked glint in his blue eyes.

"No!" I shouted, "Reaver don't you dare!" Ethan lost it and started howling with laughter as high spots of color appeared on my cheeks. Dragon looked from me to Reaver and back again and said,

"Oh, now I *have* to know…"

Oh God.

I set down my half-finished drink and covered my face with my hands as Reaver launched into the story of barging in on me in my kitchen naked. Dragon fell out of his chair laughing and I wanted to sink into the floor and die of embarrassment but I did my level best to take it like a good sport and in stride.

It helped when Ethan tipped my chin in his direction and pulled my mouth down to his. I don't know what it was about his kiss, but as my eyes slipped shut in bliss and our mouths melded together, it felt as if the seal on a vault door deep inside me finally cracked and the desire, the want and the craving… the sheer *need*, came pouring out of it, rushing to the surface of my skin. I broke out in a tingling rush from the crown of my head to the soles of my feet. I couldn't decide if I was hot or cold or both at the same time.

The air was stolen from my lungs and the room spiraled down to nothing. I couldn't hear the laughter, the talking, the music… it just all narrowed down to Ethan's mouth against mine, the feel of his hands on my skin as his hand slid against my back. The other had found its way beneath my shirt and splayed against my stomach and ribs. I suddenly couldn't get enough of him. He was my air to breathe, my water to drink my food to eat, my nourishment. I broke the kiss and clung to him, putting my lips beside his ear as the noise of the party came rushing back in, crashing over us.

"Do you still have a room here?" I asked, knowing full well that he did.

"Yeah," he said, voice low and gravelly with need, a bass rumble I could feel pressed to his chest as I was. I shivered from the sensation.

"I need you to take me to it, Ethan. I need you to touch me and I need you to not stop touching me until we're *both* satisfied," my lips traced the shell of his ear with each word I spoke and his hold on me tightened. He seemed like he was struggling with the decision and I squeezed my eyes shut.

"*Please...*" I begged, "If I don't feel you inside me, I'm really afraid I might die," I said. Melodramatic? Maybe, but it had the desired effect. He lifted me in his arms and stood in one powerful, fluid movement and was striding across the room, bikers, club girls, prospects, it didn't matter who, all of them parted like the red sea, coming back together in our wake like we hadn't even passed.

He ducked into the hallway and went straight to the room we'd shared. He stooped and I twisted the knob for him. He kicked it open and passed through the portal, kicking the door shut hard behind him. The door slammed but latched and the noise of the party became a distant thing, a throb of bass thrumming through the floor and walls keeping time with the air I dragged in and expelled from my lungs.

"You're sure you want this?" he asked.

"I'm sure I want *you*," I told him and our mouths clashed. He set me gently to my feet and pushed my new jacket off my shoulders, I dropped my arms and let it slide off and to the old ratty brown carpet. Not caring. His fingers moved quickly, deftly pulling my top from the waistband of my leather jeans and over my head.

I worked the worn leather of his belt through the buckle while he shrugged out of his jacket, both of us swept up in a frenzied need to be skin on skin. He had his jacket and the vest he called a 'cut' off and on the floor. His shirt was halfway over his head before I could start working on the fly of his jeans. He dropped his shirts the same time I dropped his zipper and he pushed me back. The edge of the mattress hit the back of my thighs and I fell onto it.

He looked down from his standing height, something feral and hot and possessive sliding behind his cool silver gaze and I felt my desire for him ratchet up a notch. He pulled off my boots and let them drop to the floor and toed off his own, all the while his gaze never leaving mine.

He reached down, a knee between my own, and unfastened the button on my leather pants. Each movement was slow, methodical and deliberate and I realized he was gauging me. Making certain I was all right with this. I was more than all right, nothing had ever felt more right in my life up until this point. His thick fingers hooked into the waistband of my pants and I raised my hips off the bed. He peeled the leather down my legs, stripping them from me in one swift, borderline violent movement and I loved it.

I sat up swiftly and scooted my ass to the edge of the mattress over the covers and pressed my lips to his stomach. I hooked my fingers into the front of his boxers and pants and pulled them down in one fluid movement mimicking what he'd just done to me with the exception that I left him nothing while I sat here in my cotton bra and boy shorts.

He sucked in a breath and I rolled my eyes up to his. He was looking down at me, hands loose at his sides but very nearly shaking with the need to touch me. I leaned forward and kissed his hip, the heat from his erection kissing the side of my face. I pressed another kiss next to the first, my hands pressed flat to his oblique abdominals; sliding around to his lower back.

He watched me with a naked desire in his eyes that turned me on even further, my cotton boy shorts already soaked through, I could feel more heat and moisture gather between my thighs. I sighed, breath puffing out against his skin and he threw back his head.

"Oh god!" he groaned.

I let my hands roam over the tight globes of his ass and he dropped his gaze back down to mine. My fingers encountered a change in texture in his skin on the back of his right thigh. It was cooler to the touch, ridged and slick with scar tissue. A vision tore from my memory and flashed before my eyes vividly. The night I burst into Ethan's room the nightmare… the scar was on the same leg he had clutched, screaming as he'd twisted in his sheets.

He flinched when I found it but I didn't give him time to think about it. I pulled back and let my eyes drop to the gorgeous thick length of him resting against his stomach and before I even realized what I was doing, I flicked my tongue against the base of his cock and licked a long, fierce straight line up its length, taking the tip into my mouth and sucking, working my mouth down his shaft, playing the velvet of my tongue along the underside.

"Oh fuck! Ashton!" he cried and I loved the sound of my name, breathy and passionate from his lips. I sucked him, loving the taste and the feel of him in my mouth. He gasped, his hands finding purchase in my hair, gently holding it back from my face so he could watch me. I rolled my eyes up to look at him and he cried out, hips jerking once before he regained control.

"Enough," he growled low and deep and drew himself from my mouth. I let him but not before kissing the tip of him before he could fully pull away. He leaned over me and I walked myself backwards up the length of the bed. He hooked his fingers in my panties and drew them off of my legs. He unsnapped the front closure on my bra with only two fingers and I shrugged out of it. He looked me over and bent, nipping my hip bone deftly while reaching for the bedside table.

He rummaged through the drawer and extracted a foil wrapped package and my blood heated. God yes! I wanted him inside of me. He tore the package with his teeth, one arm bracing himself above me and expertly rolled the condom down his length. I reached up and captured his face between my hands and dragged his lips to mine. I kissed him deftly, his mouth warm and alive and tasting faintly of beer. He switched arms, supporting himself with his left and trailed fingers down my throat, between my breasts, to the nest of curls between my legs.

I opened for him eagerly and he dipped his fingers in my wetness, he groaned into my mouth and I smiled.

"You taste like strawberries and sunshine, Baby," he whispered against my mouth and guided the head of his cock to my entrance. He knelt between my thighs and grabbed them pulling me sharply down the bed to him to get a better angle. I gasped, hips arching to meet him as he pushed the head of himself inside me.

Oh. My. God...

I closed my eyes and he stilled.

"Am I hurting you Ashton?" he asked softly and I moaned with despair at his stillness, wiggling my hips to take him in further. I heard him smile and he eased forward some more. I gasped, a deep, wanton and throaty moan escaping my body as he stretched and filled me. It was the most incredible sensation I had ever felt, having Ethan Howard inside me. His big hands gripped my hips as he reared up above me and he thrust forward until he was fully seated and I arched off the bed.

"Ethan, god yes!" I cried and it was echoed by the deep bass rumble of a moan of his own. He found a rhythm of long, slow, lazy thrusts and I felt things low in my body slowly coil tighter, growing heavy with the weight of a coming orgasm. He leaned down over the top of me, enveloping me in his warmth, his lips playing over my own, softly sweetly and I twined my arms around his neck, along his shoulders and rocked my hips to meet his.

He held me just on the edge in a state of complete bliss for so long, I never wanted it to end but at the same time my body craved release. I moaned and sighed and opened my eyes to him watching me intently, a smile gracing his lips, cool, liquid silver gaze sweeping my face lovingly.

"Please Ethan, I need to come..." I begged him breathlessly. He reared up and it forced him deeper inside me. I cried out from the pleasure of it and squirmed as he trailed his fingertips down the length of my body. He lightly pressed his thumb to the top of my slit, slicking it in the moist heat of my arousal, teasing the bundle of nerves there. I cried out, legs twitching unbidden around his hips as everything sharpened, heightened to new levels.

"That's it Baby, squeeze my cock," his voice was low and base, as he spoke between gritted teeth. He teased me gently, lovingly, my back arching as my body filled with pleasure. I thrashed, sailing over the edge, every nerve ending caressed by heat and stars and the feather light stroke of Ethan's fingers.

Tears slicked the hair at my temples at the beauty of it and I couldn't even muster a sliver of panic at what he might think to see me crying beneath him. He kissed me tenderly, and stroked my body through wave after wave of aftershocks as I completely shattered beneath him and came together again...

# CHAPTER 15

*Trig*

Oh she came apart beautifully. I pressed myself fully into her sleek heat and held her in my arms as she let out this little gasping, trembling sob beneath me. I kissed away the salt of her tears, surprised to find I wasn't worried but rather found I was elated that I could make it that good for her. I wasn't done though.

"We're not done yet, Babe," I whispered in her ear. She looked at me with her molten golden gaze, boneless liquid grace beneath me and smiled the most angelic smile.

"Can you ride me?" I asked, hopeful, and she nodded. I withdrew from her and laid out beside her. I'd had visions of this for too long, I was way past want, I *needed* to see her moving above me.

She straddled my hips and I pulled the condom more securely onto myself. She sank down slowly and I moaned. The angle was sharper this way, deeper somehow... She let out a shuddering little sigh and my hands found her hips, caressing over the ridges of the bones with my thumbs. Her hands warm on my body as she rocked and at the sight of her doing it, damn I almost came right there.

I held back through sheer force of will alone. I wasn't ready to stop. Hell I wanted to stay like this forever if I could. Her skin almost glowed in the light of the overhead and I was glad I had left it on. She stroked up my length nearly coming completely off of me before letting her body weight take over so she'd plunge back down over me.

The sweep of her hair over her shoulders was hypnotic, the sway of her hips mesmerizing and I wondered when this siren had found her way into my meek, shy little Ashton. I swept my hands up her body, her skin like living silk beneath my fingers and palms. I cupped her breasts and played the pads of my thumbs over her dusky nipples and she gasped, head thrown back the ends of her long auburn tresses tickling the tops of my thighs.

She was a goddess, my goddess and I shuddered when she looked at me. I was a captured man and I knew it. She laid down against my chest and I held her, taking over, rocking my hips, pushing up into her tight little pussy with barely controlled thrusts. I felt that tingle at the base of my spine, my balls drawing up tight against my body and with a groan I jerked up hard inside her, losing my rhythm, coming completely off my rails and plunging headlong into the warm bliss that was Ashton Granger.

She lay atop me for a long time, both of us panting, sweat cooling our heated skins. I was loathe to pull out of her and so I didn't right away. Instead, I rested with her, her head tucked perfectly under my chin. I smiled to myself, she fit against me like she was made to be there.

"I love you," the words were out of my mouth before I even realized I intended to speak them. I was seized by a momentary panic that I may have just committed an irreparable wrong. Her voice came almost immediately, soft and lilting…

"I love you too."

She drew back to look at me and I could see the mirror image of my feelings for her in her beautiful golden eyes. I relaxed, not one hundred percent sure what this meant in the grand scheme of things but one thousand percent sure that we would make it work somehow.

I'd promised her that when I finally did take her body that I'd love her and I was as good as my word. Complicated or not, some things were pretty simple and that was one of 'em. I kissed the crown of her head and stroked lazy circles on her back and she sighed in contentment.

"I gotta get up, Babe," I whispered and she whimpered in protest but moved for me. I reached down between us and held the condom in place as she slipped off of me. Holy god that felt good. She collapsed beside me equal parts sated and exhausted and I smiled. I stripped off the rubber and ditched it in the small trashcan by the bed.

"Stay here," I whispered and went out to the bathroom, Ashton's hysterical giggle following my naked ass out into the hall.

"Whoa hey! What the fuck man!?" Data called as I went past him and some club chick he had backed against the wall, hand up her shirt.

"Just passin' through, Brother," I went into the bathroom and shut the door but not before spying Ashton, sheet clutched to her chest, eyes bright, hair mussed in that freshly fucked look that *I* just put on her dissolving into high, musical hysterical laughter.

I grinned and turned on the tap, waiting until the water was gently steaming. I wet a washcloth and wrung it out and went back to clean up my girl.

"The fuck, Trigger!? Put some damned pants on!" Someone protested...

"Like a damned tater tot in yellow Easter grass," Dragon grumbled and I guffawed, slamming my bedroom door behind me. Ashton grinned impishly up at me from the middle of my bed. I got in beside her and lovingly washed her down with the warm damp cloth. She sighed and squirmed and I nipped her shoulder.

We settled beneath the sheets and I lovingly cradled her against my side. She lay with her head on my shoulder, eyes closed and I kissed her forehead. Neither of us said anything but finally she ventured with...

"Did it hurt a lot?" her fingertips played along the top of my right thigh and I knew what she was thinking about.

"Yeah. Bullet lodged in the bone, had to have surgery to get it out," I sniffed and cleared my throat but didn't say anything more. A couple inches higher and I would have been shot in the ass, I really wished it had gone that way. May have hurt less and I may have been able to do more, go back out again before the end of my tour had come up. It had been my third but man, getting shot once had been enough for me. A few of the guys in my unit didn't come back at all.

It was their screams that echoed in my brain. The haunted eyes of their loved ones that haunted my dreams. I closed my eyes and Ashton snuggled closer, kissing my chest where she could reach it with her lips. She was like a balm to my scarred soul in so many ways.

We fell asleep like that and I don't think we moved at all because we woke that way in the morning, light streaming in from the high window through the slats of the blinds. I smiled down at her where she rested completely comfortably on my chest. I liked waking up with her in my arms so I made note of what I needed to do to wear her out to keep her there.

She was a bit of a mess and in need of a shower, her eye makeup smudged in deep dark circles under her eyes. I kissed her forehead and the movement shifted her enough that she jolted softly awake, golden eyes flickering open to meet my own. She smiled lazily and the ember of her fire stoked to life.

"How you feel?" I asked her.

"Mmm, good," she smiled like the fucking Cheshire cat and I rolled her on her back. Ruined make up or not she was fucking beautiful. I reached into the drawer and pulled out another condom and she reached her arms up.

She was ready for round two. Fuck yeah!

I kissed every supple inch of her small body until her arousal perfumed the air and her lips parted to beg and then I took her, making love to her until neither one of us could stand it anymore and we dissolved into a sweating, panting mess that you couldn't discern where one of us began and the other ended. Then I took my girl in to shower with her and loved her with my hands and my mouth under a hot shower spray. I couldn't get enough of her, I wasn't really sure I ever would and it looked like the feeling was mutual.

I left her in the kitchen making breakfast for the masses when Dragon beckoned me into the Chapel.

"Yeah man?" I asked.

"You good to go on this run brother?" he asked me plainly.

"Yeah! Yeah! I'm good. I got Ashton all squared away. Why?" I asked. Dragon's dark eyes roamed my face and he chewed the inside of his grizzled cheek considering.

"Just never seen you this… happy," he said finally. I grinned and

144

looked out the Chapel door where Ashton stood in my tee shirt serving up Reaver some coffee, the tart he picked up last night on his knee. She laughed at something he said.

"She's something Pres.," I told him, eyes never leaving her.

"Yeah. I remember lookin' at Tilly like that." I sobered and sighed. This run we had coming up, was to disrupt a heroin supply chain coming up through one of the North East chapters. We were trying to get other chapters of the MC to go legit, leave the illegal shit behind and it wasn't going well.

Once men got a taste of the money... the power... well that was kind of it. A couple of the chapters had listened and turned a new leaf like ours, the old timers like Dragon, running them having lost enough in their own lives to see the benefit, the gain, of going legit. Some of them though, were a different story. Either too headstrong or too ingrained or too corrupt to save. None of them had figured out that our branch of the MC was going so far as to actively disrupt distribution yet. It was a risky game we played. Dangerous not only for us but for the people out there that we cared about. People like Ashton that had no idea what we were capable of.

We were drawing down to that moment with the North Eastern chapter where we were going to have to consider doing some very bad fucking things in order to serve the greater good. We all knew it. I huffed out a sigh.

"I'm good for the run man," I said, turning back to him. He nodded.

"We got to cut and run, we'll do it, anything happens out there or here at home but I hate like hell the thought of that poison reaching its destination. Gettin' in the hands of some kid," he clapped me on the shoulder.

"Yeah man I know what's at stake," I said, and I did. All too well. I'd gotten hooked on that shit for a time when I got back stateside in an attempt to dull the pain, the memories of over there. Reaver was on it and that's how we hooked up. We both went through hell getting off of it. It's what cemented our Brotherhood. He'd been on it a lot worse than I had. It had taken longer for him to kick the habit and he'd lost a lot more than me because of it. I looked across the club house at Ashton.

There was a lot that she didn't know about me. A lot of skeletons in my closet that she *needed* to know about. I raked a hand through my hair and hoped like hell when they all came out that she would still love me because the thought of losing her now kind of killed me. Her golden gaze swept across the room and caught mine and her whole face lit up with a smile. I pressed my lips together but couldn't help the answering smile of my own. God damn she was beautiful.

Dragon made a noise like something was confirmed and I looked at him.

"One day someone walks into your life and makes you realize why it didn't work with anyone else," he grunted. "Tilly was like that for me. I think Ashton is like that for you," he said.

"Old man, why the fuck you gotta be so insightful?" I asked, he put a hand on my shoulder and squeezed and smiled into my eyes and socked me in the gut.

I doubled over and wheezed, the wind knocked clean out of me. Ashton was coming around the bar but Reaver caught her arm holding her back. Dragon bent and looked me in the eye. "How's that for an old man?" he asked dark eyes sparkling with way too much happy.

"You still got it," my voice strained out on another wheeze and he chuckled, slapping me on the back and waltzed out of the room whistling. Reaver let Ashton go and she strode across the room to me.

"Are you all right?" she asked gently, voice tinged with concern.

"Yeah. That's what I get for being mouthy," I grinned rakishly at her and straightened, tucking her beneath my arm.

"Boys are stupid," she said frowning and her proclamation was met with laughter and a few chuckles. I dropped into a seat at a table.

"Won't argue with you there," I said.

She kissed me lightly and went back to feeding people, setting a plate of sausage and eggs in front of me. I let her do her thing because it obviously made her happy. I gave her warning when we had to get ready to go and some of the other women pitched in to help.

Ashton got dressed in record time and so did I and we headed straight for the shop in the clothes we'd had on the night before. Wasn't like we had worn 'em all that long to warrant going home and changing. I had a full day of one piece and it was promising to be grueling.

"You good Babe?" I asked her as she settled behind her desk, her jacket hanging from the back of her chair.

"Yes," she intoned, smiling softly, that lush bottom lip of hers clasped between her teeth.

I nodded and took my customer back to my station.

"She your girl?" he asked me.

"Yeah," I told him quietly, "She's my girl."

I was worried she would take it the wrong way but I think she heard, her head bowed and a sigh of contentment slipped from her, a light blush painting her cheeks. It wasn't the reaction I expected to the possessive comment... but it elated me just the same.

# CHAPTER 16

*Ashton*

I missed him, but this was his life before I had come into it. So I had done the only thing I could do. I had kissed him on Sunday morning, pouring all the love and happiness that I could into his mouth and let him drink it down. He'd climbed onto his bike, swore we would go cell phone shopping when he got back and had ridden away.

Andy had kept me busy the rest of the day. We'd gone to a check cashing place and cashed my paycheck on Saturday during our lunch break. I had set aside my portion of the rent and then we had gone shopping with a little bit of the extra Zander had given me for his tattoo. It still baffled me why he wanted my face permanently inked under his skin but to each their own.

Monday I had spent at home unpacking, my thoughts drifting to Ethan's and my time spent making love. I had come across Ethan's medals and put them carefully in the bottom back corner of his closet where he had requested they go. He said he didn't feel like a hero, but he didn't have it in him to dishonor the honor done to him by getting rid of his purple heart and what have you. He'd shown me photographs of his unit and of his earlier days in the MC.

He was careful not to speak on his ex, just said that it hadn't worked out. I knew about her, that she'd cheated, hadn't stood by him no matter how hard he'd tried to get better. Zander told me. Ethan made my heart swell with love and pride and I'd fallen in love with him just that much more that he wouldn't bad mouth her even if it was the truth.

I'd shared a little more of my pain with him. He'd asked why Chadwick and I hadn't had any children. I told him that I'd gotten pregnant by him in college... Chadwick had said he wasn't ready for children and had talked me into an abortion. I'd fallen prey to an opportunistic infection even though he'd taken me to a reputable clinic, and... well... The doctor had told me adoption would always be an option to me.

I sighed.

It was warm out today and I checked my make up in the mirror; then checked to make sure I looked good in my jeans and tank top. The jeans were mine from before but the tank top was new. It was black and ribbed and fit like a second skin. It had an anchor and roses silk screened on the front along my hip, angled across my stomach, the rose vines crawling up the anchor and my ribs. Andy had called the design old school and said it looked good.

I had smiled and agreed to buy it from the second hand store we were in as it was only .99 cents. A knock sounded at the front door and I almost skipped in my new black and white Chuck Taylor's to the door. I pulled it open and where I expected lanky tattooed and grinning Andy two men in suits, one in gray and one in blue, stood.

My face fell and dread crept across my heart.

"Yes?" I said quietly.

"Ashton Granger?" one of them asked, the one in gray... he was looking at a spiral notepad in his hands, the kind with the black leather cover you see police detectives carry on TV. My heart seized in my chest.

"Yes," I stated and my voice sounded funny.

"I'm Detective Rodgers and this is Detective Lawrence," he flashed a silver official police badge at me and I blinked.

"What is this about?" I asked carefully.

"Does an Ethan Howard live here with you, ma'am?" the man in the blue suit... Detective Lawrence asked me.

"Yes," I said, I felt hot and clammy, my heart fluttered in my chest as a bubble of panic rose.

"We're sorry to have to make the notification ma'am, but there was an accident out on the interstate, the next state over..."

"No," I said. No, this wasn't happening. My eyes filled with tears.

"Ma'am Ethan Howard has died," the detective said and I crumpled to my knees as the whole world tilted violently on its axis.

"Ma'am is there someone we can call for you?" the detective asked.

"No," I said, denial forcing its way out of my mouth. This wasn't happening.

"Very well ma'am, again, we're sorry for your loss," the detective in gray said and they left. They left me sitting in my open doorway, hot tears spilling down my face. A high keening sound filled the upstairs landing outside my apartment door and I wanted to slam the door and shut it out.

Footsteps on the stairs, Andy came into view. I wanted the keening noise to stop. I looked at him with horror painted all over my face, silently begging him to make it stop.

"Ashton," he knelt down and pulled me into his arms and the keening got louder.

"Ashton, what's the matter!? Baby, tell me what's wrong!?" he held me at arm's length and the keening turned to screaming as I felt myself break in two. Andy's mouth was moving but I couldn't make out what he was saying as awful noises tore out of me. He had his phone out and was dialing.

"Ashton, what's wrong!?" he demanded and shook me hard by my shoulders and my grief filled mind pushed it out of my mouth in a torrent of sobs.

"Ethan's dead!" and my whole safe world collapsed in a pile of burning timber around me.

Doc came, so did Chandra and Reaver. Dragon and Dray were out on the run with Ethan and I remember wondering if they were okay or if they were dead too, before Doc jammed a needle in my arm. Finally that god awful keening stopped and as my eyes drooped and I was lifted, I prayed that whatever was in the shot would kill me too, because I'd finally found my other half and I never wanted to live without him again.

# CHAPTER 17

## *Trig*

"Yo Trig!" Reaver yelled from the gas station's minimart. My head snapped up. He sounded equal parts pissed, scared and panicked.

"What!?" I yelled back. Dray and Dragon were behind him inside, heads together over Reaver's phone listening and barking the occasional demand into it while I pumped my gas.

"Trouble on the home front brother! Where's your phone!?" I frowned and pulled my phone out of my cut. Thirty-two missed calls! What the fuck over!?

"What the fuck is going on?" Panic seized my nads in a vice. The three of them trouped across the cracked cement moving as one, all black leather and thunderous looks, anger radiating off of them like heat lighting ready to strike.

"We're scrapping goin' to the way point. Ride all night if we have to," Dragon said.

Ashton…

"What happened, what the fuck did that prick do to her!?" I demanded.

"Sent people dressed like cops to your place. Told her you were dead." I blinked at the sheer audacity and just plain manipulative dirty mind fuck of it.

I stared at the numbers racing in circles on the pump's read out. They weren't racing fast enough. Ashton was hurt, I could see it in all of their faces, that whatever damage the lie had done it had done it but good. I did the breathing exercises they taught us in the corps and finally the pump kicked in my hand. I thrust it back onto the dock and screwed on the gas lid, wrenching it savagely tight.

I got on and kicked my baby to life. My brothers flanked me as we took formation and wound back onto the highway going the opposite direction back towards home. We'd ride all night if we had to... just as Dragon had said.

I had my Pres., my VP and my brother's backing and blessing but I still felt like shit. Torn, in two equal directions. On one side for leaving Ashton alone knowing her prick of a soon to be ex-husband was a sadistic mother fucker, and the other for selfishly scrapping the last part of this run, even though we successfully did what needed doing and had the cargo with us.

Ashton was my only objective now. I didn't know why or how or when in the short time we'd known each other that these feelings took root and started to grow but I learned a long time ago sometimes you didn't question these things. You just looked to the open road in front of you and dealt with the hazards and changes in the road conditions as they came up.

We had a long ride ahead of us and maddeningly had to watch our speed and keep it inside the limit. Dragon was taking the risk this time and none of us were interested in doing the amount of time the amount of drugs we had on us would bring down. About halfway through the night Dragon had us all pull in to a rest stop.

"What up Pres.?" I asked and he looked at the three of us judiciously.

"This shit is slowing us down," he said.

"What are you sayin'?" Dray asked.

"I'm sayin' we either, get rid of it now or split up and go two by two," he said.

"Get rid of it now," we all three chorused in unison. We had too many enemies and were too far out of our territory to make going just two by two an option. Solo runs were different, you could pack your cut into your saddlebag and make yourself look like just a dude on a bike if you had to.

"Or I can go it alone," I said.

"No good. We go in four and then we're suddenly three, anybody spots that and you're a sitting duck," Dragon put out there.

We made use of the men's room and started flushing, pouring the poison slowly. Who gave a fuck if anybody thought we were circle jerking it in here. It was late enough. Only thing we had to worry about were cops. Staties came up into rest stops all the time checking for illegal activity. We got lucky, and got the hell out of there fast but not before I placed a call to Doc.

"Yeah?" his voice sounded irritated.

"How is she?" I asked.

"Had to sedate her. When we got here she just kept screaming this god awful sound, never heard anything like it before. Your boy Squick couldn't get her to calm down. She came out of it about an hour ago but just lays there staring at the wall," he said.

"Can you put her on the phone?" I asked.

"Naw man I think its best you just get here. I've never seen anything quite like this and I've seen some shit before. I don't think a phone call is gonna cut it," someone said something and Doc's voice was muffled he came back on the line, I could hear that wounded animal sound in the background.

"Is that Ashton?"

"Yeah man, I gotta go," the line went dead and I traded looks with Reaver who had been close enough to hear.

"I'm going to kill that motherfucker," I said savagely, stuffing the phone back in my pocket.

"Slowly with my knives. Your way is too neat, too clean and too quick for this," he intoned. We rode out, and for once, I fuckin' agreed with Reaver. My way *was* too quick and painless for the likes of Chadwick Granger.

We rode all night and broke what speed limits we could and arrived back by mid-morning Wednesday. I took the stairs two at a time. A very tired looking Squick pulled open my door.

"Where is she?" I demanded by way of greeting.

"Your room," he answered and I thrust my helmet and glasses into his hands, never breaking stride. I stopped in the door way. Ashton was curled in a ball on her side facing away from me. She looked so tiny and frail.

"Ashton," I called but she didn't stir. I went around to the foot of the bed. She looked wrung out. Almost worse than when I'd first met her. Her eyes were closed and she clutched my pillow to her chest. Her nose buried in it, a wrinkle set between her eyes. I got up on the bed from the other side and slid my arm in the grove between her neck and shoulder gently lifting her. I leaned back against the headboard in a sitting position and laid her head atop my denim clad thigh and just petted her silky hair.

"What the hell did you put her on?" I asked Doc when he appeared in the doorway.

"When the horse tranquilizers wore off and she started up with that noise again I switched to elephant tranqs," he said, his special brand of black humor coating his words like molasses.

"When will she come out of it?" I asked. He sighed and shrugged.

"Hard to say man, everybody reacts differently," he sucked his teeth and went back out. Reaver came in and sat down on the floor against the wall between the dresser and the closet, stretching his legs out in front of him.

"She looks like hell," he commented.

"Yeah," I agreed.

"What are we going to do about her douche bag ex?" he asked.

"What can we do?" I asked bitterly.

"Something highly illegal," Dragon suggested from the door way. Dray frowned at his father and then frowned harder at Ashton's back.

"He's got money," I said.

"Money ain't everything," Reaver said judiciously.

"We'll talk about it later," Dragon said sharply as Ashton stirred. I stared down at her and willed her to open her eyes.

"Reaver?" she asked softly and her voice sounded like it'd been through a cheese grater. I winced to hear it.

"Yeah doll, in the flesh," he grinned at her.

"You're okay?" she asked.

"Yeah Babe, so is Dragon and Dray they're behind you," she pushed herself up and I could tell she was groggy from the drugs. She looked down at my denim clad leg in confusion then up at me.

"Am I dead, too?" she asked, golden eyes full of surprise.

I laughed and said, "No Baby," and pulled her against me kissing the top of her head. A high keening noise escaped her throat and

Doc appeared behind Dragon and Dray.

"Shhhh, it's okay," I used the sooth-the-frightened-animal tone.

"It's not okay!" she cried and broke down into huge wracking sobs. She was right it wasn't but it was the best I could come up with. I rocked her gently the leather of my jacket and cut creaking.

"Shhhhh, shhhhh, shhhhh," I soothed repeatedly.

I held her like that for a long time. Her arms around my neck, she crawled into my lap and stayed there clinging to me like she'd never let me go.

"Promise me you're really here," she said against the side of my neck, her tears slipping down into my collar, soaking my shirt.

"I'm really here Ashton, I promise," I said and she sniffed but didn't let go. Dray wandered off somewhere and Dragon leaned against the door frame, bearing witness along with Reaver.

"Call the cops," I whispered and Reaver pulled out his phone. Ashton wouldn't let me go. It took an hour for the police to get there. Ashton answered all their questions and gave the police officers the names the fake detectives had given her and descriptions of what the men looked like. The description matched the one Andy gave of the two men he'd passed on the stairs.

"Who are you?" one of the cops asked Doc when she and Andy reached that part of the story.

"I'm her primary care physician," Doc said and he had the credentials to back it up. Reason we call him Doc is that he is a licensed practicing doctor. The cops were surprised. So much for their stereotypes of the bad ass bikers.

"I thought I'd never see you again," she whispered and it sounded so thick with grief, so broken that it tore my heart out.

"Baby, I'd walk through Hell in gasoline boots to get back to you," I murmured and meant every word.

The cops were pissed and one of them knelt down to look at Ashton.

"Mrs. Granger..."

"Fletcher," she stopped him cold.

"I'm sorry?" he said.

"Ms. Fletcher, it's my maiden name. I don't want any part of him anywhere near me." I was so damned proud of her in that moment.

"Ms. Fletcher," the cop amended, "You need to know that a detective's badge is gold, not silver, but it sounds like whoever was in that suit may be a real officer and that doesn't sit well with me. Is there someplace you can go? Family out of state or..." Dragon stopped the man right there.

"We're her family now. She'll be fine. We'll keep an eye on her," the cop looked at Ashton dubiously but she was staring up at me, her face was so open, raw and vulnerable that I would give anything to fix it. I bent my head and kissed her gently. She kissed me back carefully.

"Not leaving you again, Baby Girl. Not until this is settled," I whispered against her mouth.

I pulled back and fixed a steely gaze on the cop. "Anything else?" I asked him.

"No I think we've got it," he and his partner left our bedroom and apartment.

Doc racked his neck from side to side.

"I'm goin' home," he stated. Squick looked ready to drop.

"Andy go stay in my room, get some sleep," Ashton murmured.

"I'm leavin'," Dray snorted.

"Thank you for coming, for bringing him back to me," Ashton murmured at him though she wouldn't meet his gaze. He nodded curtly and he and Dragon left. Reaver got slowly to his feet.

"Takin' the couch," he said and trudged into the living room. Squick shut the door to Ashton's room and we were alone.

"I'm okay," I intoned and pressed my forehead to hers.

"I really thought you were gone," her voice broke and more tears spilled.

I was hot and so I shrugged out of my jacket and cut, then I figured to hell with it and sliding Ashton to the bed, I pried her arms from around my neck, stripped her, stripped me and got into bed with her after shutting the bedroom door, not caring who heard what.

She gasped when I pulled her close and I kissed her. I needed her to know I was alive, that I loved her and to reinforce that I wasn't going anywhere and this was the best way I knew how. I pressed her back into our bed and licked, kissed and nipped my way from her mouth to her mound. Her skin was silky soft and sweet she smelled like orange blossoms but below that, purely of Ashton. An intoxicating mixture of summer and sunlight that gently tickled my nose. I slid a finger into her folds and found her wet and ready but I wanted to make sure.

I nudged her thighs apart with my elbows and gazed up the alabaster length of her body. I let how beautiful she looked to me settle into my eyes and licked her slowly and deliberately and holy fucking hell the woman tasted amazing. I pressed my middle finger deep into her sweet wet heat and closed my eyes, stroking her clit with my tongue searching for that sweet spot just... there. Her hips arched off the bed and she cried out, fisting her hands in my hair she pulled my mouth tighter against her body and I loved it.

I made my Baby come three times until with a cry she tried to scoot away from me. I grinned and settled myself between her thighs and it was as if my cock knew where to go, finding her opening of its own accord. I sank into her sleek wet heat until my balls met flush against her body.

She dragged my face down to hers and kissed me deeply with the taste of herself still on my mouth and I swear to god I stiffened just that much more inside her. She felt like sin made flesh with no barriers between us. I knew I was clean and at this point I didn't give a fuck. I didn't have to worry about pregnancy, and fucked if I was going to let that slide when it came to her ex either, but for now, right now, none of that bullshit mattered. Not one fucking tiny iota because right now it was just me and my girl and I wanted her to feel *good*.

I set a fast but gentle rhythm, thrusting without slamming into her. I hooked one of her legs high over my hip and held it there, keeping my weight off of her by bracing my other arm on the bed. She stared me in the eyes, lips parted, gasping for breath, expression filled with love and lust and I grinned savagely. God she was perfect! The sun to my moon, fire to my ice, she was just fucking everything to me and I poured that into my body, into moving over her and inside her, into loving the ever living shit out of her.

"One more time Baby, come for me one more time," I moaned into her ear and she cried out, her walls clenching around me, milking my cock. I groaned and went over the edge with her, feeling my cock jerk in counterpoint to her body's grip.

She was, just… so… *perfect.*

We came back to earth slowly, holding each other. She stared at me with her ethereal eyes and I stared back.

"What are we going to do?" she asked softly.

"You don't worry 'bout that," I kissed her forehead and her eyes drifted shut.

"I can't go through that again," she whispered brokenly and it wrenched at my heart.

"I know babe, I know," I held her tighter against me and thought hard on what could be done. I sighed and cuddled her close. "I'm here Ashton," I whispered into the dimming room and was met with a sigh that was one part contentment and one part relief.

# CHAPTER 18

*Ashton*

"Lake run next week, right?" Reaver asked, I turned from my place at the sink and looked at them both with apprehension. The last run was only two weeks ago and my husband sent those people pretending to be detectives. The phone had rung in the shop the next day and I had answered it. Chadwick's cultured voice had crackled over the line, he'd said,

"You see how easy it would be? He can't protect you forever Ashton. You belong to me and I keep what's mine…"

I'd slammed the phone down and Zander had taken one look at my face and yelled for Ethan. I'd told them what had happened and Ethan had snorted, going as still and cold as Death himself and said he'd like to see Chadwick try. Now, a bubble of panic was rising in my chest but Ethan knew and was already undoing the effects of Reaver's innocuous question.

"A lake run is different baby, you go too. Happens twice a year, once in the late spring, early summer, and one at the end of summer before the kids go back to school. We make the day's ride out to the cabin and lodge out at Lake Eversong. It's one of the club's legit business ventures. We take over the lake; party, live music and barbeque, some fun in the sun and swimming. It's a blast," his silver eyes smiled at me from the table where he and Reaver sat while I fixed breakfast.

"Sounds like I need a swimsuit," I murmured and both of them smiled bigger.

"Yeah you do! A two piece. Preferably something really slutty," Reaver gave a sidelong look at Ethan who was glaring at him, "You know, because Trigger would like that," he finished. I laughed.

"You get what you want babe, I love you any way you look," Ethan said and I felt a surge of love myself for the man. He looked absolutely delicious sitting there, jeans riding low on his hips, shirtless, hair in a wild blonde mane around his face making his light eyes seem even lighter.

I finished making the coffee. It was a work out day and so breakfast would come later. The boys measured out their protein shakes or whatever while I went and changed. Over the last two weeks, Ethan and I had grown closer. He had gone cell phone shopping with me the day after he'd come home from the run and I was still trying to figure everything out on the fancy smart phone.

We hadn't been parted for more than eight hours in all that time, and the time he had spent away from me was spent dealing with club politics. He was trying to work out a deal with other chapters of the MC, over what I didn't know and the fact that he wouldn't talk to me about it and seemed even more stressed out than usual was very telling to me that it was not going well.

I came back out of my bedroom where I still kept all my clothes and found Reaver and Ethan waiting. I took up my yoga mat which was propped by the door and went out with them. The sun was shining and the birds were singing and the trees were a riot of green. Spring may have come in like a lamb but it was going to go out like a lion. I scanned the parking lot as I went down the stairs looking for anything out of place.

We had come to the conclusion that my husband had sent people to watch us. How else would he have known Ethan was gone, to send those two men? The police were sure that one of them was an officer or related to one somehow but they had yet to catch anyone. Reports had been filed and a lawyer contacted. God knew how I was going to be able to afford one if Dragon and the club hadn't stepped in to help. I wanted a divorce but they didn't come cheap or easy.

"We gotta get you a car Sunshine," Ethan groaned when the old truck he borrowed from Dragon didn't turn over right away. It finally fired up, backfired, which made me jump, and we pulled out of the lot to head to the 'Y'.

Hayden met me at the door and was nearly jumping out of her skin. She and I had made fast friends after my second time to yoga, and Ethan had even taken me to meet her for a lunch date. Staying out in the parking lot smoking his e-cigarette, talking or playing games on his phone, patiently waiting for me. Hayden had thought it was weird and I agreed that it was but then I had explained about when he'd gone on his run and her compassion for my situation took over.

"He finally asked me!" she squealed at me excitedly and thrust her left hand in my face. I squealed in delight with her and looked at the ring, a simple band of white gold with a diamond solitaire set in it. Reaver and Ethan exchanged looks and rolled their eyes, but they were smiling, well Ethan was, Reaver's face was shuttered and his eyes distant and cool.

Hayden and her boyfriend had been together for three years and she had confessed she was growing unhappy, that she really wanted him to propose so she could take that next step with him into forever. I'd sighed, she was twenty-four. I had been married two years by that age. It took me until I was thirty to escape and find my prince charming, the man I felt I was really supposed to be with. I smiled at Ethan and he smiled back.

I shared in my new friend's joy despite my own misgivings, which, truth be told, were likely just a byproduct of my own story. My own insecurities and damage... I turned and waved at Reaver and Ethan. Ethan's smile got wider and my whole world suffused with warmth, the dark clouds of my past scudding quickly overhead and off into the distance again.

*I love you*, he mouthed at me as Hayden hauled me around the corner and into the yoga class room so we could set up. She was already asking about colors and flowers and gushing about venues she'd been thinking about. I wasn't even sure that she'd set a date with him yet! I listened patiently, smiling and nodding until the instructor for today's class took her place at the front of the room.

We were set up near the pool and so the class was accompanied by the sounds of water and the ethereal piped in music. I rolled out my mat and took off my shoes and breathed deep the warm humid air that brought with it the chemical tang of chlorine. The class began and my focus honed inward. I breathed, deeply and evenly, following the cadence of the instructors soothing voice as she took us fluidly from one pose to the next. My world narrowed to the beat of my heart, ebb and flow of air in my lungs and the rush of blood through my veins. Peace descended on me, a warm blanket insulating me from all of the chaos swirling outside these moments.

The class ended and I felt centered and refreshed. I opened my eyes and we did our traditional exit ritual. I rolled up my mat and was sitting putting my shoes and socks back on and I turned to say something to Hayden.

A shout from out in the weights area and a crash had all the heads in the class room turning as one.

"Son of a bitch!" Reaver's voice… adrenaline surged in my body and I barely heard Hayden say,

"Ashton stay here!" but my feet were already carrying me to the door out into the rest of the facility.

"Ahhhhhh!" I heard an angry male grunt and rounded the corner to see Reaver sitting on a wiry man's back. Another, burly man lay sprawled on his back on the carpet. Ethan stood over that man, bleeding from a cut over his eyebrow. He looked down on the man dispassionately, that icy cold faraway look on his face that he sometimes woke up with after one of his nightmares. I shivered.

"Cops on their way?" Reaver asked one of the gym attendants. The man nodded mutely and I looked back down to Reaver on the floor. He had a reckless grin on his face, turned rictus and frightening by the coat of blood on his teeth. The glint of his blue eyes was cold and something all around horrifying. I swallowed hard. I'd never seen my friend this way, and if at all possible I never wanted to see him this way again.

"Ashton!" Ethan said sharply and I looked up at him blinking. He hadn't moved from his place above the unconscious man but his gaze had shifted to where I stood. I was under the impression that this wasn't the first time he'd called my name.

"Go back to your yoga classroom," he said. An arm went around me and I jumped and let out a little yip of surprise.

"It's just me!" Hayden said and I looked over into her green eyes, the color of new spring leaves.

"He's going to get you! You stupid bitch! Only a matter of time, he has the money and the power and he's going to find you!" the man Reaver was sitting on screamed at me, tauntingly and it dawned on me what was going on. These men, Chadwick had sent them.

"Shut up!" Reaver snarled and bounced the man's head off the carpeted floor. The man cursed and started struggling anew. I started shaking. Hayden led me into the women's locker room.

"What happened?" I asked and my voice came out a ghost of a whisper.

"I don't know, Sweetheart," she said, "I'm sure the boys will come get us and tell us after the police get here." I nodded the careful calm I'd spent an hour cultivating and had just achieved minutes ago cracked but held true in the face of the current predicament. My heart thudded heavy in my chest and my hands shook with the effects of the adrenaline but I was okay. I was okay and Ethan was okay and Reaver was okay. I closed my eyes.

"I really hate that man," I murmured.

"Who is he?" Hayden asked, taken aback and misunderstanding.

"Not the man in the next room, I don't know who he is, I'm talking about Chadwick," I opened my eyes and stood up. The man's screaming was growing fainter as he was dragged out the front of the building. I assumed by the police.

I went out into the hall and spotted Ethan giving a statement to a uniformed police officer. Reaver was talking to an officer of his own. I went to Ethan and slipped my hand in his where it hung at his side. He pulled me against his side and kissed the top of my head.

"Where were you?" the police officer asked me.

"She was in yoga class with me," Hayden said, her arms crossed over her stomach.

"And you are?" the police officer asked.

"Hayden Michaels," I tuned out the rest of their conversation. Ethan's hand smoothed up and down my arm, warming the chill that stole over me. My gaze had been captured by the small black and white monitor behind the reception wrap in the lobby where an attendant was replaying the security footage from the weight room.

The two men stood in the doorway and had said something to Ethan and Reaver. Reaver hefted the weight and put it back on the rack. He said something back to the men and sat up. The men exchanged looks and stepped into the room. They spoke back and forth. Ethan said nothing, letting Reaver do all the talking. Ethan studied the two men who looked like bikers too, but not like Sacred Heart men. No these men looked rougher, sinister. The smaller one, twitchy, brandished a short length of pipe. Finally, the men flew at Reaver and Ethan who stood empty handed. I jumped as Ethan put up an arm to block an incoming length of chain. The chain wrapped around his thick forearm, the bend in it connecting, glancing off his eyebrow as it swung round.

Ethan pulled the man forward by the chain, his opposite hand plowing forward into the man's face and the man dropped like a stone. The skinny man had the pipe and swung at Reaver who dodged the pipe but caught the man's other fist in his mouth. He pulled back and grinned and twisted the man's wrist savagely. The pipe dropped and Reaver wrestled him to the ground.

I looked up at Ethan but he was looking down at me, his eyes slowly warming as he came back from where ever he'd went. What did the men want, why were they there? I searched for answers on my lover's face and found none though I was certain he'd read my questions clearly.

The police officer left us and Reaver came over. The police held a little powwow of their own by reception.

"Are you all right?" I asked.

"Those guys? They were pussies," Reaver looked like he was going to spit on the floor but Hayden made a noise and he thought better of it.

"What was that all about?" she asked and the men both looked at me.

"They were looking for a fight, trying to get us arrested," Ethan stated.

"Why?" Hayden frowned.

Because the honeymoon was over... The media frenzy had died down surrounding Chadwick and now it was time for retribution.

The thoughts and emotions must have gone across my face like a reader board.

"Hey, Babe, no worries," Reaver said, smile one sided.

"We aren't ones to lose our cool," Ethan said.

"Helps that I'm one majorly annoying prick and got them to attack first," Reaver grinned and I couldn't help myself, I gave a little laugh. Hayden frowned at him.

"I'm not sure that's a brag-worthy quality," she commented dryly.

"Worked this time," he shrugged and she frowned harder.

"What now?" I whispered but before they could answer the police came over to us.

"These two," he said jerking a thumb over his shoulder, "Say they have no idea who Chadwick Granger is." He frowned, "They say they belong to The Laughing Skulls. Isn't that a rival of you guys?" he asked.

Reaver cocked an eyebrow, "Never even heard of such an MC," he said and Ethan looked equally confused.

"Well that's what they say. The surveillance system doesn't have audio but it's pretty clear who attacked who. You're free to go, try to stay out of anymore trouble for a while," he wrote down a final note in his little book and walked away. Reaver snorted. Ethan hugged me close. Hayden made an incredulous noise.

"Don't sweat it Sexy," Reaver said to her, "Comes with the territory."

"I just want to go home," I said and both men looked at me.

"Yeah, okay. We can get cleaned up there," Ethan held me close. I said good bye to Hayden and promised her that I would call soon. We piled into the truck and got it going. I held one of Ethan's hands and one of Reaver's on the ride home, staring at our linked fingers. Ethan's knuckles were swelling and purpled and I worried about it effecting his work.

Reaver's fingers, I was startled to realize, were laced with silvery scars. The realistic looking open switchblades tattooed on the inside of each forearm, blades pointed towards his wrists, hilt at his inner elbow, rippled over muscles corded with tension. I sniffed, staring at the tension radiating down that arm, the stress it contained. This was my fault. All my fault.

"Hey, no. Whatcha crying for?" Reaver asked.

"This is all my fault!" I gasped.

"No, Ashton this is *his* fault. Don't do this, don't give up now, Baby. You don't get to own this," Ethan's hand squeezed mine and he turned into our apartment's parking lot and parked the truck. The careful calm I had cultivated in yoga shattered into fine pieces around us.

"No, don't you get it!? You got *hurt* today! He came after *you*! To try and take you from me... to *get to me*! I never should have left the side of that road! I should have just frozen, or made it home, or let him come back for me! I should have taken his correction and been better behaved for it! Then none of this would be *happening* to you!" Ethan dragged me into his lap and crushed me to his chest and I sobbed.

"No Babe, don't say that, don't feel that way. You're the best thing that's ever happened to me. Don't say you never should have happened to me. You're a blessing, no matter what kind of shit that happy bastard pulls you're a blessing to me, not a curse. Don't ever forget that." It was the first time I'd ever heard Ethan panicked or scared. I felt a hand smoothing up and down the side of my shin and realized it was Reaver trying to throw in his comfort and support as well.

They let me cry it out and it wasn't a pretty cry. When I was done we sat for a long time, the three of us grimly silent before Ethan shifted and opened his door. He was going to carry me and I said no, that I could do it. We three trudged wearily up the stairs and stopped in front of our apartment door.

"Sit down at the table," I said indicating to Ethan he should take a seat. I went into the kitchen and extracted some frozen vegetables from the freezer and placed them carefully over his battered knuckles.

"I'm gonna go shower," Reaver said and went into the bathroom, shutting the door behind him. I got the first aid kit and dealt with the cut over Ethan's eye, he sat still and didn't as much as flinch when I dabbed it with antiseptic.

"Talk to me Babe," he whispered.

"I'm scared," I said, taking a deep breath, "The only thing that scares me more than going back to him is that he's going to do something really bad to you." I sniffed.

"Baby you gotta trust me, nothing bad is going to happen to me," he put his left hand, his good hand, over mine and gently pulled his head back away from my fingers as I continued to dab at the cut over his eye with the cleanser.

"You can't promise that," I said helplessly and he was silent.

"You're right, I can't," he sighed.

"Is that what you really want though? To give up? To go back to that piece of shit?" he sounded angry with me and I looked up sharply.

"No!" I said, startled.

"You going to let me handle this?" he demanded sharply and his expression was cold, calculating and overtly terrifying.

"I... Yes," I said, surprised I meant it, whatever him 'handling it' meant. He stood up.

"Are you going to kill him?" I asked calmly.

"Better if you don't know," he said, then after a moment asked from the bedroom doorway... "Do you care?" I thought about it for a heartbeat and he let me and I looked up at him somber and cold to the bone and said the utter truth...

"I don't want you to go back to that place, so yes... but do I care if he died? Not after everything he's done," he searched my face and nodded slowly and disappeared into the bedroom. Reaver came out of the bathroom rubbing a towel over his head and looked across the hall.

"We going hunting?" he asked all smiles as if he were asking about something mundane like, golf.

"Something like that. We gotta be smart about this. Call the guys in for Church," Ethan said and went into the bathroom, the shower started. Reaver dropped into the seat Ethan had vacated all smiles that didn't reach anywhere near his wintery eyes.

"Don't sweat it Babe. Things are going to be fine," he said with a smile, his split lower lip and bruised chin looking fierce against his light skin tone. The funny thing was, I believed him and I was really okay with whatever happened.

Ethan came out a time later, in jeans and bare feet. He and Reaver exchanged looks. He pulled a shirt on over his head, the ends of his wet hair dripping onto the faded cotton of his light blue tee, the water soaking into the collar. Even angry, he was beautiful. Like some kind of avenging angel. I got up while the two men stared at each other, silently communicating somehow. I shut myself into the bathroom which was humid from their showers and hoped there was enough hot water left for a quick one of my own. I washed my hair and got out, wrapping in a towel. I peeked out into the apartment but Reaver was already gone. Ethan was shrugging into his jacket and cut.

"Leaving?" I asked softly. He came to me and kissed me gently.

"Back in a bit, be ready for work," he whispered against my mouth.

"Okay," I murmured.

He left, locking the door behind himself and a minute later I heard him fire up his motor cycle. I dried my hair and dressed in jeans, boots and a tank top for work. I put on Phantom of the Opera while I waited and watched through until Emmy Rossum stood sparkling under the lights as Christine in her solo debut. A key grated in the lock and I stood up facing the door, half afraid which poured out of me with relief when Ethan stepped half way in the door.

"Ready?" he asked me.

I scooped up my purse and shrugged into my jacket. He picked up my helmet and we went down to the bike.

"So what happened?" I asked, fastening my helmet into place.

"Went to Church," he shrugged. "Whatever happens, happens. Club thinks its best that I sit this one out, plausible deniability is important here. The less either of us know the better and this conversation never happened," he got on and looked at me hard until I nodded slowly that I understood. I felt boneless with yet more relief. Maybe they knew what they were doing, maybe they would scare Chadwick so bad he would forget all about me. I got on the bike behind Ethan.

"I love you," I said hugging close to him.

"I love you too, Babe," he said and fired up the bike.

We went to work, we went home… It was just another day after that and it was almost surreal. I was half afraid it was the calm before the storm but when Ethan looked at me with those cool silver eyes I felt stronger and realized that what storm may come, we'd weather it together which was more than I had ever had before.

# CHAPTER 19

*Trig*

The thrill of a long ride was calling to me, even more so because Ashton would be taking it with me. I leaned out of our small bathroom and looked down the hall into the living room with shaving cream still half on my face. She stood over her small packed bag chewing her lush bottom lip and I smiled. I loved how the leather pants I'd bought her hugged her tight ass. Her jacket and helmet sat on the arm of the couch and she fairly vibrated with excitement.

I chuckled and went back to the task at hand, drawing the razor carefully up my neck. I hated shaving, putting it off as long as possible most of the time.

"Ethan, have you seen my sunglasses?" Ashton's soft voice called from the living room and I grinned at my reflection.

"Try the kitchen babe!" I called back, her lyrical voice came a short minute later...

"Thank you!"

I smiled again and rinsed off the last of the shaving cream, patting my face dry and mopping stray water droplets off my chest. Ashton's sharp intake of breath had my head turning quickly.

"What?" I asked alarmed, but I didn't need to be. My baby girl stood in the bathroom doorway her golden gaze molten with desire as she skimmed her eyes over my exposed chest. I grinned and pulled her to me by her belt loops. I pressed her between me and the bathroom sink's counter.

I covered her mouth with my own and drank deeply of her, my cock rising in my pants. She gasped into my mouth and ran her hand over the front of my jeans. I started walking her across the hall to the bedroom but she stopped me with a laugh.

"No, no, no!" she said, skidding to the side and bouncing out of my reach. "We'll be late," she admonished.

"We can catch up," I said and tried to pull her to me. Two knocks and Reaver barged in.

"Figured you two needed a chaperone if you wanted to make it on time!" he called and spying us in the hall raised an eyebrow. "Looks like I was right."

Ashton laughed lightly, "In all fairness I started it," she said.

"Don't care, let's move. I want us all to be a part of the ride," he gestured at me to hurry up. I pulled on my shirt and went out in the living room. Ashton had us all packed which wasn't saying much. Everything fitting into a large waterproof messenger bag. She hefted the bag and slid it cross ways across her body over her jacket. It looked like it was about to drag her over but once she was on the bike she'd be okay.

"All right man! Lake run!" Reaver cheered and we went down to the waiting bikes.

I put my guns into the saddle bags, ammo on the opposite side. I had my permits for everything and it wouldn't be a lake run without shooting. Ashton handed Reaver the bag with our clothes in it and got on behind me. She adjusted her helmet, put on her glasses and Reaver slid the bag over her head. She put her phone in the pocket for it on the strap and I put the final adjustment on my own brain bucket.

Reaver and I fired up the bikes, tugged on our cuts and jackets to get comfortable and pulled out for the club house. The club was a flurry of activity. The van was stocked with tools and parts for road repairs if needed. Chandra and Shelly found Ashton and everyone got in some final touches.

"Here Sweetheart," Shelly handed Ashton a tube of something.

"What's this?" Ashton asked.

"Goth block," Shelly grinned.

"What?" Ashton asked plaintively.

"SPF 666. Put it on Girl so you don't burn," she sauntered over to Reaver.

"Gimme a ride cousin dear?" she asked.

"Get on Runt," he grunted.

Ashton was smearing the sunblock on her hands face and the back of her neck.

"Thank God for Shelly! I didn't even think about sunscreen," she said and put the sunblock into her inside pocket. I smiled over my shoulder as the smell of coconuts and shea butter assaulted my nose, sickly sweet. I preferred her orange blossom scent.

Dragon gave the announcements and the opening speech and led the way down the drive. We fell into line according to rank behind him. I looked over at Dray beside me, Reaver behind me in my side view, Doc and Chandra beside Reaver and so on down the lines.

Ashton hugged me tightly and we drove down the highway, open road in front of us, sun shining above us. My heart lightened and I did a deep cleansing breath. I was getting us both out of town for some much needed rest and relaxation. The club had handled business with her husband midweek. I knew nothing which was the way it had to be. Reaver seemed happy as a pig in shit over it though so I know some justice had been delivered. Probably a beat down from hell if I had to guess, but no one needed to know what I was thinkin'…

We had agreed that as much as we wanted him dead, dead would be too messy and we just weren't in that business anymore. That was the extent of my knowledge and that was as good as it was gonna get. I wanted so bad to beat the brakes off that son of a bitch myself but I trusted my brothers delivered.

I felt Ashton sigh behind me and checked her out in the rear view. She was smiling, long auburn hair streaming in the wind, golden eyes obscured by dark lenses. She'd settled in and was enjoying the ride and it felt awesome. It was a four hour ride to the lake across some state lines. Short for a lot of us guys not so much for the women unused to doing any kind of run so we made it a point to stop halfway at this little bar and grill for some lunch. We packed the place as a club and they looked forward to it every year so it worked out fine.

I helped Ashton down and she was grinning. She popped her headphones out of her ears and unclipped her iPod shuffle from the front of the messenger bag. She stuffed it and the wires into her pocket.

"Well, you're new!" our waitress exclaimed, handing a menu to Ashton once we were seated. Ashton flashed her a brilliant smile.

"Yeah," she agreed shyly and I smiled. Usually she said 'yes' all prim and proper like.

"Well welcome! These guys aren't such a bad lot when you get to know them but I'm sure you figured that out," she winked, took our drink orders and wandered away.

We ate and laughed and joked, generally enjoying each other's company and the run. It was a four day weekend for the club and its affiliates. Zander was down the back of the line on his custom bike. Derek was thinking about becoming a prospect and was on as an affiliate too. Even Squick was following up in his car. Most of them were gathered at my table.

"How did you get that name?" Ashton was asking and I tuned into her conversation.

"It's actually kind of embarrassing," Squick was saying, "When I was a teenager, like seventeen to nineteen I used to do a bunch of stupid shit, things that would gross people the hell out," he turned red, "Anyway I used to squick people out, that's what 'squick' means. It stuck and I've had it ever since," he shrugged.

"What about you?" she leveled Reaver with her steady golden gaze.

"Well Sunshine," he leaned back in his seat, tipping the front legs off the floor as was his habit, "Once upon a time I was not a nice man," he said, "…and I like knives," he shrugged.

"That's it?" she asked.

"Don't make me spell it out for you Baby. I want you to still like me," he flashed her a grin and her gaze turned compassionate.

"What about you?" a club whore whose name I didn't know looked at me and I shrugged. Derek was happy to tell her.

"Trigger was the best damned Marine Corps sniper I've ever worked with. He was the trigger man, and so it stuck," Derek grinned. Ashton looked at him.

"You keep saying that… that you worked *with* him, I thought snipers worked alone," she was curious and I could tell she'd been that way a while.

"Derek was my spotter," I said.

"What's that?" the new girl asked and Ashton was watching me carefully.

"A spotter is a trained sniper too and goes out with a sniper in a two man sniper team to help the sniper by locating and identifying targets. He also gives the sniper information to adjust his fire on targets so he can improve his shot. As a spotter I'm also responsible for close range security meaning I protect the sniper from anybody that's found us so he can keep picking off targets," Derek explained. His knee was bouncing excitedly and Ashton's hand gripped mine under the table.

The difference between me and Derek was pretty vast but at the same time pretty simple. He wanted to go back and I wanted to stay. He loved reliving what were the glory days for him and what was pure hell for me. Ashton got that about me and I could see why. I kissed her temple, pulling her against me and she smiled.

"So what's your nickname? Spotter or Spot seems kinda lame," the new girl asked Derek, smiling.

I snorted. "Douchebag works for the most part," the table erupted in laughter and Derek threw his balled up napkin at me. I half dodged but it hit me. Ashton smiled and whispered something.

"What?" Derek asked her and she blushed.

"I said 'Loyal'."

"Loyal?" he asked.

"Yeah, if I had to call you anything I would call you Loyal." The table was quiet as people thought it over.

"Cool," someone said as people started to get up.

"See you at the lake Loyal," the new girl said over her shoulder and Derek looked at Ashton.

"Why?" he asked.

"Because you are," she shrugged as if it were obvious, which it kind of was to everyone that wasn't Derek.

"Come on Sunshine, he might figure it out by the time we get there," I said and we went up to the counter and paid for our meal.

Outside I bent down and kissed her to howls and cat calls and a round of cheers. She smiled against my mouth and her lips traced the words 'I love you' against mine.

Damn she didn't know how hard she made me.

The next two hours felt like two days with how badly I wanted to get her to the cabin and lodge and to a room of our own. The cabin had seven bedrooms and three baths, the lodge had twelve bedrooms, each with their own bathrooms. The cabin was reserved for the council. The two extra bedrooms reserved for the presidents of any MC's that joined us out here. The lodge was used for the other club members or the ranking men of any other MC's that joined us. In the event other MC's joined us, the rank and file club members, affiliates and friends of the clubs set up in camps on the grounds. It's the way we'd been doing it for the last five years.

We parked in front of the lodge in long lines and three bikes deep, all gleaming chrome and sleek lines. The walk down to the cabin was pretty short. It was further from the lakefront set off to the side like it was, but it was more private to facilitate any Church meetings.

I took Ashton by the hand and we followed Dragon and Dray down to the cabin, Doc and his Old Lady Chandra, and Reaver brought up the rear. We were a council of five. It's the way it had been in the beginning and it was the way it would stay. Odd number, always, to facilitate never deadlocking on an issue. One vote to sway. I took Ashton up to our room and set the heavy bag down.

"God I want to love you," I said pulling her against me, and I did, something fierce.

# CHAPTER 20

*Ashton*

"I need you to love me," I murmured against his mouth. I slipped the jacket from my shoulders and let it land in a heap on the floor. His joined it a second later.

"Fucking hell, shut the damned door before you get started," Dray demanded and our bedroom door shut.

Our mouths locked, hands scrambling to touch one another we danced in place. It was hard to get undressed with both of us feeding at one another like we were. He broke the kiss and hauled me up his body and I obediently wrapped my legs around his hips. I loved his strength. He was so *different*, using it to protect me, shelter me... It was extremely erotic and I grew too warm in my leather riding gear.

Ethan walked me backwards and sat down on the edge of the bed with me still twining around him like ivy. He lifted my thin tank top and camisole over my head and dropped them carelessly to the floor, his big hands smoothing over my heated skin. He peeled the straps of my bra down my arms and I pulled them free, promptly burying my hands in his hair to hold his mouth against mine. He chuckled, a low, deep sound that rubbed along my body thick as fur.

I gasped and he swallowed it, he broke the kiss so I could pull his shirt over his head, he raised his arms and once it was clear I dropped it forlorn beside mine. He crushed me to him, skin on skin and went for the clasp at the back of my bra. Once unsnapped he let his hands smooth up and down my back uninterrupted sending chills through me. I buried my hands in his hair, holding it off from our faces while we kissed passionately as if it might be our last chance at one another.

Our desire for one another grew to a fevered pitch. Ethan picked me up, standing in one powerful fluid movement, pivoting on his booted feet to lay me down on the scratchy hotelesque comforter. His hands went to my belt, fumbling both it and my fly open. He peeled the leather and lace of my pants and underwear off my body, pausing to tug my boots off my feet before dropping the whole mess with a thud.

I giggled but it was quickly stifled when he covered my body with his. I reached down between us to free him from his denim and cotton prison but he stopped me, preferring to do it himself. He didn't even bother with getting completely undressed, he slid the material down his hips and mouth sealed to mine positioned himself between my thighs.

His urgency startled me and flipped some primal switch in my brain. I arched my hips to meet him and we crashed together. I was wet and turned on but not quite as ready as he usually made me and so it was a tight fit, riding just this side of the line over into painful. I felt an erotic little pulse in my pussy and ground my hips just the way I knew he liked. He groaned and buried his face in the side of my neck, sucking gently, nipping with his teeth and I cried out.

That seemed to be the only invitation he needed. He drew back and surged forward powerfully invading my every sense. Touch, smell, taste, sight and hearing were all for him. He was warm, his body sliding against mine in a near punishing ebb and flow that had a sheen of sweat breaking out over our skins. He smelled of the wind and open road, of moving machine parts, rubber and asphalt but mostly the clean, crisp scent of the outdoors.

I kissed him and beneath the slight chemical tang of his e-cigarette he tasted like Ethan, hot and salty sweet, primal and male. He found that spot inside me and my mouth tore from his so I could arch provocatively against the swell of his muscular physique. A low wail of pure bliss escaped my throat, spilling from my lips to swirl out into the small room and it was met with masculine cheers faintly out in the rest of the large cabin.

I didn't care. I held onto my lover with legs and arms, twining myself as completely as I could around him. He smiled and nipped my shoulder and ground himself over that place inside me, exploiting it. One of his hands braced on the bed beside my face he levered himself up some and let the other one stroke down the center of my body. The pad of his thumb slicked through my folds and then began to torturously spiral around my engorged clit in a feather light touch that maddeningly set me on edge but did nothing to push me over.

"Please Ethan..." I begged breathlessly and he grinned playfully.

"Please what, Baby?" he asked, innocently.

"Please touch me harder," I begged and he levered himself up a bit more and gripped my shoulder, pulling me down onto his pounding cock as he simultaneously thrust a bit harder. Oh my god it felt good, but that's not what I meant and he knew it. I palmed his shoulders and tried to arch into his teasing thumb which was maddeningly close to but not touching that not so secret bundle of nerve endings.

"Please?" I begged.

"Please what?" he smiled, he was going to make me work for it, beg for it.

"Please touch my clit!?" I gasped.

"Oh, you want to come?" he asked me and I let out a frustrated wail. I couldn't deny it though, his little game had me coming apart at the seams... it was incredibly sexy at the same time it was incredibly maddening.

"Yes!" I cried desperately. I heard laughter out in the cabin and I colored furiously. Ethan, though... Ethan lit up. The fact that his brothers were out there listening to us was turning him on, making this better for him and I was surprised to find it was me too. I felt bold, sexy and beautiful... but I didn't have time to dwell on it. The need for release was becoming a sharp and grinding thing, grating across every nerve ending, I couldn't take it anymore.

"Say it Baby. Tell me you want to come and I promise to make it good for you," he was out of breath but his stamina wasn't even close to flagging and I knew that if I didn't say it, I didn't ask, then he would keep me like this indefinitely.

"Ethan I want to come, please! Please make me come!" I begged and he smiled the most beautiful victorious smile I'd ever seen on him and gave me just what I needed. His thumb slid over those few millimeters and he stroked lazily across my clit. Sparks of pleasure ignited the inferno that swept through my body and blasted me apart into a million tiny pieces. I screamed with the sheer mind blowing intensity of it and Ethan jerked, stilling inside me and for a brief second I thought I may have hurt him but the pure bliss that came over his face told me just the opposite.

My voice died in my throat and I lay beneath him, completely boneless carried away on the current of our pleasure and mutual satisfaction. Ethan's legs trembled and he let himself down gently over me. I wound my arms around his shoulders and held him to me as we both panted, our mingling sweat cooling on our bodies. Loud and rowdy cheers came from the other side of our bedroom door but I was too spent to even blush let alone work up enough energy to be embarrassed.

"In case you haven't noticed, I'm a bit of an exhibitionist," he panted into the side of my neck, he dropped his lips to my shoulder and placed a kiss there.

"I think I just figured that out," I panted.

"You okay?" he asked and concern clouded his expression when I didn't answer right away.

"You know, I think I am, but mostly because I know and trust everyone out there," I said speculatively. Ethan grinned.

"Can we have a conversation about some of 'em potentially watching someday?" he asked and I could tell he was serious, I could also tell the idea *really* appealed to him when I felt him stir where he was still inside me.

"No cameras or anything right? Nobody else joining in or trying to?" I asked frowning.

"No! Nothing like that, I wouldn't do that to you Babe," he said smoothing my hair out of my face. He looked me in the eyes and his voice when it came was low and intense.

"It's not about humiliation or making you uncomfortable, I'm not into that shit. It's about heightening the experience, showing you the fuck off. You're beautiful and I love you and I want you to feel beautiful and sexy, that and I'm kind of a dick... I want some of these guys to see what they can't have," he grinned at the last part and it was so boyish and open that it made my heart light and I laughed.

"It's a far cry from knowing some of them are listening to knowing they have their eyes on me," I said thoughtfully. Ethan didn't say anything.

"Can I think about it?" I asked softly, surprised that the idea wasn't totally unappealing in fact I felt a little thrill of adrenaline just at the notion.

"Yeah Babe, sure. You think about it as long as you like. No pressure, it's just something I like to do. Can't help it. I'm a kinky bastard that way but I get that my kink might not be your kink and it's not like it's something I need, just something I like to do at the club house or on lake runs with people I know and trust," he shrugged and I think it was a mark of how well we fit together that I completely understood where he was coming from.

We kissed and I filed this new development away for later. Ethan withdrew from me and slid to the side, awkwardly kicking off his boots and pants. I laughed and he kissed me silent, drawing it out, bringing my body back to a slow rolling simmer.

"Again?" he asked softly and I nodded and so we made love again only slower and more deliberate this time. We napped for a short time in each other's arms before someone started pounding on the door.

"You guys are not spending the entire weekend locked in there!" Reaver yelled and Ethan and I laughed. Ethan looked at me to make sure it was okay, I nodded and hid behind his much larger body.

"Come on in Reav!" he yelled and Reaver opened the door, stepped in and shut it behind him like we weren't just on top of the covers wrapped up in each other naked. He was totally cool about it. He did give me a good once over and smiled.

"Freshly fucked looks good on you Sunshine," was his only comment.

"What's going on out there?" Ethan asked and Reaver stood there and crossed his arms.

"Everyone is heading up to the lodge for some grub. Sun is still out and will be for a couple more hours. Hotter than hell so wear shorts," he looked us over one more time eyes lingering on my ass and a slow grin spread across his face. "Damn, hotter 'n hell in here too," he said and ducked out the door. Funny thing was I didn't feel gross… I felt… appreciated, sexy, like some kind of siren and it felt pretty good. After a near lifetime of not being good enough I felt pretty and desirable. It had me thinking.

"Shower and food?" Ethan asked. I nodded and he smiled. He stood up and stretched, and I drooled a little. God he was beautiful. Gorgeous in fact, all masculine planes and angles, body ridged in all the right places. He bent and scooped me up shrieking, throwing me over his shoulder cave man style and I laughed. I struggled a little and he swatted me on the ass, the light sting making me yip.

Before I could think to protest he was out the door and striding up the hallway, ducking us into the bathroom. I heard Dragon's familiar masculine chuckle from further up the hall as Ethan shut the door behind us and I blushed furiously.

"Love you, Babe," he said with a rakish grin and started the shower. I put my hands on my hips and tried to put on a stern look but failed miserably.

We showered quickly and wrapped in the towels provided. Back in the room I donned my swimsuit which was a white bikini with cherries on it and pulled on a pair of olive green shorts over the bottoms. The shorts were *very* short and made my legs look longer than they actually were. I slid my feet into some white flip flops and found Ethan eyeing me from across the room. A pair of old dessert camo fatigues cut off just below the knee hung off his lean hips, that delicious muscular V shape disappearing into the waistband made me want to go peel the shorts off him.

"We keep lookin' at each other like this we're not going to make it to the party," his voice was low and sultry and did things low in my body, but I really wanted to join the others so I put my sunglasses on my head and went for the door. Ethan shrugged his feet into a pair of black Nike skids and we went out, his hands resting lightly on my shoulders.

The cabin was deserted and we trudged down the drive towards the back deck of the lodge which was two stories. Underneath the deck, tables were lined out in the shade for sitting. Up on the large wooden structure's second story the food and drink was being passed out. We went up and got our plates.

When my plate had a sufficient amount of barbeque ribs, green salad, and an assortment of fruit we went back down stairs. I carried napkins and silverware, Ethan had two bottles of beer and a third bottle of hard lemonade for me. We found a seat at the table with Reaver, Chandra, Doc, Derek, Andy and Zander.

"Came up for air?" Doc asked smiling and I blushed, Chandra smacked him in the shoulder.

"No seriously, that was hot to hear you two," she said, unlit cigarette bobbing between her lips. She raised a Bic and lit the end sucking in a long drag.

"Thanks," I mumbled, blushing deeply and cast my eyes down to my food. I could feel Reaver's eyes on me as I ate. Ethan seemed perfectly comfortable and I thought about it. If he wasn't embarrassed why should I be? I mean it wasn't like I was ashamed of making love to him… I looked up as Dragon settled his bulk next to me. He cleared his throat and I looked up.

"I was wonderin' if I could ask you somethin'," he said.

"Sure," I replied and set down my fork. I wiped my fingers on my napkin and gave him my full attention.

"Anybody tell you how the lake runs got started?" he asked gruffly.

"No, just that you do two, one in spring and one at the end of the summer…" I said.

"Well the summer run we've been doing longer but this one we're on now, the spring run, is our memorial run. Tilly, that was my wife, she died around this time of year along with some of our brothers. Happened five years ago. We been doing this ever since as a way to sort of celebrate their lives and to remember." The big man choked up and I did the only thing I could think of, I hugged one of his massive arms and waited for him to ask me whatever it was. I was already sure I would say yes. Dragon took a deep breath and pressed on…

"The last night we're here, that'll be Sunday night, we do a memorial service. Send some paper lanterns out on the lake, say a few words, that kind of thing. I was wondering if you'd sing something," he looked at me anxiously and I smiled.

"Of course, I'd be honored," I said, even though my stomach was doing back flips at the thought of singing in front of so many people.

"What would you like me to sing?" I asked.

"Whatever you think is best, just not Amazing Grace. Tilly hated that song," the look he gave me was so grateful it melted my heart. Dragon kissed the top of my head and I let his arm go.

"Thanks Sunshine," he said and moved off, lumbering through the tables, the club's logo on the back of his jacket stark on the plane of his broad back.

"Thanks Baby," Ethan said softly. The sentiment was echoed around the table.

"Of course," I murmured and finished my meal.

Later on we were gathered around a large bonfire on the beach closer to the cabin. I leaned against Ethan's chest, warm in the circle of his arms and stared into the flames, contemplating what I would sing in two nights. I settled on something and happy with my choice tuned into the conversation around me.

"Can't wait to go shootin' tomorrow," someone was saying.

"Oh yeah? Think you're gonna take Trig?" someone asked.

"Gonna try," he said. I looked up at Ethan but he was looking at the man, that cold gleam in his eyes. He'd gone still, so very still I wasn't even sure his heart beat in his chest. He'd slipped into his own head and was looking the man who'd spoken over. Reaver jumped the log Ethan was siting against and settled in next to us.

"Got one of the prospects motoring across at dawn to set up the targets," he proclaimed. I looked out into the dark. Across the lake from us was a high bluff and in front of the bluff a strip of beach but it was awfully far away… like ridiculously far away.

"How big are the targets?" I asked.

"We use melons. Closest thing to a human head," Reaver grinned and I quailed.

"How can you hit something the size of a melon from the beach here?" I asked.

"Oh, we don't shoot from the beach, baby, we shoot from the deck," Ethan said softly and the cadence of his voice was strange. Low and concentrated, almost mechanical. He wasn't Ethan anymore, *this* was Trigger. I shivered and that seemed to snap him out of it.

"You cold?" he asked and just like that, my Ethan was back.

"No," I said and he frowned. He kissed the top of my head and cuddled me in closer anyway and I sighed, a happy woman.

"We have a shooting range set up out that way for hand guns and to throw knives too," Reaver grinned and indicated a path leading back into the woods alongside the lodge opposite the cabin. I nodded.

"I want to teach you gun safety and how to shoot this weekend," Ethan said, "We got 'em in the house, you need to learn how to be safe around them," he proclaimed and I didn't argue, I thought it was a good idea.

"Okay," I said softly.

We went to bed around midnight, the day promising to be a busy one. I got up before Ethan and went for a swim about the time that two prospects loaded into a motor boat with supplies and took off across the lake. I came back up onto shore and Ethan folded me into a towel.

"Ready to watch your man show off his sniping skills?" he asked me. I blinked.

"Are you sure you're okay to?" I asked.

"Yeah Babe, I love shooting. Don't get to very much anymore. Enough booze and sex tonight and the nightmares should stay away. Up for it?" he asked grinning.

"Well when you put it that way," I said sarcastically, rolling my eyes, but I let him lead me up to the deck. I quickly realized I was the only woman present.

"Ready? One two three!" Reaver, Zander and Dray muscled a wide picnic table up against the railing, and Ethan climbed up on it, laying down on his stomach.

"Yep, that'll do," he bounded up and started assembling a weapon from what looked like a pile of little pieces. Derek was fiddling with a bunch of scopes next to him. Reaver came up behind me where I stood dripping on the deck, it was still cool right now but was promising to be a hot day. He hugged me and I leaned back into him.

"What are they doing?" I asked in a whisper.

"Trigger's putting his rifle together and Loyal is calibrating equipment, he's going to spot for him," I let Reaver keep me warm while I watched what my lover and his friend were doing. I swallowed hard. Ethan was methodical, more sure than I had ever seen him, totally aware and it was a little frightening to watch. He positioned the rifle, a nasty piece of work, on a stand on the table and did some final checks. Derek set up a scope on a tripod next to Ethan and both of them got onto the table.

Derek started rattling off some technical jargon at Ethan in a low controlled voice. I watched them fascinated. Ethan was so still that if I didn't know any better, I would say he'd perished. Reaver handed me some binoculars and I tried to see across the lake to what they were aiming at. Even with the aid, it still looked far away. A line of melons on what looked like fence posts sat on the spit across the water. Derek gave a command and the rifle cracked, I jumped. Ethan called his shot and I watched the melon explode in a fine pink mist. I felt chilled to the bone.

"That was a catastrophic brain injury if I ever saw one," Reaver said grinning and I looked up to see him peering through a set of binoculars of his own. The shot was impressive but also terrifying. Ethan lined up his next one and Derek walked him through it. I didn't watch this time.

Both Derek and Ethan were emotionless, quick and efficient and it was scary. Reaver hugged me around the shoulders and smoothed a hand up and down my towel covered arm. He smiled down at me reassuring and I gave him a brave smile back. I watched Trigger take the place of my beloved and marveled at his skill. He didn't miss a single shot and I couldn't even fathom how far away we were from the targets.

Finally, he stood up, and began disassembling and cleaning his weapon. His cold silver eyes met mine and something passed between us. His look said "I'm a killer," but in the same breath it was like the sun came out behind his gaze and it said "...and I'll use it to protect you." When he was done with putting everything away he came to me and wrapped me up in his warm embrace.

"I love you, Baby," he said.

"I love you, too," I answered.

"Scare you?" he asked.

"Yes," I said honestly and I felt his heart drop through his thin tee shirt.

"We okay?" he asked tentatively kissing the top of my head and I could tell he feared the answer. I looked up into his ghostly silver eyes and smiled.

"Absolutely," I said, and I meant it and I could see the apprehension drain out of him. I could accept this part of him. I would accept this part of him, even as frightening and alien as it was to me.

"I think you'll feel better once I put a gun in your hands and you know how they operate," he said judiciously.

"Okay," I said softly. He kissed me. People had crowded the beach, watching by the time he was finished and I saw Shelly waving at me.

"Go on, have some girl time," he said grinning and I smiled back grateful.

She and I slathered on her Goth block sunscreen and sat out on towels talking. Chandra joined us tanning and the dark clouds brought on watching Ethan shoot slowly drifted away. Several others took their shots at sniping throughout the morning but once again, Ethan was declared the best shot. We did breakfast and went and watched Reaver and several others compete at throwing knives. Reaver was just as terrifying to watch with a blade as Ethan had been behind the scope of his sniper's gun. Reaver was deadly accurate and as feral as anything I had ever seen and that included Chadwick in one of his more dispassionate moods.

When the knife throwing was done and Reaver declared the

winner; Ethan, Reaver and Dragon took me aside.

"Time to learn how to shoot," Ethan said.

The three of them went over gun safety. How to always check and see if a firearm was loaded, how to always assume one was loaded when I found one. They went through taking one apart and putting it back together. How to load it and make it ready to fire and finally how to aim properly.

Ethan showed me how to fire, how to start low, let the kick bring my arms up for the next shot and so on. Most importantly, he taught me how to breathe. I fired two clips, or thirty shots, and got more than half onto the paper target and more than half of those in the black area. Everyone agreed that it wasn't bad for a first time shooter and a girl but I think they were just trying to keep me from feeling bad.

Lunch was served and Ethan went swimming with me. Finally, it was time for dinner and the guys were getting amped up and excited again. Talking animatedly about who was going to take who and whatnot.

"What's going on?" I asked.

"Saturday night's fight night," Reaver explained, grinning.

"Oh," I said and looked at Ethan, he smiled sheepishly.

"It's tradition," he explained.

A circle was being drawn on the beach and I realized they were seriously going to fight… I paled.

"Ethan, no," I whispered.

"Hey, it's okay babe. No one ever gets anything other than a minor cut or bruise," he kissed me softly and despite my misgivings I nodded cautiously.

"Besides, most of us are too drunk to feel it anyways," Reaver said grinning impishly and I rolled my eyes.

"That is *so* comforting!" I exclaimed.

True to his word, by the time men started squaring off inside the circle in the sand ringed with tiki torches, most of them were too lit to actually land a punch. Finally Dragon and the only guy in the MC big enough to match him, a man they called Moose, entered into the ring.

Both were shirtless and both looked pretty sober as compared to the others who had faced off. They grappled, they punched they kneed each other in the face and they were just scary brutal. I quailed, and became frightened for Moose at one point. Dragon punched him a good one to the jaw and Moose sprawled out on his back into the sand. Dragon let out a primal bellow at the crowd and I blinked. Now I knew where he'd gotten the nick name Dragon. He *looked* like a Dragon when he let out that bellow, he certainly fought like one, too.

The crowd cheered and Ethan kissed the top of my head. Moose was dragged off to the side where Doc was tending to the fighters and I was glad he was here. Data got into the ring, he was serving as the de facto announcer.

"Who wants to see a marine in action?" he asked the crowd and I sighed.

The crowd went nuts.

"Who wants to see *two* marines in action!?"

The crowd went double nuts.

Derek got into the ring and Ethan squared off across from him. Both of them wore just their shorts. Ethan's hair was pulled back into a loose pony tail, the firelight gleamed satiny off their skins. Ethan's pale, freckles brought out by the sun across his broad shoulders. Derek turning a deep tan. I closed my eyes and decided I loved Ethan but that now would be a very good time to use the bathroom. I waved at him and indicated my need to pee in an unladylike and fairly childish manner.

He laughed, pointed at me, blew me a kiss and made a shooing motion with his hand. I shook my head, rolled my eyes dramatically, dipped a curtsey and went in the direction of the cabin. I could hear cheering and jeering from the shore all the way up on the porch and slipped into the building. I used the restroom washed my hands and was on my way out the cabin door when I ran headlong into a solid wall of muscle covered in black leather.

"Oh! I'm sorry!" I cried as hands gripped my upper arms to keep me from falling. I backed into the wall to the side of the door and looked up into Dray's ominous dark eyes.

"Hey, Sunshine," he slurred my nickname and the way it came out sounded more like 'Shunshine'. He hadn't let me go yet and I stilled.

"So, you're Trigger's Old Lady now, huh?" he said, a cruel grin twisting his lips. I scoffed.

"I'm not old!" I said laughing lightly. He cocked his head to the side.

"So you don't belong to Trig?" he asked and swayed a little unsteady on his feet.

"Ethan wants me to be my own person," I said brightly, a creeping dread stealing between my shoulder blades. Dray dipped his head to bring us eye to eye.

"If you don't belong to Trigger than you're anybody's meat," he bit the last word off in my face and my heart sank.

"Dray, let me go, you're scaring me," I tried.

"I'm a scary guy," he said and crushed his mouth over mine. I recoiled as he forced his tongue past my teeth, the bitter bite of stale booze and cigarettes flooded my mouth and I winced. I tried to shove him but he was bigger and outweighed me. I made a noise of protestation and felt hot angry tears well in my eyes.

I wanted him off me! I tried to bring my knee up between his legs but he deflected. I struggled and screamed into his mouth and finally I bit savagely down on his lower lip. He yelled and jerked his head back and I tasted blood.

"Stupid bitch!" His hand flew out and landed in a stinging slap across the left side of my face. I opened my mouth and screamed in fear, the sound long and loud and piteously high and I prayed someone, anyone would hear it in time...

Beefy hands covered in a smattering of dark hair across the knuckles captured Dray by the shoulders and pulled him backwards off of me. He flew down the steps and landed hard on his back and I looked down into the tempestuous eyes of his father.

*Oh no.* My heart sank.

# CHAPTER 21

*Trig*

It didn't even occur to me anything was wrong. One second I'm throwing a jab at Derek and the next Dray is sprawling at my feet. I looked up and over from the direction where he came from to see Dragon, and he was fucking heated. Just behind him Ashton stood hugging herself, looking dazed, eyes wide and glimmering with tears, the outline of a red handprint across her jaw and cheek.

Derek caught me in the mouth with a half pulled punch and I leaned back from it. I was already moving in Ashton's direction.

"Babe, what happened?" I asked her and she launched herself at me, small arms going around my waist where she could reach. She sobbed into my chest and Dragon looked sorrowful.

"Dude, what the fuck happened to my girl!?" I asked him. A hush fell over the crowd and no one dared to breathe.

"I happened," the voice came from behind me and I turned slowly with Ashton in my arms. Dray stood in the center of the ring. Reaver was suddenly beside us and I passed Ashton into his arms.

"Ethan," she said but her small frightened voice was carried on the wind because I was already launching myself at Dray.

"No women, no children!" Dragon called behind me his deep voice intoning, "Dray tried to force himself on Trigger's girl. I came up on it with my own eyes! Trigger take your retribution. Boy you take your lesson!" but I was already laying into Dray.

I punched him in his god damn mouth which was already bleeding and he went to his knees in the sand. I kicked out and connected with his chest and the air left him in a whoosh. Angry shouts broke out around us as I lit into him. It was Ashton that finally stopped me. The fucker had attacked her, *hit her* and there she was, throwing herself over his head and shoulders in an effort to protect his worthless ass with her small body.

"Ethan stop!" she screamed and I did. I wasn't about to hurt my girl. Dray groaned and lay there which was good. Fucker better stay down.

"Church in fifteen. I need a fucking proxy," Dragon said bitterly, looking down dispassionately at his son.

The crowd dissipated and I went to my knees in the sand and pulled Ashton to me. She let me.

"Why'd you stop me?" I asked, chest heaving.

"Because it was enough," she said, voice strangled.

"No. Not enough. Never enough for anyone that lays a hand on my girl," I said and picked her up. Doc and two prospects moved in to deal with Dray's worthless ass who was coughing into the sand. Ashton looked down at Dray with pity in her eyes and I couldn't fathom it. Later though. It would have to be later. I took us up to the cabin and got her inside and into the light. The handprint on her face was already fading and didn't look like it was going to bruise.

"What happened?" I asked her.

"I was coming out of the cabin and I ran into Dray, like literally ran face first into him. He grabbed onto my arms to keep me from falling over and I ended up back against the wall," she took a deep breath and let it out slowly, dried her tears and took several more breaths before continuing.

"He said something about me being old and I laughed and said I wasn't old, I'm only thirty... Then he said something about me belonging to you like I was your property and I said no, that you let me be my own person," she looked at me, golden eyes bright with tears. We had a full council of five in here. The next man down the line taking Dray's place. Reaver sat next to me and Ashton on the couch. He put a hand on her knee to steady her.

I ran a hand through my hair. I knew what was up, what's more I knew it was my fault. I'd kept Ashton ignorant all this time... I grimaced.

"Then he said if I didn't belong to anyone that I was anyone's meat and he kissed me. I tried to push him off but he's bigger'n me," she sniffed and tears welled. Doc laughed.

"Sunshine, everybody is bigger'n you," he said and low chuckles swept the room.

"I know," she said dejectedly.

"Then what happened, Sugar?" Reaver asked gently.

"I bit him," she said and I was proud of her. She sighed and went on.

"You should have seen the hurt in his eyes. Then he got mad to cover it and he slapped me and I screamed and then Dragon was there," she looked up at Dragon.

"I'm so sorry," she said and he shook his head.

"Not your fault, Chica," he said.

"No, it's mine," I sighed, "I didn't explain to Ashton what an Old Lady is or what being an Old Lady means. I didn't want to put any kind of tag of ownership on her like her douchebag ex," I looked at her. "You're nobody's property, Baby. Least of all mine, but for all intents and purposes when it comes to the club or any other biker, you're my Old Lady to keep you safe. I should have told you," I said. I searched her face while she processed things.

"I am yours," she said finally, quietly, "Not because of stupid club politics or because you want me to be… I'm yours because *I* want to be yours. I have been for a while now," she gave me a brave little half smile and I wondered if she was ever going to stop amazing me.

"This is all very touching but what are we going to do with Dray?" Data asked acting as Dray's proxy.

"I'm satisfied. I set everybody in this up for failure," I said miserably, "I put myself up for judgment and punishment under our code," Ashton hugged me tighter and looked at me stricken.

"All right," Dragon sighed… "Two issues. Dray's behavior and Trig's lack of common sense for thinking with his pud," Dragon smirked at me. It was a fair jab and seeing as he just let me beat the brakes off his only child, I could deal.

"I vote 'satisfied' on Dray," I said.

"I second," Reaver said.

"Aye," Doc.

"Aye," Data.

"Nay, but I'm out voted. So entered," Dragon knocked on the coffee table.

"I vote no punishment on Trig," Data.

"Yay, no punishment," Reaver.

"No punishment," Doc and Dragon together.

"Looks like I'm outvoted," I smiled. Ashton was quiet on my lap.

"So entered," Dragon knocked.

"I need a fucking drink," Data said and pushed to his feet.

"I'm with you," Doc said and they went out.

"Where's Dray? Is he okay?" Ashton asked.

"Yeah, he'll be sore in the morning though," Dragon commented dryly and pushed to his feet he smoothed some hair out of Ashton's face and she looked up at him bewildered. "I love my boy but I can admit when he's done wrong. I'm sorry he did that to you, he gets real screwed up around the time of his momma's death," Dragon sighed.

"I could see the hurt," Ashton said softly, "Dray is an intense person but I don't think he's a bad one, can't be with a daddy like you," she smiled up and Dragon grinned down at her.

"Tryin' to butter me up, Sunshine?" he asked.

"Never know when it might come in handy," she said softly and he laughed.

"Yer a trip," he said and went back out into the night leaving Ashton, me, and Reaver.

"You two going to fuck?" Reaver asked lazily.

"Maybe," I said, gazing at my girl, who was mine because *she* wanted to be mine.

"Why?" she asked softly.

"'Cause I wanna watch, duh," Reaver gave her a lazy grin and she laughed.

"You're incorrigible," she said.

"No idea what that means," he said shrugging, "But it sounds badass so I'm in," he kicked his feet up onto the coffee table and put his hand down his shorts Al Bundy style.

"Have you watched Ethan before?" she asked softly.

Reaver laughed, "Yeah, we've even shared a girl or two in the past," he said and I smacked him in the shoulder for oversharing. Ashton didn't look outraged or disgusted though, she looked thoughtful.

"You want to watch me and Ethan," she said finally. Reaver rolled his eyes up and over to look into hers.

"Ashton, you're gorgeous. The only thing better than watching Trigger's cock disappear inside you would be watching *my own* go there," he said frankly. I rolled my eyes.

"Tact, brother, you need to learn some," I said.

"No, I appreciate his honesty," Ashton shrugged.

"Does that mean I get to join in?" he asked hopeful and she laughed.

"I'm still trying to wrap my head around letting another man watch me while I have sex with my boyfriend. Slow down!" She cuddled into my chest then looked up at me worried. I was still glowing from her calling me her boyfriend. Juvenile but true.

"Wouldn't you get jealous?" She asked.

"Of what? Reaver is my best friend and you just said, you're my girl because you want to be... what is there to be jealous of?" I asked her. She squeezed her eyes shut. Reaver looked at me like I'd grown a second head and I shrugged.

"Never said I was consistent Bro," I told him thinking back on the day in the 'Y', Ashton's words echoing in my head. *I'm yours because I want to be yours...*

"I can't believe I'm having this conversation," she muttered.

"Hey," Reaver nudged her leg with his shoulder, "That's all this is, is a conversation. Just let me know if you ever want to go there and like I said, I'm game. Leastways until I get a girl of my own which I see happening, oh say, never," he grinned but it was sharp and cold with self-deprecation.

"Wait, so you two have done this before, does that mean," she trailed off but we both laughed picking up at the same time what she was putting down.

"No, we're not into each other. We're into *girls*. We just know how to share," I shrugged and she chewed her lip. I was growing hard just thinking about it. Didn't do devil's threesomes very often but when I had they had always been fun times. Reaver shifted in his seat and I could tell he was just as hot for the idea as I was. Still it was up to my girl.

"Would you be okay with just watching?" she asked tentatively.

"Sure. I'm'a stroke it though," he said, she smiled.

"I don't know. I still have to think about it," she said chewing her lip.

"No worries, Princess." Reaver said getting up and going for the kitchen, "You want a beer?" He asked.

I was watching Ashton's thoughtful face, she was really considering this...

"Sorry what?" I asked.

"Beer?"

"Yeah," I said and he brought me one.

He flopped back down onto the couch and held his bottle against the fading red mark on Ashton's cheek. She closed her eyes and sighed in relief.

"That feels good," she murmured.

Reaver smiled at me and I smiled at him. Maybe she would, maybe she wouldn't but I thought she'd had enough excitement for one night.

"Tired?" I asked her.

"Yeah," she said softly.

"I think you need some cuddle time, Girl. No sex. Just a man sammich with you as the filling. Come on," Reaver got up and picked her up out of my lap. I trusted him so I let him. We went into our room and shut the door. Reaver set Ashton down and she rooted around in the bag for one of my tee shirts.

"Uhm, do you mind turning around?" she asked Reaver and he took a pull off his beer.

"Yeah, but I'd do anything for my best friend's girl," he said and grinned before turning around. I laughed at him. She stripped out of her swimsuit and shorts and pulled my shirt over her head. God I was hard. I resolutely told my cock to shut up and Ashton sighed.

"Okay," she got up into the bed which was queen sized. It was going to be a tight fit but that wasn't a bad thing.

I stripped down to my boxers and got in on one side. Ashton curled tight to my side, one leg going over mine, her head on my shoulder and I sighed, at peace. Reaver left his basketball shorts on, knowing him he was commando anyways, and set his beer on the dresser. He got in behind Ashton and spooned her kissing her where her shoulder met her neck.

"This is nice," she said sleepily a moment later. Reaver's eye's sparkled over her shoulder at me his grin hidden from view but I knew it was there. We fell asleep, the three of us and were comfortable. It wasn't awkward and I was in awe of my girl one more time.

The next morning I woke up to a thoughtful looking Reaver, chin propped in one hand, the other caressing the dip in Ashton's side before the swell of her hip. He had his hand under the hem of my shirt against her skin, I raised an eyebrow and he sighed extracting the hand and settling it on top of the thin cotton material. I let the eyebrow go back down.

Ashton was warm and soft where she was fetched up against me, her breathing steady and even. She slept like the dead, I swear to god, and it was a mark of how much the day before had taken out of her that she was asleep now while Reaver and I were both awake. She was *always* up before me.

"What 'cha thinkin' man?" I asked quietly.

"You know she's your one, don't you?" he asked.

"Yeah," I murmured, careful not to wake her.

"So it surprises the hell out of me that you'd be willing to share," he said and it was his turn to raise an eyebrow.

"Only 'cause it's you. Anyone else asked I'd punch them in their god damned mouth." Reaver laughed softly but cut it short when Ashton stirred.

"You almost *did* punch me in my god damned mouth so why the change of heart?" he asked, after she settled, expression darkening.

"You know her douchebag ex is the only other man she's had?" I asked him.

"Seriously?" he asked.

"Yeah. She hasn't had a whole lot of positive experiences,

sexually or otherwise. Who the fuck am I to deny her any experimentation?" I kissed the top of her head and stroked a hand through her auburn tresses.

"Doesn't have anything to do with her sayin' she's yours?" he grinned at me, insightful bastard. I grinned back. Okay yeah, so that had taken care of a big chunk of my insecurity. I glossed over it and said,

"She seemed turned on at the thought of being watched."

"I was surprised she contemplated letting us share," he said.

"I'm adventurous that way," she murmured and opened one eye.

Reaver laughed and said, "Busted."

"Put your hand back where it was. It was warm and I liked it," she complained.

"She always this bossy?" he asked and did as she told him.

"I get it from him," she said before I could answer and both of us laughed at her.

"How you feelin'?" Reaver asked.

"Mmm warm and safe," she answered, cuddling between us.

"I love you," I murmured and kissed her forehead.

"I love you, too," she said softly.

"Anybody love me?" Reaver pouted.

"Are you in the bed with us?" I asked.

"Good point," he said and took his hand back out from under Ashton's shirt and stretched luxuriously.

"I gotta piss," he rolled out of the bed and left the room. Ashton sat up and stripped the shirt off over her head in one fluid movement. She reached into my boxers and brought me out and I put my hands behind my head and watched her, amused.

"What 'cha up to, Baby?" I asked. She smiled sweetly and straddled me, bending to kiss me. I held her hair back with one hand and kept the other behind my head comfortably. She broke the kiss and reached down between us and slipped me inside her.

Holy god, she was wet and ready. My eyes slipped shut and I palmed the top of her thigh with the hand I had out.

"He's coming back," I whispered softly.

"Do you want me to stop?" she asked gently.

"You sure?" I asked.

"Yes and no," she answered honestly and rocked her hips. I sucked in a breath and let it out through clenched teeth. Fuck she was turning me on and working my wood. The door opened and closed; Reaver looked up and froze.

"Holy shit," he said. Ashton turned calmly and said "You can watch," Reaver grinned and went over to the armchair in the corner.

"I'm down," he said, smiling.

I looked up at my beautiful, brave, sexy girl and closed my eyes and just concentrated on the feel of her for a moment. I opened them and leveled her with my gaze. She was staring at me.

"Ashton," I said.

"Yes?" she answered.

"Ride me," I ordered calmly and she smiled faintly and did what I told her. She rolled her hips and arched her back. I grasped her hips and she threw back her head and gasped. I heard Reaver let out a shuddering sigh across the room and glanced his direction. He had his cock in his fist and was stroking it, his eyes lovingly roaming over the line of Ashton's lean body as she slowly rose and fell. I felt a primal growl escape my throat and raised my hips to meet her downward momentum, shoving my cock even deeper up into her. She felt like heaven, hot and unbelievably slick against my cock. She moaned and I smiled.

"Make yourself feel good baby, I got all day," I said and I did. I really *could* watch her like this all day. She held her hair up off her neck and used her legs to push herself up and let herself drop back down. I smoothed my hands up her sides and cupped her small breasts, teasing the nipples, pinching and rolling them between thumb and forefingers. She cried out and I heard Reaver moan from the corner.

I loved being watched, I loved that someone else was getting something out of watching my girl move above me. I felt my cock swell just that much more inside her and she let her hands drop to my chest.

"Oh god Ethan!" she gasped, leaning forward. I surged my hips forward and slid up into her harder.

"Oh, man. That's nice," Reaver commented and I realized he could see me sliding in and out of her better from this angle.

"Touch yourself baby, put those fingers on your clit," I commanded gently and she reached down between us.

"Oh god, yeah," Reaver said when she threw back her head her fingers playing against the front of her body. I could feel her constricting around my cock. She was close, really close and I didn't know how much longer I could hold off.

"Oh god, oh god, ohgodohgodohgod!" Her voice rose into this epic blissed out wail and she shattered beautifully above me. Her pussy spasmed around my dick and I felt my balls tighten. I drove into her once, twice and let go. I came gently inside her, stars sparking at the edges of my vision. I only vaguely recall Reaver making a satisfied grunt in the corner as he spilled too. Ashton lay against my chest, panting softly and I cradled her to me.

"You okay, Baby?" I asked softly, with no little emotion edging my voice. God she was fucking incredible, fearless and fucking gorgeous.

"That was... uhm... wow..." she panted out and I smiled.

"I second that motion," Reaver said and she laughed.

"I don't know if I should feel bad that you just watched..." she said.

"No, god no! You two are fucking hot as hell," he said.

I raised her up and kissed her long and languorous. I was so proud of her for being brave, for flying in the face of convention, for trying things outside her comfort zone... but truth be told that was the magic of a lake run. People did things here they would never normally do. What happened on a lake run usually stayed on a lake run. It was like a mini Vegas experience.

"Again," she whispered into my mouth and I smiled. That was my girl...

# CHAPTER 22

*Ashton*

I felt amazing. Sexy, beautiful, empowered and all because I'd made love to one man and let another watch. Reaver stayed a respectful distance but I could feel his eyes on me caressing every curve with his gaze as he stroked his cock in his hand.

I was so turned on that I asked Ethan if we could go again. He smiled against my mouth and sat up, with me still straddling his boxer clad hips all though admittedly the crisp cotton was pretty well soaked from us.

"You want Reaver to stay?" Ethan asked me and I looked over to him. I held out my hand and he raised his eyebrows. He got up and came over to me. I turned my face up and asked him with my eyes to kiss me.

"You got a condom bro?" he asked Ethan.

"Don't need one as long as you're clean," I murmured and his eyebrows drew down into a frown.

"Why not?" he asked.

"Sterile," I whispered and I felt Ethan's hands rub up and down my body in comfort and reassurance.

"I'm sorry," Reaver said and brought his lips gently to mine. I carefully wrapped my hand around him. He was soft and needed some coaxing to get hard again. Ethan had slipped out of me but I could feel his cock stiffening between us.

Ethan sucked a nipple into his mouth and I gasped into Reaver's, he moaned back into mine and grew harder in my hand. I stroked him and he thrust into my hand, the moisture from his come coated my palm and made it easier for him to slick through my fingers. He broke the kiss and threw back his head, Ethan turned me and devoured my mouth with his and I moaned a little helplessly into it. Ethan broke the kiss after a time and whispered for me to get on my knees in the middle of the bed. He slipped off and took off his boxers. He and Reaver murmured back and forth and the bed dipped on either side as they both climbed on.

"Do you trust us?" Ethan asked me.

"Yes," I murmured and I did.

"Okay, Babe."

Reaver got in front of me and Ethan behind me. He slicked the head of his cock through my folds and sank into me slowly, deeply...

"Will you suck me?" Reaver asked softly and I nodded, taking him into my mouth. He moaned and held my hair gently back from my face. I rolled my eyes and tipped my head back to look up the length of his body into his deep blue eyes. He gasped and the look of adoration he cast down on me warmed me to my toes. I moaned around Reaver's long cock as Ethan gently and carefully thrust into me from behind. God it felt so *good*.

Their hands, caressed and massaged their way across my body and I closed my eyes, and just felt them. Reaver pulled his hips back and freed himself from my mouth. I swallowed and closed my eyes as Ethan slipped free of my vagina. I felt their loss keenly. Ethan propped his back against the headboard and pulled me against him, my back to his front. He held my arms across my chest and wrapped me in his embrace. He whispered encouraging things in my ear, telling me I was beautiful and how much I pleased him.

Reaver knelt between my thighs and Ethan claimed my mouth in a kiss. I expected Reaver to push his way inside me, I wanted him to, but instead he lowered his face to my curls. He found my clit with his tongue and lapped at it with gentle teasing strokes. I writhed but Ethan held me fast. A finger slid into me and I cried out into Ethan's mouth. He smiled against my mouth and I felt Reaver smile against my pussy.

Reaver sat up and came forward on his knees. He was at a bad angle to enter me so he lifted my hips, fingers digging into my ass.

"You're sure?" he asked and I loved that he did. Ethan freed my mouth and I gasped...

"Yes!"

It was all the encouragement he needed. He pressed to my opening and pressed deep, the wetness of my arousal making him glide effortlessly inside.

"Oh god, yeah!" he said and threw his head back.

"Harder please," I begged and he indulged me. He drew back and surged forward and I was pressed back further into Ethan's arms. Ethan kissed my shoulder and Reaver set a powerful rhythm. I felt my arousal heighten and I clenched down around him.

"Ohhh fuck..." he breathed.

Ethan held me with one powerful arm, the other drifted down my body, gliding against my skin, his fingers found their mark and he teased my clit gently. I shuddered in his embrace and with a cry came apart. Ethan locked his mouth to mine and kissed me deeply while Reaver pulled out of me with a final cry and hunched on the mattress, breathing hard. Ethan hauled me up higher on his body and guided himself into Reaver's place of a moment before.

I sank down on to his familiar length and he rolled his hips. I gasped and he moved a bit to get a better angle, his arms sliding beneath my thighs so that he could lift me better.

"God, I love that I can do this!" he growled into my ear and I laughed which broke and turned into a cry of pleasure as he thrust up into me over *that spot*. Reaver watched us smiling and put his fingers against my stomach, playing the pad of his thumb over my clit. I jerked in Ethan's arm, the nub still over sensitive from my last orgasm. Reaver let up on the pressure just a little and I felt that growing warmth and heaviness in my womb signaling another build. I tightened around Ethan and my breath came faster. The feel of him slipping and pressing against my walls was incredible and I couldn't get enough. I cried out his name and could hear his smile as he encouraged me.

"That's it Baby, come for me just one more time," he crooned next to my ear in a low sexy growl and it was all I needed. I felt myself tighten, and my whole body shudder as wave upon wave of pure blissful energy swept across my body, radiating out from my core. It took Ethan just a few strokes more before he was crying out, crushing me against his body with near bruising force. He bit into my shoulder and I pulsed around him with an aftershock.

The three of us collapsed against the bed gasping and boneless, lazy with satiation and satisfaction.

"We need showers," Reaver stated succinctly and Ethan laughed.

"Better let Ashton go first," he said, "Bathroom's not big enough for all three of us and I want to make sure she has some hot water."

"I need to get my legs back first," I groaned. I was pretty sure if I tried to stand right this second I wouldn't be able to keep my feet under me. I closed my eyes and reclined against Ethan who held me lightly. I felt a hand caress up my calf and I opened my eyes and smiled down at Reaver who was on his back sprawled across the bed where there was room for him.

"Thank you," he said simply.

"For what?" I asked.

"Sharing yourself with me," he said simply and I smiled.

"I should be the one thanking you two," I said softly.

"For what?" Ethan asked.

"For giving me one of the wildest experiences of my life and not making me feel dirty for wanting it is a good start," I said. Ethan kissed me on my shoulder over the stinging impression of his teeth. Reaver kissed the side of my knee.

"Nothing dirty about what we just did," Reaver said, "You're a beautiful, wild lake nymph, and as such we did our duty as a mere mortal men and worshiped you accordingly," he said matter-of-factly, patting the side of my leg and I laughed a long peal of laughter that made both of them laugh too. He was ridiculous, sweet and ridiculous.

"Shower before we get any ideas," Ethan said grinning and I rolled off the bed and landed in a crouch beside it, standing slowly. I was sore, happy but sore. I picked out a pair of shorts and a tank top, bra and panties out of the bag and went for the door.

"I've created a monster," Ethan mock bemoaned and I shot him a grin over my shoulder before padding barefoot and naked down the hall and into the bathroom. It was early enough yet that the common areas of the cabin were still deserted.

I showered and dressed and was rubbing my hair briskly with my towel when the door opened and Ethan slipped in.

"You doin' okay, Babe?" he asked and I smiled up at him he smiled down at me and kissed me.

"I'm better than okay," I breathed and he laughed.

"I'm glad," he gave me a swat on the butt.

"Coffee on the kitchen counter. The sun on the lake is pretty spectacular, good view from the porch swing," he smiled and I ducked out of the bathroom. It was a lovely suggestion. I poured myself a cup of coffee and added cream and sugar. I slipped out onto the porch and sat at one end of the long porch swing and kicked my feet which didn't touch the ground.

It was peaceful and cool out here and I sipped my coffee and appreciated the view. It was beautiful and comfortable and idyllic... I sighed in contentment and the ugly of the last few weeks slid off my shoulders and ran like sand between the cracks of the wooden decking of the cabin's wrap around porch.

The scrape of a boot in the door way had me looking up, I expected Ethan or Reaver but it was Dray. He looked a mess, one eye and cheek bruised, the crust of a scab at the corner of his mouth. He held one arm tight against his side as if it pained him. He wore a black tee shirt with the sleeves and sides cut out and more bruising peeked out of the gaping holes along his ribs. His deep night-dark eyes looked sorrowful and I went to stand.

"Please no, don't get up," he put out a hand the movement too swift, and winced.

"Careful," I intoned. He looked at me gravely.

"I was wondering if I could talk to you," he said. I opened my mouth and shut it. Finally I nodded. He came around and sat down on the opposite end of the swing leaving a healthy distance between us. I took a drink of my coffee.

"I am so sorry, Ashton," he said, and his eyes closed as if the apology pained him. I raised an eyebrow and before I knew what I was going to say it was out of my mouth.

"I don't get it, why don't you like me?" I asked softly. He looked at me startled.

"You don't think I like you?" he asked, surprised.

"Well, no… you've never been nice to me, you're always glaring at me or mad at me and I don't even know what I did to offend you," I shrugged.

"Oh," he said and sounded thoughtful. I looked him over, I mean really looked at him and realized he was a lot younger than I gave him credit for initially. I thought he was twenty-five or twenty-six but now I wasn't so sure.

"How old are you, Dray?" I asked softly.

"Twenty-one," he said, and again I'd caught him off guard. His anger made him seem a lot older. I thought about it then decided nothing ventured, nothing gained…

"Why are you so angry?" I asked.

"What, with you?" he asked frowning.

"With me, with the club, your dad, at the whole damned world… You're just pissed off all the time. Why?" I asked.

"Because I miss my mom," he said and I could see the answer surprised even him. We looked at each other for a long time.

"Tell me about her?" I asked carefully.

"Promise me something first," he said and the look on his face, so lost and scared made me want to promise him anything. Dray Trujillo was hurting, a lot…

"What?" I asked.

"Promise you'll still sing at my mom's thing tonight," he said.

"Of course I will," I said, softening.

"My mom was small like you but she was a pint sized power house," he started, haltingly, he looked up at the porch ceiling.

"She always had the answers, to everything. She helped me with my homework, fixed my cuts; drove me to my sports, always made sure I had food in my stomach and clothes on my back. She was just everything, my mom, my best friend… Dad was out on runs a lot so for a good chunk of me growing up it was almost like living with a single parent," he shrugged a shoulder.

"Can I tell you something?" I asked cautiously.

"Not sure why you would want to after what I did," he said and the look he gave me was full of remorse and misery. I ignored the comment and said what I had to say…

"It was just me and my mom. My dad skipped town when I was three, I don't even remember his face," I shrugged. "I was nine when they first diagnosed the breast cancer. They did surgery and radiation and we thought she was okay but it came back when I was ten, she died by the time I was eleven," I looked at him.

"Sorry," he said.

"I finished growing up in foster care," I whispered, "I didn't have a dad, or an adoptive family of rough around the edges motorcycle gang members to lean on," he smiled and I smiled and huffed a laugh.

"They didn't protect her," he said with a shrug.

"I still don't fully understand *what happened*," I admitted.

"Uhhh, it was five years ago. My dad and the club were into some heavy shit back then. I was sixteen and on the verge of going from hang-around to prospect. My mom, me, a bunch of other guys... we were all sitting in the old club house," he shifted in his seat and took a minute before he got started again.

"I guess a buy went south and some of the buyers got busted but my dad and the guys doing the sell got out, no one got identified or arrested so these buyers, some of their people decided to get some retribution. Sayin' shit like my dad and the others were rats, which is why they didn't go down in the bust. They drove out to our club house. I was behind the bar pouring my mom a drink when they opened fire on the place with automatic weapons," he swallowed.

"I hit the floor, all this glass and booze and shit raining down on top of me. My mom took two hits in the initial onslaught. Hit her," he choked on a strangled sob, "Hit her heart. She was dead before she hit the floor," he looked at me and his loss was sharp, agony radiated from his dark eyes and I waved at him.

"C'mere," I said and he just sort of fell over sideways on the bench laying his head in my lap, looking out over the water. I smoothed his chin length hair out of his face while his tears soaked the top of my leg.

"So why are you mad at me?" I asked.

"I'm not," he sniffed. "You're just small like her. I don't know, if I had to guess, I'd say I was tryin' to scare you away from this mess. I don't think you need to get hurt anymore." I was quiet. "I know it doesn't make any sense," he said.

"Actually it does," I said softly. It was a child like mentality or logic but grief does funny things to people, especially when a parent is involved. For years I secretly harbored the belief that my bad grades had stressed my mom out which was what had allowed the cancer to win. It's what had turned me into an instant over achiever. Like by getting better grades, going to college, I would somehow atone for the bad grades that had helped end her.

Stupid? As an adult, yes… but as a confused child that had just lost her only parent it had made perfect sense at the time. By the time I had reached high school I had just wanted to keep busy, keep my honors status and thought by doing so I would make my mother proud where ever she was. My success was how I measured being a good daughter for my dead mother, and then it became all about being a good wife for Chadwick.

Now… with Ethan's help, I was figuring out how to live for me, love for me, and just be a better me for me. That didn't mean I had to stop being there for other people or doing things for other people and with that realization some of the shattered shards of me fell back into place.

"How can you get it when I don't even get it myself?" he asked, and sniffed.

"Life doesn't come with an instruction manual Dray, plus I've had a little more time to figure some things out," I said softly. I was definitely living proof of that. The rustle of cloth had me turning my attention to the doorway. Ethan stood there glowering. I smiled faintly.

*You okay?* He mouthed in my direction and I smiled genuinely and nodded my head. Dray sighed, he hadn't noticed Ethan yet, his dark eyes troubled and far away as he looked out over the water. I was still petting his hair and startled when I realized how soft it was.

"I should have done something, anything that day," he said, the guilt lacing his voice a caustic thing. Eating away at him.

"So what? Your father could be here mourning two deaths

instead of one?" I asked softly. Dray jolted at the harshness in my tone.

"Your father loves you Dray. More than you probably realize. He's proud of you, but hearing you talk, I think you two just don't know how to relate to one another," he shook with a fresh sob and more tears wet my leg.

"He won't talk about her with me. I think I need that," the younger man said.

I looked up and over startled at a soft swear. Dragon stood just behind Ethan and I frowned. Dray sat up startled and I could tell it hurt.

"Easy," I said.

"Sorry," he said and looked embarrassed, "Look what I did and here you are listening to me spill my guts like a fucking pansy."

"Do you feel better?" I asked as he raked a forearm over his eyes.

"Yeah," he said startled.

"Then that's all that matters," I said softly and stood up. I went and took Ethan's hand, my cup of coffee in the other and stood square in front of Dragon.

"You and your son need to talk," I said pointedly and dragged Ethan back into the cabin.

"What was that?" he asked me once we were safely out of earshot and in the kitchen.

"Do you trust me?" I asked him softly.

"Yeah Babe, of course I do," he said.

"Then it's none of your business," I said and grimaced at how sharp I sounded. Ethan laughed gently and pulled me against him.

"I think we put a little of Reaver in you in more ways than one," he said, teasing and I realized I really had just sounded like him. I laughed and hugged him back.

"I get it Babe, some pains are private and for whatever reason Dray picked you to confide in," he kissed the top of my head.

"That sums it up much better and nicer than I could have," I said softly.

"What's going on?" Reaver asked, coming into the kitchen.

"Dragon and Dray are talking on the porch, best we give them some time," Ethan said and I smiled at him.

"Cool. I'm starving though," Reaver said.

"I'll fix breakfast here," I said. The kitchen was fully stocked so why not?

"Mmmm Ashton breakfast, I'm down. Your cooking is way better than anything they got up there," he sat down at the table and I glowed under the praise.

"What am I fixing?" I asked.

"Bacon," the men said in unison and I laughed.

The rest of the day was spent sunning, swimming, and reading for me, while the boys went off and played with their guns and motorcycles some more. I lay out under the warm rays liberally smeared with sunscreen all over and relaxed listening to Shelly and Chandra make fun of something a prospect did the night before.

"What'd you do last night?" Shelly asked me and I smiled.

"From the sound of it this morning Trigger *and* Reaver," Chandra said and I was surprised to find my smile widen without a touch of embarrassment.

"Oh ewe! Change of subject quick! I so don't want to hear about my cousin's sex life!" Shelly said waving her hands in front of herself as if to ward off a nasty insect. Chandra and I laughed and if it was possible I felt even better about myself than I had earlier.

I knew that most people would be shocked or dismayed at what I'd done but I wasn't around those people and those people need never know. I sighed contented and we talked about what we were going to do when we got back from the weekend. I craned my neck back and smiled when I caught sight of Ethan up on the deck of the lodge, looking down at me.

I was so lucky he'd found me.

# CHAPTER 23

## *Trig*

I was looking down at Ashton hanging with some of the other girls, her bikini clad body glimmering in the sunlight from the liberal amounts of sun screen she'd applied. God I was lucky I had found her. Taking her away from all the bull shit with her ex had been a good move. She was thriving out here with us, some of the bold and adventurous woman she'd probably been before the douche bag had gotten a hold of her was peeking through in some really unexpected ways but damned if I didn't like it.

I'd been surprised as Hell this morning. I'd expected it to take her a lot longer to realize that what she wanted was okay with me. I'd struggled with a few doubts and worries in the beginning but the way she was looking up at me know had her words echoing in my head from the night before.

*I'm yours because I choose to be yours...*

"Yo Trig!" someone called and I turned away from the sight of my girl reluctantly.

"Yeah?" I asked.

"You gotta come look at what Lucky's done to his bike this is totally sick!" I went over reluctantly but what was said was true, the bike looked like a rat bike, which is to say something straight out of a scrap heap but to a trained eye you could see it was built for performance and speed and to keep on running.

Reaver came up next to me. I hadn't seen him since breakfast.

"Hey man," I acknowledged him.

"Hey," he grinned and knelt down checking things out.

"I wanted to say thanks," I said. He looked up at me and gave me a chin lift, the one that meant 'keep talking'.

"For goin' easy on my girl," I said he stood up and frowned.

"I don't think Ashton would ever be game for some of the

things I like behind closed doors," he said.

"Yeah," I said knowingly, "Which is why I'm saying thank you."

Reaver grunted, "Dude, it's no problem. I like Ashton, she's different. Does the MC some good, does *you* a lot of good. I love her just for that. She makes me wish there was such a thing as second chances," he shrugged.

"There are brother, her and me... we're living proof," he looked me over and nodded carefully considering my words and I wondered if he was ever going to get over Aimee. She'd been his high school sweetheart and had left his dumb ass with good reason. I sighed. He hadn't let anyone get close since. I knew the story, been there for some of it, but I'd never met the girl. Reaver and I clasped hands and pulled ourselves into each other, but then he moved off. Moody bastard.

He was back to his smiling self at dinner. Squeezing himself onto the bench on the other side of Ashton, sandwiching her between us. Her leg fetched up against mine and her orange blossom scent wafted over to me, mingling with the smell of her sunscreen and my prick stirred in my shorts. Damn. When didn't this woman get me hard? I grinned as she giggled.

"You write yours yet?" Reaver asked me over her head.

"Yeah," I looked over to the table where white paper lanterns sat. Everyone wrote their wishes and memories on them for the MC's fallen. At dusk we all filed down along the dock, lit the candles inside and let them float out onto the lake. Ashton fidgeted between us.

"Nervous?" Reaver asked.

"Singing in front of a few people is one thing, but doing it in front of the entire club is a *little* daunting," she confessed. I kissed the top of her head and breathed deep her smell.

"You'll do fine," I promised.

"What if they don't like the song I picked?" she asked softly.

"Whatever you picked will be better than silence," Reaver said sagely, gnawing on a leg of chicken.

"You're a friggin' barbarian you know that?" one of the girls asked.

"Yeah but I'm amazing in the sack," he winked at her and she rolled her eyes. Ashton blushed a deep crimson and I smiled.

"What does that have to do with anything?" the girl asked, but Reaver had accomplished what he'd set out to do. Ashton was too busy thinking about this morning to be too worried about tonight. I held out my fist behind her and Reaver bumped it with his own with a grin.

About an hour later it was the moment of truth. We all stood at the start of the dock. Dragon stood on the worn wood with Dray beside him and looked out over his MC.

"Every year for the last five years we do the spring lake run to remember our dead," he said, and a hush fell over the crowd.

"It's supposed to be a time of remembrance, but also of healing. At least that was what the council of five intended. This year, our fifth year, I came to realize that for me, and my boy... A lot of remembering was happening but not a whole lot of healing was. It took a new member of the Sacred Hearts family to show us we needed to do more than just cover our hurts and keep on truckin', so I wanted to say a heartfelt thank you to Ashton, Sunshine... Our boy Trigger's Old Lady."

A murmur went through the crowd and some applause and whistles. Ashton cringed back into me but I gave her a little shove forward.

"I asked Ashton to sing something for us as we sent our remembrances out into the water this year." Lighters came out and lanterns started lighting up, held in everyone's hands. Dragon steered Ashton onto the dock and nodded. She swallowed and took a deep breath.

I recognized the song as one of her Phantom of the Opera show tunes but I couldn't tell you the name of it. She led the procession down the dock and took up sentry at its end, singing into the dark. One by one we stopped at the end of the dock and gently set our lanterns to drifting out into the lake. Ashton sang on, her gentle voice echoed across the water and the last few lanterns were set adrift.

There wasn't a dry eye in attendance. Dray went over to her and hugged her. Dragon began to intone the name of each of the fallen. His voice hollow as it carried out over the crowd and water. It was probably the most perfect ceremony we'd carried out to date.

Afterwards, Ashton found me.

"Hey," she said softly.

"Hi," I pulled her against me and smoothed my hands up and down her back.

"I love you," she said, her voice muffled by my chest.

"I love you too, Baby," I said back. We stood for a long time like that on the lake shore, just holding each other and drinking in the night.

"I don't want to go home tomorrow," she said finally and I smiled.

"What do you want to do then?" I asked.

"I want to stay here like this and have this weekend just be forever," she tilted her head back, the moonlight washing her golden eyes out, turning them to a pale yellow imitation of themselves.

"Sounds like paradise Babe, but reality awaits," I sighed.

"Reality bites," she wrinkled her pretty little nose and I laughed.

"I hear that!" Reaver said walking up with two beers in one hand and a girly drink in the other. He handed the drink to Ashton and held out a beer to me. I took it.

"Ashton Baby, I have something for you," Reaver said and my eyebrows went up. Oh he was fucking lit already.

Ashton laughed, "For me?" she asked, "What is it?"

"This here is my very favorite knife," he pulled a slim stiletto switchblade knife out of his back pocket and held it out to her.

"I want you to have it," he said. She took it and smiled.

"Uhm thank you," she said blushing prettily.

"Reaver giving you a knife is like a normal guy giving a girl flowers," I whispered into her ear. She giggled. I grinned.

"I will treasure it always," she said gravely and he kissed the top of her head.

"Atta Trigger's girl," he said and I laughed.

"Come on brother. Fire is callin' our name," I said putting an arm around his shoulders.

Ashton was looking in the direction of the lake. Dray was sitting on the dock with his dad, she smiled and turned to me and Reaver and we left them to it, me steering my best friend and my girl over to the gathering around the fire.

"There she is!" A cheer went up around the blaze when we reached it and a smattering of applause went around. Ashton blushed and tucked herself into my side shyly.

"How come you changed the words?" Squick asked, but he was smiling. She blinked.

"I only changed one," she said.

"Yeah, but why?" I settled her down into my lap.

"That was for Dray," she said softly.

"What word did you change?" I asked.

"She said 'mother' it was supposed to be 'father'," Squick explained.

"Oh," I looked down at Ashton who was beaming up at me. "Good call," I told her and kissed her nose. She laughed. We relaxed by the fire and listened to stories. Finally we called it a night. As we were walking back to the cabin Ashton looked back wistfully.

"I really do love it here," she whispered.

"We'll be back in a couple of months," I promised her. She hesitated and then smiled.

"Feels like forever from now," she said as we climbed the porch steps.

"Naw, not that long."

We cuddled into bed together and slept tightly entwined. In the morning I woke to Ashton already up, she was dressed in her riding gear and looking lovely, packing the rest of our things away into our bag.

"Sore Babe?" I asked, hoping she wasn't but she nodded ruefully. I sat up and saw she'd laid out my clothes for me. I smiled. Her hair was tightly braided over her shoulder and damp. She'd already showered.

"Gimme ten," I said gently and kissed her.

Standing under the hot shower spray I realized how much I loved her, how much light and laughter she brought to all of our lives. She was shattered when she came to us but had built herself back up seemingly effortlessly over the weeks she'd been here. I was in awe of her. Not only had she done an amazing job putting herself back together, shit, she put several others back together to some degree too.

I shut off the water, squeezed more of it out of the ends of my hair and grabbed a towel. For the first time in a long time I didn't feel as scarred up and ugly on the inside. Ashton Grang- Ashton Fletcher was a balm to my tortured soul. I got dressed and found her in the kitchen, she handed me a cup of coffee.

"Thanks," I grunted. I took a drink and set down the cup on the counter and pulled her to me. She laughed and resisted a little but I grabbed her tight ass and tugged her flush up against me.

"Do you know how happy you make me?" I asked.

"No," she said softly.

"I thought I knew what laughter and light were," I said tipping my head to the side, considering her, "But then you came into my life and proved that I didn't know shit." I think she stopped breathing for a second but then she melted against me, putting her ear to my chest.

"You taught me… You teach me every day what it is to live again," she murmured.

"You and me 'til the wheels fall off?" I asked.

"You better believe it mister," she said, trying to sound tough and I laughed. Sounded like heaven to me.

Why, when you go out on a ride, does it feel like forever getting there? But when you head home, it feels like it takes half the time? This particular run was no exception. Before I knew it we were pulling into the lot out front of our apartment building. I took the bag off of Ashton and followed her up the stairs. Mostly because of the view. We reached our landing and I handed her the key to our door. She stuck it in the lock and the door swung inward. She slipped into the cool twilight of our place and I smiled. Our place. I liked the sound of that. I followed her in and she stopped and groaned.

"I think I need a vacation from our vacation."

I laughed, "Tired?" I asked her.

"Unbelievably," she said.

I dropped the bag by the couch and set the saddle bags from the bike with the guns next to it.

"Go grab a hot shower Babe, wash the road off," I told her, "I'll see you in the bedroom. Going to bed early sounds about right," she smiled at me and went into the bathroom. I heard her peeling off leather and a minute later the water started.

My phone rang.

"Yeah?" I answered it by way of greeting.

"Hey man, its Dragon," The Pres. sounded a little irritated.

"What's up?" I asked.

"Can you swing by for Church before you head to work on Wednesday?" he asked, "Council only," he added. Council only meant serious business.

"Yeah man," I said.

"Thanks," he said.

"No problem, can you give me a heads up?" I asked.

"Wish I could but not this time," he said.

"Okay," I said.

"See you."

"Yeah, see you then," we hung up.

That was odd. The shower stopped and I sat down and took off my boots. She hadn't washed her hair, I noted as she crossed the hall and went into our bedroom. Our bedroom. I *really* like the sound of that.

"Ethan," she called, "Hurry up and come to bed, I need to be close to you." I smiled.

"Okay Babe, gimme ten to rinse off," I was out and between the sheets in five, pulling her small body into the curve of my own larger one. I loved how she fit. She sighed contentedly and I think we were both asleep inside a couple of minutes.

# CHAPTER 24

*Ashton*

"Lock the door behind me, don't answer it for anyone. I don't care if they claim to be cops or look like anything official," he told me.

"Okay," I whispered, he bent down and kissed me.

"I'll be back to pick you up just after whatever needs discussin' gets discussed," he kissed me one more time and I smiled.

"I'll be fine," I promised.

We'd spent yesterday morning in bed to the point we were going to be late for work but it was worth it. We'd put in an easy day at the shop, come home and I'd cooked dinner. Just me and Ethan. It had been beautiful. Now reality was biting and whatever he had to go to the club for wasn't sitting well with him. He reluctantly let me go.

"I love you," he said and I smiled.

"I love you too," I shut the door and immediately and obediently locked it. I listened to his boots descend the stairs and sighed. I took a shower and went in my room to figure out what to wear. I'd just pulled on my jeans and was reaching for a shirt when a loud boom shook the apartment. I dragged the ladies cut MC tee shirt over my head and snatched the knife Reaver gave me off the top of my dresser. I slid it into my back pocket just as a voice called from my living room...

"Oh Honey! I'm hooome!" My blood turned to ice water in my veins. I slipped out the bedroom door and faced one of my worst fears standing in the hallway, the shattered remains of my front door jamb littering the living room carpet behind him.

"You seriously thought that you could send your new friends to beat him and that there wouldn't be any consequences for you?" Maynard asked, he was stalking across the living room at me.

"Well, I've been sent to collect you," he said coldly.

My throat closed and I tried to push my options through my fear and into the front of my brain. My phone was on the dining room table. Ethan's handgun in our bedroom end table. I went for the gun, darting to my right and flinging myself at the night stand but Maynard was too fast and had me around the waist in no time. He flung me into the dresser, my hip bouncing off the wood, sharp immediate pain radiating out from it.

His hand shot out and he grabbed me by my face, fingers digging into my cheek, thumb into my chin, shoving me back against the wall between the dresser and closet. Tears started in my eyes partially from pain but mostly from my anger. I was not doing this! I would not die today! I thought about Ethan about having a life with him and anger twisted my heart. I was my own person and I would be damned if Chadwick would take that away from me anymore! I gripped Maynard's wrist with both of my hands and looked at him. I laughed coldly.

"Oh, you think this is funny do you?" He seethed and cocked back his fist. I jerked my head to the side with everything I had in me and his blow glanced off my cheek, raking along the skin, the majority of the force behind the punch being taken by the wall behind my head.

I screamed in rage and fought. Twisting and kicking in his grasp, I raked nails down his arm and scratched at his face and he dropped me. I slid down the wall and darted low past his legs but he was ready for it and drew back his leg. He let fly a vicious kick to my ribs and the air whooshed from my lungs. My chest locked down and I curled into a ball on my side and fought to get air into me. I crawled across the bedroom floor; fire lancing into my side, licking along my ribs and Maynard laughed coldly. I wrapped myself in my anger, reveled in my fury as he stood over me.

"Where you think you're going Ashton?" he asked me, the arrogance in his voice grating against my nerves.

He hauled me up by my hair and I shrieked my hands going to his in an effort to disengage him.

"For weeks you've been a pain in my ass. I thought sending those cops he bought would scare you back to him. I was surprised when that didn't work so I figured I needed to get you alone but you always had one of those Neanderthals with you," he picked me up by my hair and flung me onto the bed.

"So I hired a couple of men to get them arrested but good help is *so hard* to find these days. They underestimated the bikers," he put his hands on his hips and looked down his nose at me.

"Where were you all weekend?" he demanded and I wheezed a laugh. For once I *wanted* to tell the truth.

"Fucking those two Neanderthals on a lake run," I rasped. He went still, like a snake in the grass.

"Oh Ashton…" he said, advancing on me, I drew my legs to my chest curling into a ball… "Chadwick has no use for damaged property sweetheart. This might be beyond some time spent in a locked room," he said and reached for me.

I let fly with both feet and caught him squarely in the chest. I kicked with everything I had in me and I caught him off balance he stumbled backwards and tripped over his own feet landing on his ass. I scrambled for the bedside table and got my hand around the gun when he pulled me backwards. By some miracle I held onto it and I rolled, he loomed over me and sneered.

"You don't have the nerve!" That's where he was wrong. I pulled the trigger and the world erupted in a cacophony of sound and heat and burning gun smoke. Maynard flew back and slumped against the wall between the dresser and closet. I scrambled for the dining room and my phone. I set down the gun and with shaking fingers took up my phone. I was shaking so bad I just tapped the screen until it started ringing, I didn't even know who I was calling.

"Ashton?" a male voice asked.

"Help me! Please help!" I said desperately, "Maynard broke down the do…" I didn't get the rest of the words out because fingers wrapped into my hair and I was being dragged to the ground. I screamed and shrieked. I could hear the buzz of someone's voice faintly on the phone but I didn't know who I had dialed…

Maynard was straddling me, "You missed!" He screamed and his hands circled my throat squeezing. I fought, clawing at his wrist and felt something dig painfully into my ass.

*Reaver...*

I slid a hand under me and pulled out the switchblade. Maynard was straining and I was choking and kicking and fighting but I was too small he was too big. I couldn't breathe! I fought down the panic and managed to hit the button on the knife with my thumb. I felt the blade snick free and with a silent scream I brought it up, stabbing it deep into the side of him, I couldn't see where. He shouted and wrenched to the side and the blade went with him.

I dragged air into my lungs and twisted, flopping onto my stomach beneath him. I tried to pull myself away from him, towards the back of the loveseat, but his fingers tangled into my hair. I screamed and struggled and fought, thrashing back and forth beneath him. He wrenched back on my hair and my spine bowed until I thought it would snap.

I screamed and kicked and fought as he dragged me to my feet, lifting me clean off the floor by my hair, a steel like band of an arm locking around my middle, pinning me to his hard chest. Tears of fury and fear mingled on my face.

"Ethan!" I screamed as he dragged me from our apartment and down the stairs...

# CHAPTER 25

## *Trig*

The drive to the clubhouse was uneventful except for the nagging feeling that something just wasn't right. The feeling swelled and persisted over the ten minute ride until I pulled up the steep gravel drive in a thoroughly pissed off mood.

"Hey Trig," Reaver greeted as I went in the front door and I nodded.

"What the fuck we doin' here?" I asked.

"Beats the hell out of me," he shrugged and we went into the chapel. Dragon and Dray were at the table and we took our seats.

I set my phone on the table and watched another couple of minutes tick by while we waited for Doc.

"Sorry I'm late," he said and slid into his seat. Reaver swung the door shut behind him.

"What're we here for?" he asked.

Dragon sighed, "Dray wants to step down as VP," he said and my eyebrows went up.

"Given what happened at the lake," Dray started, shifting in his seat, "I don't think I'm fit to be VP, leastways until I get my head on straight." I frowned and wondered if the kid was feeling okay or if I'd knocked him harder than I thought.

"Put it to a vote?" Doc asked quietly.

"All in favor of me stepping down as VP... Yay," Dray started it off.

"Yay," Doc.

"Nay," me.

"Nay," Dragon.

Reaver opened his mouth but my phone buzzed violently across the table. Ashton's smiling face came up on the caller ID screen and I frowned. Before anyone could tell me not to I hit the button for speaker.

"Ashton?" I asked and her voice sent a shot of fear and adrenaline straight to my heart.

"Help me! Please help!" her voice was tinged with desperation, and swamped with a whole lot of panic. "Maynard broke down the do…" but whatever she said was cut off by a terrified shriek.

"You missed!" a voice snarled and the phone clattered then thumped. We could hear them struggling and all of us rose as one.

"Ashton!" I screamed.

"Forget it man, let's go!" Reaver said and I scooped up the phone and vaulted the table. We poured out of the Chapel and went for our bikes. We drove like mad men, breaking every speed limit, running red lights… It didn't matter. We arrived at the apartment just as a black Cadillac Escalade pulled out. Dragon and Dray peeled off to follow it, while Doc, Reaver, and me; we went for the apartment. The front door was dented and the frame splintered. My gun sat on the dining room table and blood spattered the dining room carpet into the living room.

"Ashton!" I screamed and went back into the bedroom. A fist sized hole was in the drywall about head height for my girl but she wasn't there. The smell of gunpowder hung heavy in the room and I looked up, there was a bullet hole in the ceiling. She'd gotten off a shot, thought she'd hit him and gone for the phone in the dining room. She was always leaving her damned phone on the table…

"Bathroom clear!" Doc called.

"Ashton's room clear!" Reaver called.

"Let's go," Doc said. I snatched my Glock 23 off the table and stuffed it into the back of my waistband under my cut.

I shot a text to Dray and my phone pinged back almost immediately.

"Highway 23," I said and we went.

"They're headed for the 'burbs," Reaver intoned.

"Back to her fucking husband I bet," Doc muttered.

This was beyond fucking ballsy. The guy had to be fucking certifiable. We rode out, the three of us. I plugged my headphones into my phone and into one ear so I could listen for any other incoming info. My phone pinged about five minutes later with a location. Sure as shit it was her husband's swanky neighborhood up in the hills.

We met up with Dragon and Dray a few streets over in a semi deserted cul-de-sac under development. Their jackets and cuts hung off the handlebars of their bikes. Reaver, Doc and I did the same. I pulled a red and black checkered flannel out of my saddlebag and put it on over my short sleeved gray Henley. The flannel hid the gun riding at the small of my back.

"He got her," Dragon said, eyes dark.

"Saw him carry her into the house, she was out like a traffic light," Dray added.

"Was she bleeding?" Doc asked.

"Didn't look like it, but he sure was," Dray said and sounded impressed. Dragon was on his phone while I shot a text out over mine to Derek.

"So what's the plan?" Reaver asked me, he pulled on loose fitting track pants, the kind with the snaps on the sides over his jeans, he had thigh sheaths strapped on over the denim and a brace of knives in a tactical like vest over his tee shirt. He was going all out. He pulled on a slightly oversized zip up hoodie over the tee and vest and voila, he looked like any typical jogger. He wore running shoes all the time anyways. He pulled the hood up on the hoodie, hiding the teardrop tattoo at the corner of his eye.

"The plan is I'm goin' in there and gettin' my girl," I said.

"Does this mean we're doin' this old school?" Dray asked.

"Fuck yes we're doing this old school," Dragon pulled out his weapon and checked it, I pulled out mine and sure enough only one round missing. Reaver pulled out a knife and tested the edge. Dray was in a tee shirt and cargo pants, he put on a baseball cap from some landscaping business from one of his saddlebags and made sure his hair was tucked up into it. I blinked at him.

"Hopefully the rich folk are stereotyping correctly today," Dragon chuckled.

"How many the douchebag keep on hand?" Dray asked.

"Only the one that I know of," I said, "But that's why I texted Loyal for backup. We need to do some recon," I asked Reaver, "You

223

and Dray?" I looked at each of them in turn. They nodded.

"You sure you want to do this?" I asked all of them.

"Does the Pope shit in the woods?" Reaver asked with a grin and Doc laughed.

"Pretty sure a bear does, Pope just wears a funny hat," Dragon said.

"Oh, well… fuck yeah! Does that answer your question better?" Reaver said and I smiled. He was half fucking cracked to be making jokes at a time like this but he'd always been that way.

"Let's get to creepin' and hope that none of the neighbors are nosey," Doc said.

Reaver and Dray nodded and went out on foot. Around the time that Derek pulled up in his truck, the first text from Dray buzzed in my hand.

**Dray: 3 ttl 1 in frnt 2 in back.**

Three guards, one in front two in back. My phone buzzed again, Reaver this time.

**Reaver: Ashton, 2 fl mstr br**

"Ashton is on the second floor in the master bedroom, Dray says there's one guard in front, two in back," Dragon snorted.

"Dumb shit, ain't he?" he asked.

"Who the fuck cares?" Derek asked. "We picking them off?" he asked.

"No I want you to provide cover. Gonna try to do this non-lethal but if shit goes sideways I want you covering my six. Don't fucking shoot me," I said. He gave me a one fingered salute. I knew he was a good shot, I was just better, that's all.

"Get in the truck," he said. Dragon and I got in back, laid down and he threw a tarp over us.

"Be ready Doc," I intoned, and he said, "Always am boy," and he got in the driver's seat. The truck started and Doc drove us close to position. Doc would stay with the truck and drive. Derek would take up position to provide cover. We'd do our best to do this ninja style. We found a suitable spot for Derek up on higher ground and he bailed out. I handed him the soft case holding his rifle and he made tracks.

The drawback to rich neighborhoods is that people like us look totally out of place. On the plus side, rich people like their privacy and tended to surround their houses with fences and shrubs, neither one of which really did a whole lot to keep people like us out if we really wanted in, but provided lovely cover once we were.

We had knowledge of the area, or at least some of the boys did, from when the MC served up Chaddy-boy his ass whoopin'. It made this shit a lot easier but right now anything could be happening to Ashton. I let the calm creep in and take over. Chadwick Granger didn't know it, but some really awful shit was about to go down in his world.

We weren't the kind of MC people were used to seeing on popular television series. We didn't go into neighborhoods with guns blazing, wearing our cuts advertising to the whole fuckin' world what badass motherfuckers we were.

No, we did shit quick, clean, and quiet; with as little flash as possible. Doc pulled up to the curb behind the Granger mansion and lifted the tarp on that side and pretended to root around in the back of the truck for something. I heaved myself up and over the side under the cover of the tarp and knelt like I was tying my shoe.

My phone buzzed.

**Reaver: Clear**

I scooted out up over the curb and I stood up and walked down the sidewalk like I'd been there all along. The street was clear, peaceful even. The sky was clouded over and threatening rain which worked to our advantage. Sunny skies meant more people out and about. The other bonus on our side was that it was late morning/early afternoon. Folks were out at their jobs, so we really only had to worry about nosey housewives and retirees. This neighborhood... Housewives were the real danger.

A bird chirped off to my left and I cut my eyes in that direction. Reaver's cold blue gaze glittered out at me from the shrubbery. I stopped, pulled a piece of paper out of my pocket and made like I was checking an address and moved forward. I turned the corner and cut sideways into the bushes and made my way back to his position under the cover of the thick shrubs and trees lining the back of the property.

He unzipped his hoodie and I ditched the red and black flannel. The red was too eye catching. I shoved it under the leaf litter and shrugged into the hoodie. Glad I'd gone with dark jeans that morning.

"How'd you get her position?" I asked.

"Watched him carry her up," he said with a grimace, adding, "She's in rough shape."

Fuck, fuck, and double fuck.

I looked through the line of trees and the back of the wrought iron fence. There were two men in suits and glasses standing near the pool. My phone buzzed.

**Derek: In post. Got a bead on 2 in back.**

I flicked my thumbs across the touch screen, hit send and made sure the message went through to all recipients.

"Show time," I muttered and Reaver gave me one hell of a nasty grin. We slipped on wraparound sunglasses and pulled bandannas up around our noses and mouths, mine was just your generic black, no flash no designs but Reaver was always go big or go home. He looked at me and nodded, the lower half of his face covered by a black triangle of cloth silk screened in white with a skeleton's rictus grin, one of the damned eye teeth embossed in gold.

Whatever man...

We stood up and pulled ourselves over the fence.

"Hey, you!" one of the men shouted.

Hey me... it was fucking on! My boots hit the ground and my hand found my piece at my back, the man who'd shouted was going for his and it was like the world slowed down. Reaver let a knife fly at the one reaching for his gun to aim at him and my weapon was out and pointed at the one I had to deal with.

"Put it down," I said. The other suit was holding his wrist, Reaver's small throwing blade protruding from the back of his hand. The man looked pale and I heard a sharp snick as Reaver freed another blade from his vest. It never ceased to amaze me how freaking fast that bastard was.

The hired suit with his gun trained on me cut a sideways glance to his partner and raised his weapon skyward, hands up and out. Reaver went and disarmed him first and then pulled the other man's gun out from under his arm.

"Pull it out!" The guy said, voice high and a little frightened.

"Nah, have 'em do it at the hospital. Don't know if I hit anything important," Reave said and tossed their guns into the pool eyes sparkling in that way that told me he was smiling.

"We aren't getting paid enough for this shit," the one I was trained on said and I could tell he was pretty much done. He looked about two seconds from wetting himself. Civilians then. Reaver punched the walking wounded in the face. Hard. The guy went down like a ton of bricks and Reaver pulled out a pair of cuffs from the back of his vest. I tried not to laugh. They were the fuzzy pink kind for sex.

"C'mere junior," he said and I jerked my head at the guy I was trained on to do what he said. He went over and Reaver fastened one cuff around the unconscious guy's good wrist and snaked it through the wrought iron support pillar for the back deck above our heads. He fastened the other one to my guy and held out a key on a necklace chain in front of the dude.

"Stop fucking around!" I hissed. The guy made to snatch for it and Reaver sent it sailing into the pool with their weapons.

"You never saw us," I grated and the guy shook his head rapidly.

"Didn't see nothing," he agreed and we let ourselves in the back door just as Dragon and Dray came in through the front. They had bandanas of their own over their faces. Dragon wore dark wraparound sunglasses while Dray had his hat pulled down low over his face.

"Guy out front?" I whispered.

"Out cold," Dragon muttered.

I took point going up the stairs, Reaver right behind me Dray and Dragon on his six. We had four doors between us and the master suite. We checked them all carefully and methodically.

The moment of truth had arrived. I prayed hard and harder that she was okay and stood to the side while Dragon made the breech.

You never follow your own breech so I was first through the door, weapon pointed. Chadwick turned from the window, a glass of amber colored liquor in his hand. His security man held one hand to his bleeding side the other had a gun trained on me.

Ashton lay sprawled on the bed. It looked like she'd been tossed there carelessly. She was too pale and wan and I was half afraid she was already gone. Dray was hot on my heels, his gun pointed at the security man's head, my weapon was pointed at Chadwick's head and I felt it all drain out of me into the floor as that still quiet place crept in, filling me up. Dragon's voice came from behind me.

"Now I know you were told what would happen if you touched her again, friend," he said, and his tone was all business and decidedly unfriendly.

"I had nothing to do with this," Chadwick said and took a sip from his glass. He had deep bruising around his eyes and a cut across the bridge of his nose. He looked... tired... deep lines bracketing his eyes and mouth.

"Maynard here got a little... overzealous, but I supposed that doesn't matter to you much. *I*, on the other hand, heard your earlier warning loud and clear. Oh you can check on her, please do," I caught Reaver out of the corner of my eye moving to Ashton. He put his fingers to her throat which bore a dark shadow of bruising and his shoulders slumped. My heart dropped, I squeezed down slowly on the trigger.

"She's alive!" he declared and I snapped the tension out of my finger before the gun could go off.

"You're lucky I have a stiff trigger," I growled.

"So it would seem," Chadwick pursed his lips.

"Hey, Bud..." I said.

"Already on it," Reaver said and he was, he slipped his knife back into his vest and slid an arm carefully beneath my Sunshine girl's knees and one behind her shoulders. He bent at the knees and lifted her. She looked frail in my best buddy's arms.

"How can you not love someone like her?" I found myself asking aloud, my question was rhetorical but he answered it anyways.

"I don't require love. Love is for the weak. I require obedience and when I don't get it, corrective action is required. Ashton was, for the most part, a good girl. Was. Then she met you," he smirked a knowing little smirk and swirled the liquid in his glass.

"Damn fine thing she did," Dragon muttered.

"We're taking her," I said and Chadwick shrugged.

"I have no use for her anymore and her dying here would just be... messy. Difficult to clean up," Reaver and I exchanged looks and even though I couldn't see the lower half of his face his eyes said 'I got this.' Before he stepped back out of my sight.

"Take him with you. I have no use for disobedience. Feel free to be my correction," he turned back to the window and sipped his drink. Dragon growled. I think we were all a little speechless. This was some serious James Bond level villainous shit.

Dray went up and fetched the bleeding man, pointing his piece at his bald head. The man was staring incredulously at the back of Chadwick's. I almost felt sorry for him but then I glanced at Ashton; small, pale, and frail in Reaver's arms and all I wanted was to have him a broken and bleeding pile at my feet. Yeah, this needed to end.

"Let's move," we backed out of the room, Dragon first, then Reaver with Ashton, Dray with the security man and finally me. Dragon shot off a text and we went out the front door he hit the switch on a panel by the door for the front gate. Doc drove up in Derek's truck.

"What did you do to her?" I demanded and the security man stared at me, lips compressed into a thin line.

"Phenobarbitol, she wouldn't shut up," he glowered at me, and we deadlocked into icy stares.

"Doc, you get that?" I asked never taking my eyes off the security man.

"I got it," he said from the open window of the silver pickup. Dray moved up to the security man.

"Your lucky day," Dray said to him, "We aren't like your boss. We aren't in the business of hurting or killing people. Where's your car?" the security man looked at Dray hard, you could see the wheels turning in his head, and he finally jerked his chin in the direction of his SUV.

"Keys," I said and he pulled them out of his pocket. He continued to hold his side but didn't complain about his injury. Doc and Reaver were already gone, tail lights blinking out as he made the turn out onto the street at the end of the drive. I got into the driver's seat, Dragon the passenger and Dray and the security man in back.

"What's your name friend?" Dragon asked as I pulled out onto the street.

The man said nothing. We picked up Derek and the man seemed genuinely surprised. Derek slid his gear into the back and got into the SUV's back seat sandwiching the security man between him and Dray.

"Had a good bead on that douchebag, why didn't you give the signal?" Derek asked frowning.

"We've got other ideas," I grunted, and we did.

We dropped Derek off at the bikes so he could watch 'em. Dragon would have some of the rest of the MC come out and get 'em. We were busy. I drove us out to the rally point where we did all of our illegal dealings of yesteryear and did our nefarious but noble deeds of now. It was a remote piece of property out near some farms about an hour outside town. I turned off the paved road and bumped us along the long dirt drive watching the plume of dry dust and dirt kicking up behind us in the side view. My heart sank a little.

This wasn't the kind of man I wanted to be anymore. Dragon and Dray were equally grim, but I could see it in the set lines of their expressions, they were as equally set on what needed to be done as I was. My phone buzzed in the hoodie's pocket and I pulled it free.

**Reaver: At the MC. Doc is working on her now.**

"They're clear," I told Dragon and Dray.

Dragon got out and opened up the big sliding door, wrestling it to the side, and I pulled into the modest warehouse barn looking aluminum building. I shut off the engine.

"What branch?" I asked the security guy, watching him in the rearview. He raised his cold blue eyes to the glass and we stared at each other.

"Army," one word but it was progress from the silence he'd maintained on the way over.

"USMC," I muttered and sighed.

"Out," Dray ordered and raised his gun to the man's head to make his point. He slid out of the SUV, Dragon waiting for him. I thought about Ashton's broken doll body on the cover of that plush bed and closed my eyes.

*God give me the strength* not *to kill this fucker.* I prayed.

Seems He was off answering somebody else's prayer today.

# CHAPTER 26

## *Ashton*

I opened bleary eyes to icy spring skies. I blinked, wait, no that wasn't right... I squeezed my eyes shut and opened them again. Everything tilted on its axis and I very nearly threw up.

"Easy, Baby," I opened my eyes again and those cold blue skies I'd seen resolved into Reaver's eyes.

"Reaver?" I asked confused.

"Yeah?" he asked and I gasped and struggled to sit up.

"Ethan, did he hear me? Did I call him?" I continued to try to sit up but Reaver gently pressed me back into the bed.

"Shhhh, he's here. He just went to the bathroom," Reaver smiled ruefully and I lay back. My mouth felt cottony and so dry.

"Can I have some water?" I asked.

"Hey, is she awake?" Ethan's voice sounded through the small room and I went limp with relief, I opened my eyes and he was standing in the doorway, I frowned.

"Why can't I remember anything?" I asked and it was true, I remember Maynard breaking down the door, I remembered fighting back, I remember grabbing the gun from the night table but then nothing after that.

"You were drugged, Baby," he said and came near the bed. He knelt down beside it and I reached out. He smiled and took my hands in his own.

"You came and got me?" I asked and my voice sounded small.

"Damn right I did," his look was dark, murderous.

"I'm going to go get her some water," Reaver murmured and slipped out leaving me and Ethan alone. I closed my eyes and sagged with relief.

"What do you remember, Babe?" Ethan asked.

I quickly recapped everything I remembered and looked at him expectantly, willing him to fill in the blanks…

"I'm proud of you, Baby," he whispered and tears glittered in his silver eyes. He pressed my hand to his lips and closed them I blinked, taken aback.

"Proud of me?" I echoed.

"You're damn straight. You fought like a wild cat. That son of a bitch had scratches all over him. You even stabbed him with Reaver's stiletto," I wiped his tears away with my fingertips and marveled that my big strong biker was crying in the first place.

"Oh," I said softly and smiled, "I think I learned that from you, too," he laughed and it hitched in his throat from the tears and he leaned forward carefully and kissed me gently. I let my hand rest along the side of his face and kissed him back. He leaned back.

"How do you feel?" he asked eyeing me warily.

"Like I've been hit by a truck," I admitted softly. Reaver tapped on the doorframe, a mug with a bendy straw sticking out of it in his hand. I smiled and waved him in. Ethan helped me to sit up carefully, shoving pillows piled on the floor next to the bed behind me to prop me up. I think I hurt worse than I ever had before. I winced and took shallow breaths. It had never hurt so much to breathe in my life!

"Doc is on his way in. He might be able to give you something for the pain," Reaver said gently, putting the straw to my lips.

"Go easy," Ethan admonished and I took a sip, then another, and another.

"Did Chadwick send him? How did you find me? Is he dead, please tell me he's dead and you killed him?" I laid back and looked at them anxiously. Both looked grim, Ethan had a look of satisfaction on his face.

"Chadwick said he didn't send him, but I believe that about as much as I believe that he's a saint like me," Reaver said and grinned wickedly. I smiled again I couldn't help it. Reaver had that effect.

"You got a call off to me, Babe. We got to the apartment just as he was pulling out. Dragon and Dray were on your tail the whole time. He took you to your husband's house," Ethan looked bitter as hell, his mouth twisting around the word 'husband'. I couldn't agree more.

"We went in after you like the ninja badasses we are," Reaver put in. "Your husband told us to go ahead and take you; that you weren't worth the trouble. Trust me baby, you are *so worth it!*" he sang out the last in a falsetto and I tried not to laugh, laughing hurt, oh my god it hurt. Like a lot.

Ethan frowned at him.

"The bastard that attacked you looked poleaxed at that one," he said eyeing me carefully. I sniffed, tears welling. Chadwick was planning something awful, it was how he was, I just knew it.

"Hey now, no tears. You're safe," Ethan sad softly, thumbing the moisture from beneath my eyes.

"He's planning something awful. I can feel it," I said.

"Yeah well, unlucky for him we're planning things too and they're probably way worse than anything he can come up with," Reaver said and leaned nonchalantly against the door fame.

"We tried to play nice with that fucker," Ethan agreed looking me over and it was as if he were asking permission with his cool mercurial gaze.

"I don't care what you have to do," I said sniffing back more tears, "I don't want to die and I don't want to lose any of you which is what he'll do. Do what you have to do," I consented. Reaver pushed off the wall and went out without a backwards glance.

"Done, Baby," Ethan said and kissed my forehead and I was surprised to find I didn't feel bad in the least for whatever was going to happen to Chadwick.

"What's going to happen?" I asked, unable to help myself.

"Can't say Babe, but as soon as Doc says you're good to travel we're going until some of this shit blows over," he said and his look was grave. I nodded. Away sounded good.

"He might come after the club," I said softly.

"We've thought about that. Don't you worry, Dragon's got the clubhouse on lock down. Your husband doesn't know what he's messing with," he kissed the back of my hand where he cradled it between his two much larger ones. I closed my eyes. I was getting tired again. Doc came in a moment later.

"How's my patient?" he asked eyeing me.

"Tired, hurt and scared for all of you," I answered truthfully.

"Well, sleep if you're tired, take these for the hurt," he said holding out one of those little paper pill cups. "And as for the scared, don't you worry about at thing. It'll all be over sooner than you think," he smiled at me and winked.

I took the paper pill cup and tipped the two tablets into my mouth, not caring what they were, trusting in Doc. Ethan held the mug Reaver had left on the dresser to my lips and I sucked water through the straw, getting the pills down. I leaned back against the pillows and closed my eyes, sighing out.

"Get some sleep, Baby," Ethan said and kissed my brow.

"Where are you going?" I asked, the stab of panic sharp and immediate.

"Just out to the common room. I'll be back before you know it I promise," he said. I nodded, lip between my teeth.

"Okay," I said reluctantly. I really didn't want him out of my sight. Not yet. I forced myself to let go of his hands and he stood up, following Doc out of the room and shutting the door behind them.

Anxiety gnawed at me. I closed my eyes and felt tears slick down my temples and into my hair. I hated Chadwick, I hated even more that I knew he was toying with us. Making these little feints and jabs intended to torture me psychologically as much as physically. I hated even more that these wonderful people, Ethan, Reaver, Doc, Dragon and yes even Dray and by extension everyone else of the Sacred Hearts Motorcycle Club were dancing on eggshells to keep me safe.

He could hurt any one of them. He *would* hurt any one of them. Chadwick saw himself as being above the law and had the money and the power to back it up. I sniffed and shuddered and tried not to sob. The pain in my side and the rest of my body was dimmed to a dull roar but it still hurt. I was sure I had at least one broken rib on the side that he'd kicked me on. I'd had one once or twice before and they were awful. Filling my chest and side with so much broken glass.

I don't know how long I lay there, watching the light grow dim until it diminished completely with the setting sun. An hour? Two hours? It felt like an age. Where had Ethan gone? I was sure they were talking about the situation, what to do, how to do it and I was grateful, I really was because no matter how badly I felt I did *not* want to die, and as selfish as it might be, I couldn't, I *wouldn't* go back to him. I had told Ethan I wanted to fight weeks ago and that was exactly what I had done, against Maynard, against Chadwick, against all comers.

I would be no one's property anymore, I'd kill myself first.

The door opened as if he sensed my train of thought and he came to me, kneeling gently beside the bed. He took my hand gently in his and smiled thinly at me.

"We have a plan," he said and I closed my eyes in relief at the determination and love shining out of his liquid silver gaze.

"Am I supposed to know?" I asked softly.

"Some," he said softly, "You might not like parts of it, but everyone involved is on board and taking up for you. They know the risks and are willing to take them, it just depends on if you're willing to take it too."

I fixed him with a hard stare, "I'm willing to do whatever it takes to be free of him," I said and Ethan smiled *his* icy smile, the warmth leeching from his eyes leaving the cold killer behind, looking out at me.

"That's my girl," he said softly and brushed his lips against mine swiftly, and even in my broken, injured and hurting state I felt a thrill at the contact.

"So what's the plan?" I asked.

"We called Hayden. We're pretty sure he doesn't know about her. We're going to do some evasive maneuvering and set you up at her place to heal. She's all in. Knows the risks and is willing to put you up," I blinked in surprise. Hayden and I were becoming fast friends sure, but this was a lot to ask of anyone, especially a new friend you only saw at yoga and had gone to lunch with once!

"Okay," I said cautiously.

"Once you're there, you're there until this is done," he looked me over and it was as if he was willing me to understand.

"You aren't going to be with me at Hayden's are you?" I asked feebly.

"No, Baby. The guys need me to watch their six. I promised you I wouldn't let him hurt you again and I failed. There is no such thing as failure a second time around," he swallowed hard, "It should only be a couple of days," I felt myself nodding rapidly, my hands clutching tightly to his where they rested in my lap.

"How will I know if you're okay?" I asked and my voice was strained.

"I got you a burner," he said and at my perplexed look explained, "A prepaid untraceable cell phone."

"Oh," I whispered, feeling stupid.

"I'll text you with updates as best I can," he promised.

"What happens if something goes wrong?" I asked quietly.

"No," his voice was solid, bordering on stern, "Don't even put that out there, Baby. Everything is going to be fine." He stood up abruptly and toed off his boots. He came around the other side of the bed shrugging out of his jacket and cut and hanging it on the hook set in the back of the closet door. He got onto the bed on top of the covers and I tucked myself into his side gratefully.

"I don't want to tell you too much," he said, cuddling me close and I nodded against his chest. Laying against him like this wasn't exactly comfortable with the fresh battering my poor body had taken, but at the same time nothing I did, no matter which way I moved *was*. I made myself as comfortable and I could and still be near him and I soaked in his body heat, grateful that he held me. Grateful that I was alive so he could.

"Just come back to me safely," I begged and he kissed my forehead.

"You know it Sunshine," he said fiercely. I lay against him quietly for a time.

"I thought I was never going to see you again," I confessed feebly.

"Like to shave twenty years off my life when I heard you through that phone line," he shared, his breath warm as he spoke against my hair.

More silence.

"He knows how many of you now, doesn't he?" I asked.

"He thinks he has an idea of how we operate, but he doesn't. We got a few more tricks up our sleeves," Ethan assured me.

"I hope so," I said and the constant roller coaster of emotions, the battering my body had taken, the medicine Doc had given me, just *all of it* had taken too much out of me. I struggled to stay awake but failed, slipping into the deep and dreamless sleep of the truly exhausted against the warm, hard body of the man I loved. When I woke, sunlight streamed through the slats of the blinds. I reached out and found the bed beside me cold and empty.

"I'm right here," he said and his voice quickly soothed me. He sat beside the bed, his tall large frame folded uncomfortably into a battered brown metal folding chair.

"How are you doing?" he asked me. I blushed faintly.

"I really need to pee," I admitted and he laughed.

"Okay. Let me help you," he made to pick me up and I waved him off a bit.

"Just help me to stand please?" I asked, explaining, "Its better if I move around on my own as much as possible, I'll get too stiff otherwise and it'll be worse," he nodded, expression grave knowing that this bit of knowledge came from experience. He let me brace against his outstretched forearms and lever myself up off the bed.

I bit back a cry of pain, moving first thing the next morning was always the worst, and gave an experimental shuffling step towards the door. Okay, not so bad. I looked down at myself and for the first time realized I was in Ethan's blue button down shirt he'd given me. I blinked, wasn't that at the apartment?

"The apartment," I groaned. The door had been half off its hinges the frame shattered, anyone could have gone in…

"Taken care of, Baby. All our stuff is moved out and in storage. A lot of the club's Old Ladies and bitches saw to it," I sagged with relief and took one determined shuffling step after the other in the direction of the nearest bathroom.

"I need a hot shower, it will help loosen me up," I said slipping into the bathroom.

"Okay, I'll get you some towels," he said softly, he laid a kiss over my left eyebrow and I shut the door. I did my business and when I opened the bathroom door again it was to Ethan standing outside with his knuckles poised to knock. He grinned at me.

"Good timing, Babe," He set the towels on the closed lid of the toilet and slipped past me, bending to crank on the old shower knobs. I admired how his jeans molded to his ass as he bent to do it and smiled to myself, biting my bottom lip.

"Why you blushing?" he asked when he straightened back up, his thick fingers going to the buttons on his shirt.

"Admiring the view," I said quietly and he smiled and let out a laugh.

"Babe, you mean to tell me you're standing there looking like death warmed over and you were still checking out my ass?" he asked, a teasing twinkle in his eyes.

"What? Not my fault you created a little monster," I said and we were both smiling. He bent at the waist and placed his lips above mine, a hair's breadth from touching.

"I like that you check out my ass Ms. Fletcher," he said softly and touched his lips to mine in a sweet soft kiss that had my muscles turn languid.

Steam started to fill the small bathroom and he drew back. He held out his hands and helped me over the edge of the tub which was a lot harder than under normal circumstances. I stepped under the hot shower spray, and instantly relaxed the rest of the way, the heat finishing what Ethan had started.

"Take your time, Baby," he said and drew the clear shower curtain closed around me. He crossed his arms over his chest and I realized that he had every intention of staying with me for which I was grateful.

I could feel our time together trickling like the last grains of sand through an hour glass. When the sand was gone, our time together would be up and I felt like I would be plunging headlong into the unknown. Ethan had been my rock the last month or so, my strength when I'd had none and now he had to leave for who knew how long to clean up the mess I had gotten myself into and had been in since college.

I felt a sudden molten surge of anger both at Chadwick and at myself for staying with him for so long. I bowed my head beneath the shower spray and let the water run down the back of my head, my long hair guiding it away from my face. I scrubbed at my face with hot water and my hands. I smoothed my hair back and straightened. Washing my self-pity and useless anger down the drain.

I was physically small, my size and stature working against me when it came to any physical altercation with Chadwick, but I had other things to fight back with. Ethan and the brothers of the Sacred Hearts MC didn't have to go against Chadwick completely blind. I'd lived in that house, been a prisoner of that house for the better part of eight years. I knew everything about it. Where the cameras were, and truth be told, there were few. I also knew all of the combinations and passwords for the alarm company. I may not be able to fight physically but it didn't take me out of the equation completely.

"Ethan," I said softly.

"Yeah, Babe?" he asked, perking up on the other side of the curtain.

"I think I may be able to help more than I have been," I said.

"How's that, Sunshine?" he asked, curiosity coloring his tone. So I started to tell him, everything. Chadwick was a creature of habit, I told him when he went to bed, when he got up, what time he left the house, the route he traditionally took to leave the neighborhood, how he could be expected promptly at what time, and how even if he were going to be late, *still* I would know what time he would arrive...

"Hold on, hold on, hold on, Babe!" he ducked out of the bathroom and shouted down the hallway to someone. A moment later he ducked back into the bathroom and sat down on the closed lid of the toilet with a notepad in his hands. I smiled at the blurry steam obscured image of him furiously scratching away, pad and pen balanced on his knee.

"Go ahead," he said at last, and I did. Every last freaking detail. I don't know why I hadn't thought of it before just like I didn't know what scared me more, the fact that I was helping these men likely plot the murder of my husband, or the fact that helping these men plot the potential murder of my husband *didn't bother me in the slightest*. No, I was beyond done with Chadwick and his cruelty and if that meant I needed to take a different sort of lesson from him, adopt a bit of the coldness I saw in the men around me into myself, then so be it.

I stayed under the hot spray until it began to turn tepid and I was beyond pruned. When I stepped out Ethan was waiting with a large fluffy towel which he laid gently around me. I patted myself dry, carefully over the really tender parts of me and let him carry me back to his room. He set me down gently and truth be told, with my ribs in the shape they were in, it hurt more to have him carry me than it did shuffling at my slow half-pace on my own. I gently told him as much and he looked sorrowful.

"I'm sorry, I wish you had told me I would have put you down," he looked mournful and I wished I had said nothing I smiled and laid my hand over his heart.

"I love you," I told him, and the thin veneer of ice caused by all of the stress and negative emotions we were both feeling cracked a bit, and he smiled.

"I love you, too, Sunshine," he said and held me carefully and close, "I love you, too."

# CHAPTER 27

*Trig*

I let Ashton get dressed, helping only when her body wouldn't allow her to do it herself. She was a fucking mess. Her entire right side painted a deep purple from her hip almost all the way up to her armpit. Her left cheek had a scrape along her cheekbone, under her eye and was puffy and bruised as well. She'd said it was a glancing blow, that the wall had taken most of the impact but still...

I zipped up the back of her dress, I'd needed to hold it to the floor and raise it for her after she'd stepped into it. Bending was proving to be difficult. She'd amazed me when she'd started blurting everything she knew about the house and it's lay out, surveillance, guard habits and the habits of her husband while she'd showered. We were going to ask her about all of it when she was clean and into some fresh clothes. Before taking her to Hayden's, but she had been one step ahead of me.

I'd passed the notebook off to Reaver in the hallway. He'd taken it to the chapel where we had Data set up and a virtual tactical war room going. We were still trying to figure out what exactly we were going to do about Chadwick Granger. I mean sure, we were going to end him one way or another but we had to be careful. Plan it meticulously so none of us got hit with any blow back.

Everyone knew he and Ashton were going through an ugly separation. We'd tried fighting it out through the proper channels but when one of the 'proper channels' had shown up at the apartment to tell her I'd died as a way to fuck with her head... and later, when the cops had let the two bone heads from the gym go without so much as a single charge being filed even *with* the video tape of them attacking us. Well, let's just say the proper channels weren't so proper anymore. Leastways not for us.

It was time to do it old school, which none of us wanted, but fuck! We felt painted into a corner and we either did something or one of us was going to suffer way more than Ashton already had. That just wasn't going to happen. That decision had been unanimous in every way. Dray hadn't so much as blinked and he was usually our only hold out. Consistently voting against the majority just to be a pain in the ass. Ashton sank onto the edge of the bed with a gusty sigh. I knelt in front of her.

"Whatcha thinkin'?" I asked her. A million different things crossed her pretty little battered face and I could read every single one of them. Which presented another problem all of its own.

Ashton couldn't lie to save her life and this time, her life really might just depend on it.

"I'm scared for all of you. I want to know what's going to happen but I know you can't tell me because I can't lie and I need to be surprised and if I know too much well..." Damn, it was uncanny how she could read my mind sometimes. I took her hands in mine.

"All you need to know is that we're going to hide you. We're going to protect you and he really is never going to hurt you again," I kissed the backs of her knuckles and stood slowly, supporting her so she could pull herself up to her feet.

"I believe you," she said softly and I smiled down at her.

"Good," I leaned down and kissed her and drew her out to the common room of the club. She moved painfully slow, like a woman three times her age and I let her take her time. Dragon, Dray, Doc, and Reaver were standing on the little stage we had for live band performances. A good portion of the MC in attendance. Dragon was giving the rundown.

"We've got three panel vans and whatever other vehicles we can get our hands on out there. We don't know what kind of surveillance the club may be under but we figure better paranoid than sorry. We set up one of those tent carport things, I don't know what you call 'em..." Dray leaned in and mumbled something and Dragon turned to him sharply.

"Eh, whatever you smart ass," Dragon grumbled and racked his neck to the side. Dray grinned and chewed his gum and looked all too pleased with himself. Those two were always at each other with the barbs and sarcastic comments. Laughter tittered through their audience and I couldn't say it was a bad thing. Shit was pretty much as serious as it ever got around here with this.

"Anyways, before I was so rudely interrupted, vehicles need to line up, back into the station one by one. We'll load Ashton into one of them. Everybody keep your trap shut! We'll pull a train out of here, every other car go left or right, they won't be able to track us all and it'll give us a better chance of gettin' her to the undisclosed safe house," he crossed his arms in that awkward way of his.

"She gets found we'll know we got a rat," he intoned. "You all know what we do to rats," silence swept through the MC. Yeah, we all knew what happened to rats and it wasn't pretty. We'd caught one a couple years back. The one responsible for selling out the club, causing Tilly and those two members' deaths.

He'd been taken apart, one little piece at a time. He'd died screaming in a lot of pain. I palmed the back of my neck and pulled trying to ease some of the sudden tension in my back. While we weren't *all* bad men, enough of us had stained our souls with enough black we weren't at all sure where we'd end up when the reaper came calling, but we would do what we could in the time we had left to make up for it in some small part.

"Right, let's get to it," Dragon said.

Ashton looked up at me.

"Which van am I going to be in?" she asked softly. I put my finger to my lips. We weren't at all sure what kind of surveillance we were under. Data, who came by his name honestly as our tech-wizard, had swept the building for bugs and had come up empty which freaked us out more because it pointed to us having some kind of rat.

I picked up her small suitcase and we went out to the temporary carport erected outside the front doors. We were being over the top paranoid which wasn't paranoid enough as far as I was concerned. Not when it came to Ashton's safety.

The first van backed in. We made a big tedious show of opening doors, moving around closed it up and it pulled out and down the drive, starting the line. Next came a member's Durango, same deal.

This went on and on until Loyal backed his pickup in. I stashed Ashton's suitcase in the bed of the truck and shut the lid of his new bed cover. He got out and came around. He smiled at her and nodded and she looked up at me with surprised golden eyes. I took her to the passenger side and we got her situated in the cramped back seat, which wasn't as bad as I thought it would be with how small her body was.

I kissed her gently once, twice, a third time and then I had to let her go. I'd be damned if it was going to be forever. I put my lips against her ear and told her to stay down for the entire ride. She nodded her understanding and when I pulled back her golden eyes were swimming with tears. I backed up and she mouthed at me, *"Be careful."*

I nodded and we closed up the truck. I rapped my knuckles on the roof twice and Derek pulled out to join the line. We went through about ten more cars, vans, and trucks and then it was time to open the gates. The long line of vehicles began pulling out, left then right, left then right they went up either direction of the highway and I tried very hard not to look too long at any one car in particular.

Ashton had the burner phone and was instructed to text me as soon as she was at Hayden's. Derek was under the same instruction.

We finished loading up the last van while cars pulled out and shut the doors. Data started her up and the rest of us took to our bikes. We left the clubhouse behind, locking things down tight with a couple of brothers and took ourselves to our rendezvous point.

As Dray got off his bike and unchained the gate and pulled it aside, the texts came in from Derek and Ashton one on top of the other.

**I'm safe. I love you.**

**@ The safe house.**

Reaver rode through first and was opening up the old corrugated steel door, sliding it aside so we could use the old warehouse building.

"We good?" Dragon asked as Data jumped down from the van.

"Yeah, got some radio traffic, confused the hell out of the guys

245

watching the clubhouse. They went for the Durango. Texted Smalls to let him know," Data was grinning. He was a hardcore nerd and tactician. He spoke, we listened for the most part. Only ever had to reign him in once or twice. I sighed.

"They're clear. We clear here?" I asked. Everyone already knew who *they* were so I didn't need to explain.

"I think so, yeah," he said.

"You think so or you know so?" Dray demanded gruffly.

"I know so! They only had one sedan with two guys watching the club. Amateur hour out there," he had the back of the van open and was pulling out computer crap and some folding tables.

"Help me get his shit set up so we can plan this," he demanded and we all grimly complied. We all wanted this over.

After about an hour of discussion and Data pecking away at his laptop keyboard we realized we were fairly short on some crucial information.

"So what do we do?" Dragon grunted.

"Observe and report. Simple surveillance. Find a good spot for Trigger to set up camp and go from there…" Data shrugged.

"How long?" I asked.

"Couple of days maybe three?" he ran a hand through his hair for the umpteenth time and I raised an eyebrow.

"Let's get to it," I said and we broke apart to do what needed doing. I shot a quick text to Ashton's burner.

**Gonna be a few days baby. Hang tight. Stay near Loyal and out of sight. I love you.**

The response was immediate and I couldn't help but smile at the thought of her clutching the burner like a lifeline.

**Okay. Be careful! I love you, too.**

I wanted to text back, but instead I stuffed the phone into the pocket of my worn old BDU's and set about parsing through equipment.

"Let me know when you have satellite imagery up so I can find a decent vantage point," I called to Data.

"Uno momento pro favor," Data said, fingers flying across keys. Dragon snorted and Dray looked like he'd sucked on a lemon.

"Don't ever do that again, your accent blows," Dray commented dryly. Reaver laughed.

"Here," Data said and spun his laptop around for me to come look. I went over and scanned the topography of Ashton's 'hood. I pointed to a ridge.

"How far?" I asked. I could never freaking tell on a damned screen.

"Less than a thousand yards. Should be cake for you," Data commented. I nodded.

"Reaver, you and me," I said and he leapt down from the battered old desk he'd been perched on. The knife in his hand disappearing god knew where.

"Radios," Dragon tossed a black bag at Reaver and he caught it. I put my scopes and rifle case into the back of the old Jeep Wrangler we kept around. The registration was clean and wouldn't trace back to the club.

Reaver got into the passenger seat and unfolded a map. Data came over with some printed sheets and handed them to him. He wasn't a bad navigator. I got into the driver's side and we went.

The ridge was high and wooded and looked down on the housing development from around 900 yards away. Using one of my detached scopes I picked out Ashton's house and smiled. We hiked around a bit to find a good vantage point and settled in to watch. Well I did. Reaver got the communications set up and settled in next to me.

"Don't think this could be any better if we wanted it to be," he said and I gave a grunt in reply. I looked down my scope and had a clear view of the back of the house and side yard. I scanned around and blinked in surprise. The place was deserted.

"It's empty," I said quietly.

"Whaaaaaat?" Reaver sounded like one of the little, yellow, pill shaped men on that kid's movie that was being advertised all over TV. I cast a side long look at him he grinned and settled a scope to his eye and looked over the place for himself. He got on the radio and spoke to someone on the other end.

Dragon and Dray came out of wherever they'd been hiding at

below us and sauntered up to the gate. Dray nonchalantly punched in the five digit code and it rolled aside and they walked up the drive like they belonged there. They were dressed like a couple of gardeners, reprising Dray's earlier role and given the neighborhood they kind of did look like they belonged. Stereotypical, sad, but true.

We watched them scout the perimeter pointing at things and writing on one of those yellow legal pads standing in plain sight and Reaver and I shared a laugh. Ballsy motherfuckers but hey, they got it done. Leaving with neighborhood denizens jogging right on past them as the gate rolled shut behind them, none the wiser. They walked back towards where they came from and disappeared. Dragon's voice crackled over the radio, "Come on back." Reaver looked at me and I jerked my head at him to go ahead and go.

"Copy, en route," he said and I set about putting on the headset for the radio. I left the mic open and settled back down to keep watching. Reaver retreated and a few minutes later I heard a branch snap and him curse. I smiled. We'd parked far enough off that I never heard the jeep fire up.

I kept watch through the night and into the next morning. I watched Chadwick come home, his modest security detail getting out of the car with him. He went into the house but they stayed outside which baffled me to a certain extent. I mean the guy was arrogant sure but this was arrogant to the point of being suicidal...

That gave me an idea.

"Hey guys," I said quietly, a moment later the radio crackled to life in my ear.

"Go ahead," Data. I rattled off my idea in so many words and listened to a long silence.

"Copy, we like it,"

So many times I watched that arrogant prick through my scope. Talking on the phone, standing on his deck, staring out the bedroom window, glass of whatever he was drinkin' in his hand and every time I had to resist the urge to line him up in my crosshairs and pull the trigger. I stood sentinel the rest of the night and into the late morning, by the time Reaver and Loyal showed up, he could have been dead at least a hundred times over and that pissed in my Cheerios hard core.

"The fuck you doin' here?" I grunted at Loyal when I realized he wasn't where he was supposed to be, which was with my girl, being her guardian, keeping her safe...

"Relax, your girl's fine. Sleeping still when I left. There's a club member there with her keeping an eye on things," he put a scope to his eye and surveyed down below. "Go on, Sir, get some chow and some sleep and I'll see you later," he settled in and I crawled back from our perch.

"Don't call me 'Sir' and she better be fucking fine or it's your ass," I stood up from my crouch near the line of trees and followed Reaver back to where he'd parked.

"We've got a plan," he said once the Jeep was started.

"Hear it once we're back at base," I said. He nodded smiling which was disturbing as all get out, considering we were talking about ending a man's life, but that was Reaver for you.

I hunkered down in my seat and took a damned nap on the ride back. Sitting for that long behind a scope usually put me in a foul mood and knowing Ashton was being watched by some random club member put me in an even fouler one.

I sighed and studied the insides of my eyelids. I hoped she was as Derek had said, sleeping peacefully. I pictured her perfect face, smiling, happy, eyes filling with that light that rivaled our sun's and I sighed.

I loved her and I needed her. Her resilience, her laughter... I flashed on the image of her sadness, her fear and her pain and felt myself slide a little in Reaver's direction. A cold smile parting my lips. Chadwick Granger was going to pay if it was the last thing I ever did.

# CHAPTER 28

## *Ashton*

"Don't get up just in case, but I think we're clear," Loyal said from the front seat. I sighed. The ride was less than comfortable and I was growing weary. I didn't know how long we'd been driving, but it wasn't long… a half hour, forty-five minutes, maybe? He slowed to a stop and put it in reverse, his arm curving around the passenger seat like an awkward date at the movies. His face was a study in concentration as he backed the truck into what I guessed to be a garage. He didn't look at me. It was as if I wasn't even there. He was good at this. Gears ground, a mechanical sound and the interior of the truck grew darker and darker as the garage door closed, Derek smiled down at me.

"I think we're good," he said brightly and I tried to smile back.

"Good, can we get me out of here?" I asked breathy, "This hurts," he frowned and jumped into action, his door opening and the driver's seat sliding forward.

"Can you get out on your own or do you need help?" he asked.

"I think I'd better do it on my own, that way you won't hurt me. If I hurt myself I can only bite my own head off," he laughed but the tightness around his eyes showed his concern. He stood back and I pulled myself to a sitting position. That was unpleasant.

"Is she okay?" I heard Hayden's voice from nearby.

"It's alright I'm o- ouch god damn it!" I winced and slid to where I could dangle my feet out the truck. I took as deep a breath as I could and leapt the short distance to the ground. Derek's hands went out to steady me and I grabbed on. Tears collected in my lashes from the smarting discomfort.

"I'm okay, really," I said to try and squash the growing look of concern n Hayden's bright green eyes.

"Okay, I believe you," she said in a tone that clearly stated she was humoring me. "Come on inside, take your time," she stood to the side and I shuffled forward toward the door that looked as if it led into her kitchen. She tossed her dish towel over her shoulder and stayed near me and I appreciated it. I took the two steps carefully and made sure I was steady.

"Make yourself comfortable," she said soothingly and pointed through to a small and comfortable looking sitting room. I went in and sank onto the chaise lounge which was upholstered in a luxurious tan fabric and tastefully matched the rich, brown leather couch and ottoman. I texted Ethan that I was safe and once that was done, settled in to have a look around me.

The carpet was a frothy cream and the large television sat on top of what appeared to be an antique buffet. The room was done in rich earthy tones. A large painting of an antebellum southern mansion hanging over the fire place. Ladies in their pastel colored hoop skirts taking tea on the front porch, gentlemen in their finery engaged in a game of croquet on the lawn. It wasn't something I would have picked for Hayden to like and it surprised me.

"Oh! Honey, you look awful." She knelt down next to me and saw me studying the painting. "Home sweet home, that's where I grew up," she smiled and her face lit up with fond memories. I smiled back and sighed.

"Okay, time for you to put your feet up and to relax!" she declared and before I could protest she had my shoes off, my feet up on the lounge and was tucking a bed pillow behind my back all the while chattering away, asking questions a mile a minute, one flying out of her mouth after the other.

"Are you hungry?" I opened my mouth to answer but before I could she was asking a different question and another and another. Derek laughed, his liquid brown eyes softer, lighter for it and he grasped Hayden by the shoulders and gave her a gentle shake.

"Slow your roll, Sister," he said and his smile and laughing eyes took all the bite out of it. Hayden erupted in a pink blush that dusted her cheeks and made her seem just a little bit ethereal. I smiled and answered her barrage of questions.

"Hungry? A little. Comfortable? Yes, thank you. Thirsty? Beyond belief. In much pain? Yes, I should probably take one of the pills Doc gave me and as for anything else? No, I think you're amazing for taking me in like this. You hardly know me." Hayden smiled at me and turned luminous. Derek's hands dropped from her shoulders, his eyebrows shooting up under his ever present backwards baseball cap and he looked at me.

"How the hell did you keep track of all that?" he asked me and I gave him a sad one in return.

"Perfectionist husband. God forbid I get his instruction on anything incorrect. You see the result," he scowled and swore under his breath. Hayden sobered.

"Right, um," she looked to Loyal and then shot me a little sideways look that begged for help.

"Oh! I'm sorry. Loyal this is Hayden, Hayden, this is Derek but the club calls him Loyal," Hayden stuck out her hand and Derek shook it.

"Pleased to meet you, Loyal," she smiled, "Make yourself comfortable. I'll be back with some refreshments in a minute." She breezed out of the living room and disappeared into the kitchen and Derek looked at me and laughed a little. I smiled and he sat down on the end of the couch, shifted and pulled a handgun out of the back of his waistband and set it on the large leather ottoman that doubled as a coffee table so he could sit back. He looked at the gun on the leather, picked it up again and sat with it on his knee, at the ready.

I sighed. That more than anything brought home just how much danger I was in, almost more so than my physical state.

"What 'cha thinking about, Sunshine?" Derek asked me.

"About how watching you with that gun makes the danger I'm in so real," I whispered.

"Have you gotten a look in the mirror?" he asked incredulously.

"I was thinking that, too," I said grinning ruefully.

"Thinking what?" Hayden asked setting a tray of iced tea down on the ottoman. She handed me a glass and froze when she went to hand Loyal his.

"Sorry. It was digging into my back," he mumbled.

"No, it's fine," she said and handed him the glass.

"We can go if it makes you uncomfortable," I murmured.

"No, I guess I just hadn't really realized how bad this was for you until I saw it," she said and sank gracefully to the floor to sit.

"That's what I was thinking," we all fell silent as things came full circle.

"So, what would you like to do?" Hayden asked brightly.

"Honestly, a nap would be great," I said. She stood up and frowned but nodded.

"Sure. Guest room is upstairs, can you make it?" she asked. I nodded wearily and drank some tea to assuage my thirst.

"I'll get your suitcase. Pills are in there. Let's get one in you before you start moving."

Loyal stood up and tucked his gun back into the back of his waist band. He went out to the garage and returned a moment later with the small suitcase I'd never seen before. It was purple and about the size of a carry on. He set it on the floor and crouched over it and fished a bottle of pills with no label out of the front pocket. A note had been rubber banded around it and he handed it to me.

"Take one pill every four to six hours as needed for pain," I read aloud and smiled at Doc's spidery handwriting.

"I'm amazed you could read that," Hayden mused. I took one pill and washed it down with a draught of tea.

"What else is in there?" I asked. Loyal looked up and shrugged a shoulder indelicately and unzipped the case's lid and flipped it back.

I could tell immediately that Ethan had packed it even without the benefit of the letter on top. The items resting just inside the case told me so. Both *Les Mis* and *Phantom* DVD's were perched lovingly on top of one of Ethan's tee shirts. Tears sprang to my eyes at the thoughtfulness of it. Loyal handed me the note. I opened the envelope.

*Hey Sunshine,*

*I know this is hard and I miss you already. I put some*

*things on top that might help take your mind off of things. Tell Hayden hi for me. Tell Loyal to keep his hands to himself. I'll see you soon. I love you.*

    *Ethan*

My phone buzzed in my hand.

**Gonna be a few days baby. Hang tight. Stay near Loyal and out of sight. I love you.**

I texted back quickly.

**Okay. Be careful! I love you too.**

"What's that look for?" Hayden asked dubiously.

"Ethan texted, said it was going to be a few days," I sighed and looked up at Hayden bleakly. She smiled.

"No worries!" She said brightly.

"Reaver told me to keep it business as usual for myself. I have some clients I need to go out and meet with but it'll be nice to have someone to come home to. Andy is going to be gone for the better part of two weeks," she shrugged and looked a little troubled but it passed quickly.

"I say we watch these tonight with a giant bucket of popcorn," she picked up my movies and flashed them at me and I couldn't help but smile. Derek groaned. She rounded on him with a stern look, "Suck it up, macho man. By the time this is over you're going to be drowning in a sea of estrogen. I don't get girl time often and I plan on making the most of this bad situation and you're just going to have to live with it," she shook her finger at him and I laughed which I bit back into a moan of pain. Stupid ribs. Hayden wrinkled her nose.

"Sorry," she said.

"It's okay," I said and her bright enthusiasm was contagious, I was smiling and thinking that perhaps this lock down wouldn't be so bad, "Thank you," I told her and she smiled indulgently.

"You bet," she took my hand in hers and said, "I don't have many girlfriends, so this is nice and it's going to be great. You'll see," she put my movies on top of the DVD player and came back to sit on the living room floor near me.

"How are you feeling?" she asked.

"So far so good. I'll probably get a little woozy from the pill in a few minutes," I confessed. Medicine always had a big effect on me which was a double edged sword.

"Okay, I'll go turn down your bed," she zipped the suitcase closed and took it up to my room with her.

"Keep an eye on her," she shot over her shoulder at Loyal. He grinned.

"Yes Ma'am," he said and gave her a half assed little salute. She stuck her tongue out at him and it was cute. I tried not to laugh and half managed to keep it to a chuckle.

"Some sleep and your chick flicks looks to be about right for you," Derek said to me and sighed. He came over and took my drink, setting it aside on the tray it had arrived on. He held out his hands and helped me to my feet. We trudged in the direction Hayden had gone and up the stairs.

"Take your time," he intoned when I started what seemed like a very long climb. He called out to Hayden when we reached the top of the stairs and she called back from an open doorway just down the hall. I stepped into a lavender room with a big bed and smiled.

"Out," she clipped at Derek and he smiled putting up his hands.

"Bossy little thing," he muttered and she smiled her impish smile. He left and she shut the door behind him.

"Need help?" she asked and I nodded. She unzipped my dress for me and hissed.

"I thought you looked rough the day I met you... What happened exactly?" she asked and so I told her. She helped me into Ethan's tee shirt and as it slipped over my head I realized it was one he had worn and it smelled like him. I was grateful for that.

"I'm so sorry, Ashton," she said and I could tell she wanted to hug me but she refrained.

"Me too," I said and she helped me into the bed. She lay down next to me on top of the covers, slipping off her flats. We lay on our sides and faced each other, talking until I grew too drowsy.

"How long has he, I mean, has it always been this bad?" she asked.

"Started a little under a year into our marriage. We've been together for ten years, so… about eight?" she looked horrified.

"Eight years!?" she asked aghast.

"It wasn't all bad," I tried, "It's not like it was a beating every time I misbehaved. Sometimes I was just locked in our room or…" Hayden looked aghast.

"Ashton! Do you hear yourself?" she asked horrified and I stopped. I thought about it, really thought about it and tears rushed to the surface.

"Oh! Don't cry! I didn't mean to make you cry! It's just nobody deserves to live like that. You treat your dog like that not a person… Hell, you don't even treat your dog that way! Bad analogy, but I think you know what I'm saying," she looked distressed.

"I guess I try not to think about it too much. I always told myself I could do better, that I would be better but things just kept getting worse. Pretty soon I was being punished for things I hadn't even done wrong!" I sobbed.

"Like what?" she asked brow wrinkling in confusion.

"One time, he called to say he would be home late so I delayed making dinner so it wouldn't be cold… he came home on time and took the switch to me for not having his dinner ready when he got there," I sniffed.

"Jesus!" she crowed, "I'm glad the boys called me, I think you need this," she rubbed a hand up and down my arm.

"When did Ethan call you?" I asked.

"He didn't, this was Reaver's idea. Reaver called me, explained some of what happened and said you needed a place to hide. He explained it could be dangerous but I didn't care. I wanted to help," she shrugged a shoulder.

"Why?" I asked softly.

"I come from money, that's no secret," she waved a hand as if to use her opulent townhome as an example.

"My dad is an oil tycoon and knows how to make money, except he uses his power and money for good. He didn't raise an overly

256

sheltered fool for a daughter. I know the warning signs when money and power go straight to a man's head. Sounds like your hubby has both in spades."

I snorted, "Courtesy of *his* daddy." I said derisively, "Which I don't get. Chadwick's dad was a good man." I twisted my lips.

"What about his mom?" Hayden asked softly.

"She was a piece of work, just like her son," I huffed a sigh.

"That explains it then," she said, then asked, "What happened to them?"

"His dad's sailboat disappeared in stormy weather, presumed to have gone down last year. His mom was an alcoholic and her liver gave out about five years ago. His grandparents are all gone, we have no kids... He's sort of on his own," I shrugged.

"Well, he *had* you... He's a damn fool," she said succinctly.

"I miss Ethan," I said and wiped my tears out from under my eyes with my hand. She smiled.

"Tell me about him... What did you guys do last weekend?" she asked and I smiled a real smile then. Lake run. I had a lot to tell her.

We talked until I could barely keep my eyes open, I fell asleep in the plush and comfortable bed and when I woke it was alone, in the dark. The sounds of running water and the clattering of dishes wafting up to me from downstairs.

I got up stiffly and carefully and padded down to the kitchen. Hayden was at the sink rinsing plates and pans and stacking them in her dishwasher. Loyal was nowhere to be seen. Hayden turned and smiled and slid a plate across the counter at me. It was saran wrapped but the food inside looked fantastic. I was starving. I sat down at the counter on one of the tall stools and she poured me a glass of sweet tea from her refrigerator.

"Where's Loyal?" I asked.

"Asleep on the couch. Food coma," she smiled and looked pleased with herself. I peeled the plastic from the plate and she whisked it into the microwave, setting out a napkin and silverware in front of me. The microwave chimed and a steaming plate of Salisbury steak and mashed potatoes and gravy was set in front of me. There was even a side of asparagus. I smiled and tried it.

"Mmm, this is good," I declared and it was. Comfort food at its finest.

"Thanks! Donisha, my daddy's cook, taught me. I spent a lot of time in her kitchen growing up. My mom wasn't much of a cook or baker," she grinned. I didn't reply, I was too busy feeding my growling stomach.

"How are you feeling?" she asked when I had paused in my eating.

"Better," I was surprised that it was true. I had slept like the dead and for a long time and now I was wide awake.

"What time is it anyways?" I asked.

"A little after nine," she smiled.

"Oh."

"Not tired?" she asked.

"Not anymore, feels like the first time I've really been awake in a while," I answered.

"That will probably be short lived. You still have a lot of healing to do. How about a movie or two?" she asked and I smiled.

"Sounds good," I slipped off the stool as she took my empty plate. She rinsed it and added it to the dishwasher.

"I'll meet you in the living room," she smiled and I went back to the chaise lounge and sat down. Loyal was out cold on the couch. I smiled, got up and covered him with the throw artfully draped on the back of the thick leather sofa. He didn't stir.

I sat down and put my feet up. Hayden returned in a matching pajama set with some pillows and blankets. I laughed a little. She tossed them down on the floor by the lounge and handed me a blanket to snuggle down with. She put on *Phantom of the Opera* and sat down next to me. We kept the volume to a dull roar on account of the sleeping Loyal and before we knew it, *Phantom* turned into *Les Mis* and *Les Mis* into a movie I'd never seen before called *Pitch Perfect* which I absolutely adored.

"Don't you need sleep?" I asked Hayden gently as she went to put on *Fried Green Tomatoes*.

"Only have one appointment, tomorrow afternoon. The rest of

my work I can do from home on my laptop," she confided. "Besides, this is way too much fun," she said in a conspiratorial whisper.

"Maybe for you two but, honestly, you just convinced me that I am *never* having a girl. Woman comes to me and says she's pregnant, okay. Girl pops out, I'ma be like 'you better put that back!' Nuh uh. Not happening. Not now, not ever, *no girls*," Derek's sleepy tirade from the couch had us both dissolving into a fit of giggles. Which hurt but was worth it. Hayden got me a pain pill and we watched *Fried Green Tomatoes* and by the end, I was ready for sleep again.

When I returned downstairs, Loyal was gone; in his place was a thin older club member with a scraggly beard and rotten teeth. His blue eyes were getting a touch milky with age but he looked like he knew his way around the revolver sticking out of the front of his waistband.

"Who're you?" I asked sleepily, rubbing my eyes.

"Go by Gypsy. I work at the garage with our VP. Nice to meet 'cha," he said and looked me up and down. I recognized him from the lake run but we'd never been formally introduced. He took a drink of coffee out of the mug in front of him and I smiled.

"Nice to meet you, too."

"Got a gracious hostess," he remarked and Hayden came in from the garage in some yoga gear. She smiled at me.

"Didn't want to deviate from the routine like Reaver said. Went to yoga," she set a briefcase on the dining table and said, "Be right back, let me shower. Make yourself at home!" She went up the stairs two at a time.

I slipped onto the stool next to Gypsy. He was a man of few words but a pleasant conversationalist just the same. Hayden returned and when she did I had sandwiches waiting along with fresh vegetables sticked into finger food. She smiled and said thanks. We all ate together.

"When did Derek leave?" I asked.

"About ten when I got here," Gypsy explained, "She set me up with some coffee before she dashed out the door for some yogurt," he looked perplexed and Hayden and I laughed.

"Yoga," we said in unison.

"Well, whatever the hell the damned thing it is," he said and smiled showing all three of his brown and broken teeth.

"Well! I have some work to do, a meeting in about two hours and then I'll be home," Hayden said. I nodded.

"Then you have a date with a pedicure, I'm giving you one. You need to relax! You have worry written all over your face," she smiled and I could tell I was at her mercy.

Hayden Michaels was a force to be reckoned with and a whirlwind of positive energy. Truth be told, I was worried and her personality was just the thing I needed while I continued this awful waiting.

I missed Ethan so much and I was so afraid not only for him, but the others as well. I would be glad when this was over. I closed my eyes and did something I didn't often do anymore. I prayed.

*Please God, let it be over soon and let them all come safely back to me.*

Amen.

# CHAPTER 29

*Trig*

I woke from one of my nightmares midafternoon, maybe early evening. I sat up on the old cot set up in the corner of the warehouse and looked over. Reaver, Dragon, and Dray were leaned over drawings we'd made from memory of the floor plan of the house. At least I'd been quiet.

"I think we know how we're going to do it," Reaver said when I approached.

"Yeah, how's that?" I asked.

"We need Ashton to be surprised, so I think you're on track with the whole suicide thing," he said judiciously, rubbing his chin thoughtfully.

"We just need to make this shit believable," Dragon grunted.

"Any ideas how we're going to do that? Chadwick Granger ain't the type to off himself and I think the world knows that," I said. Dray snorted.

"World didn't think he was the type to beat his wife either but we proved that," he crossed his arms. Reaver snapped his fingers and held his arms out like a magician revealing the results of his finest trick.

"I got it," he said.

"What?" We three asked in unison. Data came in from the outside, zipping up from taking a piss.

"People with a drug habit do some funny ass things. I'll shoot him up enough to put him out of it and we'll finish him off suicide style," he drew his index finger along the inside of his forearms wrist to elbow.

"He's not going to hold still while you shoot him up," Dray said dubiously.

"Which is why you're going to hold him the fuck down for me genius," Reaver said grinning.

"I should go in with you," Dragon said.

"No. I want to do it," Dray said hastily. "I need to atone for what I did to Ashton," we all exchanged looks and settled on the healing bruises on his face, bruises that I'd put there.

"Son, I don't think you want to atone for it this way. You'll just be covering a gray mark on your soul with a much blacker one," Dragon's dark eyes were sorrowful and Dray met it with an obsidian look of his own. Dray jerked his head to the corner and he and his dad went off. Reaver, Data, and I exchanged looks and shrugged. They came back a time later and Dragon looked both unhappy and resigned.

"Dray's going in with you," he said and then went on with, "I'll be on the ground giving you a distraction so you can get out. Trigger will be behind his scope in case shit goes sideways, providing you cover."

"How we getting you in?" I asked, was it just me or had we skipped that?

"We're going in during the day using all the codes to disable and reset alarms. We're going to hide in the fucker's own panic room. He'd never think to look there. There's no security in the house after hours, just posted outside. When he's out we'll do what needs doing, Dragon will provide a distraction luring security to the front of the house. We'll go out the back."

"That's actually pretty sound," I said impressed.

"Cool, let's roll," Reaver grinned entirely too excited to end this piece of shit.

"Let's roll," Dragon agreed and an hour later I was coming up on Loyal, combat crawling my way to our ledge.

"Hey," he said.

"Got eyes on Reaver and Dray?" I asked.

"Naw man. Wait… Affirmative, there they are Sir," he said and I switched him places taking up at the rifle while he spotted for me.

"What did I tell you about that 'Sir' shit?" I grunted.

"Sorry. Habit," he grunted back. I chuckled. Reaver and Dray were in coveralls with tool bags in hand. They were going in as exterminators.

"Reaver is a fucking riot, man," I said.

"Exterminators? Really?" Derek asked.

"He does love a sense of irony," I commented.

"So what's the plan?" he asked me and I quietly filled him in.

"Ballsy," he said.

"Yup," I grunted. We watched and waited but nothing... all quiet. Two hours later the man of the house came home. Security settled at their posts. The evening wore on, then night fell, the clouds rolled in, threatening rain. I got nervous. Rain meant mud. Mud meant footprints. Something traceable.

The light turned on in the bedroom. Chadwick pulled back the sheets and got into bed in his monogrammed pajama set and I wanted so badly to pull the fucking trigger and splatter his brains all over his expensive, likely, Egyptian cotton sheet set. More time crept by. One hour, two, a light sprinkle damped our backs as we continued to watch. Another hour, then two and then a shadow passed across the bedroom window.

"Show time," I muttered. I could tell a struggle by the violent movement and nervously I scoped out the security men around the outside of the house. They didn't even stir. Good.

The bathroom light clicked on and the door shut muting it. A security man looked up but paid it no never mind and I let out a slow controlled breath. I had never been so damn nervous looking through my scope before. Never. Not even when we'd been over in the sand trap with hostiles every which direction around us.

Then it had been all business but this, this was personal on so many different levels. We waited, and waited, and waited some more. I swallowed hard and we waited, and waited, and waited. Finally, two shadows slipped through the room and out of sight. Shouts carried over the houses and the security men out back whirled toward the front.

"Come on, come on!" I muttered. They took off running for the front and I felt a surge of adrenaline.

The back door opened and shut and two figures darted low across the back garden for the fence line. They made it up and over and disappeared without a trace. Fucking flawless.

"Shit, is that it?" Derek asked.

My phone buzzed in my pocket. I waited. It buzzed again a minute count later. I waited and it buzzed a third time. I waited. Nothing else. I didn't dare pull it out of my pocket. The light would be a beacon with how dark the night was, and would give away our position.

"That's it," I intoned.

"Burn in fucking Hell, you happy bastard," Derek uttered and I smiled an icy cold, soulless smile.

"Ooh-rah." I said and we packed it in. Crawling back from the precipice of the bluff and melting into the tree line. Dragon picked us up. Dray and Reaver were on their own and showed up before we did back at the rendezvous point.

"We got alibis?" I asked.

"Yep, all out on a run together, we are each other's alibis. Add to that we all have room charges on our credit cards for San Antonio and a bunch of bikers in Sacred Heart's colors vaguely matching our descriptions stayed there tonight, well, we hole up here until day after tomorrow and we're golden," Dragon said.

"Thank you San Antonio chapter," Dray said but his usual boyish grin was watered down.

"Doin' all right, Son?" Dragon asked quietly.

"Nope," was his only reply but the look he gave us said plenty, that he just wanted to be left alone to make his own peace with what he'd done in that house. Reaver was like he always was after a kill. Uncharacteristically quiet. Somber. The most at peace you'd ever see him. His eyes met mine and the predator in him slid behind his bright, icy blue eyes. Yeah, his inner demon was satiated for now.

"You make sure?" Data asked and Reaver turned that disquieting gaze on our tech junkie. Data held up his hands and stepped away, going back to his PC.

"I better go relieve Gypsy," Derek said and we clasped hands and pulled ourselves into each other for a burly hug.

"Take care of my girl," I said quietly.

"Your girl and her friend are happier 'n pigs in shit and up to their eyeballs in girly ass movies. I had to try and sleep through three musicals and a tearjerker last night," he fumed.

"Liar. You fucking watched 'em!" Reaver said, a grin peeking through.

"How do you fuckin' know? Were you there?" Loyal demanded.

"Don't need to be," he stated, then asked, "How else would you know they were three musicals and a tearjerker if you didn't?"

Derek looked like he sucked on a lemon and flipped Reaver the bird. Chuckles and outright laughter swept the room. Hell, if they made Ashton happy I would have watched them, but you'd never catch me admitting it to these jerk offs.

"Go take care of my girl D," I said and he nodded.

"Sir, yes, Sir," he said and I pinned him with a look.

"Fucking knock it off!" I said and he smiled.

I waved him off, a table was cleared, chairs put around it and a round of cards started while Data monitored the news outlets and police scanners for the fall out. We wouldn't know if foul play was suspected otherwise. Now it was just one big giant waiting game.

The news broke late the next morning. I texted Ashton's burner.

**Turn on the news.**

She came back a few minutes later with…

**OMG**

I smiled.

**We'll be in San Antonio until tomorrow. It will take us at least another day to come home. Day after tomorrow baby.**

I sent her, hoping she would understand.

**I understand.**

She sent back and I smiled. That was my girl. My regular phone buzzed in my pocket and I frowned I looked at it.

**Omg the news says my husband killed himself Ethan! When will you be home!?**

I broke into a huge grin and texted Ashton's regular cellphone back.

**We'll be in San Antonio until tomorrow. It will take us at least another day to come home. Day after tomorrow baby. Just hang on.**

"Smart little shit," I said all smiles. Reaver peeked over my shoulder.

"Hells yeah," he said.

"What'd she do?" Dragon asked and I showed him.

"Heh. Outlaw spirit that one," he commented and handed me back my phone. She'd just reinforced our fucking alibi. It was going to be a long couple of days before I could kiss the shit out of her for it too.

# CHAPTER 30

*Ashton*

The phone Ethan had given me buzzed across the kitchen island between me, Gypsy, and Hayden late the next morning. Hayden was fixing us breakfast and we were all sharing coffee and chatting.

**Turn on the news**, flashed bold across the screen. We all leaned over to look at it and then all looked from one to the other. The scraping of the kitchen stools across the hardwood was loud in the bright kitchen as we three went to the living room as one. Hayden picked up the remote control from one of the trays on the ottoman and turned on the region's 24 hour news channel.

I gasped.

My house was on the screen, ambulances, fire trucks, and police cars spilling out the front gate, piled in the circular drive behind a pretty blonde reporter.

"Circumstances surrounding the death of prominent defense attorney Chadwick Granger aren't being released at this time citing that his wife and family haven't been notified. No one knows *where* Mrs. Ashton Granger is located at this time. She and her husband were recently in the news…" I sat down on the edge of the chaise lounge, my knees suddenly shaky.

"Wait, yes, a source inside the investigation is saying that this looks like a potential suicide. I repeat, it looks as if prominent defense attorney Chadwick Gregory Granger has been found dead of an apparent suicide and that drugs and or alcohol may be a factor here. Of course any official findings will be up to the medical examiner's office…" she prattled on and with shaking fingers I texted Ethan back.

**OMG**

The phone buzzed in my hand.

We'll be in San Antonio until tomorrow. It will take us at least another day to come home. Day after tomorrow baby.

I blinked in momentary confusion.

"San Antonio?" I murmured. Gypsy grunted.

"Anyone asks you, that's where they're at," he said. I blinked and looked up at him.

"I'm a horrible liar," I said panicked.

Hayden snorted, "I'm not. Where's your real phone?" she asked.

"In my suitcase, turned off," I answered immediately. She gave me a feral grin and disappeared up the stairs, when she returned she handed it to me, the startup screen lit.

"Send Ethan's phone a message, something about your husband committing suicide and ask when he's coming home," she smiled her impish smile and it was pure deviousness.

I texted out: **Omg the news says my husband killed himself Ethan! When will you be home!?**

A return text came in on my phone immediately: **We'll be in San Antonio until tomorrow. It will take us at least another day to come home. Day after tomorrow baby. Just hang on.**

"Smart," Gypsy commented.

"Let the electronics do the lying for you," Hayden said softly. I looked at her and wondered just what Reaver had told her.

The police came much later that day. Gypsy disappeared upstairs and into the guest room when the sharp knock landed on the front door. Hayden motioned me to stay on the chaise lounge in the living room and went to answer it.

"Yes?" she asked when she opened the door. I could see her but not the officers.

"Hayden Michaels?" a man asked.

"Yes?" She was unerringly polite and sounded curious. My heart hammered in my chest and I wondered if I could do this. Tears gathered in my eyes and spilled over.

"According to our records you were with Ashton Granger on April 22 when an incident occurred at the YMCA on Rucker Avenue. Is that correct?" a female voice this time.

"Yes, that's right," she concurred nodding her head.

"Do you happen to know Mrs. Granger's whereabouts?" The male voice asked.

"Of course, she's right here," she said gently and stood aside to let the two plain clothes detectives in. Their badges were clipped to their belts, gleaming golden in the soft light of the entry way. They looked my direction and the woman frowned.

"Mrs. Granger?" The woman asked.

"Yes?" I said and the tears spilled over. Hayden strode across the creamy carpet in her comfortable ballet flats and sat down beside me on the chaise lounge. She'd covered my bruises with expert makeup and I wondered if mascara was now running down my face. She'd told me not to worry that if the police found me here to just try to cry and she would do all the talking.

I trusted her. We'd done some serious bonding over the last day or two and now here I was about to be put to the test. The officers stood a few feet from us and gave me their condolences.

"We're very sorry ma'am but we have a few questions we need to ask."

"Of course," I said, more tears slicking down my face. I stayed silent and prayed the stricken look on my face would be interpreted as the shock of a new widow.

"Ma'am, were you aware that your husband had begun using drugs?" That one was easy.

"Drugs? I… I know he…" I let out a shuddering breath.

"It's okay he can't hurt you now," Hayden said gravely, she looked up at the detectives and I clutched her hands in my lap.

"Ashton's told me that she suspected his drug use in the past, why?" she asked them.

"Is that true Mrs. Granger?" I hid behind my hair and nodded rapidly.

"Okay. Well preliminary tests indicated your husband had heroine in his system at the time of his death. I'm sorry to have to tell you that it looks like suicide…" they tried to break things to me as gently as possible, Hayden put her arm around my shoulder while I cried they didn't need to know my tears were those of relief.

Finally I was free. Finally I didn't have to worry or be scared. It looked as if the detectives really believed that he'd killed himself. I was shocked. *That* I didn't have to fake. They wrapped up their interview and took my phone number and where I'd be staying. I gave them the address to the club house since that was where I would be staying with Ethan and they left. I texted Ethan on my phone as soon as they were gone.

**The police were just here. I miss you. Please ride safe.**

The burner phone rang.

"Hello?"

"You're a fucking genius," Ethan's voice was a low rumble filled with pride and love over the phone line.

"Oh, well it was Hayden's idea," I said embarrassed.

"Tell her she's a genius," he said.

"I heard you loud and clear," she said loud enough to be heard. Ethan chuckled.

"How are you doing baby?" he asked me.

"I'm just feeling so much, I don't know... I wish you were here," I sniffed and shook.

"I know. Won't be long. Have the club member you're with destroy the burner you're on. I'll call you in a few hours from my phone. Keep the texts coming updating me but be careful what you send. I'll call you when I can. Derek is on his way back and will take you to the clubhouse," he said.

"Okay," I said.

"Cops suspect anything?" he asked. Hayden took the phone from me.

"Doesn't look like it," she said grimly into the line. I couldn't hear what Ethan said.

"No, she did great. She's a little shell shocked I think. A lot to have happen to a person in a short amount of time," a long pause, "Are you sure that's a good idea? I'm happy to have her here," she said. I frowned and she smiled at me. I didn't want to put her out any more than I had.

"Okay," she handed me back the phone.

"Sunshine?" Ethan's voice warm and sweet came through the phone.

270

"Yes?"

"You're going to be fine. I'll see you the day after tomorrow. Hayden's pretty great."

I smiled, "Yes, she is," I agreed.

"I love you. I can't wait to have you back in my arms," he said.

"I love you too. I miss you," I began to tremble. I didn't want the call to end but I could tell it had to.

"Day after tomorrow," he promised.

"Day after tomorrow," I repeated and the line went off. I was glad he hadn't said goodbye. I sighed, Gypsy came into the living room and I looked up.

"You're supposed to destroy this," I said and held up the temporary pre-paid phone. He nodded and took it from me.

A few hours later Loyal showed up freshly showered and changed. He helped me out to the truck. I texted Ethan asking if it was okay to have visitors at the club house and he texted back that it was okay with him and the boys, that I should have people around me at a time like this. It was nice to be back someplace familiar. Chandra and Doc were waiting for me just outside the club house doors when Derek pulled the truck into the lot. The big tent thing had been taken down. I went inside and sat with them talking softly for a little while. They asked me how I felt and I didn't really have an answer for them, I felt just… so many different things.

Elated, until I realized I was elated that a man had died, then guilty for feeling that way, then angry that I should feel guilty for being glad that I was finally free. Sad, a keen sense of loss, not over Chadwick being dead but for other things… for the life we *could* have had together. For the life that was stolen from me by his unrelenting cruelty. For the life of the child that could have been had I been stronger. Had I left his sorry ass the moment he even suggested an abortion.

I mourned the loss of that child long ago and I thought I had mourned the loss of the ability to ever have more, but now I was with Ethan and I worried about it. What if he decided he wanted a child? I couldn't give him that. I pressed those thoughts back down deep into my secret vault of despair I kept locked in the far recesses of my heart to deal with another day. I told Doc and Chandra about the rest and Doc told me it was natural to feel all of those things. That it would take time to come to grips with all that had happened. Ethan called me an hour or two later and I excused myself to his small bedroom to take the call, away from everyone else. I needed to speak with just him. Hear his voice. No other people, no other distractions.

"Ethan?" I asked quietly.

"Yeah Sunshine, I'm here," he said.

"How long do I have to talk with you this time? Everything has just been so short," I sniffed and dashed at my eyes.

"Oh, Baby, I know. We got time. We're stopped for the night and so a long conversation is okay," he said and I smiled. I laid down on the bed and settled in.

"I miss you," I confessed.

"I miss you, too. Being away from you right now is killing me. Feels like I'm so close but so far away," I could hear him sigh.

"I've been thinking about a lot of things," I whispered.

"Tell me," he said and it all came out in a giant soft spoken rush. Everything. My trials, my fears, my tortured mind. He listened. His voice, when it interjected some bit of sage wisdom or other, or when he soothed this fear or that worry, was liquid and deep. I confided in him everything, the hour growing late, the time ticking by but still he was patient and loving and kind and everything my now dead cruel husband was not and had never been.

I realized that there were two kinds of monsters in this world. Evil ones who hid behind beautiful masks and shrouded themselves in darkness. Monsters like Chadwick. Then there were the monsters like Reaver and Trigger and me now too, I suppose. The monsters who were honest about the brutality and awful thoughts. Who didn't hide it, didn't lie about it, but rather embraced those ugly parts of themselves and tried their best to wring what good they could out of them while they yet breathed.

"You sound like you're getting tired," Ethan said gently when I'd paused for too long.

"Yes and no," I said honestly.

"Okay, well, I'll try to keep this short, Sunshine. I want to address some of your fears. One, you are not a bad person. You are a good person who went through some very bad things and there isn't a single person on god's green earth who could go through the things you went through and *not* come out the other side with some kind of stain on their soul. You are some kind of angel, at the very least some kind of saint to be as well-adjusted as you are after living in that hell," he was quiet for a long time and I realized that he was waiting for me to acknowledge what he'd said.

"Okay," I said hesitantly. I wasn't really sure *what* I should say to that.

"Second, I love you. *You*. For who you are, *as you are*. Kids aren't a deal breaker for me. If you want a child we'll find a way when we're both ready, when *you* are ready,"

"Okay."

"Lastly, you haven't even been free for twenty-four hours yet, Baby. I'm in no hurry to put any kind of ring on your finger or collar around your heart. I suspect you aren't ready for it either. Marriage, like children isn't a deal breaker for me. That's not to say I never want you to be my wife but I'm just happy you're even in my life. Grateful that you want to be," he paused.

"What?" I asked alarmed, this silence was different from the rest. Heavier somehow.

"Make you a deal Ashton," he said.

"What?" I asked again.

"When you're ready for me to ask you to be my wife you come to me and say 'ask me'. I want to do right by you so I'm not going to drop to one knee right then and there and shit. I'm going to plan it and I'm going to do it right. You get me?" he asked.

"I get you," I said softly, the tightness around my heart easing with his reassurances.

"We have a deal?" he asked me.

"Deal," I said and I smiled my first real genuine smile not weighted by sadness since this whole new mess began.

"Good," Ethan said resolutely into the phone.

"Thank you," I said.

"You're welcome, Baby," he said and nothing else needed to be said.

He told me to rest, to heal and that he would call again in the morning. I must have been exhausted because I slept through three missed calls. When I got up a note had been tacked to the outside of the bedroom door.

*Sunshine,*

*Trigger called the club house, had me check on you since you weren't answering your phone. You were out cold, told him as much, he said to let you sleep and to tell you 'I love you'. Please wake up next time so I don't have to pass girly and embarrassing messages.*

*Loyal*

I laughed a little and shuffled slowly to the kitchen for some coffee and cereal. Chandra was out in the common room reading one of her paperback romance novels.

"Hey Girly," she said looking up. She pulled off her red framed rectangular readers and set them down. She was sitting at a table by the window to take advantage of the natural light.

"Morning," I said.

"More like afternoon but only by a bit. Still coffee in the kitchen want me to get you some?" she asked.

"I can get it," I said and moved off that direction.

"Suit yourself," she said and put her glasses back on. I returned with a steaming cup with liberal amounts of cream and sugar and took the seat opposite her.

"Mmm," she said and pulled herself back out of the book. She took off her glasses and marked her page.

"Good book-boyfriend?" I asked and she smiled.

"Think I may have a new favorite," she said with a grin. A soft knock landed on the club house door.

"What the hell?" she said getting up. I felt a surge of panic which quickly swirled away… *Chadwick was dead.* I had to remind myself. It still wasn't real yet. Chandra opened the door.

"Help you?" she asked in her hard stand offish way.

"Oh my, um, yes, is Ashton here?" Hayden's sweet voice.

"It's okay Chandra, that's Hayden," I said brightly.

Chandra stood aside and Hayden stepped through the door looking about as out of place as a sheep in a wolves den. She wore comfortable looking ballet flats, a pair of khaki cargo capri's and a light pink polo shirt. She even had a cream sweater, sleeves tied around her shoulders. Country club perfect in the middle of a biker's club house. I hugged her and she hugged me carefully back.

"Well, I feel out of place!" she declared.

"You look out of place," Chandra confirmed and lit a cigarette between her lips.

Hayden blinked and asked, "Should you be doing that?"

I smiled. I had asked the same thing all those weeks ago and Chandra smiled around the cig and said the same thing she'd said to me then… "Private club."

"Oh," Hayden said softly, her green eyes swept the club house considering.

"The things I could do with this place," she said and took a few steps further in.

"Just don't go opening any closed doors," Chandra warned her. Hayden nodded absently and let her finger tips slide along the bar.

"What's back there?" she asked me.

"Private rooms and restrooms. My room with Ethan is back there," I said.

"Where's the kitchen?" she asked me.

"Behind the bar, come on I'll show you and get you some coffee while I'm at it," I linked arms with my new friend and we went back into the kitchen. She started commenting on how she would better lay out this or that, paint colors and flooring and I giggled.

She and Chandra talked while I showered and dressed and I could tell they were becoming fast friends too. It was hard not to like Hayden. By the time I came out of the bedroom in a spring time dress and my white flip flops they had made plans to kidnap me.

"You need to relax," Chandra complained.

"Pedicure is as good a start as any. Since I didn't get the chance to give you one we're all going now," Hayden said.

"Don't look so panicked! It'll be fun," Chandra said and they linked arms with me on either side. I made sure to have my phone in my pocket in case Ethan texted or called. I texted him the girls plans and that I would be out, not expecting one in return. I got one.

**Stopped for gas. Have fun with the girls. Sounds like a fine idea.**

Hayden and Chandra, and even Reaver's cousin Shelly kept me extremely busy the rest of the afternoon. First it was smoothies, and then it was manicures and pedicures, and then it was lunch, and then a trip to a book store. By the time we were through there they took me back to the club house and it was time for a much needed nap.

I woke long enough to cook some dinner for myself, Doc and Chandra and to speak with Ethan on the phone. Tomorrow would be spent with Doc and Chandra making arrangements for Chadwick's body. I was waiting for Ethan before going back to the house.

He and I spoke on the phone about what would have to happen next. The important documents residing in Chadwick's office safe. I knew where he hid the combination. I'd known a lot of things I wasn't supposed to know when we'd been married. When he'd grown complacent that I was too stupid or that I wasn't paying attention. Ethan bid me good night and said that he would see me the next day but couldn't tell me what time. Said he would have to check with Data who was drooling on his keyboard which had made me laugh.

I slept, but it was a fitful sleep. My mind turning over and over just everything that had to be done that I didn't wish to do. I was awake for most of the night, my eyes finally sliding shut as the room began to grow light with the coming dawn.

I woke from a sharp pain in the side that Maynard had kicked as I was being dragged back across the bed into a warm, hard chest. I struggled to sit up.

"Easy Girl, just me…" I closed my eyes and slumped back into Ethan's warmth as his low growl of a voice vibrated up my spine. *He was here. He was home. Thank God.*

"Didn't mean to wake you, I just wanted to feel you against me," he murmured and I felt a little thrill at his words.

"I missed you," I whispered.

"I missed you too, but I'm here now Babe. Go back to sleep. You look like you need it," he cuddled me carefully and I snuggled back into him and immediately fell into a deep and dreamless sleep. Safe in the circle of his arms, forever at last...

# EPILOGUE

*Trig*

I couldn't wait to see her face.

"Don't move," I said excitedly and she sat as still as a stone, her generous lips curving into a gentle Mona Lisa smile beneath the black bandanna tied tightly over her golden eyes. That part was a shame but a necessary evil to complete the surprise.

Her douchebag husband had met his fucking maker three months ago and though his life insurance policy had been null and void because he'd 'committed suicide' it didn't matter. The dick had been loaded. Ashton had been so still and quiet at his lawyer's office, silent with the weight of her feelings. She'd been married to him when he'd died and with no children and no parents or siblings on his side of things to fight over it, everything he'd had in his possession when he'd kicked it had been declared hers.

It was about time she'd gotten something good out of him and she'd sat there in stunned silence when all was said and done. The house, the cars, the art, the *yacht...* Yeah the fucker had a secret yacht for Christ's sake. All of it she'd told the lawyers to sell, which they'd accomplished in record time. Her ex had been a douche but his lawyers and accountants were surprisingly good people. She'd put her name to the check for *twelve million dollars after all the taxes were paid* and looked at me.

"I want to find a house, a small house just you and me," she'd said gently and I'd done just that.

I opened the door to the brand new Jeep and helped her out, swinging her out and over the cracked sidewalk under the tree dappled light of the brilliant summer sun. She squealed with joy and laughter and her arms slipped around my neck and shoulders and I laughed with her. I kissed her and she kissed me back and I suddenly couldn't wait to get her out of her bright yellow sundress and underneath me to christen her new surprise.

I set her on her sandaled feet oh so gently and turned her to face the little three bedroom two story cottage-like home. I stood behind her and placed my hands on her bare shoulders smoothing my thumbs over her silky skin. My cock swelled in my jeans, I couldn't help it. I couldn't get enough of my Sunshine Girl no matter how hard I tried.

"You ready?" I asked.

"Yes!" she cried equal parts excited and exasperated. I whisked the blindfold off and she blinked while her eyes adjusted and when they did her reaction was fucking flawless. She gasped. Her manicured nails going to cover her mouth her golden eyes flying wide. The lawn was perfectly manicured, the fence low, white and freaking picket. The flowerbeds overflowed with blossoms and the drive leading back to the detached garage glowed just about as white as the fence.

The house though, that was the main attraction. It was a soft dove gray and trimmed out in lavender, the front porch was white and meant for sitting, a porch swing, like the one at the lake cabin, which she'd expressed she'd loved, hung from the porch's covered rafters. Two end tables for coffee in the morning, tea in the afternoon, and wine or beer in the evening, sat to either side of the swing, still and waiting.

The windows were white and set into all sides of the house to allow as much natural light as possible. The chimney to the side wasn't brick but rather stacked round river stones in grays ranging from light to tans giving the place that natural woodland feel. A giant oak tree took up the majority of the front yard dappling the light and casting the shade that we'd both be craving each summer. She took a hesitant step forward.

"Go on Babe, it's your house. It's not going to bite you," I laughed. She went up the driveway trailing fingertips along the fence and opened the latched gate that opened onto the flagstone pathway that led to the porch steps. She looked up at me.

"It's everything we talked about," she whispered and looked like she was about to cry.

"Nothing but the best for my girl," I said softly. She wrapped her arms around my waist and a little sob broken by a laugh bubbled out of her. I laughed, "Hey now, come on now, none of this I want you to see it all." I said. Which was only true because I wanted her to see it all so I could get her nude and writhing underneath me. She nodded against me and reluctantly let go taking a step back. She went down the little path and up the stairs. I pulled a key out of my pocket and pressed it into the palm of her hand. She slid it into the lock with shaking fingers and opened the door.

The place was empty. I'd thought of furnishing it but then decided that with her BFF, Hayden, being an interior designer and a total spitfire besides... Well, I decided I rather liked having my balls firmly attached and that the decorating could come later. Besides, it was Ashton's money and I could honestly give two fucks about how she decorated as long as it was her that I was coming home to every night.

"I love it Ethan," she'd said after she'd toured every room. We were in the upstairs master bedroom. She'd cried in the kitchen. I'd made sure to have it redone to her every specification. She came to me and tipped her face up for a kiss and greedy bastard that I am I lifted her, her lithe legs curving around my hips in the way that drove me wild.

I broke the kiss and said against her mouth, "You and me until the wheels fall off Sunshine," she smiled against my mouth.

"I like the sound of that," she whispered.

I pinned her against our new bedroom wall and pressed into her, fingertips digging into the soft pale skin of her outer thighs. Holy god she wasn't wearing any panties. Now I know why she'd insisted on taking the Jeep rather than my bike. This woman drove me nuts.

"I'm going to make love to you against this bedroom wall," I growled into her ear but her small hands were already working the fly of my jeans. God what this woman did to me.

"Okay, but I want you in the kitchen next," she murmured and I smiled as I pushed my way inside her.

Her. Me. Forever.

Still, I loved that she was in such a rush.

"I love you, Ashton Fletcher."

"I love you, Ethan Howard."

We christened every room in the house and the bedroom twice before the afternoon was over.

Her and me until the wheels fell off along the open road called life.

Fuck yeah.

## THE END

Hear that sound?

# BROKEN & BURNED

is roaring in…

# CHAPTER 1

*Everett*

Worst.
Day.
Ever.

It started with me being late to work, cue ass chewing from my manager... I finished my day job burning myself with the steam from the espresso machine only to find out the first aid kit had been out of burn gel. What's more, I didn't understand a god damned thing in my statistics class, which I was pretty sure I was going to fail, my boyfriend won't answer his phone, and now my car was wheezing its death rattle and I was terrified I wouldn't make it into the mechanic's lot!

I could barely afford to keep a roof over our heads and me in my classroom, I had no idea how I would afford to fix my car and if I needed to call a tow truck to go two blocks I was going to implode.

The mechanic's shop was *right there...*

"Come on baby, come on baby; come on baby..." I chanted under my breath as if it would help anything.

I cranked the wheel and pulled into the lot with a little shout of triumph and my car just died... I stepped on the brake stopping with a little lurch and one of the mechanics, a man about my age, looked up from under the hood of an ancient old brown Ford pickup in my direction.

Tears pooled in my eyes. I was frustrated, embarrassed, stressed out, and just everything all at once. I took a deep breath and grabbed the strap of my overloaded backpack to heave it off the passenger seat. The zipper gave way at the seam and with a mighty ripping sound my text books, notes, pens, and pencils all spilled out onto my shabby, if tidy passenger side floorboard.

That did it.

I burst into tears.

The mechanic, a Hispanic man with chin length, stick straight, black hair looked on with detached interest as I bent and tried to scoop everything back into my bag.

*God Everett get a grip, girl!* I thought savagely to myself.

I shoveled everything back into my bag and as I went to straighten, my driver's side door opened. I jumped and let out a little startled shout. My hand, moving unbidden, pressed to my chest.

I looked up into a pair of intense dark eyes, so dark a brown you couldn't differentiate where the iris left off and the pupil began. The mechanic raked me once over with that smoldering dark gaze of his from my head to my feet and his lips quirked up on one side. I swallowed hard, my heart doing a somersault in my chest.

"Having a bad day?" he asked and his voice was even and deep without a trace of an accent.

"Yeah." I nodded.

"Put it in neutral and steer," he commanded and disappeared around the back of my forlorn little Toyota. I did as he told me to and put the gear shift in neutral, taking my foot off the brake. He pushed, I steered, which was a lot harder without power steering.

"Pull up in front of the center bay!" he called and I put some elbow grease into cranking the wheel in that direction.

"That's good!" he called and I braked, put the gearshift into first and threw the parking brake.

I sighed. This was going to take the last of my savings and then some. I didn't know how I was going to do it, but I would just have to cross that bridge when I came to it.

"Come on into the office." He started walking that direction and I hung my head for a second. I pulled my permanently open backpack into my lap and holding the overstuffed bag like a toddler in my arms, shuffled to the office dejectedly...

Could this get any worse? Any more humiliating?

I set my messy pack onto one of the old scruffy waiting room chairs. The office was small but neat and smelled heavily of stale engine grease and metal.

"The diagnostic is fifty bucks and includes a full vehicle

inspection," he said and was filling out a carbon copy sheet listing out everything that was included. His printing was neat and orderly, flowing out from the Bic stick pen in block letters. He only used capitals. I fished out my phone and sent yet another text to my boyfriend, Jerry.

"Name and address?" he asked me.

"Oh yeah, sorry." I was kind of blank. I went to my ruined backpack and unzipped the smaller front pocket, glaring at the gray canvas-like material for its betrayal. Although I suppose I shouldn't be *too* hard on it, it had served me pretty well since my sophomore year of high school.

I extracted my small black leather wallet and pulled out my driver's license and handed it to him. He looked down at it and then back at me then back down at the small plasticized cardboard rectangle.

"Something wrong?" I asked. His intense dark eyes raked over me and I swallowed as the hair stood up on the back of my neck. I felt a slight blush brush my cheeks with a kiss of heat.

"No," he said simply, but that didn't stop his stare, so I boldly stared right back at him in a vain attempt to give as good as I got, which of course, only made him smirk at me. It was a sexy smirk and judging by the gleam in his eyes, he knew it too.

He was a couple of inches taller than me. Maybe five eight to my five six. His black tee shirt hugged his muscular shoulders and was tucked into the light blue grease stained coveralls, the arms of which were knotted around his waist. His black hair shone with blue highlights under the bare overhead bulb and I realized that even though it was fall it was awfully dark for it being early afternoon.

I dragged my eyes from his bronze skin noting that his jaw was just barely kissed with the beginning shadow of dark stubble. I turned with some difficulty, I didn't want to stop looking at him. I looked out the window behind me with some effort. The uniformly neutral colored venetian blinds were in the down position but the slats were open to let in the natural light from outside. The sky hung heavy with dark rain clouds, threatening a deluge. I sighed. *Of course.*

I tried Jerry one more time, but after several rings his phone just went to voice mail. I hung up without leaving a message. I would try again when my business with the hot as hell mechanic was concluded.

"What kind of name is Everett?" he grunted.

"It's where my dad ended up. A city north of Seattle." I sighed. Not much of a name but my dad had kind of been stunned and when they'd asked him what to put on the birth certificate it was the first thing to come out of his mouth and I was forever branded.

"Long way from home," he commented. I rolled my eyes.

"Grew up here, well not *here* specifically, but in the state." I looked him over.

"What's your name?" I asked, noting the lack of a name tag. Likely it was stitched on his coveralls but in their current position that wasn't a lot of help.

"Folks call me Dray," he said and I tilted my head to the side. An unconscious gesture.

"Dray? That short for Andre?" I asked.

"Naw, short for Draven." He made a face.

"What kind of name is Draven?" I echoed his earlier question and he smiled.

"My mother's last name is my first, I carry my dad's surname. She wanted me to have both names and my dad wasn't on board with a hyphenate." He looked up and a flicker of surprise crossed his features.

"Not sure why I just told you that," he said gruffly, and dare I say, looked a little embarrassed himself.

"Secret is safe with me, so long as you don't tell anybody mine." I held out my pinky finger and he looked at it like it was an alien being from another planet. I self-consciously tucked my hand back over the edge of the counter.

"Well Ms. Moran," he said oddly formal all of a sudden, "You can pay when the diagnostic is complete, should know what's up with it tomorrow afternoon. Got a number I can reach you at?"

I wrote down my cell number on the paperwork and thanked him, handing over my car key. My house keys and key ring I stuffed

4

into my jeans pocket. The spikey metal lump unfamiliar and uncomfortable there, but it was only until I got home. Dray the mechanic handed me back my driver's license and I tucked it back in my wallet and my wallet back into my traitorous bag.

"Thanks," I muttered and picked up my torn backpack, attempting to crush it closed at the top. Talk about an exercise in futility. I went back to carrying it like a toddler and walked out to the street. I looked up at the forbidding steel gray autumn sky and scraped my bottom lip between my teeth. I juggled the bag and got my phone to my ear.

"Pick up Jerry." I swore under my breath and stood at the edge of the shop's driveway by their sign.

"*Hi! You've reached Jerry, I'm doing something right now, leave a name and number and I'll get back to you.*" The recorded voice of my boyfriend of four years played out of my phone and was immediately followed by an obnoxious tone.

"Jerry! It's Everett, I'm stranded at..." I looked up at the sign, "The Open Road Garage on 39$^{th}$ street. Please come get me? I love you. Thanks, bye." I ended the call and my shoulders slumped as the first fat drops of cold rain began to fall.

Great.

I looked back towards the garage but the open sign was out and the bay door was inches from the ground and closing fast. I hugged my bag to my chest and tried to keep the top closed as the rain fell faster.

Frustrated tears stood out in my eyes as the first trickle of cold water ran down the back of my neck. I was cold, I was tired, having been up since three thirty that morning and my left hand hurt from my thumb to my wrist where it was burned just shy of blistering. I glanced over at my car and sighed... Can't wait there, key was in the shop. I looked up and down the street for some cover.

Nothing. All the buildings were industrial and warehouse like with flat fronts in brick or stucco, not an awning to be seen. I sighed and hugged my bag tighter. I was soaked through to my skin in a couple of minutes but longer than that dragged by.

What the hell was Jerry *doing*? He didn't have any afternoon

5

classes and it was his scheduled day off from his non-existent job. I rolled my eyes. I loved him dearly, I really did, but he couldn't stay employed for longer than a couple of months and when he lost whatever piecemeal dead end job he'd had, it was always someone else's fault. His mother coddled him, and honestly, at least his dad paid his portion of the rent, that was something... I sniffed. My nose was starting to run from the chill. I was going to kill him when I figured out how to get home. I tried his cell again. Voice mail... again.

A sleek and shiny, black, fully restored 70's Trans Am, complete with gold firebird on the hood pulled up beside me. The engine was growling in that rumbling purr that declared '*I am a mechanical bad ass, just step on the gas and I'll prove it.*' The passenger door popped open and I bent. My lip was trembling with the chill and I gritted my teeth to keep them from clacking together.

"Get in. I'll take you home." Dray, the sexy as sin mechanic, was leaning over the center console. His dark and burning gaze straddling the line between brooding and angry. I swallowed hard.

"That's okay, my boyfriend Jerry will be here any minute." I forced a smile onto my face and he scowled.

"You can't bullshit me, Sweetheart, get in the car. You're freezing and your boyfriend ain't comin'." I debated for one heartbeat, then two. The man made a harsh, impatient noise and I got in, shoving my bag on the floor between my knees and shutting the door firmly on the cold downpour outside.

"Thank you." I murmured.

"No problem." He said as I fastened my seatbelt.

I turned to look at his profile as he drove. He'd taken off the coveralls and he wore butter soft, light colored blue jeans that clung to his muscular thighs, falling straight legged, the frayed cuffs covering the tops of the laces of his well-worn steel toed work boots. The leather pitted and scarred from use, a patch of the shiny steel showing through a ragged hole in the leather.

Watching those worn boots work the gas and clutch suddenly became really fascinating if it meant I didn't have to meet those deep dark eyes that were casting sidelong looks at me. His hand interrupted my view of his feet as it reached out and hit the switches on the heater console. Warm air blew over my feet and legs and the feel of wet denim against my skin made me grimace. I hated being in wet clothes. The sensation bothered me, the clinging dampness just... ewe.

His hands were clean, I noted and the leather of his jacket creaked with the movement. My eyes traveled up the well-worn black leather sleeve, the leather turning brown and scaly with too much time spent in the elements. He had a vest on over the jacket, hiding the shiny silver snaps and zippers behind equally well-worn leather bearing patches for a motorcycle club. I shifted nervously in my seat and my eyes continued flowing up that sleeve, past his elbow to his shoulder to his smirking sensual lips.

I shivered.

"She'll warm up in a sec," he said but his lips twisted and I just knew he knew that little shiver hadn't been from the cold.

"I live in an apartment above Vale's dry cleaning with my boyfriend. He should be home, I don't know why he didn't answer the phone." I swallowed. Dray's presence was, in a word, intimidating as he steered the growling muscle car through the rain slicked streets.

"Yeah. I know where you live." He muttered and I blinked. The sound of the pounding rain and the *swish-shush* sound of the windshield wiper blades filled the sudden silence in the interior of his car.

*Swish-shush.*

*Swish-shush.*

*Swish-shush.*

"You gave me your license, I just wrote it down, I have a knack for remembering things I read." He shifted uncomfortably in his seat.

"Oh." I said.

"Sorry, didn't mean to make it all creepy and awkward." He gave me a lopsided grin that made his face go from harsh to endearingly boyish and handsome and I couldn't help the shy answering smile of my own.

7

We lapsed back into silence and it was comfortable enough that I didn't feel a need to fill it if he didn't. He piloted the old muscle car deftly through the streets and I felt myself stealing glances at his vest, secretively trying to read some of the patches nearest me. One over his breast declared him the vice president and I felt my eyebrows raise. He was young... Maybe twenty five to my twenty, wasn't vice president usually a position reserved for a grizzled older biker with a big beard, who was going soft around the middle?

I turned back to the window and stared out as we turned onto my street. He pulled smoothly up to the curb in front of the dry cleaners and I gripped my bag together at the top, shoving some damp papers into the side where they'd tried to spill out sometime during the short ride.

"Thank you for the ride Dray," I said softly. He looked me over one more time, face serious, half smiles and smirks fled from his lips.

"No problem, give him hell." He grunted and I opened the door and got out. I shut the door behind me and dashed to the glass door to my apartment. I slipped inside, bypassed the four mail boxes set in the wall and took the shabbily carpeted steps two at a time up to my apartment door.

I fished my keys out of my pocket and opened it.

Did I mention that this was the worst day ever?

"Jerry?" My voice sounded small, wounded and I hated it. I blinked slowly and heard my bag hit the floor just inside the door, the contents spilling out over the tired brown carpet in a slosh of paper and books.

I blinked slowly as my boyfriend stood up from the couch, spilling the woman who'd been straddling his cock to the living room floor. My face felt hot and flushed and I shook, tears traced their way from my eyes to my chin in twin hot lines.

"Shit! Everett! What are you doing home!?" he demanded.

"That's what you have to say to me!?" I screeched outraged.

"Baby, who is she?" the girl asked. I blinked at her as she pulled her too short jean skirt down over herself. Her long legs terminating in a pair of clear plastic platform stripper heels. She wore a fire

8

engine red lace bra and her matching thong lay in a damp puddle on my coffee table. I shuddered with revulsion.

"I *was* his girlfriend! Who the fuck are you!?" I demanded.

"Girlfriend!? I thought you said you lived here with your sister!" she glared over at Jerry who was trying to fasten his pants.

I put my hands on my knees and doubled over and tried to breathe. I gagged both on the smell of sex permeating the air and the fact that he was decidedly *not* wearing a condom as he shoved himself back into his pants.

"Oh my God, this isn't happening," I heard myself say.

"Baby come on, she doesn't mean anything; she's just some chick I met when I was out with the guys last week. Let's talk about this." I straightened and raked him with a cold hard glare.

"You want to *talk about this!?*" I shrieked.

"God! Fuck you, you fucking jerk!" the girl pulled on a tight fitting red top and grabbed up her panties and her purse from the coffee table. "I'm out of here," she muttered and I closed my eyes.

"God, yes, please... get out," I said, swallowing hard to keep my gorge from rising.

She made a derisive noise.

"Shit, maybe if you were a better lay he wouldn't have had to come to *me*," was her parting shot as she brushed past me and went out the door. I crumbled a little on the inside but I would be damned if I would let it show.

"Seriously Jerry!?" I demanded. He leveled me with his unremarkable brown eyes and ran a hand through his sex mussed dark hair. I closed my eyes so I didn't have to see him standing there shirtless and barefoot, but closing my eyes just brought the image of the woman with the long dark hair riding him on my couch. I shuddered in revulsion.

I so needed to get tested.

"Babe, it's not like that, I was weak. I mean, she has a point, I have needs and it's not exactly like you've been there to meet them." Cold laughter filled the small apartment and I realized it was pouring out of me. I snapped my mouth shut.

"For the last two or three years I've been getting up at three

9

o'clock in the morning to *go to work* Jerry! To keep us in this shitty apartment, when I'm not working my ass off to make ends meet, I'm in *school*! I'm fucking *tired* and it's not like you do anything to make it better! You sit on your ass playing video games and live off your daddy's money! So excuse me if after putting in sixteen hour days for weeks on end my fucking panties won't drop for your half assed notion of foreplay!" I crossed my arms more to hold myself together, hold myself in, than anything. I felt blasted apart, angry, hurt and exhausted like a piece of rope frayed to its last string and that last string was at its limit.

I stared across the small space at the man I'd loved since high school and wondered when and where it all went wrong.

This was easily the worst day of my life so far.

# BROKEN & BURNED
KINDLE AND PAPERBACK
## OUT NOW

# ABOUT THE AUTHOR

A.J. Downey is a born and raised Seattle, WA Native. She finds inspiration from her surroundings, through the people she meets and likely as a byproduct of way too much caffeine. She has lived many places and done many things though mostly through her own imagination... An avid reader all of her life it's now her turn to try and give back a little, entertaining as she has been entertained.

You can stalk her through the following links:

*Facebook*
Author Page: http://www.facebook.com/authorajdowney
Fan Group: http://www.facebook.com/groups/ajsfanbase
Street Team: https://www.facebook.com/groups/sacredstreetteam

*Goodreads*
https://www.goodreads.com/author/show/7871309.A_J_Downey

*Amazon*
http://www.amazon.com/author/ajdowney

*Pinterest*
http://www.pinterest.com/authorajdowney

*YouTube*
https://www.youtube.com/channel/UCzGTqQBySgwixrj6-PQsERw

*Blog*
http://authorajdowney.blogspot.com

*Mailing List*
http://eepurl.com/blLsyb

Made in the USA
San Bernardino, CA
08 February 2017